Praise for *The Witch King*

"Edgmon's ebullient debut depicts a variety of trans perspectives with tender sensitivity, and quintessential walking disaster Wyatt's self-deprecating humor, punk glee, and surprisingly level head are vividly lovable.... Readers will adore this revolution-tinged celebration of trans joy, which refreshingly builds its conflict without jumping for trauma tropes."

—*Publishers Weekly*, starred review

"This romantically charged, anti-fascist fantasy presents a diverse cast of queer characters.... The page-turning resolution promises an irresistible duology closer to come."

—*Kirkus Reviews*

"A complex fantasy debut, rich in nuanced LGBTQIA+ representation and timely social commentary, perfect for fans of Adam Silvera, Holly Black, and Rin Chupeco."

—*School Library Journal*

"Edgmon's debut is a spellbinding duology starter, ultimately driven by its core cast of complicated and lovable characters who will keep readers laughing with deftly written, witty dialogue that never veers into cliché, and a richly layered world that feels incredibly real, with high-stakes fascism, corruption, and oppression. Readers will be left eager for the sequel to this fiery stunner of a fantasy."

—*Booklist*

An Indie Next List pick

Best Book of the Year pick by *Publishers Weekly* and the New York Public Library

**Books by H.E. Edgmon
available from Inkyard Press**

The Witch King
The Fae Keeper

THE FAE KEEPER

H.E. EDGMON

inkyard
PRESS

ISBN-13: 978-1-335-42591-1

The Fae Keeper

For questions and comments about the quality of this book, please contact us
at CustomerService@Harlequin.com.

Inkyard Press
22 Adelaide St. West, 41st Floor
Toronto, Ontario M5H 4E3, Canada
www.InkyardPress.com

Printed in U.S.A.

For every trans elder who should be here but isn't.
I'm sorry. I love you. I will not stop fighting.

A Note from the Author

While there was so much of my personal story in *The Witch King*, there is so much of *us* and our history as a community in *The Fae Keeper*. And I won't lie to you—it's brutal. At times, it was painful for me even to write it. And I guess that makes sense. Queer and trans history, too, is brutal and often painful. This particular story contains violence (including murder), gore and body horror, on-page panic attacks and dissociation, graphic discussions of infanticide, discussions of cannibalism, off-page rape and discussions of childhood sexual abuse, animal death, discussions of gender dysphoria, discussions of real-world racism and transphobia, and emetophobia. Please be gentle with yourself.

But understand, this is *still* not a queer pain story. It's a story about queer survival, and queer revolution, and queer love. I will never promise you a happily-ever-after, but I will promise you hope, and humor, and a group of people who care enough about each other to grit their teeth and stare down impossible odds side by side. After all, our fight may be bloody, but it isn't one we have to fight alone.

Thank you for fighting with me. Now let's get to work.

H.E. Edgmon

A Note from the Author

CUT THE DECK

Two weeks after my boyfriend dies in my arms, we go to the woods in the middle of the night to close a portal to another world.

Emyr—my boyfriend, now less dead and more of a king—brushes his knuckles against the back of my hand as we weave through honey locusts, moonlight making puppets of our shadows. He doesn't say anything, but there's no need to.

Briar and Jin, walking side by side a few feet ahead, fill the silence for us, their yellow and purple energies batting back and forth at each other as they do.

"So, we'll do this one, and then—"

"Right, these three, yeah. Are we sure about—"

"I don't know. Maybe we should go back to—"

"I was just thinking that, yeah, and I was also thinking—"

Their conversation is both about me and not, and I only manage to half follow it. They're still knocking out the logistics of what we're about to do, making last-minute decisions on the sigils they're going to use to close the door to Faery.

"What if it doesn't work?" Briar asks, and she's still talking to Jin, but her eyes meet mine when I look her way. I can only face her dark, tender stare without an answer.

Because I don't have one.

This isn't the first time we've tried closing the door. Briar, Emyr, and I have been out here a few times on our own. But Briar and I can barely come up with an ounce of magic between us, and Emyr is a fae *Healer*. None of us is exactly perfect for the job.

"It *will* work," Tessa snaps, pushing past Emyr and me to force her way to the front of the group. "So, that's a pointless question."

My charming sister. We brought her into this endeavor the same time we told Jin, once we realized we were never going to fix the problem on our own. Tonight's the first night we'll try all together.

And it *has* to be tonight.

In the morning, Briar leaves Asalin, the fae kingdom hidden in upstate New York, for her home in Texas. She and her mother, Nadua, are going to start tracking down their family's changeling contacts, gathering more information on the secret network of their people around the world. Changelings keep their true nature hidden, pretending to be human to avoid fae eyes, not wanting to face the same mistreatment the witches do.

But Emyr is king now, and he wants something better. With Briar and Nadua on his side, maybe we can make allies out of these creatures we didn't even know existed.

Which would be fucking great, because allies are something we're desperately in need of. Briar might be leaving Asalin tomorrow, but so are the rest of us. Emyr, Tessa, Jin, and I are heading to North Carolina, to follow up on a lead on the whereabouts of Derek and Clarke Pierce.

The sibling duo who killed Emyr. Who then escaped from Asalin and went on the run.

Under *normal circumstances*, hunting down his own assassins would not be the king's job. But since one of Emyr's first royal decrees was to finally shut down the Guard—the corrupt fae police force, previously led by Derek—in a move that *wildly* pissed off most of his kingdom, and the people he trusts not to murder him (again) are basically limited to the five of us in the woods right now...

Well, we don't have a lot of options.

"Yeah, it's gonna be fine." I am trying to get better at sounding all confident and positive about things, even when the hamster in my head is screaming and its wheel is on fire. I've learned recently that being intentionally shitty about everything is not a personality, actually, or at least not one that's fun to be around.

When Emyr's knuckles graze mine again, I lace our fingers together. He squeezes, his gold energy wrapping like a cuff around my wrist, his claws digging into the fragile skin on the back of my hand. I don't pull away, even when it starts to hurt a little.

We're greeted in front of the door by Boom. The hellhound sits twenty feet away from the opening, red eyes sharp and keen as he keeps watch, black hackles raised along his back. He hates this place.

Which really makes me feel good, you know, about what the hell is over there.

I reach over with my free hand to scratch the top of Boom's head, nails scraping the base of his ears. "You can go home, bud. You don't have to be here for this."

He huffs, tilting his neck back to nip gently at my fingers, and then returns to his superimportant task of glaring at the door.

Though I'd really rather not, I turn to look in the same direction.

If you don't know what you're looking at, the door to Faery isn't much of a door. It isn't much of anything at all except a feeling—a *wrongness*. Two elm trees, ancient but long dead and blackened, have grown twisted together in the middle of the woods, their branches tangling into ugly knots to form an unnatural archway.

Before, when I looked at the door, I would see nothing. Not beyond it, to Asalin's forest on the other side of the trees. Not through it, to the world of Faery inside. Just…nothing. It was as if my eyes couldn't, or wouldn't, focus on it. It was the same for all witches, while Emyr, like the rest of the fae, could see through it to whatever desolate wasteland was on the other side. But there was nothing for me here except the heavy feeling of something forbidden.

Now it's the same, but it isn't. I still don't see Faery, not really, I don't think. But I see…flashes. Sometimes, there is that strange, elusive, almost staticky nothing that sets my teeth on edge. And sometimes, for the briefest moments, there is something else. Something just as difficult for my brain to process, something so abhorrent that my eyes simply refuse to register it's there until it's gone again.

I want this fucking door *dead bolted*. Immediately.

"Alright. Let's get to it, then." Tessa claps her hands together and turns to look at Jin, raising her eyebrows. "You bring the thing?"

"Oh, right, yeah." Jin digs a hand into their oversize mesh cargo pants, pulling out a small metal box, passing it over into Tessa's waiting hand.

Tessa turns back around, and her soft lilac energy jumps to life, slicking from her fingertips and up her arms. She lifts the box to the base of one of the branches, and, with a deep breath, shoves it into the bark. The black elm allows her to do it, the tree opening itself up to her magic to accommodate the strange little device, making space for it to nest perfectly in the wood as if it'd grown there.

As soon as she does, the doorway begins to flicker. Once, quickly, and then a few more times in rapid succession, and then, a soft blue light fills the archway and doesn't dim again.

This is why we needed these two.

Jin's pet project for a while has been taking human technology and finding ways to integrate it with witch magic. They've invented cell phones that allow them to send spells through cyberspace, and laptops that let them share magically binding documents in the cloud. And this? This is a security system, ripped off from human designs, programmed with witch magic, that we're about to install with sigils for a passcode.

Yes, we are, in fact, going to close the five-hundred-year-old door to the magical fairy-tale planet with a dressed-up ADT alarm. Because of course we are.

We need Tessa to make sure Jin's spellwork is able to weave itself into the forest properly. As an Influencer, Tessa can shape the world around her.

It's also nice to have a fae on hand who *isn't* about to lose her shit at the sight of the tech magic.

Jin and Emyr worked on these projects together. He helped them with their design, their shared visions.

And then Clarke and Derek used Jin's cell phone to send the magic that killed him. Now, even watching this display unfold in front of us, I can feel the way Emyr tenses at my side, the way his hand tightens around mine even more.

I wince when his claws prick blood, and he jerks away. I snatch his hand back with an *absolutely not* scoff. He doesn't squeeze this time.

"Okay, it's all yours." Tessa waves her arm out, ushering Jin and Briar forward. "Make it quick."

I know I should be helping them with the sigils. I'm supposed to be learning this shit, too. It's important, and I'm already seventeen years behind, and if there were a witchcraft final exam, I would fail it. *Big* fail it.

But I don't let go of Emyr's hand to join them. I just stroke my thumb against his, watching the way his energy tightens like armor around his chest and hoping my touch makes him feel anchored to his body, because I love him, and I need to do this right now. And I let our friends close the door, and I don't worry about not doing my part, because I know they love me anyway, and they need to do *that* right now.

Minutes later, the blue light in the archway flickers again and then disappears.

"Okay...um. Okay, it's done." Briar's words are soft, and she takes a few steps back, tilting her head to consider the elm trees.

"Are we sure?" Tessa demands.

"Positive." Briar nods. She looks over her shoulder at me, offering a lopsided half grin, flashing one little dimple when she does. "It's over. We did it."

Next to me, Emyr exhales. Boom rolls onto his back in the dirt.

"It's just a shame we couldn't even take a peek inside." Jin's voice is a taut whisper, each word seemingly pried from their throat. Their eyes flit across the twisted tree branches covering the now-closed doorway, and I notice the way their hand gives the smallest of twitches at their side. "Not even a look."

"If my father's account of Faery is to be believed, we don't ever want to go through this door." Emyr sounds exhausted at the mention of Leonidas, his father, who lied about what was behind this door for decades. My black energy winds up and curls around his throat, stroking through the curls at the nape of his neck. "Besides, we have more important matters to deal with right now."

"Whaaaat? C'mon." I huff sarcastically, reaching down to pat at his backside. "Personally, I don't think we have *enough* going on. What if we got another dog?"

I pretend not to see the scowl Emyr slides me. But Boom's ears perk up with interest.

"I don't give a shit what's over there," Tessa snaps, balancing her hands on her hips, still eyeing the doorway with contempt. "I'm more concerned about what might've already come through."

Right. That part.

We *definitely* don't have time to deal with that part.

Here's hoping it doesn't come back to bite us in the ass.

CHAPTER ONE

THE TOWER

The next time I see Derek and Clarke Pierce, we're in the outskirts of Nowhere, Appalachia, and I'm pretty sure my arm is broken. Emyr would have healed it by now if it weren't for us barreling up this freaking mountain after them.

If you get away again, I quit.

Two weeks we've spent playing cat and mouse with these assholes, up and down the East Coast, in and out of little nothing towns, and I'm *tired*. I want to take a nap. I want to take several naps. I miss when I got to do things that weren't hunting wanted criminals, or helping my undead-king-boyfriend try to reconfigure his kingdom, or keeping very big world-altering secrets about doors to other worlds.

I miss Briar.

But all I have to do is think about Emyr's lifeless body in my arms that night, and I'm pushing past the pain to hurry in the siblings' direction.

Fifty feet away—or maybe twenty, or maybe a hundred, I cannot possibly be expected to do any kind of mental math— Derek turns so sharply on his heel that he kicks up ash. He wheels toward us, black wings blowing out at his back, blue eyes glowing like headlights in the center of his face. This is the most disheveled I've ever seen him, dressed down in jeans covered in muck and blood, white T-shirt snagged down the chest where Emyr almost managed to catch him moments earlier by grabbing a fistful of fabric between his claws. He looks like he hasn't managed a decent night's sleep in the month since he ran.

The fact that I once thought this man was the epitome of male beauty is unbelievable to me now. There is no way that wasn't a direct result of the Influencing he was wielding over my head. Giving him a second of my time when *Emyr* was right there? I'm a clown, but I'm not the whole circus.

I can make jokes about it. But the sight of him this close, rancid as he is, still makes my stomach hurt. This man was *in my head.* Clouding my own thoughts, making me *want* him, just so he could play with me, a pawn in his little political game.

What else could he have Influenced me to do? How much further could he have taken his coercion?

Derek raises his hand, energy sparking along his fingertips, and the sugar maple trees surrounding us start bending in his direction.

"WYATT, DOWN!" Tessa shouts from behind me, and I

barely manage to dodge the boulder that comes flying over-head. One jagged edge brushes against my shaved scalp and my stomach roils at the *almost* of the sensation.

At the same time, Derek rends a tree straight from the ground, roots and all, and sends it hurtling right at my body. Before it can wipe me off the map, it collides with Tessa's rock in midair. The *BOOM* of the Influencers' magic clash-ing is enough to set my teeth on edge, and I stumble back, blinking away stars in my vision.

Wait.

Pause.

"Where's Clarke?"

Emyr grips the hilt of his sword, casually slung over his shoulder like it's just another one of his accessories. He's started carrying one since not long after they put the crown on his head, an ancient relic from Faery itself. It would be very sexy if it weren't because he felt the need to protect himself from another assassination attempt at all times. (As it stands, it's only moderately sexy.) He slides it down and in front of his torso, wielding the weapon with practiced ease. "Where's Jin?"

Well, *fuck* me.

Tessa rushes past. She and Emyr circle closer to Derek, try-ing to back him up against the stone face. He smiles, teeth bloodied from some earlier collision, tilting his head back as blue energy snakes up his body. Emyr and Tessa respond in kind, gold and lilac draping itself across their shoulders, curling around their throats, twining together in the air be-tween them.

As much as I don't want to leave Emyr or my sister to

fight the evil Ken doll alone, I have my own pressing problem. Why the hell did we not assign someone to keep their eyes on Clarke?

Okay, correction. Why the hell did we not assign someone who wasn't her *ex*? Jin insisted they be the one to deal with her, that they be responsible for making sure she was brought in safely. (Never mind *whose* safety they were worried about there.) We never should've let that happen. They shouldn't have even been on these recon missions in the first place. Their head's been screwed on wrong since they found out the truth about their fated mate. Now they've gone and disappeared without backup.

And if Clarke does anything else to hurt Jin, Briar is going to string me up by my toenails. So, when I catch a flash of electric purple just past the tree line, bobbing farther up the mountain, I grit my teeth and race off in the same direction.

"Jin!" I push past tree limbs with my good hand, my clothes and skin snagging on brambles all the way up. Everything hurts and I'm dying, or at least exhausted. And it doesn't matter. "Where the hell did you go?!"

"Wyatt." Someone giggles, a chirping, harmonic little sound. "So nice of you to join us."

Ah. Not Jin.

The air at the top of the mountain is cold and sharp, like ice fractures settling into my heaving lungs. It's quiet, too much so, or maybe I just can't hear anything over the sound of my breathing.

Clarke Pierce stands in front of me with her hands on her hips and a fat, self-satisfied smirk on her glossy pink mouth. Unlike her older brother down there, she somehow looks Pinterest perfect. Her tanned white skin is unmarred by a single scratch, her white-blond curls perfectly pinned behind her head. The blush tracksuit looks like the early 2000s spit up on her. And she's wearing heels. *Bejeweled* heels.

I would be impressed by her dedication to the vibes if I did not hate this bitch with every itching, furious inch of me.

"Hey there, handsome." She grins, raising one hand to wiggle her fingers in my direction. Those fluffy white wings shimmy at her back. I get the feeling she's enjoying being the center of attention. "Was just telling Jin here how much I've missed them." Those round blue eyes flick to Jin's face and I think, maybe I'm imagining things, but it's almost like something in them softens. "And I have missed you, sweetheart. More than you'll ever know."

"Jin." My teeth grate, and I bare my sharpened fangs. "She's a liar. Every word out of her mouth is a lie. You know that now."

Jin isn't looking at me. They only have eyes for Clarke, twin black holes drinking in everything that this manipulative asshole is spinning for them.

"Not everything," Clarke assures them. "Some things. I've done a lot of lying. I've hurt a lot of people. But could I lie about what we have? Do you think I ever really wanted to hurt *you*?" She shuffles closer, tilting her head to blink up at Jin like some kind of wounded fawn. "No one else is in this relationship but you and me. No one else knows what it feels like. You know I couldn't fake this. Not even *I'm* that good of a liar."

Clarke is a tiny thing, dwarfed by Jin's height and muscles. But it's clear, looking at the two of them only a few feet apart, who's in control. Clarke's pink energy hisses with venom, and Jin looks like they might just disappear into the dirt.

"Jin…" Blackness creeps from under my fingernails and crawls up past my wrists. I reel it in before it slides the rest of the way up my arms, stifling the embers that flicker just beneath the surface of my skin. I've been working with the witches in every spare moment I have, but those moments are few and far between. I didn't have that many brain cells to begin with, and the ones I have left, with everything else going on, don't seem interested in learning Witchcraft 101.

See, witch magic is fueled by emotion. We draw our power from what we *feel*, the way fae draw theirs from the earth around them. But we need conduits. We need something to channel our magic, like sigils, or spells, or potions, otherwise…you know, we accidentally burn villages to the ground.

Not that I'd know anything about that.

Anyway, I've been studying when I can, but I still have no idea what I'm doing. At this point, all I can do is try for emotional self-control (*clearly* my strong suit) and hope for the best.

"Jin, look at me."

"Wyatt." Their voice hitches. They don't look away from Clarke's face, even as they speak my name. "What card did you draw when you woke up this morning?"

Every morning, I pull a single card from my tarot deck. Most mornings, I tell the others about it, a glimpse of insight into the rest of the day. Today, I didn't. It's been sitting in my gut like lead.

I swallow. "The Tower."

Chaos. Violent upheaval. An awakening that can't be stopped.

A single tear streaks, wet and hot, down Jin's cheek, and

drips from their chin. We both know, no matter how this encounter goes, Jin doesn't get what they want. Because what they want is a world that doesn't exist anymore. A world where Clarke is innocent, and she loves them.

"Hmm." At length, Clarke turns away from her mate to face me. "Okay, let's talk. What do you want, kiddo?"

"Huh?"

"Well, I want to leave this mountain without my hair singed off. I know I have a pretty face, but I'm thinking I wouldn't rock the shaved head look nearly as well as you do. Now, what do *you* want?"

She cannot be serious, except she is, and I know she is.

"You killed Emyr. The only thing I want is for you to get everything you deserve, *peaches*."

Jin makes a warbling sound of distress at my words.

Clarke's tongue flicks out against her razor-sharp teeth. After a beat, she giggles again, like nails on a chalkboard. "You know, Wyatt, you and I have so much more in common than you'd like to believe."

"We absolutely fucking do not."

"No, really. Look at us. We're constantly underestimated. We're small, and cute, and people think that's all there is to us. They think they can push us around. And we keep getting caught up in all these awful little conundrums just because we're trying to do the right thing." She shrugs. "Sure, maybe we have different ideas of right and wrong, but that's neither here nor there."

I stare at her for a long moment. She stares back. Sweat drips down the side of her forehead, creasing her foundation.

Finally, I smile. "Appreciate you thinking I'm cute. But I can tell you're stalling."

Clarke raises one eyebrow. "Pardon?"

"You're trying to buy yourself some time, wait for Derek to show up. You're… Oh, Clarke, are you *afraid* of me?" That shouldn't send a thrill through my body the way it does, but I've always known I'm a little messed up in the head. I take a step forward, and I don't miss the way she shifts her weight to the other foot, easing herself back a pace. "You've seen what I can do, and you're scared. After all, I did almost kill you once already, didn't I? Don't think Emyr would waste the magic healing you if it happened again. And now that I've had time to train…"

Now that I've had time to train *absolutely nothing*, but she doesn't need to know that.

Clarke tilts her head and shifts her weight again. I can actually see the moment she decides to stop playing coy, her shoulders tightening and her pretty face twisting into a grimace. "Fine. I think you're a creepy little weirdo and I don't trust you or your magic one teeny tiny bit. I'm a survivor, honey. That's what I do. That's what we both do. We survive. And sometimes that means making a deal with the devil. Isn't that exactly what you did with Derek?"

"I made that deal before I had any idea who Derek *or* Emyr had become."

Okay, look. Clarke's stalling, but so am I. She's afraid of the power that nearly took her life the night of the riot, but I don't actually know how to control that power. I need backup, and Jin sure as hell isn't it. "And that doesn't change the fact that you don't have anything I want."

"What about a new face?"

The words are just unexpected enough to throw me for a loop. "What?"

"I'm an Influencer, Wyatt. I can shape the world into whatever I want, and that includes you." Now she's sidling closer again. "So, tell me. What would turn this body into a more comfortable place to live? A dick? A flat chest? A deeper voice?" She flicks her wrist at my face with a grin. "Maybe you want all those scars to disappear."

My heart pounds hard enough I can feel the reverberations all the way down my broken arm. I know Influencers can control the world around them. I've *heard* of ones who could shape-shift. But could Clarke possibly be as powerful as she's claiming?

Something saccharine and sinister sneaks into the corner of her smile, and she gives a quiet little hum. "Hey...maybe that's not what you want at all. Maybe what you really need are sharper teeth. Claws as deadly as Derek's?" She's close enough now that I can smell her perfume, sweet like candy. "Maybe you want everyone to finally see you as the biggest monster in the room. And I could make that happen. I could turn you into anything you wanted."

Anything I wanted.

I refuse to bend to the cis logic that my body is wrong, that I am a boy's soul stuck in a girl's bones, that the only appropriate way to be trans is to hate myself. I don't *want* to be cis. I don't want the magical penis Clarke is offering me, and I wouldn't go back and give up the experiences transness has given me, either.

Seriously. *Me*, a cis man? No thank you.

And yet…there is a part of me that wants to buy what she's selling, and I hate myself for it.

I know who I am, but how much easier would it be if the rest of the world knew it, too? If I didn't have to listen to their uninteresting apologies over pronoun slips. If I didn't have to wonder where it was safe for me to exist in full.

Besides, transness isn't the most interesting thing about me, and it's definitely not the only reason I might want to make some renovations. At seventeen, my body has already survived more than it ever should have had to. Maybe it'd be nice to have skin that didn't feel marked by the things the world has done to me. Maybe it'd be nice to be the kind of monster that could stop it from ever happening again.

"Wyatt." Jin's voice this time, startling me out of my reverie enough to look over at them. They haven't looked away from Clarke. The first tear has been joined by others. "Maybe we should just let her go."

"You're absolutely not going to do that, Jin."

Not my voice. Tessa steps up to the top of the mountain with us, arms already outstretched, soft lavender energy resting in her hands and ready to throw down. She shoves herself in front of both us witches, her small body like a shield. Her translucent wings sparkle a thousand different colors in the low afternoon sun.

If Clarke and I are similar, Tessa and Clarke are, too. It's more obvious with the two of them, I guess. Little blonde girls, always draped in shimmer and pastel. Both of them far deadlier than people might assume at a glance.

Only my sister isn't pure evil. For the most part, anyway. We're still working on our relationship.

"Where's Emyr? Derek?" I can't believe I was actually standing here fantasizing about Clarke's offer. In what world would *anything* she could give me be worth letting her go?

Tessa doesn't look at me. "On the way."

When the trees behind me rustle with movement, I jerk around in time to see Emyr joining us and my body nearly goes limp with relief. I didn't realize I was holding tension in every muscle, not knowing how things were playing out down below, until I saw him again.

He looks exhausted. Shaken up. But okay. Alive.

Emyr is alive. He's breathing. Sometimes, I have to remind myself of that over and over again, even on the good days.

"Derek?" He must've gotten away. It's not like they would've put him in cuffs and left him somewhere to be picked up later. And that just means, even if we manage to get Clarke back to Asalin, we're going to have to keep doing this. Round and round the fucking mulberry bush.

I just want a *nap*.

Emyr stops at my side, reaching out and curling his fingers around my wrist. A golden glow emanates from beneath his palm, and suddenly the pain in my arm is gone. I hadn't even realized I was still in pain until I'm not anymore. Magic or not, he has a way of doing that to me. His thumb claw strokes along the back of my hand and he sways a little closer to my side.

That's when I notice the blood.

My heart collides with my stomach as the sight of it dripping down his throat, alarm bells flaring out inside of me in every direction. I grab his arm, tilt my head back to get a better look.

My heart beats a little easier.

It's not actually Emyr's blood. I don't think so, anyway. It covers his sword, red liquid dripping down the length of the blade, droplets splashing on his skin, others falling farther to the mountain rock under our feet. A tiny river of it begins to flow from the tip, making a current that passes beneath the sole of my boot.

My eyes move from the ground to Emyr's face. Again, I ask, "Derek?"

He doesn't speak. He nods only once.

Tessa confirms what I know, her gaze never leaving Clarke. "Derek was unable to be taken alive. I hope you'll learn from your brother's mistake."

An impossibly long moment drags past us.

I reach inside my chest for a feeling, some reaction to the news, but my fingers barely grasp at loose threads.

It really is so, so quiet on the top of this mountain.

"You...you killed my brother?" Clarke's voice has no right being so soft. So weak and broken, like a flightless baby bird. "Derek's dead?"

"We did not have a choice." Emyr finally speaks, voice like honey-dipped thunder, and when his hand glides from my wrist to my waist to the small of my back, I can't help but to press tighter to his side.

"You've always had a choice, Emyr..." Clarke whispers. Pink lightning sparks around her body. A wind begins to pick up, shaking the sediment on the ground, twisting at the trees. "And, for some reason, you always choose wrong... Why do you keep doing that?"

"Clarke, you are outnumbered," Tessa warns. "Do not make the same mistake as Derek. Come back to Asalin with us."

The wind picks up harder until it's whipping at all of us, nearly yanking me off my feet. Emyr's arm snakes tight around my waist, holding me against his side. Jin seems to snap out of it, at least a little, enough to move closer to Tessa's back and brace their large hands on top of her shoulders as if to keep her from flying away.

It's a ridiculous thought. Or it should be. But when I look at Clarke, I realize her feet are no longer touching the ground. The wind seems to have lifted her into the air. Pink continues crackling all around her.

An Influencer, just like Tessa, just like Derek.

But is it possible that Clarke is stronger than both of them? Has she been the biggest monster in the room this whole time, just biding her time until this brutal power needed to claw its way to her glittery surface?

"My brother's biggest mistake was not slaughtering all of you when he had the chance." It's another whisper, but I can hear it as if her mouth is pressed to my ear. As if her voice is being carried by that unnatural wind itself. Tears well in her big blue eyes and begin to spill freely over her cheeks, dragging mascara tracks with them. "Rest assured, I will not do the same."

And then she tilts her head back and screams.

I guess, technically, she screams. It comes out of her mouth, anyway. But whatever this magic is, it's more like a seismic blast.

And it *does* knock me off my feet this time. I'm wrenched out of Emyr's arms so hard my shoulder pops out of place. Connective tissue and muscle rip apart like paper. Somehow I can't feel my arm and it's the *only* thing I can feel, pain overriding everything else. And now I think I'm the one screaming, but the sound is so inhuman my brain can hardly process that it's me.

Thrown backward through midair, my body connects, hard, with tree after tree, battering me on my way down the mountain. My head slams viciously into rock, and a *new* kind of pain erupts behind my eyes. Is my skull *open*?

Air is trapped in a cyclone in my chest, my breaking body unable to breathe in or out.

I've thought I was dying before. This time, I'm certain of it.

Thankfully, it doesn't last long before the world goes dark.

I'm not sure how long it stays dark. All I know is one minute I'm being tossed around like a dog's favorite toy, and the next I'm lying in a pile of rocks and shredded bark, and every part of my body hurts, and people are screaming my name. Somehow, though my ribs offer a vicious protest, I manage to force myself into a sitting position, spitting out a mouthful of blood and dirt to warble out a miserable, "I'm alive!"

Mostly, I think.

Emyr is on me in seconds. He scoops me against him, that golden glow erupting out from his body yet again, stitching my open wounds back together and clearing the black spots from my vision.

"Firestarter." He sighs, the palm of his hand sliding up against my cheek. His fingertips brush along the scars on my jaw, his thumb sliding over my nose, then my lips.

"Your Highness." I lean forward to stretch out my still-aching back, resting one hand on his thigh. "We've got to stop meeting like this."

I take it from his eye roll that he doesn't think I'm very funny. That's fine. I *know* I'm very funny.

Jin and Tessa join us moments later, and both of them look as shitty as I feel, covered in various unfortunate fluids, with leaves and sticks poking out of their hair.

"What *was* that?"

"I think that was Clarke in mourning," Tessa offers, grimly. She holds a hand out to me and I take it, allowing my sister to drag me out of Emyr's lap and to my feet. "On the upside, we got rid of the Big Bad. Derek's not a threat to anyone anymore."

The blast of Clarke's magic leveled the top of the mountain. While I was once standing cliffside in a clearing, I'm now at the bottom of a freshly scooped basin. It looks like some kind of giant punched down right in the center, leveling everything as it went. All around the sides, jagged edges of the mountain's walls hover over us, splintered pieces of stone looking as if they might collapse at any moment. Shredded bark and crushed rock and the corpses of animals caught in the destruction litter the ground.

Clarke is nowhere to be seen among the wreckage, but I can still hear the memory of her whispered threat.

Rest assured, I will not do the same.

Have we gotten rid of the Big Bad? Or have we created one that's worse?

CHAPTER TWO

THEY'RE ALWAYS
BESIDE THEMSELVES

Almost immediately, human news outlets start calling it a suspected terror attack, even though none of them can explain who would want to blow up a mountain in the middle of nowhere. More than a few people start screaming about aliens, which I remind Emyr is not *technically* wrong. He doesn't laugh, which is fine, because I do.

Emyr manages to get us a private flight back to New York while the Charlottesville Airport halts all travel in and out. I don't ask how much it cost him, the same way I've never asked him just *how much* money is sitting in the royal accounts. Pretty sure the answer would make me feel gross.

That's a problem for another day. Today has enough of its own.

I sleep most of the way back. I'm exhausted, the kind of

tired that makes the edges of the world feel muffled, the kind that couldn't be shaken off with all the Frappuccinos in the world. But I dream of pink claws and black blood and don't wake up feeling any more rested than when we took off.

The car ride to Asalin is quiet, each of us gazing out the windows, lost in our own thoughts. I text Briar and give her the rundown on the last twenty-four hours.

MY GIRL
Holy shit, that was Y'ALL? Wow. Uhh. Is Emyr okay? I mean, it was DEREK, but he still like…killed someone, you know?

I do know, because I've been there. Ending someone's life isn't something you just bounce back from, whether or not they deserved it.

And there's no question in my mind that Derek Pierce got exactly what he deserved. My only regret is not being there to see it happen. Sick, predatory fucker.

Yeah. My mind *knows* that. But again, I try to summon up what Derek's death actually makes me *feel*, and all I find is a hollow space behind my ribs.

Weird.

Anyway.

It's not something you ever get used to, carrying around the weight of taking a life. I've done it three times now, and I'll be happy if I never have to do it again. I don't need another ghost living rent-free in the back of my head. I don't need someone else's voice joining the chorus constantly trying to remind me of the two worst moments of my life.

Well, two of the three worst, anyway. I may not have killed

anyone the night Emyr died, but it definitely hurt more than watching Unicorn Boy get blown to bits.

And besides, there's a new heaviness to Emyr already, a shift that happened before he was forced to kill his cousin.

I look up from my conversation with Briar and find him staring from across the car at the phone in my hand, his jaw clenched, shoulders pulled up high toward his ears. When I shove it inside the sleeve of my hoodie, tucking the offensive piece of tech away from view, he relaxes only slightly. Our eyes meet and he frowns, as if only just realizing his reaction, and looks away quickly.

Kadri warned me things would change. She told me being brought back from the dead has a way of warping who a person is. And I've seen it, I think, over the last month. The way shadow clings to him, dragging him down when he thinks I'm not looking. There's something *off*, something I can't name and don't understand, even though I want to, even though I've tried.

Maybe it's death. Maybe it's trauma. Maybe it's the pressures of being king, of hunting the Pierce siblings up and down the Atlantic, of trying to do right by a kingdom that doesn't even want him. Probably it's all of the above.

Of course, if Emyr has his way, he won't be king for long.

The Guard is gone, and the Committee along with it, but he doesn't want *any* of this. He's eighteen years old. He deserves a chance to be eighteen years old, without having to save a crumbling empire from falling into the clutches of fascism.

The problem with transitioning to a new kind of government? How does one go about electing leadership in a democratic way, where the voices of the people can be heard, when those *people* have spent generations culling witches from their midst, and letting bigotry take root? How are we supposed to make sure things are fair for everyone when a huge chunk of that everyone...sucks?

For now, Emyr's put the Circle into place. A few people, fae and witches, hand selected by him, to help keep the peace in Asalin. Tessa and Jin. His mother, Kadri. The witch Lorena. And me.

It's far from perfect. It's nepotistic, and biased, and it certainly hasn't helped Emyr earn anyone's favor back after breaking up the Guard. But it's something, for now, just until we figure out our next move.

Maybe now, with Derek gone, that process can begin in earnest.

I hope so. Because Emyr can't keep carrying on like this. I'm still watching him, watching the way that rust seems to work itself into his golden energy, subtle enough I wouldn't be able to place it if I didn't already know what I was looking for. It drags him down, dulls his shine. It makes him look older, so much older than he is.

I'm afraid for him. I'm afraid of what's happened to him, the consequences of which we still don't fully understand and probably won't for a long time. I'm afraid of what's still coming, what the Throne will do to him, what the kingdom will do. He's survived so much, and he hasn't even had time to process it, instead forced right back into surviving.

I can't lose him again.

As if he hears the thought in my head, Emyr catches me staring again. Our eyes lock and he reaches over to curl his fingers over mine, bringing my knuckles to his mouth. His fangs brush over the back of my hand when he kisses me there, and, in spite of the long, hard, horrible day it's been, a shock goes straight down my spine.

God, I love him. My *boyfriend*. I love that word, too. I *love* my *boyfriend*. It took me so long to get here, to strike the balance between marrying him and running away from him. To find the version of the future where I got to have Emyr, and I got to have *myself*, too. Where loving him didn't feel like giving up, and I didn't have to go through with the impossible task of leaving him, either. And now I just want to savor it, as much as I can. I *love* him.

Maybe I'm not *in love* with him. I'm not totally sure I understand the difference. Maybe there isn't one, not really, not for us. But we have all the time in the world to figure that out.

Which is good, you know, because I really wanna keep looking at him. Emyr North is the most beautiful thing I've ever seen. Even right now, tired as I know he is, after doing an entire murder, he's beautiful. His sharp cheekbones, and the golden jewelry in his septum and ears. His full mouth, and soft curls, and perfect, deep black skin. Broad shoulders and big hands and—

Derek Pierce's blue eyes appear in my mind. I can see his mouth, his cruel smile. And suddenly, I can't breathe.

Of course, neither can Derek.

Emyr interrupts my thoughts, yanking me back to the present. "How is Briar?"

"Oh. Uh. I'll ask."

He lets go of me when the phone is in my palm again. I think it's subconscious, this fear like it might attack him if it gets too close. Either way, I don't blame him for it.

i guess we'll see. can't really talk to him about it in present company. jin's still acting shell shocked after seeing clarke.

MY GIRL
Ugh. I'll call them tonight. We'll talk about it.

Right. Because that's a thing those two do now. And they don't just talk on the phone, they *video chat*. All the time.

If I sound irritable about that, it's because I am. I'm pretty sure Briar has developed a crush on Jin. Which would be all well and good under normal circumstances. Jin is great. Not great enough for Briar, but, you know, who is?

But, right now, Jin is really, deeply, *Going Through It*, and I'm pretty sure Briar is throwing herself into yet another relationship where she's responsible for fixing someone. Where she opens up her bright, beautiful, perfect heart and lets someone else suck the life out of her until they've nearly drained her dry.

I would know what that looks like, because I've done it to her, too.

Their little blossoming *whatever* is part of the reason I was so very okay with Nadua and Sunny forcing her to come home for a while, even though it feels *bad and wrong* for the two of us to be apart. Besides, Briar's doing important work. She and her mom have found way more changelings than I think any of us realized were out there.

ok.

so, how are you doing? you think you're gonna be let off the leash anytime soon? i miss your face.

i don't get to see it nearly as much as some people do these days.

Alright, well, that last part is petty. And I don't want to sound like a jealous ex-boyfriend.

But also, it's true! So!

My phone dings again and I roll my eyes when I look down at our conversation to find a selfie of her stretched out on the couch, one of the mutts sprawled over her chest. As obnoxious as she is, I can't help the way my chest twists at the sight, anyway.

God, I miss her so much. I miss her, and the dogs, and even that ratty, secondhand couch that's probably seconds away from falling apart. I miss Sunny's cooking and Nadua's too-knowing gazes and coloring with Doli. I even miss Briar's weird, stoic grandmother and her game shows.

What I'm doing here is important. Emyr needs me, and the witches need both of us. Asalin is changing for the better, and it's because of things that *I* helped set in motion.

But it doesn't change the fact that none of this is what I imagined for myself. And all of it would be easier to handle if I had my best friend.

you are such a smartass.

MY GIRL
I love you, too.

I'm doing fine. Mom's managed to hunt down a changeling elder in NZ. Think she might be up for talking with you two.

When are you meeting with the Bells??

The Bells are the kings of Monalai, the Oceanian fae kingdom tucked away in New Zealand. Emyr's had a meeting with them on the books for a while now, but we've canceled every time to chase down a new lead about Derek and Clarke.

The night Emyr died, when he woke up in my arms and we learned the truth about Clarke and all of her scheming, we learned other truths, too. Like the fact that fae magic is taking too much from the planet. That it's killing it, right under our feet. And it makes sense. We know that fae magic nearly destroyed Faery, and that's why our ancestors had to come through the door to Earth in the first place. We know fae magic takes power from Earth, the way that witch magic takes power from emotion. Eventually, all take and no give leads to a pretty stark imbalance.

Clarke's ideas about fixing it involved ridding the world of any non-fae. No more witches, no more humans. Fewer people, more time to drain the planet dry.

Emyr's ideas are...not genocidal. He wants to put restrictions in place on fae magic. To halt how often they're able to wield their power. And he can do it, using the technology Jin has created. Human science and witch magic could replace fae power, without the planet taking any more damage.

Extremely unfortunate that Emyr is now terrified of the very magic he's relying on to save us all. But that's not the point.

The point is, Asalin slapping restrictions in place means nothing without the other kingdoms on board. We've already met with Paloma and Maritza, the queens of Eirgard, and they're willing to work with us on a plan moving forward. Now it's just a matter of winning over the other three.

Convincing fae royals to give up their magic and rely entirely on the magic of those they oppress? Yeah, shouldn't be too hard. Especially with us starting out on such a great foot, with all the canceled meetings.

　　　　　　　　　　　　　　　　　　soon, i hope.

MY GIRL
Well, let me know if you get it figured out and we'll try to get something on the books.

Mom wishes you'd come home and see US, too, you know.

　　Well. Rather than crying about that, as I would sort of like to do, I shove my phone into my pocket and ignore it.

　　We're back inside Asalin's border, anyway. The car carries us up the cobblestone path through the heart of the village, where it immediately strikes me how…empty everything seems. It's silent. No one is milling about. It's later in the evening, but not *that* late. Where the hell is everyone?

　　I get my answer moments later when we pull up in front of the palace. A crowd has gathered there, a congregation standing at the base of the steps. Kadri stands in front of the doors, her hands folded over the head of her cane, long white braids hanging down her back. Lorena is at her side, the purple-haired witch seeming to argue with the crowd, throwing her hands up and shouting down the stairs at them. Roman and Solomon, Lorena's partners, stand off to the side, as if prepared to jump in and defend her at any moment.

　　"What the hell is going on now?" Tessa growls, throwing the car door open and jumping out before we've even come to a complete stop.

She's such a *dumbass*. It's humiliating. I can't believe we share the same gene pool.

(I imagine there are plenty of circumstances where she would say the same about me, but that's really neither here nor there.)

When the car *does* come to a stop, Emyr, Jin, and I scramble out after her. The crowd has turned away from Lorena and Kadri to face us, a sea of faces with expressions ranging from fury to fear.

"How can you live with yourself?"

"What more has to happen before you make things right?"

"You've disturbed the natural way of things! This is the consequence!"

"None of us are safe anymore!"

"HEY!" Tessa throws her arms out in front of Emyr, wings slamming out as wide as they'll go on either side of her body, forcing the crowd back a few paces. "Back off!"

A bark comes from the side, and Boom suddenly appears, pushing himself up against Emyr's and my legs, a desperate, terrified whine escaping the massive wolf-dog. Emyr reaches down to scrub a hand over the top of his head. "What are you doing this close to the castle?"

I link elbows with my boyfriend, and we force our way past the crowd, Tessa and Jin and Boom helping to make a path for us, until we reach Lorena.

"Thank god you're back," she groans, rubbing her knuckles over the shaved half of her head. "They're beside themselves."

"They're always beside themselves." Roman pipes up from behind her. When I look over at him, his intense eyes capture mine. "Happy hunting?"

"Uh. Long story." Derek's dead, but Clarke is still out there, and angrier than ever, and I really don't think I can get into that with Roman right now. Weeks ago, during a riot that the Pierce siblings conspired to start, Clarke murdered Lavender, the witches' elder matriarch, and the very woman who *raised* Roman. He's not going to be happy about what went down in the mountains. "What's going on here?"

"There has been an incident," Kadri drawls, stepping up next to Lorena and staring down at me with a shrewd expression. Kadri North always has a way of making me feel like a problematic little bug. Like, more than I usually do. "Leonidas was attacked."

"Mother, what are you talking about?" Emyr straightens at my side, shaking his head. "What happened? Where is he?"

"He's alright. Shaken, but healed. He's retired to our chamber for the night, and does not want visitors." Kadri sniffs, giving a small shake of her head. "He was unable to identify who the assailant was. Your hound discovered him. We believe Boom may have saved his life."

Boom gives another long, low whine.

Down at the base of the stairs, Jin and Tessa are still trying to control the crowd, whose panic is suddenly making a lot more sense. Especially as my own fear begins to wind its way through me, body feeling suddenly cold.

Leonidas is getting up there in age, but he is still a powerful Influencer. And more than that, he's one of Asalin's heroes, one of their most revered leaders in history, beloved almost universally. Traditional enough not to upset the fae, but kind and charming enough to earn the favor of the witches. He has his secrets, the extent of which we may still not know, but those secrets aren't public knowledge. What kind of person would just *attack him*? And why?

Boom lets out a soft, pitiful whine and presses himself tighter to my legs. My eyes flick to the forest where he usually spends his time, only to find other eyes already looking back at me. All along the tree line, tucked just into the shadows, the other creatures of Asalin, goblins and hellhounds, peryton and pixies, have gathered. The weight of their stares, the eerie, silent judgment, makes my breath hitch.

"Do you regret getting rid of the Guard yet?" someone shouts from the crowd below, and Emyr and I twist our bodies in sync to look down at the man. "Derek Pierce knew you would be our downfall! He did everything he could to try and stop you! And he was right about it all!"

Emyr stares the man down for a long moment before giving one small shake of his head. "I assure you, whatever you may think of me, Derek Pierce would not have been able to save you, either."

Arm in arm, the two of us enter the castle as the crowd outside continues to yell their accusations at our backs.

CHAPTER THREE

NOTHING GOOD HAPPENS WHEN SOMEONE KNOCKS ON YOUR DOOR IN THE MIDDLE OF THE NIGHT

I'd never intended to move in with my first serious boyfriend so soon after we started dating, but I'm also constantly doing shit I don't intend to.

After Briar left to go back to Texas, our old room felt too big. The bed was too empty. As it turns out, I am a cuddly sleeper. I'm a freaking *little spoon*. Go figure.

Emyr and I had just gotten back from North Carolina, no closer to catching Derek and Clarke, and neither of us wanted to be alone. That was when I ended up sort-of-accidentally relocating to His Royal Highness's chamber and making myself comfortable.

Boom brushes against my thigh when we enter the bedroom, gliding past me to leap into the oversize black bed. He curls up at the foot, resting his chin on his massive front paws, and gazes at me with those wide red eyes. I wish I could ask him what he saw today.

"It's unsettling, seeing him here," Emyr drawls at my back, tossing his sword and scabbard next to Boom with little care. I turn in time to see him moving toward his wardrobe, deft fingers undoing the buttons on his shirt before shrugging the supple fabric from his shoulders.

If nothing else has stayed the same, I take some comfort in the fact that Emyr's clothing choices still leave me speechless. The shirt he's just taken off is made of baby-pink velvet, his pants white dragonhide with sheer lace sides running down the length of both legs. I'll know the world is finally coming to an end if he ever puts on a T-shirt and jeans.

The dark muscled curve of his bare back rolls with a lethal grace, leathery wings stretching out at either side of his tall, finely tuned frame. One sharp, golden tip catches the light and casts a warm glow over his throat.

I force myself to look away. Begone, gay thoughts. It is extremely not the time. "Tell me about it. Apparently the palace isn't as scary as whatever went after your dad."

Before today, Boom rarely wandered any farther from Emyr's cottage in the woods than he had to. We haven't seen much of him lately, with all of our running around, and I've missed him almost as much as Briar. The hellhound sighs, hard, blowing out a hot puff of air from his snout. I reach down to scratch behind his ears, and he lets his eyes close.

Emyr growls and kicks off his heeled boots with too much force.

"Who *do* you think went after your dad?" I hedge, tugging

off my own boots and clambering, otherwise fully dressed, up into the bed behind Boom. "What do you think happened today?"

"I don't know!" Muted gold flares in his hands, and he slams his palms against the wardrobe's door. Wood splinters under the force of his hand.

Boom gives a startled half growl, eyes popping open.

I only blink, unimpressed.

Death, trauma, the pressure of being king, his father being attacked, and an angry mob screaming at him that it's his fault...

Emyr's claws curl into the wood and he tips his head forward, breathing deep. Moments tick by. I study the shape his shadow makes as it hugs the wall.

Finally, he tugs his wings in against his back, turning to look at me and letting his hands fall. "I'm sorry."

Unbothered, I shrug one shoulder. "You're reaching your limit."

"I'm not *allowed* to reach my limit."

What sucks the most is that he's right about that.

Tessa's been pretty insistent about all of us needing therapy. She's probably not wrong, either. Unfortunately, fae therapists are not a thing, and human therapists are, um...not equipped to handle this.

He sighs, going back to getting undressed. "I don't know what happened. But I'll see if I can get him to tell me more tomorrow—should he *deign* to have visitors."

I don't miss the bitter edge sneaking back into his voice. I get it. Things between Emyr and Leonidas were weird *before* all of...everything.

For tonight, though, there's no getting any answers. And I'm still exhausted.

With a groan, I haul myself up out of bed to shuffle into the attached bathroom. I *hate* this bathroom. It's way too big, first of all. Like, grossly big. There is absolutely no reason we need a tub the size of a small swimming pool, or a walk-in waterfall shower that could probably fit the whole secret witch club. (Which I'm pretty sure has disintegrated into nothing since Lavender died.) There is really no need for every single surface to be made of gold and crystal, or for one massive wall to be made entirely of mirror so I can't avoid looking at myself.

There are some perks to Emyr being king, I guess. We've got more leverage, more power on a global level. We aren't as vulnerable as we were before, or at least it doesn't feel like it. But seriously, sometimes I really, really miss the tiny rundown house in Laredo.

I grab my toothbrush and spread on the paste, shoving it between my teeth as I glare at the reflection looking back at me over the sink. The dark circles under my eyes have gotten worse. Somehow, the scars painting my jaw, slicing up the sides of my cheeks and curling toward my nose, look even *more* noticeable now that I've got this death's-doorstep vibe clinging to me. I really need to get a full eight hours in. I may not be the otherworldly supermodel my boyfriend is, but damn. I used to be kind of okay-looking, at least.

After rinsing my mouth out, I strip from my hoodie and jeans, pull off my shirt and tug my binder over my shoulders. Immediately, I can breathe a little easier, my ribs expanding as I suck in a deep breath and twist from left to right. My back makes an uncomfortable cracking sound when I do. That's probably not great. This shit—read: existing—is prematurely aging me.

Standing there in nothing but my boxers, unable to get away from the sight of myself in the mirror, I consider the rest of my body. It's not as unfortunate as my face is right now. It's still pale and scarred, old burn marks from the *worst-worst* night of my life climbing the length of both my arms and sides. My chest is not small, not easily quashed even with the binder and the hoodie, but it isn't bad.

Objectively, I am kind of hot. Emyr definitely thinks so.

And still, Clarke's words roll around in my head like marbles clacking together. *"What would turn this body into a more comfortable place to live?"*

I shove that bitch out of my thoughts as deliberately as I can and grab my T-shirt, yanking it back on and heading into the bedroom again.

Emyr's settled down, sitting up against the pillows with the blanket tucked at his waist. Boom is curled against his side, head in his lap, snoring.

"Your phone went off while you were in there." I reach for my cell, but Emyr shakes his head. "No. The other one."

Ah.

The *other* one is Emyr's cell phone, not mine. Of course, he won't touch it. Barely stomachs it being in the same room as him. But the king needs to be reachable.

Which I guess makes me a glorified personal assistant. Whatever.

I dig the phone out of my bag, pulling up the only notification, a message sent through Fae-Mail. "Robin and Gordon have agreed to reschedule our meeting for next week."

Robin and Gordon. The Bells of Monalai.

Emyr hums acknowledgment.

"Let's all hope Clarke doesn't raze Asalin to the ground before then," he drawls, eyes faraway, not focused on me at all.

I knee my way next to him and take his chin between my fingers, forcing his face toward mine. "We're not talking about Clarke tonight. There's nothing to be done right now. And we both need to sleep."

A moment drifts past us before he sighs, slow and heavy, those bottomless brown eyes holding mine, black and gold energy crawling toward one another and locking together. Emyr reaches up to curl one hand around the side of my neck, trailing his claws down the length of my throat, gently scraping at the surface of my skin. I sway forward, pressing my belly to his side, tipping my head down to press my mouth to the ridged base of one horn. It tightens and twists in response.

Warmth blooms at the core of me. But it's short-lived.

When Emyr reaches his other hand to wrap around the back of my thigh, just beneath the fabric of my boxers, a memory cannonballs me in the chest. The last time Emyr's hands were on my thighs like this. His mouth on my hips, on my pelvis, dipping lower...

And then his lifeless body in my arms, so soon after.

When I pull back and meet his eyes again, I know he's thinking the same thing. That now-familiar expression of anguish and want mingled into something raw has settled on his features.

This happens every time.

"Let's turn the light off," I say, instead of asking how long it's going to be before I can sleep with my boyfriend.

Our bodies can't seem to forget what they lived through that night. Or what they didn't.

Mine remembers how perfect it felt with him on top of me just as sharply as it recalls the pain of losing him. Maybe my nerve endings are trying to make sense of how those things can exist in one memory, and I don't know how long it'll be before they work themselves out.

But it won't be tonight.

Emyr nods and rolls onto his back, stretching out one arm to create a cocoon for me against his side. I brush my fingertips against his collarbone before hoisting myself up out of bed to hit the light switch.

My hand's hovering less than an inch above it when a knock comes at the door.

And I freeze.

Nothing good happens when someone knocks on your door in the middle of the night.

A second knock comes, and Emyr throws himself out of bed, cursing under his breath. Boom disappears under the blanket, a miniature mountain of trembling anxiety-riddled fabric.

Wade Pierce stands in the hallway outside.

"What in the goddess's name are you doing here?" Emyr's voice leaves his teeth on a snarl.

"Emyr," I groan.

The cold shoulder going on here is getting old. And I get it, I do. I understand why Emyr's angry. Wade knew Clarke was a double agent. He knew she didn't really want equality for the witches, knew she didn't want to see Emyr on the Throne, and he didn't tell anyone she was a liar. And because he was so afraid of what might happen to his sister if he just did the right thing, Emyr died. He might have stayed dead. I'd like to kick Wade's teeth in just for that.

But I think he knows he fucked up. He thought he could change Clarke. He thought he might be able to help her over to the right side instead of turning her in and ruining her life. And it seems obvious to me how much he loves Emyr. How hurt he is that he's been shut out since that night.

It's not obvious to Emyr. I'm not even sure if he believes Wade's story. There's a chance Emyr really thinks Wade wanted him dead.

And if that's true? Well…Wade would get a lot worse than a cold shoulder from me.

He looks as gross and sleepless as I do, long blond hair greasy and limp around his shoulders, matching black bags on the apples of his cheeks. He winces at Emyr's tone, swallowing before he says, "Martha's had the baby."

Oh? Martha Pierce is Derek's wife—well, Derek's widow, now. She's been about to pop for a while. Honestly, I'm surprised to hear she didn't have the kid already, before tonight.

"Why could that possibly be worth waking me up in the middle of the night?" Emyr demands, and I do not point out the fact that we weren't actually asleep.

"The child is a witch."

Silence follows Wade's words. In fact, the only thing I can hear is suddenly the sound of my own blood rushing, my own heart pounding in my eardrums.

Derek Pierce's heir...is a witch.

Oh.

Oh, that's...*hilarious.*

But wait. I frown, pushing past Emyr to cross my arms at Wade. I'm sure I look very threatening in my pajamas. "So what? Why did you need to tell us that?"

He frowns, glancing from my face to Emyr's. "Ah..."

"You want a member of the Circle to escort her," Emyr says in a flat sort of tone I've never heard him use before.

Wade nods. "We're still not sure how much of Derek's plans she knew. You said we needed to keep a close eye on her. Didn't think you'd want her going out there alone. So, I thought maybe Tessa—"

"No." Emyr sighs. "I'll take care of this myself."

"Wait, take care of what?" I don't know why, but panic begins misfiring in my chest, a drumming anxiety like a car that won't start. "Escort her where? What are you two talking about?"

Wade blinks. Emyr grits his teeth.

I know the answer. Of course I do. It's doing backflips in my head right now. I just refuse to look at it. One of them is going to have to say it out loud. "Well?"

"She wishes to leave the child outside," Emyr answers in that same unfamiliar tone. He won't meet my eyes.

Wade nods, confirming what Emyr knows, what I already knew.

"You can't be serious."

Emyr takes a deep breath, pinching the bridge of his nose between two claws. He seems lost in his own head, words coming out slowly. "I hate it as much as you do. But we have no way to stop her."

"Bullshit!" I throw my hands up, and black energy flares out like a blast of ash around the outline of my body. "You're the *king*. You can do whatever you want."

"I'm the king. I'm not a dictator." Emyr finally looks at me, only to raise his eyebrows. "Isn't that what we want? For no one group to have all the power? It's her child and this is our law, at least as it stands tonight. The only person who could stop her would be the father, and Derek died this afternoon."

"What?" Wade's face turns several shades whiter.

"Emyr!" Everything else aside, the casual cruelty of telling Wade about his brother's death like *that* isn't lost on me. "What is *wrong* with you?"

Emyr stares at me and says nothing. Wade isn't even here, eyes vacant, hands shaking.

Well, fuck this. I don't bother grabbing more clothes, just storm out into the castle in nothing but my boxers and dirty T-shirt, racing off and ignoring Emyr when he calls at my back.

Being in Derek's bedroom immediately sends my fight-or-flight response into high alert. With neither being an option, my body starts leaning toward the third, lesser talked about, option of *fucking throwing up*. Saliva floods my mouth, so thick I almost gag on it.

I've only been in here once before, but the memory is still burned in my head. My back against the foot of his bed, his ice-cold energy encompassing me, whispered threats falling like a song from his mouth.

How much worse could that day have been? What could

he have done to me—and what could he have Influenced me
to think I wanted?

I can't think about it. If I do, I won't stop. And I'm here
for a reason.

Martha is in bed, only a tear-stained porcelain face and a
tangle of red curls visible over the top of the sheet, but she
sits up straighter when I barge in. "W-Wyatt? Get out! I don't
want to see anyone!"

I've only had run-ins with Martha a couple of times since
her husband took off. She's always been nice to my face. Of
course, that doesn't change the fact that she was married to
the leader of a fae terrorist group. And now she's trying to
throw her kid away, because they weren't born the way she
imagined they'd be.

"I don't really give a shit what you want, Martha."

There's a little white bassinet in the corner of the room,
tucked away out of sight, the edges adorned with lace. My
knees shake as I approach it.

I don't think I've ever seen a newborn before. At least not
that I can remember. It's so *small*, smaller than I ever thought
a person could be. (And I just barely make it over five feet tall.
So, like, I *know* small.) The little thing is wrapped up like a
burrito in a pink blanket, eyes closed, perfectly still.

"Don't look at her!" Martha's voice is choked, sobs cracking around each syllable. I could almost feel bad.

Except I don't. Not even a little.

The baby's so still, and so small, and so very wrapped up
in that blanket, I can't even tell if she's breathing. I reach out
one quaking hand and place it over her chest, to feel for the

rise and fall of her ribs, and she immediately jolts under my touch. I jerk my hand back, worried I might've hurt her.

Tiny little eyes blink up at me. Blink. Blink. Then slide closed again.

She already has hair. A little bit, anyway, blond tufts sticking up at weird angles on top of her skull. She isn't exactly cute. Her skin's all red and pink and splotchy, wrinkled like there's too much of it to fit on her tiny frame.

Her energy is *crazy*. Babies aren't born with a set color. It usually develops a little later, at some point in the first year or two. Right after they're born, the color can shift and change, bouncing from one shade to the next at random. And right now, hers looks like a freaking rainbow, an assortment of every color I can imagine just swirling around her, filling up all the space in the bassinet that her body doesn't.

I picture her dumped in a ditch somewhere. Left in the woods for animals to find. She's so small. She wouldn't be able to do anything if something got ahold of her. What would she feel? What would she think? I don't even know if babies *have* thoughts.

How would something so small process that kind of pain?

It's not a conscious decision, but suddenly I'm reaching into the cradle and sliding my hands under her to lift her toward my chest. She does that little jumpy thing again, but settles even more quickly this time. My black energy curls around her rainbow. Her cheek rests against the crook of my elbow, and her lips suddenly pop open.

Oh.

She's kind of cute.

"Wyatt." I don't know when Emyr got here, but that's his voice.

I turn to find him and Wade have come into the room. I don't like the look either man is giving me.

"She isn't garbage, Emyr." Is that my voice cracking? Why? That's weird. "She can't just be thrown away."

"Get him out of here," Martha hisses, voice sloppy with her tears.

"Wyatt, give Wade the child." Emyr takes a step toward me. "We will change the laws. We will protect the witches. But I can't just wave my hand and make a new rule on the spot. I have to gather the Circle, I have to—"

"THEN GATHER THE CIRCLE!"

Emyr stares at me with soft, sad eyes. "Wyatt, you have to let her go."

Sometimes, when I'm very quiet, I think I can still hear my mother's voice buried in the back of my mind. *Do you know how lucky you are we chose to keep you? We could have left you for dead in the woods.*

I never felt lucky. Maybe I should have.

Emyr's hands brush against my arm. I growl and show off my fangs when he curls them around the child's sleeping body.

"Wyatt, listen to me," he's whispering now. "The baby has to go beyond our border. What happens after that is not within fae control. Do you understand what I'm saying?"

"I can't believe you're doing this."

He slides her out of my arms, and I stare on in horror as he passes her into Wade's, instead.

"I'm doing what has to be done." Emyr shakes his head. "*Please* trust me."

And I do trust him. I trust Emyr with my life. He would never do anything to hurt someone unless he had to. I *know* that.

But right now, I can't understand why he has to.

CHAPTER FOUR

HOW ARE YOU GOING
TO LIVE WITH YOURSELF?

I don't end up sleeping at all, but none of us do.

Martha wants the baby gone as quickly as possible. But she has to be the one to do it, and her body is still recovering from labor. Besides, Emyr has a thousand questions to ask first. He wants her to be sure she understands what she's doing, wants to be sure she knows all the alternatives available. And there are many alternatives. Wade would take the baby. There are witches in the village who would be happy to have her.

But Martha knows, and she's sure. She does not want someone else to raise her child. She does not want to see her out there in the world, an abomination wearing a familiar face, and be reminded of her own loss.

Loss. She's in mourning. She's grieving the child she carried for nine months, the baby who no longer exists, and who never really did.

Emyr doesn't bother telling her about Derek.

When she starts to cry, big heaving sobs that rattle her slim shoulders, wailing out to the ceiling, I have to leave. I want to grab her, throttle her, tell her that her baby is there, her baby is *right fucking there*, perfect and *alive*, but I know it won't do any good. A witch baby is worse than a dead one, as far as these people are concerned.

I shouldn't go to the woods, but I do anyway. I'm not alone. Shadows move in my periphery. Eyes watch my every step from above. I'm not afraid of what the things out here might do to me, but *I'm* not really here. I flip through the possibilities to fix this but keep coming up short, like trying to solve a puzzle without all the pieces, jamming together corners that belong on opposite sides. I listen to the sound of Martha's screaming in my head until her voice turns into my mother's. Eventually, I could almost mistake the dawn fog for smoke as it starts to float up from the ground.

There's no knowing how long I spent in the Pierces' bedroom, and even less how long I wander through the trees. It takes me some time to bring myself back to my own body. And when I do, I find my feet are bloody and sore. Probably should have stopped to get dressed before heading outside, huh?

I head back toward the castle.

I'm not alone here, either.

Emyr towers over Martha as he walks behind her, the two of them emerging from the trees on the other side of the courtyard. Tessa, expression grim, follows a few paces back. I don't know when she became part of the night's—now morning's—events, but I imagine sending the king out into the woods alone with the widow of the man who tried to steal his throne would have been ill-advised.

Martha's cheeks are red, her teal energy dragging along at her feet. Emyr hasn't slept in ages, and he looks it. They're careful not to walk close enough that they might accidentally touch each other.

There's no baby with them.

I feel like I'm going to die.

The four of us converge at the foot of the steps. Martha juts her chin up at me in something like defiance, though the action is belied by the way her body trembles.

I want to summon the energy to hurt her. There is a part of me that wants to burn her alive, to watch her skin roast away and peel from her bones. And I *want* to want it even more than I do. But I go looking for the fire, for the rage that's so familiar to me, and I come back feeling cold.

Because Martha Pierce is just one terrible woman consumed by her own sadness and bigotry. She has no idea why this thing she's done is as awful as it is. And even if I'm never going to forgive her, I know she didn't end up here on her own.

The whole fucking fae world is responsible for what happened here. The entire system, built on generation after generation of poisonous lies meant to keep the witches under control, brought that newborn to the woods to die alone.

My eyes burn. My tongue feels thick, and bile threatens to climb its way up my throat.

When I open my mouth, I almost expect to lose the contents of my stomach all over Martha's shoes. Instead, I say, "You will be out of the castle by this afternoon."

Derek was afforded a room in the castle because of his position as leader of the Guard. After he was arrested, no one got around to kicking Martha to the curb. Partially out of guilt over her pregnant white woman tears. Partially because no one's had the time to even think about her, with everything else going on.

But she's not pregnant anymore. And if she's feeling well enough to walk past Asalin's border to abandon her child to the elements, she's well enough to pack her shit and move.

Her eyes widen in disbelief. She turns to look at Emyr, as if expecting him to tell her something different.

Instead, he visibly bristles as he stares down at her. I can hear the unspoken *Are you kidding me?* in his glare.

Defeated, Martha lets out a quiet little whimper and turns to head inside.

Only when she's gone do I redirect any of my anger back at Emyr. "Are you proud of this one, Your Highness?"

"Wyatt—"

"How are you going to live with yourself? How am I supposed to *look at you?*"

Emyr reaches up to rub his fingertips into his eyelids.

Tessa steps forward, joining at his side. "Seriously, Wyatt—"

"And *you*," I scowl, flashing fangs at her. "What happened to changing for the better? This isn't very *revolutionary* of you, I gotta say."

"Okay, Wyatt, that's really enough."

The last voice is neither Emyr's or Tessa's. It actually *hurts* how familiar it is, like a punch to the gut that knocks the wind right out of me. But it doesn't belong here, and my brain scrambles to try and understand how I'm hearing it.

I look up, away, past my boyfriend and sister, toward the woods again. And everything inside my body goes flipping upside down, organs doing cartwheels behind my bones.

Briar has emerged from the tree line, dressed in sweats with her long curls in a ponytail, smiling in a way that doesn't light up her eyes. Her bright yellow energy bobs along at her shoulders, restrained—but far from extinguished.

Her mother, Nadua, is following close behind her. The older woman is dressed down, too, in a white T-shirt and soft black pants, her clay red energy wrapped around her forearms like bands.

Or maybe like swaddling blankets. Because in her arms, she's cradling a bundled-up infant.

"I don't... I'm..."

"Our law states that once a child is left beyond the border, their parents reject all claim to them. It dictates nothing about what happens after that." Emyr's voice sounds a hundred worlds away. "We *will* change the law. But tonight, this was the only way."

His words make sense, but I can't understand them. Everything is happening both too quickly and in slow motion. Everything hurts.

Briar doesn't hesitate as she finally reaches the steps, her arms coming around me and dragging me to her chest. She smells like chocolate and sunlight. "Oh, Wyatt," she whispers, pressing her face against the top of my head, kissing my temple. "You seriously didn't think Emyr was going to just let her *die*, did you?"

"He—how did you even get here?"

"He called me as soon as Wade told him what was going on." Briar sighs against my skull. "Told us to get here as quickly as we could. Made sure tickets were waiting at the airport. Kept Martha busy until we landed."

All those questions, the hours spent interrogating her in that room. He was stalling, buying Briar and Nadua time to get here, knowing the baby would be safe once they were.

And. Wait. I pull out of Briar's arms, looking sharply at Emyr, eyebrows making a tight line just above my nose. "You *called* them? On the phone?"

The pointed tip of one of his ears twitches. "I didn't have any other option, did I?"

Oh.

Oh, I am the worst boyfriend in the *entire world*.

I am going *directly* to boyfriend hell.

"I'm so sorry," I say, and I know it isn't enough.

"Mmm-hmm." He looks down at Nadua when she approaches, inclining his head down at the baby. "How is she?"

"Formula and some skin-to-skin contact and she'll be just fine." Nadua pats gently at the baby's back through the blanket she's wrapped in. "Nice to see you again."

"Likewise."

Right. The last time Emyr and Nadua saw each other, we were in Texas and she'd just stabbed him. Of course, in her defense, he had wandered, all behorned and shit, into her backyard to kidnap me.

"Wyatt..." Briar's voice brings me back to her. The saddest smile tugs at one corner of her mouth, and she reaches a hand up to press against my ruined cheek. Her thumb strokes tenderly beneath my eye, and she gives a small shake of her head. "It's okay. Everything's going to be okay."

I'm here now, she doesn't say aloud. *You can take a breath.*

And I do. For the first time in weeks, I feel myself let go. I lean forward to bury my face in her chest, wrapping my arms around her waist, my fingers digging into my wrist behind her back.

I start crying before I realize I've given myself permission to. I think the others leave us alone at the base of the steps, but I don't pull away again to confirm. I just cry, and Briar just holds me, and we stay that way for as long as we can.

Inside, once I finally manage to pull myself into something person-adjacent, a member of the staff tells us Emyr has called a meeting of the Circle in the Throne room. I'm *barely* keeping myself on my feet, but somehow I manage to lead Briar through the labyrinthine staircases to get where we're going. The Throne room is near enough to Emyr's and my (luxury apartment posing as a) bedroom that I pass it often. Though, it's the kind of room I would rather avoid, if I could. It reminds me of all the parts of the monarchy I would rather forget.

Before we can actually get inside, though, we run into Wade. He's standing outside the massive golden door, hands tightening and stretching at his sides. When he turns at the sound of our approaching footsteps, the wild look in his eyes, surrounded by deep violet circles, tell me he probably never got any sleep, either.

"Wyatt," he half whispers, voice raspy and desperate. *"Please."*

Briar shoots me a look, eyebrows rising. *You got this?*

I wave her forward, and she nods, slipping past him and into the room without us. As much as I don't want to do this right now, someone has to, and it looks like that someone is me.

"Please what, Wade?"

"I need—" His hands reach out like he's trying to grab at something in the air between us. But they twist around nothing, and his fists fall again. "How is she?"

"The baby?" At his nod, I shrug. "Formula and skin-to-skin and she'll be fine."

He lets out a jagged-edged sigh. *"Thank you."*

"I didn't really do anything." Except almost make everything worse. I should really learn to stop doing that. I thought I was getting better. "You should be thanking Emyr."

"Don't you think I'd like to?" Wade's eyes meet mine, and I realize he's on the verge of tears. It's unsettling, seeing him like this. Only a few weeks ago, Wade was so put together. So on top of everything. He's been falling apart since the night Emyr died. But he can get in line. "He barely looks at me. Maybe—could you talk to him?"

Ugh.

"I really don't think that's my place." *Is it* my place? I actually have no idea what is and isn't my job, where the boundary lines are. When do I stop being his boyfriend and start being a member of the Circle? How much can I push him, on either side, before I push too far? Emyr and I should probably talk about that.

Not like we have anything else going on at the moment.

"I don't know what else to do!"

"Did you ever think about... *not* letting Clarke try and kill him?"

Wade looks like I've just taken a knife to him. (He should be grateful I haven't done worse than that, yet.) His lips have the audacity to quiver, and he opens and closes his mouth a few times before sucking in a deep breath to force himself to answer. "Wyatt... I had no idea what my sister was planning. And if I had, I would have turned her in myself. I love Clarke. I...I loved Derek." He winces. "But I realized a long time ago I could love someone and they could still be a bad person. I just hoped Clarke could change. When I saw her with Jin... I just hoped she could change."

"And your hope almost got Emyr killed. No, wait, it did get Emyr killed. I just brought him back." I press my fangs against the inside of my mouth, trying not to lose my shit here. Trying not to think about Emyr's body oozing black and gold, his eyes rolling back in his head, his light snapping out.

God, I need to hold him. I need to crawl into our bed and put my head on his chest and sleep for a year.

"You sitting back and watching and hoping nothing bad happened was as good as being an accomplice. Look, I'm not saying you deserve to be iced out forever. And what Emyr did to you tonight? The way he told you about Derek? That wasn't okay. But I'm not going to bend over backward trying to convince him to forgive you, when he still hasn't had a chance to get over the trauma *you* had a hand in causing."

Wade stares at me for a long moment, blinking back tears that slowly evaporate. Finally, he says, "You don't seem like yourself."

"Yeah, well, I'm tired. Also, I'm trying this new thing where I act like less of a piece of shit all the time."

"It's unsettling."

I wave my hand dismissively.

Wade sighs. "I understand. And I will grovel for Emyr's forgiveness for as long as it takes. But, my niece… When can I see her?"

"*That* I will talk to Emyr about." It's one thing not to want to play nice with Wade. It's another thing entirely to keep him away from the baby, especially when he's the only semidecent not-wanted-criminal family she's got left, now that Martha's dropped any claim to her. "So long as you don't plan on giving any more benefit of the doubt to people who would hurt her. People like Clarke."

"Believe me, Wyatt, that chapter of my life is over. My sister won't get the better of me. Not again."

Wade walks away with the world on his shoulders, but I don't watch him go. I turn and head into the Throne room.

Opulence. That's the first word that comes to mind in here. Like Emyr's and my ridiculously overdone bathroom, with the gold and mirrors, except worse, somehow. It's shaped like a half-moon, the floors made of solid gold, the walls a shiny white marble. The ceiling is a thick translucent glass that morning sun filters through.

On the wall now at my back, where the doors are, art and weapons hang side by side. Ancient swords, probably important memorabilia from some long-forgotten battle, next to paintings that would be more appropriate hanging in the Met or something. The fae have had a long time to secretly accrue their wealth and all the *trinkets* that wealth can provide.

I am very aware that I am standing here still in my pajamas.

Across the room, the Thrones themselves sit on a raised platform carpeted in plush red velvet. They're the only part of the room I don't actively *hate* looking at. They look less gro-tesquely rich and more like the outside of the castle, with its carved mountain stones and overgrown ivy. While so much of Asalin has changed over the five hundred years since the fae's arrival in New York, upgrades and renovations always tak-ing place, some more necessary than others, the castle's exte-rior and the Thrones themselves have always stayed the same.

They're made of trees from Asalin's forest, manipulated by Influencer magic to form two oversize chairs. The smaller of the two Thrones is made of delicately laced-together limbs of paper birch, with a high back and two arms stretched out on either side of the seat. The larger is wider, lower, and more mangled, black cherry limbs twisted together to form a nest suitable to sit in. Both are covered in moss and ivy, flowers and berries, all growing unnaturally from the bark, an amal-gamation of the woods outside.

A round table—an unbearably ugly red crystal glass *thing*—sits in the center of the room. There's an untouched plate of biebives in the middle; bite-sized cookies whose flour is made from a combination of crushed nuts and lavender pow-der, dipped in a shimmery sugar glaze and pieces of candied sour fruit.

The other members of Emyr's Circle have gathered. Lorena, Jin, and Kadri are the only ones I haven't already seen this morning.

Lorena looks almost as exhausted as I am. Her blue-black complexion has taken on an ashen edge, puffy bags beneath her dark eyes rimmed with smudged eyeliner. The long purple side of her hair is out of its usual braids, a loose chunk hanging against her throat. She's slumped against the table's edge, leather jacket tight on her muscular shoulders, short black-painted nails thrumming against the glass surface. She hardly spares a glance at me.

Jin, on the other hand, seems almost *too* awake. They've posted up next to Briar, chair turned toward hers, sparks of their dark purple energy buzzing and popping all around them. Their dark hair has been pulled into a short messy pigtail at the back of their head, their many, many tattoos seeming to *shake* against their beige skin as their body trembles with something like manic animation.

Under the table, only vaguely visible through the red-tinted glass, Briar has a hand on their knee. I pretend not to see it.

Of the three, Kadri is the only one who doesn't look like she's falling asleep on herself or overdosing on caffeine. Seated at Emyr's left side, Asalin's previous queen is put together with precision, her long white braids flawlessly framing her sharp obsidian features, every piece of her sage-green suit perfectly ironed in place. Her cane, topped with a crystal cat's head, is spread across her lap. She rests one hand on it, the other on her son's wrist.

I drop into the chair on Emyr's side as Nadua—now feeding the newborn from a bottle—continues a conversation that started before I walked in.

"There is a large group of our people in New Zealand. I've been in contact with one of their leaders. If you'll be there next week to meet with these...kings..." I definitely notice the way her lip curls over her teeth on the word, as if the idea of secret monarchies makes her want to bite. Which, same. "…I'll try to arrange a meeting with them, too."

"Thank you." Emyr reaches over and puts a hand on the back of my neck. It's all I can do not to start purring. Or fall asleep. Or both. "I would appreciate that."

"Don't be too appreciative just yet." Nadua gives a small jerk of her chin. "They're open to the things I've told them about you, but that doesn't mean they're going to trust you. They've only survived as long as they have because they've kept themselves secret from your kind."

Changelings like Briar and her mother are the descendants of witches abandoned by their fae parents, found and raised by humans in the human world. According to Nadua, there are entire communities of them around the world, raised to live in secret, hiding the truth of their existence from humans and fae alike. Until I caught Briar opening the door, *I* didn't even know what she was. Until we needed help closing it, no one else did, either, besides Emyr. Even now, the only people in Asalin who know are in this room.

"I'm still grateful for your time," Emyr answers with an inclination of his head.

Nadua huffs, clearly skeptical, and turns her attention back to the baby. "What are your plans for the child?"

"Wade wants her." I barely manage the words around a yawn.

"You trust him to care for a helpless witchling?" Emyr's hand falls away from my neck and *oh my god* I'm five seconds away from throwing a tantrum.

"*Trust* is a big word," I mumble.

Tessa clears her throat. Her expression is pinched, almost

pained, when I look over at her. "Emyr, I don't want to overstep—"

"Then don't." He raises his eyebrows.

I think I can see Tessa's teeth grinding behind her lips. "Hmm. All I wanted to say, *Your Majesty*, was that I would be happy to help Wade take care of her."

I still do not totally understand whether Tessa and Wade are in love or just best friends or some combination of the two. Their relationship feels both confusingly profound and extremely queer, but I've yet to get around to forcing my sister to explain it to me.

Emyr crosses his arms and shrugs. "The child was found by Briar and Nadua. They are responsible for deciding what happens to her."

"Pardon me?" Briar's deep brown skin nearly turns gray. "I am not ready to be a mother."

Nadua scoffs, but there's a wry, private smile in the corner of her mouth. "Explaining this to my husband will be interesting, but she won't be the first stray I've brought home."

Our eyes meet across the table and my heart cracks right on open. I'm *not* going to cry again, but I've missed her so much. Not as much as Briar, maybe. But if Briar is my better half, Nadua is the closest I've ever come to a mother who loves me.

Still. Wait.

"No." I shake my head. "No, you can't take her."

"Oh?"

It's like everything is as fine as it ever is these days, and then it isn't. I'm tired and depressed and gay, and then I'm tired and depressed and gay and panicking.

Why is the idea of this baby going away to Texas so terrifying? Like, besides the fact that it's Texas.

Finally, I stumble around with my tongue and find the words. "She needs to be raised with the witches. She needs to know about...herself."

At my side, Emyr sighs. "I'm sure you will remain part of her life."

"Me? Are you kidding? I don't know anything about myself, either." I sit up straighter, looking around the table, hands gesturing wildly as I try to find the words. "Because *I* grew up without the witches. Do you know how much it *sucked*?"

"Children like her have existed for a long time, Wyatt." Nadua tries to soothe me. "This is where the changelings come from."

"Yeah, and that's remarkably shitty. But she *isn't* a changeling, and we can do better for her." I tilt my head at Lorena, narrowing my eyes. "You and the boys ever talk about having kids?"

Lorena balks, waking up immediately. She glances between me and the newborn, still fast asleep in Nadua's arms, oblivious to the controversy of her existence. "Uh. I mean."

"Wade wants her," Tessa reminds us. "And she would still have access to the entire community of witches in Asalin."

"Wade can't *have* her."

"Does she have a name?"

"*Who* would have named her?"

"I could talk to Roman and Solomon, I guess, um—"

"Not sure that *I guess, um,* is the kind of person who should be adopting a child."

Nobody will shut up, and nobody is saying anything I

want them to, and suddenly it is so very much, too much. Black magic slicks, unexpected and seemingly unprompted, up my arms.

My brain feels like it's on fire.

The conversation around the table falls quiet.

I don't know what's wrong with me. I'm too tired for self-control, and something about this topic is slamming all the wrong buttons in my head.

She's just a baby. She's never done *anything to anyone.* And so far, in her first day of life, her mom's tried to have her killed, and her rescuers want to take her away from her people, and no one really seems to *want* her, exactly as she is, and I'm—

"Wyatt." There's Briar's voice, a faraway call to come back. Seconds tick by. I breathe myself back into my body.

Emyr's hand is on my neck again, his thumb pressing into the pulse point under my jaw.

Kadri is the one who speaks next. "We will find a solution that works for everyone involved. But perhaps now is not the time, when so much of the future is still uncertain."

I push away from the table, Emyr's hand falling as I move around to Nadua's spot. The baby's plump cheek is squished against her chest, tiny little fists gathered into balls under her chin. Her wild rainbow energy is tucked around her like a cocoon, but when I reach out to place my palm against the top of her head, a single thread unwinds from the rest and wraps around my wrist. Under my gaze, that single thread turns to a deep warm brown.

"Wyatt." Briar's voice again, this time right at my back.

My hand falls away from the baby and I turn to stare at my best friend.

She offers me that same tired smile. "Wyatt, she's okay. She's safe. And we'll figure it out. But you need to get some rest before you can do anything. You and Emyr should *both* sleep."

I don't remember Emyr standing, but then his hand is on my side and he's pulling me to him.

"Go and *sleep*," Briar says again.

And we do. Emyr and I disappear to our bedroom, and into each other, and we lose the rest of the morning in bed.

CHAPTER FIVE

JUST BECAUSE YOU DON'T KNOW YOUR OWN HISTORY

When I finally come to, it's only because Emyr is extracting his body from mine, sliding his arm out from under my waist to slip out of bed. I growl, reaching for him and coming up with a handful of pillow, still half-asleep.

"Sorry." In the dark of the room, he brushes his claws against my shorn scalp, and I hate myself for the pitiful sound it drags out of me. "Was hoping you wouldn't notice."

Emyr is warm and solid and soft and how in the hell did he think there was any chance at all I wasn't going to wake up when he *abandoned me*?

"Where are you going?" I demand, trying to grab for him again. My nails barely manage to scratch at his hip as he moves away from me to turn on the bedside lamp.

Light assaults me and I groan, giving up on reaching for Emyr to pull the blanket over my head. This is a *hate crime*.

What could possibly be more important than staying in bed with me?

"I'm going to see my father."

Oh.

Ah, well, okay, fair enough. I suppose Leonidas *was* assaulted yesterday. (Fuck, was that yesterday? My sense of time is still wobbly.) I guess Emyr probably should go and have a conversation with him.

Even though it's incredibly homophobic of him to *cast me aside* like this.

When I finally convince myself to drag the blanket back down, Emyr is half-naked across the room. Which, okay. Sometimes being woken up is worth it. I watch him from behind as he drags on a—

"Is that a skirt?"

"Yes," he says, like it's obvious, because it is, buttoning the waist of a flowy thick black skirt that hangs down to the floor. He adds an oatmeal sweater, oversize enough that it nearly hangs off him, loosely knit so it's full of holes, and white booties with a short gold heel. I think I could probably be with him for the next hundred years without seeing him repeat an outfit.

When he sits at the vanity and starts applying glittery eyeshadow, I know he's putting on armor.

"Worried about seeing him?"

"Mmm."

"Fair enough."

Ugh. I suppose if Emyr is going to go be a whole dressed-up person, I should at least consider getting out of bed. I manage to shove myself into a sitting position and fish for my phone on the bedside table.

It's already well into the afternoon. I have a handful of texts from Briar, some pictures of the baby, various assurances that everything is okay and no one is dying. And one that's not from her.

SOLOMON
Come see me when you wake up. You're overdue for a lesson.

Uuuuuugh.

He's not wrong. Solomon is one of the witches, Roman and Lorena's boyfriend, who had to disappear with Jin and a handful of others when they were arrested the night of the riots. And while everyone's been pitching in to help me when they can, trying to coax some more control into my magic, he's certainly been the most insistent.

I guess if Emyr can go talk to Leonidas, I can sit and stare at sigils for an hour, pretending to absorb fuck all of the information.

And like, the most annoying part of it all is that I *want* to learn. It's just that, for some reason, my brain doesn't seem to wanna get with the program. Maybe because it has too much other shit to focus on right now. Or maybe because I'm just broken, not like the other witches.

Oh god, I sound like a *not like other girls* bitch.

Ironically, I was also one of those at one point.

I shoot off a text to Briar asking her to meet me outside so we can go to the lesson together. Solomon and Roman don't know about her being a changeling (unless Lorena's told them behind our backs, which I guess wouldn't be shocking) but she can still sit and "hang out" while actually probably learning more than me.

Next to where my phone was left is my deck of tarot cards. I slide one finger, absentmindedly, against the black box, tracing the gold lettering. Finally, I pick it up and tug it open.

I love this deck. When I ran away from Asalin, the night after I was attacked by fae and started a fire that killed both my parents, I told myself I was going to give up magic for good. I needed to force it down, to rob the fire of its oxygen, so I would never be able to hurt anyone like that again. But it was always there, this undeniable part of me that kept trying to claw its way to the surface. And while I was struggling for control, Briar bought me these cards. Beautiful matte-black cards with gold-stamped lettering and no illustrations. Dark, and simple, and powerful.

She said they could be my one reminder. The one piece of Asalin I carried with me, the last bit of magic I let myself do. And so that's what they became. Every morning, I started pulling a single card, willing my magic to give me a glimpse at the day that was about to unfold. And when I did, controlling my magic in every other way got easier. The cards were like a release valve. I had them, and the fire was put out.

At least until Emyr showed up and doused me in gasoline. But he's always had a way of making me feel both stronger and more out of control than anything else can.

Actually, Emyr was the first person to ever give me tarot cards. Before the night I left Asalin, when we were little children, enamored with each other and our dreams of the future, and I was forbidden from learning about my own magic, the prince snuck me my very first deck. They were all I had to connect me to my people, even then. Until my parents found them and—oh, this is a cruel bit of irony—burned them.

I slide them through my fingers, shuffling their familiar weight between my hands. It's difficult to explain how well I *know* them. It would probably sound silly to anyone else. But when so much of my magic, for so long, has been in these cards, and *only* these cards, they feel almost like an extension of my own hands.

And maybe because of that, there's a part of me that knows the card I'm going to pull before I pull it. I flip it over in my lap and sigh.

Eight of Swords.

Indecision. Restriction. Playing the victim.

Sounds like today's lesson is gonna go *great*.

Emyr is just taking a blade from the wardrobe, fastening it to a leather belt around his waist, when I force myself out of bed. The last piece to go on is his crown. It catches the light from the lamp, glinting a sharper, brighter gold than the energy currently hanging from his shoulders like a cloak. I don't stare, though there's a part of me that would like to.

"Gonna head to the triad's." I grab my binder, boxers, a pair of black jeans and a new T-shirt from the dresser and start wrangling my limbs into them. I'll snag my hoodie on the way out. The sight of my outfit next to Emyr's is probably comical. (There are two kinds of queers...) "Meet you back here in a bit?"

"Have fun," he says, and I honestly don't know if he's being sarcastic—I have never once had fun at a lesson with

Solomon—or if he's too distracted mentally preparing for his conversation with Leonidas that he doesn't even know what he's saying.

"Hey." I slide my phone and cards into my pockets, then reach up to take his chin in my fingers, forcing him to look down at me. "You're gonna be okay. You've got this."

Emyr frowns, his thick eyebrows dragging down toward the base of his nose. After a moment, he sighs, hard, and gives me a forced smile, instead. "You, too."

We're both lying, at least a little.

Solomon, Lorena, and Roman live in a tiny cottage on the very outskirts of Asalin, only a few yards away from the invisible border to the human world, nestled against the tree line. There are overflowing flower boxes in every window, and a giant doormat in the shape of a frog. And there are protective sigils etched into every single log.

I know the magic is meant to keep out unwanted guests, but it doesn't do anything to me. I've been here before, a few times now, and maybe it's just used to my presence, or maybe its owners have told it I'm not a threat. (In which case: a bold assumption.) Either way, I don't hesitate to walk right through the front door like I own the place, calling out, "Honey, I'm home!"

"In the office!" comes Briar's voice, and I follow after it like a well-trained dog.

The inside of the trio's house is just as cute as the outside, and remarkably weirder. I have to pass through the foyer, the living room, and the kitchen to get to the office. Each room is painted a different dark, moody color, while all the furniture is bright and covered with far more pillows than necessary. They're very much *not* into the minimalism trend. There's just so much *stuff* everywhere. The walls are lined with built-in shelves, each one cluttered with weird knick-knacks, books, bones, and potion vials. There are temporarily discarded projects shoved in every possible corner; paintings a few brushstrokes short of completion, flowers hanging up to dry, what appears to be a handmade dining table, half-constructed and left sitting in the middle of the room. They've abandoned cups on every available surface, each of them containing only the dregs of whatever they were once filled with.

The office is a small room at the back of the cabin, the back wall half bookshelf and half glass. Solomon sits in the center of the room at a little wooden table, facing me with his back to the massive window. He's a beautiful man, a couple of years older than Emyr and a few inches taller, but infinitely more *delicate*. His warm skin reminds me of copper, his curls loose and bouncing like a halo around his face. His off-white turtleneck and cat-eye glasses look fitting on him, and his olive green energy floats out at his back, as if reaching for the books.

Briar's already seated at the table in front of him, and she grins up at me, the gap-toothed smile that shows off the dimples in her rounded cheeks.

Unfortunately, they aren't alone. Jin is poised in the chair at Briar's side, body twisted toward her, the knuckles on one hand (seemingly absentmindedly) running along her shoulder.

I don't *want* to hate this. But I *do*.

Jin's not the only spectator, either. Roman's here, sitting on the edge of the table, one boot unceremoniously propped on top of it so he can rest his chin on his knee. Roman is, like…he's hot in the way that only unstable white boys are ever considered hot. He looks like he has a nicotine addiction and hasn't slept in years, with a corpse-like bone structure and a ton of piercings in his face and unkempt brown hair hanging down to his shoulders. His scarlet-red energy twitches in my direction when I enter. It reminds me distinctly of a snake flicking its tongue.

"Wyatt."

"Roman." I don't bother with more than that, though, and turn my attention to Briar. "How's…"

I don't actually know who to ask about here. The baby doesn't have a name yet.

But she seems to get the idea, reaching up and wrapping her hand around my wrist, tugging me down into the chair on her other side. "She's fine. She was sleeping when I left. Lorena's with her and my mom now."

"Congratulations, by the way. We just heard about your bundle of joy." Roman inclines his head at me.

I ignore him.

Or I would, if I had to. I don't, though, because Solomon interjects to bite out, "Are *all* of you staying for Wyatt's lesson?"

"I focus better when Briar's with me," I offer smoothly. It's true, even if it isn't *the* truth.

"Mmm-hmm." Solomon doesn't seem all that interested in my answer. He raises his eyebrows at Jin. "And you?"

"Oh, well, I thought I could help." They smile, placing their hands against the table's surface. "I've been working with Wyatt, too, you know."

It's true. Jin was the first one I talked to about trying to harness my magic. They started working with me almost immediately, once they realized I wasn't going back to Texas. And they've been helpful. At least as helpful as they can. I've picked up a little bit on sending the spells through the phones, using technology to charge and channel what I'm doing. In a pinch, I can make some magic happen that way.

And, like...okay, I want to preface this by being clear on something. I *love* Jin. I do. Loving people in Asalin isn't a feeling I'm totally used to just yet, but I *do* love them. And I hate what Clarke did to them. I hate knowing what they've been through. It hurts. It sucks. I want them to heal, and get better. I'm rooting for them to do that.

However...

It feels like, instead of doing that, they've decided to leech onto Briar as an emotional support bisexual. And they still turn into wet, gloopy mush in Clarke's presence. Like, okay, I cannot imagine the level of grief they're going through right now, that the person they were building a future with, surprise, never loved them and actually wants everyone like them to die. But they won't get angry about it, which they should. They're just being...pitiful. And they're making it Briar's problem. Which makes it my problem.

And I would really rather they not be here right now, when I need to concentrate on my own shit.

I don't know if Roman sees something on my face and decides to intervene, or if he's telling the truth when he stands up and says, "Actually, Jin, I could use your help. Been going through Lavender's stuff and found some things I think you might want. Come sort through it with me?"

"Oh…" Their eyes flick between Roman and Briar, clearly struggling to decide between helping their own still-grieving friend go through his dead surrogate mom's belongings or continuing to soak up as much of *my* friend's attention as they can.

Briar gives them a small smile, and reaches out to brush her fingertips over their cheek. "Go. I'll meet up with you after."

Jin sighs, softly, and nods, their eyes still locked with Briar's. "Yeah. Okay."

Excuse the actual living fuck out of me, but are these two about to kiss? The maintained eye contact goes on for *faaaaar* too long.

They don't, though. After an uncomfortably, painfully long moment, Jin finally stands up and follows Roman out of the office. The dwindling tendrils of their electric purple energy cling to the air even after they're gone.

Solomon waits a beat before he huffs. *"Anyway."* He stands and starts grabbing books off the shelf behind him.

Briar meets my eye with a frown. I can read the expression on her face as clearly as if I were a telepath. *What's wrong?*

We are so not getting into this right now. Not even silently. I shrug, hoping to convey a *Nothing—I don't know what you're talking about.*

She obviously doesn't buy it, thick eyebrows rising. She looks like she wants to think some more in my direction, but Solomon's attention is back on me before she gets the chance.

"Okay, here's what we're going to do today." He drops a book in front of me, old and worn, with *Practical Sigils for Witchlings* handwritten in faded black ink across the front. When he opens it up to a page near the front, he points out a simple-looking symbol, two slightly curved lines stacked on top of each other. The instructions written on the page are clear, but he explains them to me, anyway. "You're going to draw this on a cup. And you're going to fill it with water."

"From the sink?"

"You are going to *magically fill it with water.*" I swear he's going to snap my neck with his bare hands. "You can create fire. So, you can create water. Okay?"

"Okay." There is no way I'm going to be able to do this.

He produces a bag filled with a stack of clear plastic cups and a single black marker from the floor under the table and passes them to me.

While I take the first cup and start painfully, meticulously copying the sigil onto it, Briar asks Solomon, "Do you mind if I look through some of the books, too?"

"Go ahead."

The first four times I try, Solomon makes me redo the sigil because it doesn't look right. It looks exactly perfectly right to me, but clearly I don't know anything about anything, so, I let him bully me.

The fifth and sixth times, I glower down at the cup in my hands, willing it to fill with water, until I get so annoyed that my palms light on fire and plastic melts against my skin.

The seventh time, I place it on the table in front of me—decidedly *not* touching me—and try to think about why I might want the water. I imagine being thirsty. My *friends* being thirsty. Magic comes from feeling, right? That's what I learned when I brought Emyr back to life. I can do any-thing, I just have to feel it strongly enough, and find the right channels to get it done.

So, I think about *needing* the water, try to summon up every ounce of panic I can manufacture to trick myself into doing it.

What if Briar and Emyr were dehydrated? *What then, hmm?*

Apparently they would simply die of thirst, because absolutely fucking nothing happens.

"I'm never going to get this!" My arms shoot out, sending the cup and the book flying. The cup bounces off the wall, quietly crinkling, while the book makes a dull thud beneath us.

"Wyatt…" Briar mumbles at my side, disappointment thick in her voice, more cutting than any reprimand could possibly be.

Solomon looks unimpressed. He sits calmly in the chair in front of me, hands folded over his stomach. When the book hits the ground, he barely spares a bored glance in its direction before his eyes flick back to my face.

A moment of silence drags on. I think I hear a clock tick somewhere in the house.

Finally, he asks, "Are you finished?"

I'm not sure if he means finished with the lesson or finished throwing a fit. Either way, the answer is no. "You don't understand what this is like for me. I am *seventeen years* behind already, and it's not like I have a lot of free time to devote to this shit. I'm trying to save the fucking world while studying *kindergarten-level* magic." I throw my arm out demonstratively at nothing. "It's humiliating."

Solomon blinks. "Don't take your embarrassment out on me, Wyatt. We both have better things to do."

I—

Well. He's not wrong.

When I don't actually say anything else, he leans down and picks up the book of sigils, placing it on the table between us again. "This *shit* is the language our people invented to communicate when it was dangerous to even exist as ourselves. It—"

He takes a deep breath and pinches the bridge of his nose, his eyes closing when he does. I scoot back a little in my seat and fold my hands in my lap.

"It is our magic, written in a code only for us to understand. It is the work of hundreds of thousands of hours of labor by witches who came before us, living under the constant threat of fae punishment. It was born of a love for their people, for *you*, you little shit, giving you access to your magic, and risking their own lives to do it." Solomon's hand falls away from his nose and he stares at me, shaking his head. "I am sorry you have been denied the access to this language they fought so hard for you to have. And I am sorry you are being forced to play catch-up now. But you are not going to belittle the work of those who came before you just because you don't know your own history."

Oh.

"I've never…thought about that before."

"About what?"

"That this, all of this—" I wave at the book on the table, the others on the shelf behind his head. "The sigils, and the spells, and the potions, that it was all…created by someone. It always just felt like something that…*was*."

Solomon takes a deep breath, and I know I'm wearing thin on his nerves. Or maybe it's more than that. He does seem so tired. "The fae in Asalin have done everything they can to keep us from having power. Of course we had to create this ourselves."

"Surely some of it came over from Faery, though, right?" Briar pipes up, leaning forward and balancing her elbows on the table, chin in one hand. "I mean, the witches who came through the door must have had their own practices."

"They didn't let witches through the door." He snaps the words, and immediately after, he frowns. "I just—considering how much the fae hate us, they probably left all our ancestors over there to rot, right?"

Makes sense, I guess. A bit of a jump, but not an impossible one.

I rub my palm over the top of my head, taking a deep breath. "Anyway... I'm sorry. I didn't mean to disrespect this. I know you're spending your time to help me here, and I appreciate it. I just... I don't think I'm ever going to get this. It doesn't make sense to me. I'm glad it exists. I'm glad it helps other people. But it doesn't *feel right*. And I don't know if it ever will."

The tense moment seems to have passed. Solomon considers me for a beat and then shrugs. He takes the book from the center of the table and closes it, then stands up and walks it back to the shelf.

"Like any other language, our magic evolves. These things are all just conduits; ways to communicate what already exists inside you. But there are others, of course. Witches in other kingdoms have developed their own systems. After all, look at Jin's technology—it's just another way of communicating." He turns back to us, and folds his thin arms over his chest. "You just need to find something to channel your power.

Something that does feel right, that makes sense to you, that your magic will obey the rules of. Honestly, the *what* is a lot less important than the *why*."

"So, I need to find my what."

"You need to find your what. But until you do, you need to practice what you have."

Briar puts a hand on my neck and gives a small, encouraging squeeze. I kind of wish she would just strangle me to death.

CHAPTER SIX

EVERYTHING IS ACTUALLY DECIDEDLY NOT FINE

"You heading back to the castle?" Briar asks me when we step out of the triad's house not much later. It didn't take long after my freaking out for Solomon to get tired of me and call it quits for the day.

"Yeah." I wanna meet up with Emyr, ask him how things with Leonidas went. If we have any new information on who decided to sneak attack the fallen king.

I don't actually know if he was sneak attacked, but I've certainly concocted a very vivid, fun little story in my brain.

It's not that I hate Leonidas, not necessarily. I just think he's a lying, sneaky, two-faced rat man, who gave Emyr some serious daddy issues and may or may not be a mass murderer.

"Uh." I frown, cocking my head at Briar. "Are you *not*?"

She pushes her hand into her hair, dragging black and teal waves through her fingers, and makes a face, scrunching up the side of her mouth. "Told Jin I'd meet them at Lavender's."

"Oh. Right."

Because Briar is Briar, she hears what I *don't* say and sighs. "I know. Don't start. It's just—they're going through it right now, you know?"

I do know. I'm not trying to minimize the absolute shitshow of a time Jin's been having.

But also, in case Briar hasn't noticed, I am also going through it. And I haven't seen my best friend in weeks. And this is fucking ridiculous.

I don't say any of that.

Briar is an incredibly good friend. She always has been.

When Nadua found me and brought me home, Briar and I attached ourselves to each other right away. I was…bad at being a person back then.

Of course, there's the (probably very convincing) argument to be made that I'm still bad at being a person. But back then, I was worse.

It's been months since I ran away from Asalin, and I haven't slept through the night since. For a while, that was by choice. It wasn't safe to let my guard down for that long when I was crouched next to a toilet in a gas station bathroom, or hiding behind an alley dumpster, or curled up on a park bench. Human men, I've come to realize, aren't much kinder than the fae.

But I'm safe now. Or at least that's what they tell me.

Nadua Begay-Brown found me in a library, pretending to read from an encyclopedia so no one would give me a second glance, and

brought me home with her. I've been here a week now. Nadua is…
not nice, not exactly, but she's kind. There's a difference.

She put up a curtain in her laundry room and shoved a mattress
behind it for me to sleep on. She bought me new clothes from Good-
will. She spent hours cleaning and rebandaging the wounds on my
arms, from the fire, when I told her there was no way I was going
to the hospital. (Nadua says she has no idea how they weren't in-
fected worse than they were. I think it was probably magic. Not that
I could tell her that.)

The rest of her family is kind, too. Sunny, her husband, has a
big booming laugh that takes up all the space in the room, but he always makes his voice small when he notices I'm there, like he doesn't
wanna spook me. Her oldest daughter, Briar, keeps leaving snacks
outside my curtain for me, 'cause I think she's picked up that I don't
like eating around everyone else. Doli, her younger daughter, asks
me every day if I want to play with her, even though I never say yes.
Even her mom, Ruth, who hasn't actually spoken a word to me since
I got here, looks at me with gentleness in her eyes.

This is the first time in my life I've been around humans. Really
around them, anyway, and not just forced to coincide with whoever
was out there in the world between here and Asalin. And they're
nothing like I expected, nothing like the fae always said they were.

And I feel safe here. I think.

But I still can't sleep.

Sometimes, I try. I force myself to lie in my makeshift bed with
the quilt over my head, squeeze my eyes shut, and will myself to fall
asleep. And it works, most of the time, but not for long. The dreams
always come soon after. Usually, I dream of the night I ran. Hands
on my body. Magic around my throat. Fire. Screaming. I wake up
choking. Otherwise, I dream of the human world beyond this house,

the one I wandered alone for months, and I wake up with phantom hunger pains or the whisper of adults' catcalls crawling in my ears.

Only occasionally do I dream of Emyr. Those nights, I wake up crying.

Still, there are nights I don't even bother trying at all. I know what's going to happen, and there's no use fighting it. Tonight's one of those nights. I'm sitting up against my pillows, knees pulled to my chest so I can rest my forehead against them. My arms are wrapped around my legs, dark blond hair spilling over me. Slowly, I rock. Back and forth. Back and forth.

Outside, in the Texas darkness, I can hear coyotes yipping. They call out to each other, hideous, rabid little howls that make it sound like they're surrounding the house. Louder and louder they grow, calls coming faster and faster, circling ever closer.

And then it happens. Another animal begins to scream. I never really knew animals could scream until recently. It almost sounds like a person.

The coyotes wail louder, but it isn't enough to drown out the screaming.

My teeth chatter, a chill shooting down my back, even though it's gotta be ninety degrees outside. All I can think about is the creature outside screaming.

On the other side of the curtain, someone says my name. It's quiet, almost quiet enough that I don't hear it, but when I do, it pulls me back to myself. I blink, sitting up straight. The animal noises from outside aren't as loud as they seemed a second ago. I can hear the A/C running in the walls, a TV playing down the hall.

My name again. I recognize Briar's voice the second time.

"Y-yeah?"

"Can I come in?"

I think coming in *is an overstatement, considering, but still, I say,* "Um, sure."

The curtain shifts and Briar comes into view. She's only a little older than me, maybe just by a few months. She's chubby, and her big round brown cheeks have the deepest-set dimples. ~~They remind me of Emyr's.~~ *They're cute. She's really pretty, actually. And her energy is beautiful, a bright yellow like daffodils. It suits her.*

Right now, that energy is floating its way into the space where my bed is, making itself comfortable. Settled in alongside my black, it makes the whole space feel lighter, less cramped.

"Can't sleep?" *she asks, sitting down at the bottom of the mattress, folding her hands in her lap.*

I force my body tighter into itself, staring down at the space she's taking up at the end of the bed. The thought of her accidentally touching me makes my skin hurt. Trying not to dwell on it, I shrug one shoulder. "You either?"

"Mmm." *She seems hesitant to say the next part, but finally admits,* "I was worried about you."

It's difficult to explain why I don't like that. Why the idea of being seen and looked after makes me uncomfortable, and nervous. I choose not to examine it too closely.

"Why?" *I try not to sound too defensive. I think I probably fail.*

"You seem so tired all the time." *She shifts, biting at her lower lip.* "I was wondering if maybe this space isn't working for you."

This space is *better than where I was before, but I don't exactly want to tell her that. I feel good here, with these people, I think, but I can't exactly tell them about...anything. If I start talking about where I was before this, they might ask where I was before that, and what am I supposed to say? I don't have any satisfying answer.*

At least they haven't asked. Nadua saw all she needed to see when she found me, and I'm pretty sure everyone else just trusts her judgment. But still. Better not tempt them.

I don't want to have to run again. The idea of being back out there, alone...

No. I wouldn't be able to do it again. I'd just walk into traffic.

"No, uh, the space is fine." I push my hair out of my face, over my shoulder. "I just..."

Get nightmares? Even telling her that seems like admitting too much. My voice just trails off, my mouth settling into a frown, unspoken stories hanging in the air between us.

Briar coughs, gently, after a too-long beat. "You wanna come hang out in my room?"

The question catches me off guard. I blink at her, tilting my head, frustratingly pushing my hair away again when it falls right back in my face. "Shouldn't you be sleeping?"

"Nah, it's fine. I was gonna see if I could find something new on Netflix. Wanna help me?"

I do not actually know what Netflix is. That's happened a lot since I got here, but I never know what to say when it does. I am an imposter, pretending to be human, pretending I know what their world is like while I'm really just figuring it out as I go. It's like being a secret agent, except not cool or interesting at all, and actually just extremely terrifying. Because if I screw up and they realize I'm not actually one of them... I don't even wanna think about what happens.

"Sure," is what I go with, and I follow Briar to her bedroom.

She offers me a spot on her bed, but I sit on the floor. She sets up her laptop on the dresser so we can both see, and settles on something called Queer Eye. I guess it's a show where a bunch of (gay?) men give life makeovers to sad people. Briar cries every time someone on screen does. *Or anytime something good happens. Or sometimes for reasons I do not actually understand at all.*

We sit like that, on opposite sides of her room, through a few episodes. And then something…bad happens.

It's not a big deal. It shouldn't be a big deal. The guy on TV is having a conversation with his stepmom, telling her that he's gay. And it doesn't mean anything. It shouldn't mean anything.

But suddenly he's me, and his stepmom is my mom, and I can see her face in my head, and then her face is melting because she's on fire, because I'm killing her, and I can't stop, no matter how badly I want to, no matter how scared I am and how much I don't want to hurt her, even though she's hurt me plenty, and I'm screaming, but I don't know if it's only happening in my head and—

Briar is saying my name again. I can hear her, calling me, but I can't seem to see her through the smoke. And then someone touches my arm, and I growl, throwing myself away from their skin. When I realize what's happening, I'm on all fours in the corner of Briar's room, snarling like a fucking coyote, and she's staring at me with big eyes, her hand suspended in the air between us.

I don't say anything. I go back to the laundry room and I don't sleep.

The next night, she invites me to her room again. I say no. But she starts asking every night, and eventually I say yes again.

One night, I fall asleep on her floor.

I never end up going back to the laundry room after that.

"Wyatt?"

Briar's voice—her real voice, not the one that only exists in my head—pulls me back to the present. I blink and I'm in my body again, suddenly acutely aware of every single inch of my skin. At my sides, my hands flex uncomfortably.

Her brown eyes are soft with concern, watching me from a few feet away. Her gapped front teeth sink into her lower lip.

"Sorry." I don't know why I'm apologizing, exactly. "Um." What were we talking about before? Right. Jin. Briar going to see Jin instead of coming back with me. "Okay. But we'll see each other later?"

"Of course." She smiles, reaching over and curling her fingers around the side of my palm, giving my hand a squeeze. "I'll be up soon. I missed you."

"I missed you, too." Suddenly, without warning, tears burn in the corners of my eyes. I don't know why. Nothing's happening. Everything is fine.

"Oh, Wyatt." Briar takes a step forward and wraps her hand around my wrist. "Maybe...let's go to Lavender's together, okay? I'll let Jin know I'm going back to the castle with you."

"You don't have to do that." I don't understand why my voice cracks halfway through the words, folding like it's given up. My throat aches, like someone's shoved a bunch of rocks down my windpipe.

Everything is fine, so why am I about to cry again?

I mean, everything is actually decidedly not fine, everything is at least partially, in some way, terrible, but right now, in this second, everyone is alive, so that's fine.

Well. I assume everyone is alive. It's been a few hours since I last saw Emyr.

And now there's something else out there, attacking people in the royal family. And it's not like someone didn't try to kill him once already.

No, they didn't try. They did kill him. He just didn't stay dead.

But how long can my magic keep him here? The best Heal-ers in Asalin brought Kadri back and now she's reaching the end. I'm *far* from the best Healer in Asalin. For all I know, Emyr could drop dead again at any moment.

The thought makes me burn. My heart beats so fast I can feel the rattle of it at the base of my throat, jostling free some of those rocks. On instinct, my hand reaches for the phone in my pocket, needing to text him, but I pause before I actually pull it out. He's not going to read a text.

I have to get back to the castle. I have to see Emyr.

"No," Briar says softly, and I can't remember what we were even talking about. "I think I do."

We stop briefly by Lavender's on the way up the road to the castle, just long enough for Briar to pop in and check on Jin, and let them know where to find her. Physically, I am right there in the house with them. Mentally, I am on another planet entirely.

Boom greets us in the palace foyer. It's still disconcerting to see him outside of the woods, but I don't have time to dwell on it. I *have* to get to Emyr. If I don't see him right this second, I'm going to explode.

Kadri and Leonidas have moved into a suite on the southern side of the castle. I've never actually been inside, but I've seen them come in and out of it a few times. The door comes into view while I practically run down the hallway, Briar and Boom keeping pace at my back. It's opening already as I approach.

Emyr steps out.

Fuck.

He makes one of his more inhuman sounds, a growl that caresses the tip of his tongue, and reaches for me at the exact same time that I reach for him. Somehow, it's as if he needs to be touched as badly as I need to touch him. His big hands curl around my waist and I stand on the tips of my toes to wrap my arms around his neck. I close my eyes, tilting my head forward to bury my face against his chest, dragging in the smell of him. Musk and sugar and a hint of smoke. This close, I can even hear the rhythmic *thump, thump, thump* of his heart. He brushes his mouth against the top of my head while our energies collide and swirl overhead.

Behind me, Briar sighs.

These...episodes have been happening since the night he died. I don't understand what brings them on, really. I'll be totally fine, going about business as usual, and then all of a sudden BAM. I'm convinced my boyfriend's dead. And if I don't see him, right then, immediately, I think I'll die, too.

It's not like it's exactly an irrational fear. I have every reason to worry about Emyr keeling over.

Clearly.

Sometimes, I wonder if this is what it was like for him, when I was in the human world. When he didn't know if I was okay, or happy, or safe. He says, somehow, because of the bond, he always felt I was *alive*, but there are plenty of times being *alive* isn't necessarily a good thing.

But I've always wondered what it is he's feeling. He can't explain the bond to me, not really. I've definitely asked plenty of times. I see it, in the wicked, all-consumed look he reserves for only me. And I feel it on him, in the way his hands are both tender and wild when he touches me. But I've never felt it from the inside. Whatever this thing is that, for him, makes us...us.

I know what it feels like for me. Emyr is my past, and my present, and my future. He holds a piece of all the worst things I've ever done, but somehow reflects back all the best things I could still do.

Being with him is comfortable and familiar, and it is terrifying. He feels like home. He feels like adventure. He's the lighthouse *and* the storm.

And, apparently, he's panic attacks. But I think that's probably more about my trauma than it is our bond.

After a long moment, when both of us manage to turn our insides upright again, Emyr and I detangle from each other. Briar's watching us with sad, thoughtful eyes, her finger scritching at the top of Boom's head. The hellhound appears utterly oblivious, panting with his tongue hanging out, a dog smile on his face.

I sniff, swiping underneath my eyes. "Um. How did your conversation go?"

Emyr's gaze shoots back to the door, then to me. He shakes his head. Whatever was said, I don't think he wants to get into it while we're still in earshot of Leonidas.

"You wanna head to your room?" Briar asks, picking up on the same vibe.

Before Emyr can answer, though, I pipe up, "Actually, there's something else I wanna do first."

"She doesn't really *do* much," I say, staring down at the baby sleeping in my arms.

"She is one day old." I'm pretty sure Nadua spiritually ages like ten years every time I speak. "What exactly would you like her to do?"

Nadua and Briar are staying in the same room Briar and I stayed in when we arrived in Asalin together. It looks exactly the same as it did then—seriously, you'd never be able to tell it was almost destroyed in the riots a few weeks ago—except someone's brought in a bassinet to put in one corner.

The five of us—well, six, if you count the tiny one, plus Nadua and me, Briar and Emyr, and Tessa, who was here already when we showed up—are sitting out at the table on the balcony, overlooking Asalin's southern fields. The dragons have gathered, most of them dozing in the low-hanging sun, a few of the smaller ones play-fighting at the center of the herd. (Smaller *comparatively*. When they ram against each other, it sends tiny little reverberations through the ground that I can feel all the way in my seat.) Boom's inside, dozing on the bed like he owns the place.

It feels almost familiar. This could be a few months ago, when we first came to Asalin together, right after being let free from the dungeon. Briar on the balcony, watching the dragons, while Emyr and I stood in the room. Clarke and Jin bursting in unannounced to introduce themselves.

How was that only a few months ago? I was a completely different person then.

And still, of the five people there *that* day, I might be the one who's changed the least in the time since.

Well, I guess maybe Clarke and Briar haven't changed all that much. I just didn't know who they really were at the time.

"I don't know," I finally answer Nadua. I'm not a complete dumbass. (*Well.*) Obviously, I didn't expect the kid to be like, running around and performing a stand-up routine or anything. But I did think she'd be awake more than she is.

Although, if someone gave me the option of sleeping all the time and not having to worry about anything, I would definitely take it. Even if it meant zero ability to communicate or do anything for myself? That's fine. I already suffer from that condition thanks to being a gay little bitch.

"We should give her a name," I add, looking away from her face and her multicolored swirl of pastel energies to turn toward Emyr. "Everyone needs a name."

He's watching me with an inscrutable expression. Normally, when his eyes get all dark and mysterious and he stares at me with an emotion I can't read, it's because he's being all fated-mate-possessive or some shit. It's kind of sexy. This very much does not resemble that. This is far more akin to one of those flat-faced cats who always look incredibly irritable.

"Well," he says at length, leaning back in his chair and flicking a wrist toward Briar. "She's Briar's. She can name her."

"She is *not* mine." Briar's voice is higher than I've ever heard it. "At most, she's like…half mine. My mom found her as much as I did."

"Also, if Briar had a kid, it would basically be my kid, too." I roll my eyes, like this is an obvious fact everyone should already be aware of, and only realize how it sounds after it's out of my mouth. My boyfriend is staring at me, one eyebrow arched. Tessa snickers. Briar puts her head in her hands, while Nadua just scoffs. "I don't mean that in some like…nuclear family, heterosexual, we're-registered-at–Hobby-Lobby kind of way. I just mean, you know, Briar is my family, and our family is whatever we decide it is."

Emyr blinks. "I thought you didn't want children."

"I don't." That hasn't changed. "Not right now, anyway."

"Hey," Briar cuts in, and effectively ends all talk about babies with the question, "What happened with your dad? Is he doing okay? Could he tell you anything about who attacked him?"

A very long moment drags by. I choose to stare at the nameless newborn's face, instead of meeting eyes with anyone who just heard me announce that I want to be Briar's co-parent.

Finally, Emyr clears his throat and speaks. "He's doing... alright. Physically, he's fine. His injuries were taken care of. But his pride was more damaged than anything else. He's not accustomed to anyone seeing him as weak."

No, I would imagine not. Leonidas was, up until very recently, the shining fucking gem of Asalin. After a youth spent as the heartthrob prince, some kind of kingdom-renowned warrior playboy, he went on to become their charismatic and benevolent king.

"Does he have any clue who it was?" Tessa asks, leaning forward with her elbows propped against the top of the table.

The corner of Emyr's mouth twitches, nearly twisting up over one fang before he can school his expression. "He has his theories, though they're based purely on speculation, as he was unable to actually get a look at his assailant. I will certainly look into them, regardless."

I wasn't in the room, and I don't know what Leonidas said. But if my guess is anywhere near the truth—that he blames Emyr for this, too, and thinks someone who has it out for his son was behind the attack—then he can eat a dick.

Actually, no, he doesn't deserve the privilege of eating dick.

I open my mouth, on the verge of saying *exactly* that, when someone knocks at the bedroom door. Boom growls, startled awake by the sudden noise, and comes stalking out to the balcony to lie down at my feet.

Tessa sighs and hauls herself up to answer it. From across the room, I hear the surprise in her voice when she says, "Oh, hey. What are you doing here?"

"I have a message for His Majesty. He is here, isn't he?"

"Um. Yeah." She tosses me a confused, mildly panicked look over her shoulder and steps back to let Wade into the room.

Immediately, it strikes me that he looks…different. Which is to say that Wade actually looks like himself for the first time in a month. He's clearly showered, which is a nice improvement, his pretty blond hair up in a perfect knot instead of hanging like greasy curtains around his face. He's dressed himself in a very Wade-esque outfit; uncomfortably form-fitting taupe pants, a white shirt with a low V-neck, and a dark green cardigan almost the same color as his energy, slits cut in the back to make room for his obnoxious furry wings. He smiles when he steps toward the balcony. It's the closest thing to an *actual* smile that I've seen on him in…well, since the night Emyr died.

"What do you want?" Emyr doesn't waste time with pleasantries.

I really need to talk to him about this *thing* with Wade. Because I get it, I do, and I don't want to tell him he has to forgive his cousin. He isn't ever *required* to forgive anyone. But also…he is being an asshole. And both things can be true.

Ugh.

Wade seems unbothered by the blunt question. "I've been

sent to inform you the staff have finalized your travel plans for this week."

Before Emyr became king, back when the Guard was still a thing, so was the Committee. They handled day-to-day issues like making travel plans, or acting as messengers between kingdoms. Wade was one of them. Now, with both branches dissolved, Emyr's been handling most of their tasks by himself, with his staff (or me) picking up the slack where the Circle doesn't. And Wade, in an attempt to make himself useful, has been inserting himself wherever he can.

"*And?*" Emyr raises both eyebrows.

"You leave for Auckland Airport tomorrow evening. The flight time is substantial, and with time differences, you won't arrive until Wednesday afternoon." Tomorrow is Monday. Two whole days lost on a flight, for crying out loud. "From there, a car will meet you for the three-hour ride to Monalai."

"That sounds fucking miserable," Emyr informs him, as if Wade was the one who designed...the globe. Or invented time, maybe.

"Sure does. Sorry about that." Wade is unwavering. "They've booked tickets for you, Wyatt, and Briar. I assume all three of you will be going, yes?"

"Oh! New Zealand?" Briar leans forward against the table, hands curling around the edge, an excited glint in her eye. Beside her, Nadua scowls.

"Why would she be coming?" Emyr snarls. "What is this? Some ploy to get us all away from the child?"

"*Dude.*" I take one hand off said child's back, reaching over to curl my hand around his wrist. "Enough. I'd really like it if Briar came, actually."

Especially considering the meeting with the changelings we have scheduled.

And the fact that Jin can't possibly follow her all the way to Auckland. I hope.

Emyr frowns, looking down at the place where our skin is touching. A tendril of golden energy wisps up from his fingers and threads through mine. He doesn't say anything else.

I know it doesn't actually have anything to do with Briar. The two of them get along just fine, considering Emyr once suggested I keep her as a concubine and then Briar went and opened a portal to his shitty ancestors' hell dimension. His bad reaction has everything to do with the fact that *Wade* was the one to suggest it. Emyr would argue against breathing if his cousin told him it was a good idea right now.

When I look back at Wade, I realize he *is* staring at the baby. And for a moment, that polished persona he's cobbled back together collapses. For a moment, I can see underneath, to the version of him that's existed here for the last month. There is such open, obvious longing etched across his face when he looks at her.

He loves her. He doesn't know her, but he already loves her. And if she's going to be raised by anyone, it might as well be by someone who clearly wants her *that* much.

Yeah. I really gotta have that talk with Emyr.

I want to offer her to Wade, but I don't. I know, right now, Emyr would just make it into a whole thing. And also, selfishly, I don't want to let go of her just yet. She's warm against my chest, a bundle of softness, her whole little body expanding and shrinking with every breath she takes. She's *alive*, and untainted, and there is something inexplicably calming about the feeling of her in my arms.

"Well," Wade says when the silence stretches out for a moment too long. "I suppose I'll be going now."

"I'll come with you," Tessa agrees, reaching out and sliding her hand into his, squeezing.

He looks down at their linked fingers and squeezes back. To Emyr and me, he offers, "If there's anything else I can do for you, please let me know."

"Will do," Briar chirps when no one else responds, bobbing her head enthusiastically.

And with that, the couple (Friends? Ambiguously coded companions? I need to ask Tessa about this relationship) leave, the bedroom door closing with a quiet snap behind them.

"I do not like this energy," Nadua announces, waving a hand in the direction they disappeared through. On the floor, Boom huffs out an agreement.

I glance between Emyr and the sleeping baby, my stomach aching with nerves. *Same.*

CHAPTER SEVEN

COLONIZER CHIC

Growing up, before the fire, I was never allowed to leave Asalin.

Emyr went away a lot. He and his parents would make trips around the world to other fae kingdoms, rubbing elbows with the rest of the royals. They made frequent visits to Oflewyn, the Eurasian kingdom that Kadri came from, where Emyr's birth mother still lives.

The idea of me going with them was never even entertained. At the time, I didn't question it. Emyr was the prince, and I was nobody. Why would I go?

In hindsight, I know I've *never* been nobody. Even if the fae thought I was nothing special on my own merit, I was Emyr's fated mate. I was supposed to grow up and be the next queen of Asalin. (How embarrassing for them.) It would've made perfect sense for me to be invited on these trips. To start making connections with these people, to be exposed to this world I was destined to be part of.

Of course, in hindsight, I also know exactly why I wasn't. Kadri and Leonidas may have accepted Emyr was destined to be with a witch, they may have even treated me with kindness themselves, but that's very different from taking me out in public and setting me loose on the rest of the Court. They probably didn't know how the other royals would react to me, and worried the answer was "poorly."

Whether they left me in Asalin for the sake of my own feelings or everyone else's is up for interpretation.

My first time seeing one of the other kingdoms was Emyr's and my trip to Eirgard, the South American kingdom, a few weeks earlier. I'd gotten us in hot water with their queens, thanks to a truly obnoxious protest video I uploaded to Fae TV. (Not my proudest moment. Though maybe one of my funnier ones, now that we can look back and laugh without worrying about someone starting a war because of it.)

Eirgard was beautiful, the village dotted in vibrant colors, the castle reminding me of an ancient Catholic church with modern tech sprinkled throughout. It was so different from Asalin, in every possible way.

And Monalai is nothing like either of them.

Just like Wade said, we arrive in the kingdom three hours after a driver—a fae, horns and wings magically hidden, like Emyr's, for the first hour—picked us up from the airport. Unlike with Asalin, I can't just *tell* when we cross the border. There isn't a feeling, some gut-tingling sense telling me shit is *different* in these parts. Instead, the winding road we're on just...stops.

The car slows down to a halt. We're in the middle of nowhere, as far as I can tell. There's nothing but rolling green hills on three sides of us. (Seriously, New Zealand, at least this part, is beautiful.) A few feet ahead, though, the scenery is broken up by something new. At the spot where the tar abruptly ends, a tall woman with short hair and a bored expression stands, leaning against what looks to be a barbed wire fence.

Our driver rolls down his window and leans his arm out. He makes some hand gesture at the woman that I can't make out from where I'm sitting in the back seat. I can't even lean forward to try and get a good look, 'cause Briar's dozing with her head in my lap. I try to catch Emyr's eyes, hoping to exchange an *Is this normal?* kind of look with him, but he's eyeing the fence with an unimpressed scowl. Hmm.

I clear my throat, and he finally tilts his head to look at me. At my raised eyebrows, he says only, "Iron."

Iron?

Ooooh.

My eyes flick back to the fence. Iron can't kill the fae, but it can *seriously* hurt them. It also clamps down on their magic, making it impossible to access. In Asalin, prisoners are tossed into the dungeons wearing iron cuffs.

Why would the Monalai kings make a *protective* barrier out of something that could hurt *them*?

Whatever little gesture our driver made, it seems to be enough for the woman at the fence. She uses a gloved hand to grab one side of the wire and slowly pull it back, creating a narrow, barely car-sized passageway for us to get through.

As we crawl through at the slowest possible speed, I swear this woman stares through the black-tinted windows to look right at me. And the shit-sniffing grimace on her face tells me she isn't my biggest fan.

But the feeling is mutual. This close, I can tell she's not just some random civilian. Her outfit is a Guard uniform, slightly different than Asalin's but similar enough to be recognizable, with four black stripes sewn on the shoulder to indicate her rank.

A world away, but it doesn't matter. They're all agents of the same broken system wherever you go.

Fuck the Guard.

Immediately past the fence, nothing seems to change, except the lack of paved road makes things a little bumpier. Briar makes a groggy, discombobulated kind of noise and rubs her face against my thigh before sitting up straighter. "Winm'laiye?"

I nod. "Just got here."

Emyr's eyebrows shoot up toward his scalp. "You understood that?"

I offer him my palms and a shrug. He should not be surprised, at this point, that I speak fluent Briar.

After a couple minutes of driving, the village itself starts to come into view.

And it's...

Well, it sure is interesting.

As far as I can tell, there are no actual houses, no permanent structures made of wood or stone or anything else that looks like it would actually survive the elements or the rest of time. What there *does* appear to be are a bunch of...tents? But not the kind of tents you take on a family vacation to a state park. These are like, uh. Okay. I hate myself for thinking this, but these are like *glamping* tents. Big-ass white fabric structures spread out across the hills on either side of the road, most of them pinned open so the air can flow right through. They're all decorated with assorted colorful tassels, strings of lights, braided rugs, and, seriously, are we still in Monalai? Because this is giving me uncomfortably Coachella vibes.

Somehow, the castle is even worse.

Of course, castle isn't the right word for it. It's built more like a modern McMansion, a gigantic triangle in the center with two huge wings on either side. But that's not the most disturbing part. No, no, what really gets me is that the entire thing is made of glass. Well. The entire outside. All the outside walls are completely see-through, allowing us to drive up and stare right in at the people going about their business inside. The inner rooms appear to have actual walls, so you can't actually see from one end to the other, allowing for a little more privacy, but *still*. If you squint, it looks like the people inside are just kind of floating in the air. It's unsettling.

Briar, who looks both physically far more awake and existentially far more tired, says only, "Colonizer chic."

She's not wrong. Frankly, I'm disappointed the gays in charge don't have better taste.

Inside, it's not any less uncomfortable. As we're led up a glass flight of stairs to the top of the palace, it feels like being walked through some kind of futuristic office building, ultra-sterile, devoid of any personality. It sets my teeth on edge, and I can't exactly explain why.

Or maybe I can. Look, I'm not a fucking interior decorator. (Shocking, I know.) But when I think about the places where I've felt the most loved, and comfortable, and at peace, I think about places like the Begay-Brown house, messy and in need of some repairs, but filled with love, pictures everywhere showing off their family, dog fur making it all feel extra lived in. Or I think of Emyr's cabin, small and tucked away in the woods, covered in flowers and always smelling like baked goods or coffee. I even think of places like Lavender's or the triad's houses, none of the money of fae society, but bursting with color and packed with trinkets.

It's starkly different from places like Asalin's Throne room, dripping with extravagance and lacking any real personality. Or *this* place, which feels clean to the point of being oppressive.

Makes me think, though, what my place would look like. If I had a place that was mine.

I mean, I've always had a home. (Well, almost always.) But that home was always with someone else. My parents, Briar, Emyr. And it was really *their* place, where I just happened to also live. I've never had a space that was wholly mine.

But I could. And I will. I mean, that's always been the goal, in a kind of roundabout way, right? Back when I wanted out of the contract, when all I wanted was to *not* marry Emyr, it was so I could have whatever human-ish future I wanted, carving out a place of my own in that world. Now, when the goal is creating a fae society that's fair and just, where the monarchy and the systems that support it are abolished, the end result is still pretty much the same. Carving out a space for myself. For me, and for Briar, *and* for Emyr. Where we can all be happy.

What would that look like? I can sort of picture it in my head, I think. Some little townhouse filled with plants and dogs and food. Lots of sunlight and art and definitely close to a twenty-four-hour drive-through. A cozy bedroom upstairs for Emyr and me, a bigger one downstairs for Briar.

That's about as far as I can get in my fantasies, though.

But I hope, someday, I'll be able to see it more clearly.

"Your Majesties," the driver, our escort through the building, announces as he pushes open a massive white door when we reach the upper floor, "His Royal Highness, Emyr Leonidas Mirac North, of the kingdom of Asalin."

The Monalai Throne room is just as uncanny as the rest of this place. The high ceiling is covered in built-in fluorescent lighting, and the floor and walls are made of the exact same pristine white metal. It makes everything look *too* bright, which is maybe to compensate for the fact that there are no windows in here, an awkward contrast to the palace's outer wall. There are only two chairs, in the center of the room, matching white thrones that...honestly just kind of look like oversize IKEA furniture. Each one is holding one of the kings.

The only color in the room comes from the *mounted animal heads* hanging on the wall above the thrones. Eight of them, lined up in a horrifying row, their stuffed faces permanently shaped into too-sentient expressions of horror. A gryphon's eagle-like head, with its lethally sharp beak. A chimera, a scaled face framed by a red mane and curling horns. A green dragon's open mouth, poised to breathe a flame it never will again. A phoenix's red feathers, also never to see fire again. A hellhound, so old its black fur was beginning to gray. A unicorn foal barely bigger than a newborn. A peryton, massive horns broken on one end, like it gave a good fight. And finally, at the end, a selkie—a seal with a woman's face.

I cannot stand the sight of them. When I look away, I catch Briar, eyes up at the wall, lips parted, horror and revulsion clear in her eyes.

Life, to Briar, is sacred. All life. For her, that doesn't mean going vegan or mourning terrible people when they die. It means making sure that death is also sacred. That it serves a purpose. To feed people, or to make the world a better place.

Looking through her eyes, at creatures killed for decoration… I can only guess at what she's feeling, but I know it isn't good. I reach over and take her hand, try to pull her back to me.

We need to focus. The kings are speaking now.

"Thank you, Kevin," Robin Bell is leaning back in his chair and throws an arm out in dismissal. "That will be all."

The driver—Kevin, I guess—nods and dismisses himself, stepping out through the door we entered through, letting it swing closed behind us.

I remember seeing Robin and Gordon Bell the night Emyr was crowned king, albeit from a distance. I was sitting on the balcony of my bedroom, watching the other members of the Court arrive down below, desperately wondering what was going on.

Up close, Robin, who I'd known was a giant from the first sight of him, is even bigger than I expected. Standing, he's gotta be seven feet tall, five hundred pounds *at least*. His wings are a woody brown, thick and bushy, stretching out to the sides and hanging past the arms of his chair to droop to the floor, and his horns are more like antlers, similar to Wade's. His massive beard hangs down to his lap, obscuring half his face and almost as much of his torso. His white skin is deeply tanned, even sunburnt in patches. His energy, a dull green yellow, wraps around his arms like a pet snake.

"Emyr," he says in a cheerful tone, and I can see a smile behind his mustache. "It's so good to see you. You wear the crown well, son."

I glance up at my boyfriend to gauge his reaction. I think I notice the tips of his ears darken to a plum-like shade, and he reaches up to run one finger along the finely wrought gold of his crown.

Finally, he tips his head slightly. "Thank you. That means a great deal."

At Robin's side, Gordon Bell sits eerily still. Sizewise, he could not be more starkly different from his husband. He's probably smaller than I am, maybe five feet even and dis-armingly thin. His white skin is almost as pale as the room we're in. His fluffy gray wings look like a baby ostrich's, and his horns are sharp silver blades jutting out on either side of his head. His wheelchair sits next to his throne, and his dark gray energy clings to the air around them both, like a set of shadows.

He catches my eye when he sees me sizing him up and raises one eyebrow.

I'm the one to swallow and look away.

Both men are dressed in similar styles, Robin in a beige

tunic with olive green pants and Gordon in a dark brown blazer over a white T-shirt and khakis. They look so…dull.

Especially compared to Emyr. My eyes flick him up and down, taking in the sight. He's never one to be outdone, and it suits him. Today, he's opted for the most colorful pair of pants I've ever seen, a patchwork design of different patterns and colors, high waisted and cinched at the ankles but massive and flowing at the legs themselves. He's paired them with a high-neck black crop top and black sandals. And, of course, the crown.

The only thing missing is his sword. His new favorite accessory isn't exactly TSA-approved.

"And Wyatt," Robin continues, and my eyes move to him again. "What a pleasure we finally get to meet. Though, Gordon and I did assume our first face-to-face would be on your wedding day." He chuckles. "Honestly, I'm surprised to see you two standing here together, after calling off the nuptials. Unless there's a backup ceremony we're not aware of…"

Uh. Well. I did not anticipate being asked if I still plan to marry my boyfriend.

It's not like I *don't*. But it's also not like I *do*. You know? I love Emyr. I want to be with Emyr. But I still don't know that I'm *in love* with Emyr. I also don't know how many of my feelings are wrapped up in the fact that we've survived some pretty big, capital *T* Trauma together, and how much is just…me loving him. The same is probably true in reverse. We both need time to just…live, and I assume we'll figure it all out together as we go. Maybe we'll invest in some couples therapy.

But it's not like I'm going to tell Robin Bell that.

Luckily, Emyr throws me a lifeline. "Wyatt is an invaluable asset to Asalin's Throne, whatever our future may have in store."

It is a very polite and diplomatic way of saying it, and that is why Emyr is the king and I am his traveling jester.

"Hmm." Robin's gaze slides, slowly, from me to Briar. "And you…"

He trails off, like he isn't entirely sure what to say, his eyes taking her in like he's studying some newly discovered lifeform. Briar doesn't cower under the scrutiny, though. She turns up her chin at the mountain of a man and lets herself be assessed, hardly attempting to conceal the rage flowing off her. At least she didn't say anything about the heads. Though, I don't know how she managed it.

My energy flows toward hers, black twining with yellow to create a braid between us.

Finally, Gordon continues where his husband left off. "I must admit, I was taken aback to learn Emyr was audacious enough to request a human be granted access to our kingdom. For as long as Monalai has stood, one such as yourself has never been inside these borders." Gordon's voice isn't what I was expecting at all. It's high-pitched and melodic, all soft edges and lilting cadence. "Tell me, how does it feel?"

I really hope, for the sake of international relations, Briar does not answer this man's question honestly.

She doesn't, though I think she'd probably like to. Instead, she offers him a tight smile and says, "Well, I haven't had the chance to see much of your kingdom yet. But I appreciate the invitation, all the same."

Some people have this superpower where they can say

something nice but it still sounds like *"eat shit and die."* I wasn't aware Briar was one of those people until this exact second.

Emyr, like usual, slides in to rescue the conversation. "How are Paisley and Papyrus?"

Gordon says nothing, too busy continuing to stare Briar down with consideration and a wry smile of mild amusement.

Robin, though, seems more than happy for a change of subject. "Well, you surely won't believe this, but life with twin toddlers is *not* all fun and games," he teases. "They're a handful. Always into something or another."

"Where are they now? I'd love to see them before I depart."

"Oh, they're with one of the nannies, I think."

Okay.

So, this isn't going *great*, and so far I definitely don't like these guys as much as I enjoyed hanging out with Paloma and Maritza—chaotic as the queens are—but it could be worse. They're willing to entertain polite conversation, and we have some things in common. Like, *they're* gay, *we're* gay, *they* have twin fae babies, *we* have a little trash baby we found in the woods. There's plenty to help this conversation start off on the right foot.

It's possible Emyr's mind has gone to the same place mine has, because he says, "Well, I want to thank you for having us here today. As you know, I wanted to bring to you some concerning information I've learned about our magic system. If you—"

"Hold that thought, Emyr," Robin smiles. "Why don't we send Wyatt and Briar into the village to explore while we talk shop?"

A beat passes. I glance at Emyr's face, just long enough to

see him visibly recover from being knocked out of his prepared speech. "Ah, well, Wyatt and Briar are intricate pieces
of the conversation. You see—"

"No, no, shh." Robin, still smiling, raises a finger to his
mouth, quite literally *shushing* Emyr. The way someone might
do to an actual child.

My blood turns hot. I want to burn his ugly house down.

"You see, Emyr," Robin continues, "I know you do things
by your own rules in Asalin, and I certainly cannot stop you
from ruling your kingdom however you'd like—even if that
means right into the ground." He chuckles. "But we have
standards here. We do not discuss politics in the presence of
witches. And certainly not in front of creatures like *her*."

"Briar is not a *creature*. And Wyatt is my partner—"

"He is no such thing. You broke your contract, did you
not?" Gordon tilts his head, condescension dripping like
venom from his tongue. "Your pets can play outside, or this
conversation will not happen at all."

"Hey, fuck you," Briar snaps, and I step in front of her
when she moves forward, like she thinks she's gonna fight
these men.

Emyr isn't much more composed than she is. "I am the king
of Asalin, and you will show me some respect."

"Child king, we have extended far more respect than you've
earned." Robin sighs.

Emyr's eyes go wide, his wings snapping out at his sides,
claws flexing. I watch the kings exchange a conspiratorial
glance.

"Hey." I step forward again, putting myself firmly in the
middle of the sides, and turn my back on the Thrones. Fully

facing Briar and Emyr, I hold up my hands, giving them my palms. "We're gonna go outside so you can talk."

"Wyatt, you cannot be serious." Emyr gnashes his fangs, eyes flashing gold as he glares at them over my shoulder. "They can't talk to us this way."

"Unfortunately, they can." Every single word feels like yanking a splinter out of my skin. I hate it. I hate making myself small and obedient for *anyone*, and I've worked too goddamn hard to be my own person to sit here and be treated like this by *offensively boring* rich people.

But what exactly is the alternative? Being thrown out of the kingdom before Emyr has the opportunity to make his pitch? Losing an alliance with Monalai before we've even had a chance? Starting a fucking fistfight and landing myself in their (probably terribly decorated) dungeon?

This isn't about me. This is about fae magic sucking the energy from the earth, and Emyr and Jin's technology being the solution we need to use less of it. This is about fae governments being built on the oppression of witches, and Emyr needing people in his corner to help *him* help *us*.

And if I have to bite my tongue and make myself invisible just to make sure he can get in the room to start that conversation, then that's what I have to do. Even if I hate every single second of it.

"We'll be outside. Okay?" I reach into my pocket to produce his cell phone, infused with Jin's magic, and hold it out to him.

He's staring at me like he hardly recognizes me. Though the sight of the phone is enough to knock him back to the present, at least a little. With a grimace, he reaches out and takes it, curling his fist around it so tight I almost worry it's going to fall apart in his grip.

"Thank you for respecting our customs, Wyatt," Robin says in his still too friendly tone.

I turn to glance at him over my shoulder. "I don't. It was truly terrible meeting you. Let's never do this again." Looking back at Briar, I nod toward the door. "Come on. Let's go."

By the look on her face, I know she wants to argue. She's itching for a fight, and no doubt wants to show the kings they shouldn't underestimate this particular little human. But finally, she grumbles out a surrender, turning around and stomping back out into the hallway.

The last thing I see before escaping the room is the lingering image of the selkie's face, her mouth frozen open in a silent scream.

Outside, Briar and I settle on the front steps, her leaning hard against the railing and crossing her arms tight over her chest, me sitting down at the top with my elbows on my knees.

"This is bullshit!" She stomps her foot to enunciate her point.

"Yep."

"How are you not more angry?" she demands, throwing an arm out. "You are like, the poster child for poor anger management skills. And now, what, all of a sudden you're fucking *zen*?"

I make a face, looking up at her. "I'm sorry, do you think me setting something on fire right now would be helpful?"

"Well NO, but it would probably FEEL GOOD!"

"Yeah, for like, two minutes, and then we'd actually have

to deal with the consequences." Becoming a better person is so draining. I've made one single mature decision and I feel like I need a nap.

Briar pouts but falls silent, which is how I know I've won.

In the quiet that follows, I stare out at the tent village of Monalai. People pass, as silent as we are, occasionally glancing up at us from the corners of their eyes, but mostly avoiding eye contact. They move more quickly anytime they have to walk up the steps around us, like they're afraid we might try and stop them for a conversation.

That isn't what really makes my stomach churn, though. At first, I can't put my finger on it. I can't figure out why sitting here is *so* uncomfortable, can't name why watching these people move about their daily lives, passing through their tents, just existing, makes my skin crawl.

And then it hits me.

"There's not a single witch here."

Briar frowns, turning her head to look at me, then glancing back out at the village. Her mouth tugs down further at the corners, eyebrows drawing together. "Well…surely there are some…somewhere."

Okay…but where?

I lock eyes with a passing fae, dragging an industrial-sized black trash bag across the yard. When they realize I've caught them staring, they quickly look away.

But I don't. I follow their path all the way to a massive steel structure, almost too far away to see. I can just barely make out the way they pull down a lever, dragging open a heavy metal door.

And, even from a distance, I can see the dragons caged inside, heads barely able to lift off the floor because of chains around their necks. The fae opens their bag and throws meat into the building, and the massive creatures scream, straining against their constraints to reach for the scraps.

A cold chill crawls along my shoulders. I think I'm going to be sick.

Suddenly, the iron fence on the kingdom's border makes a little more sense.

No one is safe here.

Soon after, Emyr walks out the front door. He doesn't stop when he reaches us, but keeps walking, calling over his shoulder, "We're leaving!"

We exchange a look, but get up to hurry after him.

"How'd it go?" I asked, elbow brushing his when I reach his side.

He scowls down at me and doesn't say a word.

Yeah. That's about what I expected.

CHAPTER EIGHT

IN A SOFT, TENDER, GAY WAY

I wake the next morning to sunlight spilling across my eyelids and the bulge between Emyr's thighs pressing into my back.

Though that isn't where my head goes right away. My first thoughts are more of a jumble of *mmmph, warm, good, soft, warm, warm, strong, arms, warm, good, mmm* than anything else. I yawn, rubbing my cheek against the pillow and shifting back against the solid expanse of Emyr's chest. His arms tighten around my middle, pulling me impossibly closer.

There are some moments, like this, when I think I could crawl inside his bones and only then would I feel really and truly at ease. Only if I could somehow slip my body into his skin, like a ghost possessing him, would I really be able to breathe. If I could feel the air in *his* lungs. If I could hear his pulse from the inside.

Emyr growls, a quiet rumble at my ear, and his claws rake, sleepily, against my belly. There's a suggestion of pain, but it still makes my body tighten in response, my toes curling, my backside pressing back against him on reflex. His hips roll forward to meet mine and the bulge between his thighs slides against my center. I gasp, and my eyes open.

We booked some short-term rental online the night before, a little house on the water that was probably ridiculously overpriced because of the timing. Our room overlooks the ocean, and when I blink to adjust my vision, I can see waves hitting rocks just outside our window. Everything feels warm and fuzzy at the edges, my mind trapped somewhere between dreams and salt-soaked air, my body consumed entirely by Emyr.

His claws trail up my belly, pushing up my T-shirt as they go, and my stomach tightens, my breath hitching. He stops just beneath my breastbone, thumbs making slow circles against my ribs. His hips haven't stopped their slow, torturous roll yet, and every time he brushes tighter against me my entire body cries out in an aching kind of response.

After a beat, I lift my arms over my head, resting them on the pillow, nosing against my inner elbow. Emyr hesitates, hands and hips stilling for a moment. I groan, and arch back into him, and he makes a wrecked, pitiful sound in response, before pulling my shirt off and tossing it away.

Emyr's seen me without a shirt or without a binder plenty of times, but he's never seen me sans *both*. His claw tips trail back down over my arms, starting at my wrists and dragging lower and lower, over my forearms, my biceps, leaving little white scratch marks in their wake. His hands glide across my collarbones, then lower, over my chest, and—

When he curls his hands over the part of me I usually work so hard to minimize, every cell in my body starts screaming. In a good way. I think.

I gasp, struggling to breathe deep as he gives an experimental, gentle squeeze. When his mouth brushes against the back of my neck at the same time his thumb skirts across one nipple, I let out the most deranged, inhuman sound ever. His body stills behind me, like he's worried he's crossed a line, and he has, but I want him to keep crossing it.

I *need* him. I might not actually be able to climb inside his bones, but there is another way to be inside each other.

Rolling over in his arms, I reach up to wrap my arm around the back of his neck, hand sliding between his horns to grab a fistful of his curls, and bring his mouth to mine. He whimpers against my lips, his fangs catching mine before our tongues meet, and I curl my knee around his hip in response. This time, when our hips grind forward to meet each other, our bodies hit in the exact perfect way to make us *both* growl.

"Wyatt," he whispers into the kiss, hands curling around my back to press into my bare shoulder blades.

"I know." My teeth nip at his lower lip, my own nails dragging down over his chest until my hands reach the elastic waist of his briefs. I slide my fingers past the stretchy line, my hand slowly moving down between his thighs.

"No, Wyatt," he says again, a little louder this time. "Wait."

I freeze. Our mouths part enough for my eyes to shoot to his face, and I realize he looks...less excited than he sounded a second ago.

"Hey." I tug my hand out immediately, pulling back just enough to put a little breathing room between our bodies. "You okay?"

"Yes. No?" Emyr frowns. "I don't want to do this right now."

"Okay."

"I just..." He swallows. "I *do* want to, really. It feels... I want you so badly. But I started thinking about..."

"That night," I say, because I know what he's talking about as soon as he says it.

Emyr nods. "I'm sorry."

"*Absolutely not.* You don't have any reason to be sorry." I flop onto my back, staring up at the ceiling, the little white fan whirring in circles over our heads. My body still wants to do obscene things, but my brain's been doused in cold water. I need a minute to get them on the same page. "Even if the reason was just *no*, you wouldn't need to be sorry."

He rolls over onto his stomach, and one of his leathery wings stretches out to rest on top of me. I absentmindedly run my fingers along the veiny lines.

"Okay." He sniffs. "I love you."

"I love you, too." I kiss one clawed wing tip, and close my eyes. "And good morning."

"Morning."

"You sleep okay?" Maybe if we start having a normal person conversation, my brain and body will stop trying to kill each other.

"Not really." Emyr yawns, shrugging one shoulder. "Dreamt about Derek."

Oh.

Well, if anything was going to kill my boner, it'd be thinking about Derek Pierce. That increasingly familiar hollow space in my body gives a dull throb. My stomach churns.

I wiggle out from underneath Emyr's wing to climb out of bed, snatching my shirt off the ground and yanking it over my head. "Yeah, well. Good riddance. That corpse doesn't deserve to keep you up at night."

"And yet." He sighs and rolls over.

I glance back at him, though I don't think he notices my staring. He's somewhere else, eyes unfocused as he stares at the ceiling.

God, he's beautiful. With his wings spread out, dark brown leather against the soft white bedsheets, and his head tipped back, exposing the long, perfectly black expanse of his throat. With the blanket tucked delicately around his waist, and his soft, warm golden energy dusting down his limbs and mingling with the sunlight.

For one too-brief moment, I think about kissing him.

Except, when I do, somehow it's Derek's mouth in my mind, sucking the air right out of my lungs and making me gasp to breathe.

No. Emyr and I are definitely not having sex anytime soon.

"What all happened yesterday after Briar and I left?" I ask, trying to get far away from Derek Pierce's lingering phantom touch.

Emyr makes a face, nose scrunching up over his mouth. "Nothing. I presented Robin and Gordon with all the information I have, made my case, told them the move to techno-magic could save the world *and* help the witches, and they... didn't care. They just didn't care."

"Just said, 'nah, we'd rather die than support a single progressive thought'?"

"Basically."

"Lovely. Hope they do, then."

Now that I'm awake and suitably unhorny, I grab my bag from where it's been unceremoniously tossed by the bedroom door. My box of tarot cards is shoved in the front pocket, and I open it up, pulling them out for my morning reading.

I don't usually think of myself as a ritualistic type of person. I am, by all accounts, an agent of chaos. But there's something grounding about the morning card pull. It helps me feel a little more in control.

Without thinking, I slide a card from the center of the deck and flip it over on top of the others.

Ten of Cups. Happy family card?

I look over my shoulder at Emyr, still tucked into bed, staring absentmindedly into space. I think about Briar, probably still passed out on the couch in the living room.

My family.

Fair enough, Ten of Cups.

"So, what's the gay agenda for the day?" I shove the cards back in my bag, dropping down at the foot of the bed.

Emyr sits up and rubs a hand over his jaw, shrugging. "We can't leave. Nadua got us a meeting with the changelings for tomorrow. I suppose, for today, we just...wait."

I blink. It's not like he's saying something particularly convoluted or difficult to follow here, but it sounds like a language I've never heard before. "We just...wait."

"We have nothing else to do."

"Do you remember the last time we had nothing to do?"

Emyr frowns, turning his eyes down and off to the side, like he's genuinely trying to remember. After a moment, he huffs. "I'm going to take a *nap*."

"And I'm going to join you." I crawl up into his lap, putting my hands on his shoulders to press his body down into the pillows.

He sighs, soft and warm, and curls his arms around my waist.

And we get some rest.

Hours later, when I absolutely cannot sleep anymore—in large part due to Briar breaking our door down and forcing us to entertain her—I find myself sitting on a dock over the water. When I packed for this trip, I wasn't exactly planning on a beach vacation, so I didn't bring anything resembling proper swimwear. It's a good thing I've apparently decided I'm okay being topless around Emyr, 'cause I'm stripped down to nothing but my boxers, feet dangling into the cool gentle waves beneath me.

And it would seem Briar and Emyr are both much smarter than I am, not that that's any big surprise to anyone, because they both actually brought things to get wet in. Briar's in the cutest bikini I've ever seen, white with little red and yellow mushrooms, ruffles at the chest and high-waisted shorts. And Emyr is...well, he's being Emyr. I'm fairly certain his bathing suit is either a women's one-piece or one of those vintage men's suits, in the brightest shade of red I've ever seen. He's helping massage suntan lotion into her back while she stares out at the sea.

I follow her gaze. Man, this trip absolutely isn't going the way I hoped it would, or the way I planned for it to, and I really did not expect or want to be stuck here with nothing to do for twenty-four hours, but…it's really beautiful. We're hidden away in this little cove, surrounded by nothing but lush mountains and rolling ocean water as far as I can see. Everything is clean, and clear, green and blue, and vast, and maybe it's just me but it feels easier to breathe than it has in months.

When I look back at them, I catch Emyr staring at me. He smiles when our eyes meet, and I lean over Briar's shoulder to brush my mouth against his in a quick kiss.

She sighs. "I want someone to kiss."

"You don't even like kissing that much," I remind her, flopping onto my back and putting my hands under my head.

Emyr finishes lotioning her up and stretches out on his side, our faces only a few inches apart.

"Making out was not your favorite part of being my girl-friend."

"Maybe you're a bad kisser," she suggests.

"That is not true." Emyr makes a face.

"Maybe you're just very asexual," I remind her, like it's some sort of secret.

She rolls her eyes at me. "I can be very asexual and still want someone to kiss. Making out with *you* was different. You were always looking for it to *go* somewhere. Kissing you was never just about kissing."

"Orgasms, Briar."

"Insufferable, Wyatt."

"Asexuality," Emyr says suddenly, maybe because he wants to shift the conversation away from the mental picture of Briar and me exchanging orgasms, or maybe because something had just occurred to him. "I take it we're not speaking in terms of reproduction. This would indicate you don't experience sexual attraction?"

Briar grins at me, clearly letting me know we're all good despite the teasing, and then turns her attention back to him. "Mmm, yes. In my case, specifically. No sex drive at all, really. No interest in it. But also, it's a spectrum. It can mean different things for different people."

"A spectrum?"

"Right. So, like, I just consider myself ace. But some people might use the label gray-ace, to mean they experience sexual attraction sometimes, but it's different than the way allosexuals experience it."

"Allosexuals?"

"Non-asexuals. Like Wyatt."

"I am, unfortunately, horny," I agree. Though, notably, less horny these days. Or maybe just a more *complicated* horny.

"Right." She rolls her eyes. "Some ace people are horny, though, is the thing. And like, there are also people who identify as, let's say, demisexual. They totally experience sexual attraction, but only after developing an emotional bond with someone."

"Is that not normal?" He frowns. "How can you want to have sex with someone you don't have a connection with?"

"Oh, it's very possible," I inform him.

"Wyatt. Shush." Briar sighs, hard. "Um, I think it's less about wanting to have sex with someone, and more about the fact that the literal *ability* to feel that attraction isn't there. Like...allosexual people can look at someone they don't know and experience sexual attraction. They might not want to sleep with a total stranger, but they're still attracted to them. But for demi people, that just doesn't exist. You don't feel the attraction at all until you create the bond."

"Huh." For a moment, he looks thoughtful, brow furrowed. He looks at me, then back at Briar. "So, I'm demisexual."

"Oh! Um, alright! Cool!"

I chuckle. This is not exactly surprising to me, considering the way Emyr's spoken in the past about sexual feelings for other people. But Briar's right. It is cool, seeing him find the language to talk about himself. "Congrats, Your Highness."

"I was not aware that these things could exist on spectrums," he says after another beat. "The fae have very black-and-white terms for everything."

"Yeah, well, a lot of it is also culturally enforced, right? Like, even with humans, there's not hard and fast rules for any identity. The words I have, the words I'm giving to you, they're just things we made up to try and describe a set of feelings. And people around the world use different sets of words. Even people *from* the same place, but with different *kinds* of community, sometimes use different language." She makes a face. "Like, okay. Native people and non-Natives. We're both part of the greater human collective, or whatever. But culturally, our understandings of gender are super different. Even tribe to tribe, gender isn't the same. Throw in the fact that I'm queer, and I've also spent time in a lot of mostly white, mostly Gen Z queer circles, and my *personal* understanding of gender can suddenly be so different from another human's."

"Hmm." Emyr reaches up to rub a clawed hand over his mouth, tongue flicking out to run against his fangs. "You're saying gender is something else that exists on a spectrum?"

"Oh, don't even get me started," Briar says, but it's definitely too late, she's already started. "Gender *can* exist on a spectrum, yeah. But it really depends on what system you're using to look at gender. Fae have men and women, right? Which, like, I don't understand why, of all the cultures in all the worlds, y'all decided to go with that model of gender, but whatever. Anyway. So, through that lens, yes, gender can totally be a spectrum. Look at Jin. Jin is a lesbian, and definitely leans toward the woman side if you're thinking of it like a point A to point B situation, but they aren't a woman. They're somewhere in the middle."

Emyr's hand trails lower, over his chest, claws brushing lightly at his lower stomach, over the fabric of his swimsuit.

"There are other ways of looking at gender, though. I don't think of myself as cis, or as nonbinary, or as really anything that it wouldn't require a much longer conversation to explain." Briar shrugs. "But you've been Jin's best friend for a long time… You've never thought about this before?"

"Jin told me who they were, and I accepted it. It was simple. But…the idea of engaging with anything on any sort of… spectrum, in regard to myself, was not something I'd ever given any thought to. Not until…" He trails off, but waves his hand in my direction.

I smile, waving. "Queer awakening, at your service."

"Mmm. I didn't even know I liked men. Well, man."

"Man is also a stretch," I tell him plainly. "I am an overgrown little boy at most."

"You are not that overgrown." He stands up. "I'm going swimming. Much to think about."

Doesn't even give me time to retaliate to his vicious attack

on my height! One second he's there, and the next he's div-
ing into the water, disappearing under the crashing waves. I
see his horns reappear a few yards out not long after.

It makes my stomach flip, the sight of him out there. In
a bad way, because I'm anxious about the sea dragging him
under. But also in a soft, tender, gay way, because he's smiling up at the sun, and his golden energy is sparkling along
the water, and I love him.

Briar lies down at the edge of the dock, her black and teal
curls fanning out like a halo around her face. I sit up so I can
reach down and run my fingers through them.

As if summoned by the mention of their name in our conversation, Jin's name lights up on Briar's phone, where it's
nestled next to her shoulder. She tilts her head at the sound of
the buzz and pulls away from my touch to pick it up and read
whatever it says. I grate my teeth at the smile it brings out of
her, and watch as she sends off a reply before lying back down.

I want to go back to playing with her hair, but I don't. We
sit in silence for a long moment.

After a bit, Briar bites her lip, studying me with her neck
tilted back. Without a word, she asks, *Can I ask you something?*

I raise my eyebrows. *Go ahead, then.*

"What's your end goal, exactly?" Briar's fingertips trail
over the water's surface, her shoulders shifting against the
warm wood beneath us. "I mean, I get things didn't exactly
go the way you hoped with the kings. But...let's say you *do*
get everything you want. What does the future look like?"

It's funny, that question. Funny that I was just thinking the
same thing yesterday, trying to imagine my future and what
it could look like, what I *want* it to look like. Briar has always

had a way of reading my mind, knowing where I'm at sometimes even better than I know where I'm at.

I'm trying, though, to be better about seeing the world through her eyes, the way she can see it through mine.

It's also funny, because the version of me I am today is so far removed from the version I was when I first started planning a future with her. A year ago, I was a completely different person, with completely different hopes and dreams. But honestly, so much of my response would have been the same, even then.

"I don't know," I tell her with a sigh, because I don't, really. "What I want more than anything is just…the chance to figure that out, you know? For me *and* Emyr."

She hums softly, turning her cheek to watch him. He's pretty far out in the water by now, our little sunburst in the water. She bites at her lower lip. "You want to figure out your future together."

"Yeah."

"In the human world?"

"Well…yeah, at least partly. So much of my life is there, you know? *You're* there." I let go of her hair, tugging my knees to my chest and balancing my chin on them. "And I want to show him that world."

"I think there are many parts of the human world that could be good for Emyr. Pieces of himself he could find out there that would be harder to understand in Asalin." A beat passes, and I can see her considering her next words carefully. "But are you prepared for what that's going to mean for him?"

I think the answer must be no, because I have no clue what she's talking about. I only raise my eyebrows.

She sighs, sitting up to join me. "In the fae world, Emyr is a prince. But in the human world, he's a queer, gender-nonconforming Black man. Have you ever thought about the privilege he gives up anytime he steps outside the protection of fae society? And the privilege you *receive*?"

Oh.

It's *humiliating* how obvious it is now that she's said it. Mostly because no, I hadn't thought about it at all until right now.

Sure, I face transphobia in the human world, just like I have to deal with the way witches are treated in Asalin. On some level, it's dangerous for me to exist in either one. But at least in the human world, I have options. It's bigger and, depending on the city, there are more safe spaces and more allies. Plus, I don't have a (pretty shitty) reputation looming over my head.

But human racism? At least in America? It's a plague that infects every single facet of their society. There are no *options*.

Humans see color before anything else. I might always be a trans guy to them, but I also look white. It doesn't matter that I'm not even human, because they don't know that. And my whiteness is the most notable thing about me, more notable than my queerness ever will be, and it protects me everywhere I go in their world.

Emyr's Blackness would be the first thing they saw about him. And the same system that protects me would try to hurt him. Maybe it would even succeed.

"So, what do I do?" I know as soon as I ask the question that it isn't fair to make her tell me. It isn't fair that Briar is walking me through this, when I should have come to these realizations a lot earlier, on my own.

Still, before I can take it back, she reaches over and gives my arm a squeeze. "You fight like hell for each other, in whatever world you're in. You fight for a better future. And you use your privilege when you can. That's all you *can* do."

And it isn't enough. But I know she's right. Emyr and I will keep fighting for each other's safety. In whatever ways we can. For however long it takes.

After a moment of quiet consideration, I turn my head back to her. "What about you?"

"What about me?"

"What does your life look like when all of this is over?" I wave my hand around, as if to indicate the "all of this"-ness of our lives.

"Oh." Briar looks like someone's just asked her to solve for X. "Um. I have no idea. I guess I move on to the next fight."

Of course she does. "Another lost cause?"

"You were never a lost cause."

That is yet to be determined. "What about Jin?"

"Jin is—" Briar stops, closes her mouth, shakes her head. "Jin is going *through it* right now."

"We've established that." I brush my knuckles against the warm wood of the dock. "I'm just wondering what your life could look like, without someone to save. You know. If you were your own fight."

She pulls her knees to her chest and narrows her eyes. "Are you trying to get rid of me?"

It's so ridiculous I have to laugh, letting out a wild bark of a cackle at the audacity. "Are you kidding me? Please. We were apart for two weeks and I thought about dying like sixteen times." Oh, nope, too honest and totally not the point right now, let's not do that. "I just—you deserve to be the main character in your own story."

And I'm sorry I didn't realize that sooner.

"Well," I add, when she only frowns at me instead of answering. "Whatever we do, apparently we're going to be parents. Tell Jin to send us a picture of our baby if they're gonna be blowing your phone up!"

I can only laugh at the horrified look on her face before she flings herself into the water to get away from me.

CHAPTER NINE

SOME TERRIBLE OFFERING TO THEIR GOD

There is no private driver to take us to meet with the changelings the next day. Instead, we get a text with an address from Nadua early in the morning, and that afternoon we call an Uber.

I don't have the foggiest idea what to expect from this place, or these people. They're not human, but they're not witches, either. They live in human society, I guess, but I'm pretty sure they also practice magic. And they're secretive. They keep themselves hidden, for fear of what the fae might do if they learned of their existence.

A valid fear, based on *everything* I know about fae society. And the treatment from the Bells didn't exactly change my opinion any. I imagine if *those* are the fae these changelings are used to, their feelings toward our horned overlords might be even less kind than my own.

Present company excluded, based on the fact that he is a good person and also sexy.

I flip through a few possible scenarios in my head. I imagine some supersterile converted apartment building. Or maybe just like…a cave in the middle of nowhere. Both somehow seem completely possible.

The address leads our Uber driver to a winding road about a half an hour away from where we spent the day before, surrounded by weird-looking palm trees on both sides. (They are probably not actually palm trees, but forgive me for not being a botanist.) A mile or so—a kilometer? I don't know anything, I've never known a single thing a day in my life—down the road, the trees open up to a massive clearing surrounded by forest, with houses all along the tree line. We climb out with a quick thanks, and the car books it out of there and on to the next customer.

So, I don't know what I was expecting, but it wasn't…this. It definitely was not this.

Nature clearly rules this place. It feels like stepping into some private forest commune, with all the trees, and moss, and birds. There's a rainwater collection system, tanks set up around the perimeter. There's running water, too, a massive waterfall on a cliff on the other side of the clearing.

It's beautiful. It feels secret, and sacred, and safe.

I would *feel* the way changeling magic is infused into the place, even if I couldn't see signs of it. But there are signs, like the unfamiliar symbols carved into the trees around us, almost like the sigils I've been trying to learn. And I can hear a distant song, or maybe a chant, coming from one of the houses that I swear sounds like a spell.

But there's also someone sitting on their stoop with an open laptop on their knees. Someone else is watching TV inside. There's a handful of cars parked off the main path—someone here drives a Tesla, for crying out loud. It's clear that human influence is all over this place, too.

Actually, the combination of nature, and magic, and tech reminds me of Asalin. It reminds me of all the *best* parts of Asalin. Maybe I'm looking at one version of what our kingdom could become.

The houses are not all identical, not in some weird cookie-cutter kind of way, but they're clearly all the same style, built around the same time, probably by the same people. Tall skinny white houses tucked around the trees, with big windows and porches wrapped around their sides. There's probably fifteen of them or so, clustered throughout the clearing, each of them relatively small.

There's one that's clearly different from the others. More than twice the size, this one sits at the center of the rest, made from a wood that looks almost red, with a pillar at the center of the front porch. There are already three people standing just off the steps, watching us.

Briar steps out in front of Emyr and me, holding out her hands in an open-palmed, nonthreatening kind of gesture. "Mary?"

One of the three onlookers moves forward. She's an older woman, probably in her seventies or eighties, with light brown skin marked by faded gray tattoos, and a bald shaved head. Her energy, a blue so pale it borders on white, reminds me of the foamy crest of ocean waves. She moves slowly, but with purpose, and stops a few feet away from us.

"You are Nadua's daughter?" Her voice is stronger than she looks. I get the sense, immediately, that she's used to commanding a room.

"Yes. Briar Begay-Brown." Briar doesn't turn to look at us, but waves her hand at her back, in our general direction. "This is my adopted brother, Wyatt. And our friend, Emyr North."

Okay.

I mean yes, sure, I am Briar's brother, let's go with that. It's not like it's on paper or anything, but we live together, and we basically share her parents, and it makes as much sense as anything else, ignoring the fact that we have previously made out. I've just never heard her, or anyone else, ever say it so matter-of-factly. It makes me feel all...buzzy. Don't even know if that's a good thing or a bad thing or just a thing thing.

But also, our *friend*? Ha.

Like, also yes, Emyr is my friend, it's good to be friends with your significant others, all three of us are definitely friends, but...still.

"Some friend you have." Mary does not sound impressed. Her deep brown eyes study Emyr with only thinly veiled contempt, sliding over his horns and wings, flicking down his body, before she glances quickly at me, then back to Briar. "You've been to see *our* friends?"

"The kings?" Briar asks, and at Mary's quick nod, she says, "I didn't find them particularly friendly."

Mary snorts. "No. I thought you wouldn't."

I want to ask her how she knows them. If the changelings keep themselves hidden, just rescuing witch babies at the bor-

der or whatever, how is it possible they know *anything* about
the fae kingdom? But I have a feeling I should keep my questions to myself for right now.

"These are my grandchildren, Ari and Kora." Mary flicks
her fingers over her shoulder.

Ari is…hot. Not my type, but so utterly attractive it's impossible not to notice right away. He's probably around Emyr's
height, with bigger muscles that are covered in tattoos, similar
to his grandmother's but fresher, the ink a darker black. His
brown skin is darker than his grandmother's, too, and his thick
brown hair is long, hanging in beachy waves to the middle
of his torso. His energy is a vibrant, raw red, like fresh meat.
He smiles, and, oh, yeah, of course he has dimples.

Kora could not look more different from the other two.
She's tiny and pale, with freckles all over her, and strawberry
blond hair up in a topknot. One of her eyes is black-brown,
the other bright blue. Her cinnamon-colored energy swirls in
the air over her head, the only indication she might be feeling
anything, since her face seems utterly impassive.

"First time they're seeing one of his kind face-to-face."

Emyr clears his throat, moving past me to stand at Briar's
side. If this is the first time they're seeing a fae up close, they
really aren't getting the full effect. His wings and horns are
hidden again, cloaked for the ride over here. It always makes
him look smaller. But that's not the only reason he does, this
time.

His golden energy is low, dim, pushing in on him like he
wants to appear as unthreatening as possible to these strangers. "The kingdom of Asalin is incredibly grateful for your
willingness to meet with me today. *I* am incredibly grateful.

Nadua has made it clear how much you value your privacy, and the last thing I want to do is make you feel unsafe. I assure you, whatever comes of this conversation, I want nothing more than for us to help *each other*."

"Hmm." Mary eyes him up and down again, lips pursed. She looks back to Briar. "I don't like this. But I trust Nadua. She says you've got a good head on your shoulders. That true?"

"I'd say that's probably up for debate." Briar smiles. "But these two are good boys. I trust them with my life."

"And with mine, it seems." Mary sighs, turning around. She motions over her shoulder again, shaking her head. "Well, come on. Might as well get comfortable while you ask your questions. Can practically see the little one about to explode, he's got so many."

Well...she's not wrong.

At first, I think we're going to head into the big building at the center of their village. Instead, Mary and her grandchildren lead us away from it entirely, and in the direction of a nondescript little house tucked in the back. There are dried herbs hanging from the front porch rafters, and it smells like eucalyptus when Mary opens the door. The walls inside are a dark red wood, and covered in pictures of smiling faces that I can only assume are different branches of a sprawling family tree.

She leads us to her kitchen table and motions for us to sit. When we do, she says only, "Out with it, then."

"How does this place exist?" It sounds ridiculous once it's out of my mouth, but by then it's already out there, and there's nothing I can do about it. "Like...how did any of this...happen?"

"You're not one for subtle, are you?"

"It's not my strong suit, no."

"Good." Mary shrugs. "Well...let's see. As soon as the fae came to Aotearoa, we knew. This was before colonization. Of course the Indigenous people *knew* when strange creatures arrived and built a kingdom on our land. But we gave them space. Watched them from a distance. That's how we learned of their ritual sacrifice—the infants left in the woods."

A *ritual sacrifice*. For fuck's sake.

She's not wrong. But also, who's gonna tell the fae that?

I glance over at Emyr from the corner of my eye. His jaw is tight, golden energy snapped close.

Mary continues. "At first, our people believed it was some terrible offering to their god. We rescued the children, and folded them into our families. Of course, we knew they were different than us, because of where they came from. When they showed us their gifts, it didn't come as a surprise. As years went on, and generations passed, our bloodlines be-came intermingled. The community you see today is mostly Maori, but we are *all* changelings. We stay near Monalai, and we keep our eyes open for abandoned children. Or adult witches who run.

"Those adults, we didn't meet until much later. Long after the changelings had become part of our people. These were witches escaping the kingdom of monsters, after lifetimes of abuse, and sometimes they were lucky enough to find us. My grandfather was one of them. They taught this community the *full* story of the fae. We didn't know there were other

kingdoms, all around the world, or other communities like
ours, until then. Communities like the one you come from."
Mary inclines her head at Briar.

"Is there a reason so many changelings are Indigenous
peoples?" Emyr asks, frowning as the wheels in his mind
turn round and round on this new information. My clever,
knowledge-hungry boy.

Instead of Mary, Ari answers, with a sudden laugh, "Think
maybe colonizers were too busy colonizing to notice when
demons came knocking at our doors." Immediately after, he
frowns in Emyr's direction. "Uh. No offense."

"No, no, you can call him a demon—it's hot." Someone
should just kill me so I'm not able to speak ever again.

Ari snickers, but Kora's looking at me like she's giving
some serious consideration to doing just that. "My cousin
might indulge your crude humor, but I don't think any of
this is funny."

"Oh, I agree. Being this hot is extremely serious." You
know, if no one's going to kill me, can they at least cut my
tongue out? "I'm sorry. I act like a dumbass when I'm nervous."

"*And* he has an anxiety disorder," Briar adds. I'm going to
crawl in a hole now.

Mary clears her throat, and all eyes go back to her. "The
answer to your question is no. All changelings are not Indigenous. And certainly not all Indigenous people are changelings. But it feels obvious that our communities would have
the crossover that they do. Does it really surprise you? That
settlers from an entirely separate world would appear, their
so-called magic sucking the life from our land, and we would
be the first to take notice?"

No, I guess that makes—

Wait a minute.

It seems to hit Emyr at the same time it does me, because he asks, "You know? That fae magic is taking power from the Earth?"

"Of course we know." Mary huffs, shooting him a glower.

"How? *We* didn't even know—not until recently, and even then, it was only speculation."

When Clarke, wide-eyed and deranged and speaking like some kind of genocidal prophet, told us about what really happened to Faery. What was happening again here.

"It's our job to know," Kora pipes up. "Because it's our job to try and *fix* it."

"As caretakers of the land, you mean?" Briar asks, leaning forward and threading her fingers together in front of herself.

I've heard the word *caretaker* thrown around a lot in the Begay-Brown household, along with *protector*. Something her family prides themselves on, a common thread that unites many other Indigenous people around the world; a feeling of guardianship for the lands they come from.

"Kaitiaki," Ari says, bobbing his head in agreement, though I don't know what the word means. "But also...with magic."

Emyr looks to Briar, who looks to me, and I look back at Emyr. None of us know what the hell he's talking about.

It's Emyr who speaks, though. "What do you mean?"

It's the changelings' turn to exchange looks with one another. Kora makes a pinched expression and gives a little shake of her head. Ari rolls his eyes and elbows her in the ribs, not hard enough to hurt her, but not gently, either. Mary sighs, pressing her fingertips together, and finally turns her attention to me.

The full, isolated weight of her stare is heavy and makes my skin ache.

"There is so much you do not know about your magic."

"Um." Like, it's true. It's just me and my tarot cards out here winging it. But where the *fuck* did that come from?

"It is intentional, on the part of the fae. They keep the truth of witch magic concealed." Oh, she meant *you* as in witches, not *you* as in me. It should make me feel better, knowing it wasn't a direct callout, but it doesn't. It just makes me angry, especially as she continues. "They keep your numbers down in their kingdoms, make it difficult for you to connect with one another. Your ability to practice becomes so muddled that you're never able to figure out the full extent of what you can do. Which is, of course, what they want."

A conversation I once had with Jin plays back in my mind.

"If our power comes from emotion, wouldn't that mean it's infinite? Wouldn't that make us stronger than them?"

"Why else would they hate us so much?"

It's obvious. The fae hate us, keep us under their boots, because they're scared of what our power might look like if we actually reached our full potential.

But what does that have to do with fae magic draining the Earth?

"Right, the fae suck." I roll my wrist, flicking my fingers toward my scarred face. "I'm aware."

Both Ari and Kora glance to Emyr, like they're waiting for him to argue, or at least look offended on behalf of his people. I don't need to look at him to know they're not going to find what they're looking for.

Emyr is *also* aware that the fae suck.

"I still don't get what your point is," I finish, shaking my head.

"He just means—" Briar starts, but Mary cuts her off.

"You don't need to explain your friend to me, Briar. He says what he thinks. I appreciate that." She smiles at me, more of a smirk than anything, before sighing. "There is still so much about our magic I don't understand. So much knowledge was left behind in Faery, I don't think we'll ever have all the answers we want. I don't know how witches came to be. And there is undoubtedly so much more to what our magic is capable of than we will ever know. All that being said…" That smirk is back. "Changelings, unlike witches, have lived for generations without the threat of fae punishment looming over us. This community has been given years to practice our craft in peace, in a way that fae-born witches living in their kingdoms have *never* had. And in our solitude, we've learned things. I may not know the origin story of witchkind. But I know why you exist. Fae and witches are one another's perfect counterparts."

Mary says the words with such dramatic finality, I know this is supposed to be the climactic moment when everything falls together.

Unfortunately for her, I'm a moron. I still have no idea what's going on.

"You can keep going."

Kora snorts, and then put a hand over her face, cheeks

pinkening. Ari laughs, flashing those dimples again. I totally see Briar show off her own at the sound.

Mary fully rolls her eyes at me, but she does keep going. "Fae power comes from the Earth. They draw strength from the land. The stronger the land is, the stronger they are. Unfortunately, this also means using their power takes from the world around them. Conversely, witches—and changelings—draw our strength from our empathy. Our emotions fuel us, and *their* strength gives us strength. And, unfortunately, enough magic can drain us from the inside."

"Wait, really?"

"You didn't know that?"

I think about my massive depression naps immediately following big displays of magic, my *episodes*, barely being able to get myself out of bed for days at a time. I thought I was just, you know, mentally ill.

Which, *okay*, I guess the two aren't mutually exclusive.

"No. I didn't."

"Hmm." Mary nods. "It doesn't surprise me. Witches living under fae control undoubtedly already live in fear of their own magic. Displays of great power are likely punished, either legally or socially. It would be difficult to recognize the correlation. But, yes, in answer to your question, really. Magical overspending can leave us feeling numb, hollow, depressed. It takes a toll on our emotional well-being, the same way fae magic takes a toll on the land."

"Whoa." Briar tilts her head forward, cupping her chin in her fingers. Her eyebrows scrunch together, face thoughtful. "That's…a lot."

I scoff. "Yeah."

Emyr and I meet eyes. Not for the first time, I can hear his thoughts without him speaking them aloud.

Is that really how it feels for you?

I shrug. *I mean, yeah, it's not great.*

"What do you mean about fae and witches being each other's counterparts?" Briar pipes up, dragging attention back to Mary.

"It doesn't have to be this way. Your magic doesn't have to hurt you, and fae magic doesn't have to hurt the planet. The answer lies in one another." Mary smiles, watching me with that intense stare, like she's waiting to see what I'll do next. "Witches, and changelings, are just energy movers. We take power from one place, and put it in another."

"Through conduits," I add, nodding sagely. Solomon is totally somewhere out there feeling very proud right now but with no idea why.

"Mmm. When a witch creates a connection with a fae, when we learn to tangle our magic with theirs, we can draw on it. Fae magic has the ability to refill our wells, so to speak. And witches, in turn, can take that magic and return its power to the land it was originally taken from." She inclines her head between Emyr and me. "Your kinds are one another's *keepers*. At least, you were always meant to be."

That is…so much to take in.

I think what annoys me the most about all of it is that it makes complete sense.

Of course there's a *reason* witches exist. Of course we have a *purpose*. We aren't abominations, we're necessary pieces of the puzzle who've just been led to believe we're some kind of grand mistake.

Living under the rule of the fae is draining, emotionally,

mentally, even physically in its own ways. But being with
Emyr, being loved by him, has always left me feeling re-
charged. Some of that, I have no doubt, is just *him*. But maybe
some of it is *this*, too.

And then, there's the night he died. I could *feel* the way
his energy threaded with mine. I held his body and let grief
overtake me, and the golden threads of his power entwined
with my black magic.

"This community is kept secret from the fae," Briar starts,
each word coming out slowly, like she's thinking this through
meticulously before speaking. "So, you've never been able to
form those connections."

"No," Mary agrees. "Not with the living."

Pardon me?

"What does that mean?" Emyr asks, sitting up straighter,
the tips of his wings twitching over his shoulders.

Mary exchanges a look with Ari. Her grandson makes a
scrunchy, disgusted sort of face. When she looks back at us,
she sighs. "We believe fae magic is carried in the blood. And
there is still power there, once they have left their bodies. This
is another reason we stay close to their kingdom. We save the
children they discard, yes. But we also sow their magic, once
they're gone."

"I…" That's one of the most disturbing things I've ever
heard. *"How?"*

"We've given you a lot of information already," Kora interjects, before her grandmother can go spilling some inevita-
bly disturbing, nightmare-fuel secrets. "It's your turn to give
us some answers. Nadua said you wanted an alliance with us

because you aren't like the rest of the fae. You want to *change* things. Why? How?"

Emyr's eyes are huge and glassy, staring at these people like he's definitely imagining them digging up fae bodies and playing with them like puppets or something. Which, same.

After he doesn't move for a moment, I reach over and smack a hand against his chest. The *thunk* seems to reboot his brain, and he snaps out of it, shaking his head.

"Right. Ah, the why of it is simple. I don't believe any person deserves to be treated the way the witches have been, under fae rule. I don't believe a monarchy is an equitable form of government. I want a future where all citizens of Asalin, and every fae society around the world, can live in peace. All of this was true before I knew what fae magic was really doing to the planet. And before I realized witches were the key to undoing the damage."

"You don't want to be king?" Ari asks, raising his eyebrows in surprise. "Seriously?"

Emyr shrugs, leaning back and folding his hands over his stomach. "It's not a question that was ever presented to me until very recently. I've never known any other future. I don't know what I want, not really. But I know my being king isn't fair."

"Well, shit. How the hell do you plan to get out of it?"

"Slowly and meticulously." Emyr frowns.

"Not that slowly," I argue. "We've already gotten rid of the Guard and Committee. We have a new group helping us keep our shit together; the Circle. Made up of fae *and* witches."

"And how did your people react to that?" Mary raises her eyebrows.

No one answers that question.

After a moment, Emyr clears his throat and continues. "We've been floating the idea of an election. Letting the people of Asalin determine their new leader. But there are problems with that, too."

"Mmm." Mary bobs her head, looking thoughtful. "There is a difference between equality and justice."

Emyr nods. It's a problem we've gone round and round about, over and over again, for a while now. Sure, we could let every single citizen of Asalin cast a vote, but since the majority of people have ass-backwards, oppressive views on the witches, because they've spent generations *culling them*, that's not exactly guaranteed to lead to any change. At least, not positive change. It might actually make things worse. Majority rule might *sound* fair, but it still isn't the right choice when the majority decides to hurt people.

"How do things work here?" Briar asks, holding up her hand and flicking her fingers to indicate the building we're in. "You're the leader of this community, right? How did that happen?"

"I'm sorry, but I don't think anything I have to say could help you." Mary sighs. "Our community here is not like any other. Our traditions are unique, and built on generations of relying on only each other to stay safe. I'm not sure our ways could ever be applied to a place like this kingdom of Asalin."

It's disappointing, but it also doesn't come as a big surprise. Asalin, like all of the fae realms, has done an excellent job of fucking itself over. It's going to take something remarkable to unfuck it.

Kora clears her throat. "So, you've explained the why. You

want a better world for the witches. And you want to save the planet from fae magic sucking it dry."

"Is reversing the effects of fae magic really enough to save the planet?" Briar asks, leaning forward and balancing her forearms on her knees. "You know…with the whole impending climate apocalypse and everything?"

"Oh, *definitely* not," Ari laughs. "In the long run, we're all screwed unless we destroy capitalism. Fae magic's just speeding up the timeline."

"Ahem," Kora interrupts. "Right. But, to be clear, you have no idea *how* you're going to do any of this?"

"Well, not *no* idea," I mumble, offended on Emyr's behalf. "It's coming together."

Emyr reaches over and puts a hand on my shoulder, pressing his thumb into the notch where my collar meets my throat. My pulse thrums up to meet him. I swallow.

"For some time now, I've been working with a witch, Jin Ueno, to develop a new kind of magic use. Together, we've combined witch abilities with human technology, allowing for the fae to use this power themselves. It is my hope, and my goal, that by replacing some of the fae magic that keeps our kingdoms running with this technology, instead, we'll be able to slow down the exhaust on the land. And that, with witches at the helm, it will create new, invaluable roles for them in our kingdoms." He sighs, shaking his head. "It isn't perfect. But it's a start."

"Hmm." Mary narrows her eyes, not harshly, but skeptically.

"Here." I dig into my pocket and fish out Emyr's cell phone, sliding it across the table toward her. "You can look for yourself."

Ari and Kora lean in over her shoulders, comically close, while the older woman picks up the phone and inspects it. She unlocks the screen, fingers deftly sliding across it, and I wonder what she's looking at.

When Emyr's leg bounces at my side, I reach over and put my palm over his thigh.

"I'm surprised you think your people will go for this," Mary finally says, passing the phone back to me. "From what I understand, the fae are not known for embracing change."

I snort. I can't help it. Emyr rolls his eyes at me.

It's Briar who answers, though. "Some of the fae kingdoms are more eager for change than you might think. The South American queens are known for pushing boundaries. And Emyr's mother, Kadri, is something of a revolutionary. Even before Emyr took the Throne, she was working with him to push progress in Asalin. Despite the backlash she faced, Kadri championed all kinds of innovation."

"I would like to meet this woman," Mary says conclusively.

"I'm sure she would enjoy that." Emyr smiles, but I notice the way his golden energy flicks tighter around his throat, almost as if constricting him.

Kadri probably would enjoy that…if she lives long enough for it to be a possibility. The former queen's inevitable death is looming, and there's no knowing how far out it is now.

"While I understand your point that Asalin and this community are very different places," Emyr continues, "I want to be clear that I have a depth of admiration for your people. What you've created here is beautiful. And I believe in a future where the fae can have something like this for ourselves. To that end, we can help each other. If you're correct about the symbiotic nature of our people, it stands to reason you would benefit from creating connections with the fae, with *living fae*, that would allow you to recharge your magic. And, in turn, you could help us bring balance to our kingdoms, for the first time."

Mary nods, reaching up to brush her fingers against her chin. "It is dangerous for us. We have worked hard to become inconspicuous, to humans *and* the fae. We walk the line between worlds, our truth hidden from both. You are asking us to come out of the shadows, but you know how the fae treat things they don't understand."

"I do." Emyr nods. "And I won't pretend there aren't those who would want to harm you."

"I'm in my second year of uni," Ari says with a grimace. "I'd rather not die, you know?"

"I can't make you any promises. I'm sorry." Emyr swallows, curling one hand over mine and squeezing. "But I will do everything in my power to keep you safe."

"He means that," I tack on, threading our fingers and squeezing right back.

Mary is quiet for a long moment. Finally, she asks, "Would you like to see how we sow magic now?"

We go for a walk in the woods. The changelings don't offer much of an explanation about what we're supposed to be looking out for, telling us we'll know it when we see it. Or rather—*they'll* know it when *they* see it.

It really is beautiful, here. Everything is green and lush, the sun overhead bright. The trees are ancient, massive giants looming over us all. I try to catch Briar's attention a

few times, try to make eye contact with her to silently communicate how cool it is, but she's absorbed in checking out
the woods around her. She stares up at the treetops, savor-
ing glimpses of black-and-white birds darting through the
branches, a dimpled little grin on her face.

I stare at her for a few moments before glancing over at
Emyr. He's watching her, too, and he smiles when he catches
my eye, reaching out to link our fingers together.

Finally, after walking for who knows how long, right when
I've started to wonder if this is grandma and her grandkids
luring us out to the middle of nowhere to murder us, Mary
stops and holds up a hand. I don't know what she's listening
to, or thinking, or what, but she pauses, eyes looking into
the middle distance. After a moment more, she exchanges a
look with Kora, then Ari, then the three of them motion for
us to follow them in a new direction.

"You can see energies," Mary says, suddenly, inexplicably.
"And you call this magic. Right?"

I'm not sure which one of us she's addressing, Emyr or me,
but I cut Emyr off to answer, "Yeah. Why?"

"Like the humans, we cannot see these energies."

Huh. You know, Briar told me that, back when we first
met. That she couldn't see energies the way I could, that no
humans could. It never occurred to me to ask if that had been
a lie, just a way to cover her tracks about the whole changeling thing. Apparently, it wasn't. I'm glad it wasn't.

Not because I don't want her to be able to see them. Just
because I don't want even one more secret between us.

Mary continues, "But this is not the only magic there is.
Others are simply more difficult to see, even for your kind."

"Can you explain?" Emyr asks, frowning deeply.

"Everything that lives has energy." Kora shrugs, brushing against Mary's side as they walk. "And every culture knows it. They all have different words for it. Our human relatives call it mauri. *Magic* is just moving that energy from one place to another. And nearly every living thing can do that, too. Changelings? Witches? We just help the process along, because we're the only ones who can move the energy of *other people*."

"I don't understand," he sighs.

Mood.

"You will." Ari grins and claps him on the shoulder. "Hope you're not squeamish."

"Oh, that's, like, super encouraging," I grumble. Still, I keep following.

I realize what he meant about being squeamish just a few seconds later, though. As we approach one of the smaller trees in the woods, Briar gasps loudly at my side, her hand flying to her mouth. I look to her, then to the place where her eyes are rooted.

Oh. Poor thing.

Mary kneels on the ground at the base of a tree, next to a *huge* black pig. He makes a soft, gasping noise and rustles against the ground as if trying to run. He can't, though. One of his back legs is mangled, broken and bloody and lying un-moving behind him. There's an open wound across his belly, even worse than his leg.

"Shh," Mary whispers, putting a hand over the creature's eyes. "It will be over soon."

She pulls something from her pocket, a short handle con-nected to a curved, too-wide blade. The whole thing is made from something deep green, like jade, and intricately carved with decorative symbols. To the rest of us, she says, "You won't be able to see his energy return. But you will see the immediate effect it has on the Earth."

When she presses the tip of the curved edge to the pig's throat, I can't help myself. I have to look away, my stomach in knots. Briar does take my other hand, then. I know it happens when she and Emyr both squeeze.

"Wyatt," Kora says, voice sharp. "You don't want to miss this."

And she's right. When I turn back, I see…flowers. All around the pig's body, *flowers* are suddenly blooming. They shoot up all around him, right in front of me, an entire bed of tulips.

"Whoa."

I look to Emyr, and find his eyebrows low and tight, deep in thought. Briar, though, is as mesmerized as I've ever seen. It makes my heart pang a little to see her dark brown eyes gone wet and wide, her mouth parted until I can make out the gap between her front teeth.

Ari bends down and grabs the pig's front legs, and hauls him over his shoulder. "C'mon, let's head back. Get him cleaned up."

"What will you do with the body?" Briar asks, as we all move to follow after him.

"Eat it, of course," he grins at her again, over his shoulder.

Mary sees something in Emyr's face that I don't, because she elaborates, "That is *not* what we do with the fae. When a fae is buried in the woods at Monalai, we simply find them and give their energy to the land. Their bodies go with them.

I believe it is because they are not truly of this Earth. With creatures like these, their bodies remain, because the land cannot take what already belongs to it. And so, we eat them. They help to keep our people alive, and we carry the last remnants of their energy with us."

That's bizarre.

"That's beautiful," Briar says quietly. I swear she wipes a tear from her face.

When we make our way back to their village, outside of the woods, Ari tells us goodbye and heads off to…do whatever it is that one does with a pig carcass. Kora doesn't offer us a goodbye before she heads off, too, though not with her cousin.

Mary smiles. "I would invite you to stay for a meal. But we have learned a lot about each other today. Perhaps some time apart to reflect would be good for us all."

She's right. My mind is still swimming with everything she's unloaded. It's a lot to process.

"Thank you for seeing us." Emyr nods his head, in respect. "I hope we'll meet again."

"Oh, I've no doubt we will." Mary looks over Emyr, then Briar, before her eyes settle on me. "Regardless of what happens next."

CHAPTER TEN

THEY TURN TOWARD EACH OTHER INSTEAD

What happens next is this: I'm in the car with Briar and Emyr when my whole world turns upside down.

Back up a few minutes, though.

"Overall, I give the whole trip a seven out of ten," Briar announces as our limo glides up the road toward Asalin two days later. "It did not go *exactly* as planned, but it's a beautiful country. Also? I might be in love with Ari."

"Ari's *hot*," I add emphatically, both because it's true and because Ari *isn't* currently dealing with the fallout of learning his ex-girlfriend was a witch-hating murderer who never loved him. I just think that's neat. You know, I think someone who *isn't* in the middle of the world's messiest breakup ever would be *such* a good match for Briar. Even if he does live on the other side of the world. (A bonus, really, since there's less opportunity for him to steal all her attention that way.)

Emyr raises his eyebrows.

"Don't start. I'm just doing my job as the group's token allosexual. You two need to know these things." I grin, shoving a handful of chicken nuggets in my mouth.

Finally, on the way home from the airport, I got Emyr to swing through a drive-through with me. We're splitting an order of a hundred nuggets between the three of us, *technically*, but I have definitely eaten more than thirty-three at this point. Emyr and Briar both seem less enthused to keep going in on them than I am. Cowards.

"Why are you like this all the time?" Emyr sounds like he's on the verge of breaking up with me.

I swallow but don't get a chance to answer, 'cause that's around the time the car blows up.

Well, maybe that's a bit of an exaggeration. (From *me*? Weird.) Technically, I guess the car doesn't blow up so much as it crashes into nothing. An invisible force rams against the driver's side with a brutal, worse-than-nails-on-a-chalkboard crunch of metal, and suddenly we're spinning out of control. My stomach lurches into my throat, breath stalling as my hands shoot forward, one to grab at Briar's shoulder and the other Emyr's arm.

Not that holding on to them does anything to help. The driver loses control, the car hits something, and then we're in the air. My world, upside down.

And there's a moment when everything feels suspended, when my body hasn't had time to process the adrenaline, when I'm watching dozens of chicken nuggets rain down around me and think, *This would be such a stupid way to die.*

I've survived so much. We all have. A car crash taking us out? Ridiculous.

The moment passes when metal crunches on gravel, the roof of the car caving *up* underneath my feet.

"Wyatt," Emyr groans, glowing golden hands reaching for me like he's searching for a wound to heal.

I'm fine, though. I think. I'm not worried about me.

"Briar," I answer.

One of the back doors came open in the crash. Maybe Briar opened it, thinking she could get out, or maybe it happened on impact. Either way, she went through it at some point, and I push myself through it now, while Emyr forces himself into the front seat to check on the driver.

"Briar?"

The world feels too still. There's no other traffic to make noise out here in the woods, in the nowhere's land stretch of road between human civilization and Asalin's border. It's just us and this wrecked piece of metal. The adrenaline's still pumping hard through my system, head spinning, but the woods don't seem to notice anything's wrong. A bird chirps overhead. Sunlight casts afternoon shadows through the trees.

No sign of Briar.

The adrenaline turns to something cold. Threads of ice wind themselves around my waist and move up, slowly constricting my stomach, chest, throat. I turn round and round, eyes searching the crash zone, out of control of my own body like a marionette coerced by strings of dread.

Who's the puppet master?

"Briar!"

"Wyatt."

Her voice tiptoes softly across my ears, so quiet I almost miss it, but when I do, my whole body jerks in her direction. I don't consciously make any decision to go running to her side, but then I'm there, finding her propped up against one of the trees on the side of the road, tucked just out of view of the car.

"Briar, I—"

World upside down. World off its axis. Gravity gone, strings cut. I am floating outside my body.

"It's...not good," she admits. Blood slicks over her tongue and down her chin when she speaks. More coats her side, where metal juts from her ribs.

When you die, your life doesn't flash before your eyes. I know this. The day Briar and I stole Summanus, the kings' dragon, from the field and took him for a joy ride, the day we fell from the sky, I didn't see my life unfold in front of me. I saw all the unanswered questions. The what-ifs I would never see through. The people I was leaving behind.

When someone you love dies, their life doesn't flash before your eyes, either. When I held Emyr's still-warm corpse in my arms, I didn't think about everything we had together growing up, but everything the *world* would miss without him in it.

That's what I think about when I look at Briar. A world where she doesn't exist.

No more of her dimpled smiles. No more of her sunflower-yellow energy that lights up any room she stands in. No more of her bold determination, her passion, her strength.

But it's more than that. The world would miss out on so much without her in it—but Briar would, too.

How much has she already missed out on, pouring herself into the people she loves? Giving up everything at a moment's notice to fight for the people and the causes she believes in?

She can't die. Not now. Not before she lives.

I crash back into my body so hard I feel reverberations in my toes. She's not going to die.

"Emyr!"

"Please," Briar whispers, but I don't know what she's going to ask me for, because I'm already running back toward the car.

"Emyr! It's Briar!"

The driver is still unconscious, lying over his steering wheel. There's glass everywhere from the broken front wind-shield. And more blood.

I wish I still felt sick at the sight of this much blood.

"Emyr, I need—"

I forget whatever I was going to say. Emyr is in the woods on the other side of the road. And everything is wrong.

His body is bent backward so his chest faces the sky, his wings open and crushed into the ground underneath him, head tilted so far back that his horns nearly touch the dirt. His eyes stare up, pure gold and glossy, as he claws, futilely, at some invisible force around his throat.

The thing about constantly worrying your boyfriend is going to die again, about always looking over your shoulder for the next threat that's out to get him, about jumping at every shadow, real or imagined, is that, once you see him *actually* in danger again, it feels like…

Like, *Oh, here we go. This. I've been waiting for* this.

Whatever this is. Whatever's happening here.

I race toward him, crying out his name, but I never make it there. Something unseen grabs at the back of my collar and suddenly my feet aren't on the ground anymore. This invisible force hurtles me through the air, tossing me onto the ground a few yards away. I snarl, leaping onto my hands and knees, looking around frantically for the source of this magic.

If they're watching me right now, I probably look like the same feral dog I was that night years ago in Briar's bedroom. And maybe I am. Maybe I haven't really changed at all since then, not in the ways that matter.

"I WILL EAT YOUR FUCKING HEART!"

The woods seem to soften, going even quieter, as if this thing is considering my threat.

And then the most awful thing begins to happen. Emyr's mouth falls open, and a *sound* comes out of him. I've heard plenty of noises from Emyr before. Harsh words snapped with snotty authority. My name breathed with reverence. Growls of irritation. Growls of pleasure. But this sound is…it's *wrong*. It crackles, like gravel rocks popping in his vocal cords. And I don't… I really don't think he's making it on purpose.

I leap to my feet and run headlong at him again. This time, when I feel *something* grabbing at my neck, I yank myself free.

Still, I don't make it to him. Instead, I run headfirst into nothing. An unseen wall, like some kind of force field between me and my boyfriend. I slam so hard into it that my teeth clank together, hard, maybe cracking one of them.

Emyr's groan—not the right word, don't have time to think of the right word—gets louder. He claws so hard at this invisible thing around his neck that he draws blood along the underside of his own jaw. Red slicks up the sides of his face, over his horns, and drips down off the tips. His golden energy pulses out of him like a heartbeat, filling the bubble he's captive in but unable to go any further. Each pulse grows slower and slower.

"LET HIM GO!" My throat tears as I scream, hands slamming against the invisible wall keeping me away from him.

Whatever's out there doesn't care.

Emyr's hands stop clawing at his throat and fall, weak, to his sides, bloody claws trailing into the dirt. The sound coming from his mouth finally crawls to an end.

Our eyes meet.

He's going to die.

And Briar's going to die with him.

And it's going to be all my fault.

Because I can't do anything to protect either of them. Because my magic doesn't know what it's doing, because it's useless, because *I* am useless. Any other witch could probably figure this out, could probably cast some spell to save him, but I'm stuck here, helpless, because I don't *know anything* about my own magic. I scramble with my rage, the part of me hungry for blood, and fire rises to meet me, jumping to life in my hands. But what is fire going to do? I can scorch the whole world, but that won't save the people I love.

I try reaching for the darkness inside me, instead, the blackout that took over my body the night of the riot, the night Clarke killed Emyr with our broken contract. It doesn't rise up to meet me at all. Jin once told me that darkness only existed because I was out of control. What the fuck is the point of fighting for control if it just makes me weak?

The fire sputters and goes out in my palms.

Emyr's eyes start to roll back in his skull and my heart howls in response.

Focus! Fuck! Enough feeling sorry for yourself! Fix this.

I don't know any spells. I don't know sigils, or potions, or anything I should know, but what did Solomon say? I don't actually need those things. They're just conduits, delivering energy from one form to another. All I really need is something to be that channel. He told me I need to find my *what*.

There's only one piece of magic I know. It's the only thing I've carried with me for years now, the only part of my past I let myself keep in the human world. The first connection to the witches I ever held, given to me by Emyr and destroyed by my parents. Until it was given back to me in a new form, years later, by Briar. It's as much a part of my story with the two of them as it is a part of me on my own.

And I don't know if this is going to work, but I don't have anything else. I'm grabbing the cards out of my pocket before I even realize what I'm doing. My fingers move on instinct. I've thought for a while now that the tarot deck felt like an extension of my hands, but in this moment they flow into my skin like we actually *are* connected. Like they can feel my magic, or maybe my need, thrumming through every nerve ending in my body, and they're reaching for me just as desperately as I'm reaching for them.

I need something that can tear this barrier down, something strong enough to push back and knock the power out of it.

A single card flits between my index and middle finger. I

can't see the front yet, but I don't need to. Somehow I already know what it is. I slam it, hard, against the invisible wall.

Nine of Wands.

Perseverance. Sheer will. Overcoming obstacles.

Dark energy erupts, and I know it's mine, I can feel it in the way it moves, but it doesn't come from me at all. Instead, it comes from the card itself. Tendrils leap off the matte-black paper, shooting out in every direction like a bomb going off. Even though I still can't see it, I can *feel* when the attacker's magic gets sucker punched. The force of the wall being shattered sends reverberations through the ground.

It'd be enough to take me off my feet, if I weren't completely, ruthlessly, frantically focused on Emyr. The magic releases him, too, dropping him from his suspension. He falls the rest of the way to the ground, rolling off his wounded wings onto his stomach, and sucks in a deep breath.

As if nothing happened, the Nine of Wands flutters into my hand, nesting itself back in the deck. I shove them all in my pocket as I race to Emyr's side.

The need to touch him now is overwhelming. It's worse than every panic attack I've had since That Night, worse than every other moment where my little rat brain has tried to trick me into thinking he was dead again. I *need* to get my hands on his skin, to feel warmth and muscle and a beating heart under my fingers—but I don't. Because I'm not sure he wants me to.

Emyr looks wrecked. I can see him shaking, gently, every inch of him vibrating at a low, quiet thrum. His eyes—brown again—are wide, his claws digging into the ground until he's got fistfuls of dirt in his hands. I'm not even sure he's *here* right now.

So, I don't touch him. I crouch down next to him and put my own shaking hands on my knees in case they get any ideas and try to act without my permission.

"Are you okay?" A bullshit question we both already know the answer to.

Nothing. He just keeps shaking, staring into the distance at nothing.

Briar. I leave Emyr to his dissociating, push myself back to my feet and race to the other side of the road.

The first sight of her rips a strangled "no!" from my lips. Her eyes are closed, her head tilted back against the bark of the tree. Sunlight, oblivious to what's happening beneath it, streaks across her face.

Did you know that sunflowers turn toward the sun?

Did you know, when they can't find it, they turn toward each other instead?

My knees hit the dirt next to her, and my hands find her neck. For a moment, I can't distinguish between my own shaking and her pulse, but then I feel it, faint but unmistakable, a quiet thump, thump, thump under my hand. She's still here. She's with me.

But barely.

One hand still on her pulse, my other runs down her side, brushing against the metal wedged in her body. I don't know how to fix it, and trying might make it worse. I need Emyr.

Briar needs Emyr.

I don't want to leave her, but I have to. I force myself up and back across the road. Emyr is still staring into the distance, exactly where I left him. I crouch at his side again, still not touching him, but closer than before.

"Emyr." I dig my nails into my shins. "I need you to come back to me."

Nothing.

"Emyr! Briar is going to die!"

It must only be seconds before he turns his head to look at me, but a lifetime might've passed in every silent ticking of the clock. Finally, slowly, his eyes meet mine.

And then, with impossible fae speed, he's on his feet and across the road. By the time I make it back to them, the piece of the car door that was inside of Briar *isn't* anymore, and his golden hands are lighting her body up.

There is a long moment where I can do nothing but sit and wait. And finally, the weight of everything that happened hits me. The sight of Briar's body. The sound Emyr made. What I did with the tarot deck.

I crawl away from them to throw up behind a tree, the taste of bile and fast food and a thick layer of saliva lingering in my mouth when I'm done. By the time I make it back to them, Briar is waking up.

She blinks, groggy, down at herself, and then over at me. I don't know what I expect her to say. It is not what she says, which is, "You left me."

"You...needed help."

Her eyes flood with tears. Another chord of panic strikes in my heart.

"I didn't want to die alone," she mumbles, and then slumps onto her back, breathing hard and staring up at the sky through the tree limbs.

Okay. I don't know what to say to that. She didn't die alone, because she didn't die at all, because we saved her. I take a deep breath, running a hand over my face.

Finally, I look back to Emyr.

He's watching me. The look in his eyes is still far away, his body still trembling, but I think he's coming back. Maybe.

I still don't move. I don't touch him.

Until one dirty, bloody, clawed hand reaches out to press against my cheek, and I give in to myself, throwing my arms around his shoulders and pressing my face into his neck.

I don't even know what mindless bullshit I'm whispering as my mouth brushes along his throat, pressing featherlight kisses to any part of him I can get to. I know his blood tastes like rust and salt and a hint of burnt sugar when it makes its way to my tongue. My fingers twist in the back of his shirt, holding him as tightly as I can as his shaking begins to dissolve, his body melting into mine.

I don't know what attacked us. Probably the same thing that went after Leonidas.

And I don't know *how* I did what I did with the cards, or how to make it happen again.

But I know this: the next time someone comes for my family, it'll be *their* blood in my teeth.

CHAPTER ELEVEN

A SCARED, VULNERABLE CHILD

The driver is fine, once Emyr heals him, if disoriented. I get Tessa on the phone, and she shows up within minutes in some irritatingly outdoorsy off-roading thing with no doors.

There is still so much I do not know about my sister. Like why she has this car.

Now's not the time to ask, though.

We pile in and start heading up the path toward Asalin, our driver now in the passenger seat next to Tessa; Briar and Emyr shoved into the back seat with me. I can feel the moment we pass through the barrier that separates the human world from ours, and moments later, the village starts to come into view.

"I need to speak with my parents," Emyr says against my knuckles. He's got my hand to his mouth, fangs gently pressing into the backs of my fingers, claws tenderly raking up and down my wrist. I bend forward to kiss one delicately pointed ear. "I need to talk to my father about what happened without anyone else overhearing."

And I know I'm included in anyone else. Leonidas didn't even want to tell Emyr what happened to him; he's not going to want to talk about it with an audience.

"Hmm." I don't want him to go anywhere without me. I don't want him out of my sight ever again. But I understand. "Maybe I should go talk to Solomon about what happened with the cards. Briar? You wanna come?"

Briar leans into Emyr's side, resting her elbow against his thigh and her chin on his shoulder, so she can face me. We slip easily into a silent conversation. *I'm exhausted. I need to lie down.*

I nod, reaching over to tuck a strand of black and blue hair behind her ear. *You want me to come with you?*

Her eyebrows knot together. She gives a small shake of her head.

I don't know what I did wrong, or if I even really did anything wrong, but I know Briar needs to be alone right now. And as much as I don't want her out of my sight ever again, either, it's fine. It's *fine.*

Emyr turns his face to kiss the top of Briar's head. To me, silently, he says, *We'll be alright. You need to get answers.*

Briar nods, taking Emyr's hand and squeezing his fingers. *We'll be okay.*

They'll be okay. Right. Yeah. Definitely. I have totally no reason not to believe that at all.

But there's nothing for me to do except roll with it. "Hey, Tessa, let me out."

She slams to a stop so suddenly I nearly go flying over her seat. I manage to catch myself by grabbing onto her headrest, but only after it knocks me in the chest hard enough to bruise.

"Ow," I grumble, slumping back and rubbing a hand across my chest, over the thin fabric of my long-sleeve shirt.

"Sorry." She does not sound sorry.

I jump down onto the cobblestone path, but lean forward to wrap my hands around the steering wheel before Tessa can zip off. "Maybe try not to kill my people on the rest of the drive."

"I'll do my best."

Her words drip with sarcasm, green eyes rolling. But there's a secret tenderness tucked under her tongue, a softness she's trying to hide. I only know where to look because it's the same hiding spot I use.

And that's how I know she means it. She'll do her best to make sure nothing happens to them when I'm not around to make sure for myself. And I'm as grateful for that as I am uncomfortable at the idea of being *seen* by her. By the subtle, unspoken acknowledgment that she knows she's got my world in her back seat.

As I watch them take off up the road again, winding through the village and eventually disappearing up the hill toward the castle, I take a second to just…breathe. In the shadow of everything that's happened in the last few minutes—hours, days, weeks, months, years—I need a second to just fucking breathe.

Beneath the wild summer air, Asalin smells like herbs and fire. Lavender, sage, basil, and rosemary blend together with a hint of smoke and burning wood. I can't be sure if it's from the shitty little bakery owned by an anti-witch asshole, or someone's open kitchen window, or witches making magic in a hidden nook somewhere, or some combination of the three.

Somewhere, inside one of the cabins, someone is singing. Music isn't really a big thing in Asalin. These days, most of it is Top 40 human songs that make their way here through osmosis. But there are a few old fae tunes, remnants from Faery, that have survived all this time. This is one of them, a slow, hypnotic ballad.

"The Tide, the Tide, is coming in, to claim the blood it's craving. And for the children of the air, the Tide shall be lifesaving. Beloved babes of sea and stone, for you we'll hap'ly bleed. If there be doubt of our devotion, listen to this creed."

Absolutely weird song.

Beautiful, though.

I rub a hand over my face, taking another deep breath. My chest hurts. My binder, probably on for too long since I wore it on the plane from Auckland, is digging into my ribs and underarms. My stomach hasn't found the will to unclench, nausea or nerves or both pressing up against the back of my throat. The path shifts under my feet, dozens of tiny rocks moving around the soles of my boots.

The memory of Emyr's blood presses against my tongue, faint and sharp at the same time.

When I lower my hand, planning to finish my moment of peace and head in the direction of Solomon's cabin, I see Martha freaking Pierce leaving the bakery and walking right toward me. There's another white woman marching at her side. Neither of them looks happy.

So much for taking a breather.

"Please leave me alone," I manage to say, once I'm sure they're in earshot. "I'm not interested."

Martha's eyes widen and she opens her mouth, undoubtedly to say something lukewarm and moderately offensive, but the other woman silences her with a hand to her shoulder.

Like many people in Asalin, something about her is familiar, though I can't place where we've met before. I spent my childhood being ushered in and out of the same spaces as the kingdom's high society, introduced to countless people whose names I forgot as soon as I heard them. This woman is older than Martha, maybe in her fifties or sixties. Her hair, wheat blond with streaks of gray and white, is pulled up in a stern bun. She's got on khaki capris and a floral print blouse with poufy sleeves down to the elbows. There should be nothing threatening about her, dressed like some kind of conservative private school teacher the way she is.

And *yet*. Her energy, the same off-white beige as her pants, juts off her body in sharp peaks. It looms in the open air between us like a threat.

"You're not interested?" she asks, somehow managing to hiss the words. "That's a shame, because you're going to listen. It is truly a displeasure to see you again, Wyatt. Remember me? Nancy Pierce."

"For crying out loud, there are *more* of you?" Where do all the members of this blond-haired, blue-eyed, rich asshole family keep coming from? And how do I make sure I never have to see any of them ever again?

She shows me her teeth in the most unhappy smile I've ever seen. "Derek Pierce was my son."

"Oh." Okay. Well. That's incredibly awkward.

"Now, it's very obvious to everyone that *family* means nothing to you, so I shouldn't bother trying to appeal to whatever morals you have."

Hey now.

Family does not mean nothing to me. It's probably just that my definition of family and hers are very different.

I know what she's actually saying, though, without her having to say it. *"Hey, Wyatt, remember how you murdered your own mom and dad? Remember how they were going to kill you, for being a scared, vulnerable child, who couldn't control his own power? Remember how instead that power rose up and burned them alive and you had to watch it happen, unable to do anything to stop it, knowing it was you doing it?"*

"Wow, I actually hadn't thought about that moment yet today, thank you so much for reminding me, Nancy."

Since neither of us actually says those things, she plows forward with her speech. "But you have no measure for the amount of suffering you've caused us. How much you have stolen."

"I don't remember robbing you."

She takes a step forward, a spike of that ugly energy rising over her head.

When I realize I can *feel* the tarot deck moving toward my hand, lifting from my pocket and spilling into my palm, a chill shoots through me. Black magic threads across my fingers, up the backs of my hands and wrists, and it pulses forward to meet the cards.

Nancy eyes me with disgust. At her back, Martha lets out a pathetic squeak of protest.

"First, you framed my children for crimes you committed yourself. Derek had proof it was you and that *Jin*." Nancy snarls Jin's name. I don't think she likes her daughter's ex. "Who tried to kill the prince. Yet you manipulated everyone into believing otherwise."

"Oh, okay." I seriously don't know if she actually believes what she's saying, like some brainwashed cult member, or if she's just continuing to push her kids' agenda. Either way, it doesn't really matter. I'm not going to argue with her. There's no point.

"Then you had my son slaughtered by your lies." She chokes back what might've been a sob, reaching up to put a hand over her mouth. When she shakes her head, a single tendril of hair falls loose. "Murdered in cold blood all for having an opinion contrary to yours."

I can only blink at her. Yep. That's totally what happened. Derek actually died because he wasn't politically correct enough. The ultimate victim of cancel culture.

"There is nothing I can do to bring Derek back," she continues. "Nor do I have any idea where poor Clarke has gone, chased away by the very people she dedicated her life to helping. But I *can* save my granddaughter."

Ah, there it is. I knew that's what this had to be about. I shuffle the deck between my black-slicked fingers and raise my eyebrows at her. "Oh?"

"You are a vile little snake, Wyatt Croft. You attached yourself to my daughter-in-law in a moment of profound grief. She was not thinking clearly, and you took advantage of that, so you could steal away her child, the only piece of Derek we have left. And all because you don't want to carry the prince's heirs yourself."

"I'm sorry, what now?" *This* is the story she's convinced herself of? *This* is what she's going with, of all the options?

It is becoming increasingly clear I am not dealing with a stable person.

"You heard exactly what I said. Now, I will not let Martha feel the pain you have caused me. No mother should lose her children because of one person's selfishness. You will give us the baby back immediately." She juts her chin up, as if to say *mic drop*.

But, very sincerely…what the fuck.

"First of all, Emyr is the king. Not the prince." The cards move from one hand to the other. "Second of all, it's kind of ironic that you think *I'm* manipulative and Derek was some kind of saint. The way I remember it, he's the grown-ass adult who spent weeks Influencing me to think I wanted to sleep with him, so it'd be easier to get me to do what he wanted."

Nancy opens her mouth to argue, immediately, but I don't let her get a word out. "Actually, now that I think about it, isn't that really similar to the shit Clarke pulled?" Convincing Jin she was in love with them, taking them to bed every night, all while plotting the witches' fall. "What kind of childhood trauma did you give your kids that they both grew up to be predators, Nance?"

"You continue to spew your *LIES!*"

"Uh-huh. Sounds a little victim blame-y to me, but whatever. There's one thing you can't tell me I'm making up." I tilt my head toward Martha. "'Cause lastly, you are aware she left your *granddaughter* in the woods to starve to death or be eaten by coyotes or something, right?"

"She was beside herself. She would have come to her senses,

and no harm would have come to the child. But you didn't give her the chance."

"Beside herself...because the baby was a witch." I look at Martha over Nancy's shoulder. "You know she hasn't sprouted wings since the last time you saw her, right?"

A tear drips down Martha's porcelain cheek. The perfect victim.

"Witch or not," Nancy growls, dragging my attention back to her. "As long as there is blood in her veins, the baby is a Pierce. She will never be yours."

"Okay."

When she takes another step forward, Martha finally speaks up. "No! Nancy, you don't know what he's capable of." She sniffles, reaching out and curling her hand around her mother-in-law's elbow. "Let's go back home. We'll talk to Wade. He'll know what to do."

"Wade?"

"Yes." Nancy shakes her arm out of Martha's grip. "I suppose if one good thing has come from the irreparable harm you've caused, it's that my wayward child has finally realized what you people are really like."

"What the hell does that mean?" Last time I saw Wade, he was all smiles. He was...different, yeah, but in a *good* way. Like he'd showered. Not like he was about to start championing the causes of bigots.

"You'll see." Martha is already rapidly backing away, and Nancy casts me one last hateful look before she joins her. "You'll see."

"Okay, bye!" I call after them. "Lovely chatting with you!"

Let me just add *have a potentially very uncomfortable conversa-*

tion with Wade Pierce to my mental checklist. Because, really, I don't have enough shit on my plate.

Without thinking, I pull a random card from the deck, flipping it over and then glancing down at it.

Seven of Swords.

Lies. Backstabbing. Scheming.

Awesome. Everything about today just continues getting better and better. I turn and head in the direction of the triad's house, shoving the cards back in my pocket.

I've been in and out of here enough times that I don't bother knocking when I finally reach the frog doormat, instead just stepping right inside. Maybe one day I'll walk in on something I really don't want to see, like Roman's naked ass. Hopefully they'd lock the door, in that case.

Or maybe I should just start knocking anyway. Because it would seem I've walked in on a *different* kind of something.

"How could you do this!" Lorena is screaming in the back of the cabin.

I freeze, halfway across the threshold, one hand still curled around the knob.

Solomon's voice comes after hers. "You don't understand! You aren't giving me a chance to explain!"

"What explanation could you possibly have? You're going to get us all killed!"

"Lor," Roman's voice is quieter, calmer, than the other's. Unusual for him. "Hear him out."

Shit. Uh. I should go, right? I can talk to Solomon about all of this another time, when he's not in the middle of some kind of like...marital issue or whatever the fuck is going on. They'd be pissed if they knew I was here, listening.

Besides, after talking to *Nancy*, I wanna head up to the palace and lay eyes on the baby. And Nadua, since I really don't trust that woman not to try and go through her, physically if she has to, to get the newborn back.

Yeah. Okay. I'll leave, come back later.

Except, as I'm backing out onto the front stoop, Lorena yells, "Hear him out? This *thing* tried to kill Emyr!"

Oh.

I guess I'm not going anywhere.

Quietly as I can, I slip into the living room, slowly edging the door closed behind me. The sound of the latch clicking back into place sounds obnoxiously loud, even though I know it isn't. I pause again, tilting my head, waiting for someone to realize I'm here.

Instead, Solomon says, "Vae's not a thing, Lorena."

"Oh, holy shit, Sol, that cannot seriously be what we're arguing about right now."

Yeah, Solomon, what the fuck?

The voices are coming from the back office, the same place where I normally take my lessons. I creep through the rest of the house, wincing anytime my feet hit a squeaky board, my stomach a ball of knots.

"I don't want anything bad to happen to Emyr," Solomon says, sounding exasperated, the first thing he's said this whole time that hasn't made me want to murder him myself. "But you have to understand where vae comes from. Things are different there. The story of what the Pierce family did, the people they hurt, it's biblical in proportion. Vae thinks vae's on some kind of holy quest to get rid of them."

"You gotta hand it to him, babe," Roman drawls. "That family does suck."

"But *Emyr*?" Lorena demands.

"Yes, that was bad," Solomon agrees. "Which is why we've done *this*."

"Oh, okay, but you were just gonna let vaer get away with trying to kill Leonidas, though."

"In my defense, I didn't *know* that was vaer."

"Solomon." Roman has the audacity to laugh. "Don't play dumb. It doesn't fit you."

Lorena's voice turns to a sharp stage whisper. I can only hear her because I've crept so close to the door now. "And what happens when someone discovers you're harboring the person who tried to *assassinate the king*? In *our* home?"

"No one's going to find out." Solomon doesn't sound too sure about that.

And he shouldn't. Because there I am, leaning up against the door, my ear pressed to it, listening to every word they're saying.

Emyr *trusts* these people. He welcomed Lorena into the Circle, giving her the kind of power witches in Asalin have *never* had. He covered for me, for all of us, when we broke Solomon out of the dungeons and sent him into hiding after the riots. He's hunted Clarke across the country to avenge the death of Roman's surrogate mother.

And *I* trusted them, too. I sat in this house, studying their pointless sigils, and trusted that these people had my best interests at heart.

Harboring the person who tried to assassinate the king.

Protecting the person who almost killed my boyfriend. *And* Briar.

I am going to peel the skin off their bones.

Fire, my familiar friend, slides up along my palms, black magic chasing it like smoke. I shove the office door open so hard it slams against the other wall, knocking a hole into the wood.

"Hey—" Roman turns to me, throwing up his hands, trying to block me from getting into the room.

I grip his skinny upper arms in the inferno of my hands and spin him away from me, tossing him into the wall as effortlessly as I did the door. Solomon stands at the back, eyes so wide they're bugging out of his head, his mouth open. Lorena isn't even looking at me. She's staring at the floor, arms crossed over her chest.

And on the floor, bound in iron chains that sizzle against vaer skin, is a fae.

"Wyatt." Roman's voice is quiet and steady against my back. "Meet Zai—vae's from Faery."

CHAPTER TWELVE

LIKE COMING HOME TO MYSELF

Black magic jumps off my skin like a living shadow as I stalk across the floor. Flames dance up my arms, up my throat. I can *feel* them, but they aren't hurting me.

I can't say the same for anyone reckless enough to put their hands on me.

Roman moves at my back, as if he plans to stop me, but the shadow creates a blockade between us. He can't do anything to intervene.

Lorena, next, seems to realize she should do something. "Wyatt," she starts, reaching for me, daring to put her hands near the flame. But black magic curls around her waist and yanks her back. I don't want to hurt her. I *do* want her to get out of my way.

Solomon moves in front of me, sliding his body between mine and the stranger's. "Wyatt, please. I can explain everything. Just give me a chance to—"

A single card flicks up through the flame at the tips of my fingers, unbothered by the fire.

The Hanged Man.

Rest and surrender.

I press it to Solomon's forehead, between his eyes. He crumples, unconscious at my feet.

My relationship to anger is a complicated one. It's taken everything from me, and given me back just as much. It's hurt me and the people I love. It's also protected me and the people I love.

Recently, I've been working hard to rein it in. To put my fire, this brutal manifestation of rage, on a leash. To soften the sharpened edges of my teeth. To give myself permission to be more of a boy and less of a monster. Because I never wanted to let my anger take another life. Because I wanted to prove I could grow into something more than the broken, furious thing the fae turned me into. I wanted to heal. Fighting like hell to embrace softness felt like healing.

But anger as deep as mine can never go away. Not really. Not entirely. It just waits to be needed.

Forcing myself to be smaller than I am and calling it self-growth isn't the grand solution to my problems I've been acting like it is. I played nice and bit my tongue against the Bells and they still didn't want anything to do with our plans. Now these Pierce women, with their weaponized tears and their convoluted conspiracy theories, are coming for my family. And they think they can win.

Emyr and Briar both could have died after that crash, at

the hands of this fae the triad is hiding, all because I couldn't tap into my dormant rage. Because I've fought so hard not to lose control that I've accidentally debilitated myself.

But this isn't me losing control. This is me taking it.

I am not a monster, but I am not weak. I am not a pawn in someone else's game, but I am not here to burn everything down without even caring who I hurt in the process. I am a combination of fury and exhaustion and sheer stubborn will and I am doing my *fucking best*.

Even if Roman hadn't already confirmed that this fae came from Faery, that vae snuck through the door when it was still hanging open weeks ago, I would have known vae wasn't from *here*. It isn't anything explicit, nothing I can immediately put my finger on. But there's something *wrong* about vaer.

Vae's muscled in a soft way, like someone stretched out a preschooler to five foot nine and then forced them to start lifting weights. Vaer olive skin is pocked with scars, obviously healed wounds, some fresher than others. Vae's shaved off vaer eyebrows, or maybe never had any to begin with, and vaer electric-green hair is braided down to vaer lower back.

None of this is particularly un-Earthly, though. Just looks like gay alt fashion to me. In fact, the black T-shirt with spikes on the collar and distressed jeans vae's wearing both belong to Roman, I'm pretty sure. Nothing about the outfit indicates vae didn't grow up in Asalin all vaer life.

The piercings in vaer black satiny wings are...odd, metal hoops decorating the ridges that I've never seen on anyone else before. Vae's got piercings in vaer horns, too. The horns themselves are an opalescent green that nearly matches vaer hair, three of them lined up across vaer forehead, with metal barbs hammered through their tips. It's not typical for fae, at least not on *this side* of the door to Faery.

But that's still not the reason for the wrongness.

Vae's propped up against the wall, vaer arms bound in front, over vaer legs. When I step in closer, fire licks out to brush against the soles of vaer shoes, singing the hems of vaer jeans. Vaer eyes, massive milky-brown orbs, stare at me with an expression I'm not used to having turned my direction. It's nothing short of awe.

I hope vae's afraid. And I don't care if that's something a less mentally stable version of me would have thought, if it means I'm *regressing*. I think it anyway.

The cards are back in my hands, deck shuffling through my fingers on instinct. This new magic, this *thing* that shouldn't make any sense, that should be so much more complicated than it is, just feels like coming home to myself. This has been my magic all along. I just wasn't using it correctly.

Until today. And now everything changes.

I pull a card between my index and middle finger and flick it up against the underside of Zai's jaw. Using the dull edge, I force vaer head back, force vaer to show me the line of vaer throat. Black magic pulses from my hand, beats off the paper, curls around vaer neck like a tightening fist.

The Death card is, I know, the most misunderstood card in the tarot. More often than not, it's actually a good thing. It can mean transformation, and personal growth, and coming into something new. Rarely, *rarely*, does it actually have something to do with *real death*.

But the cards are just conduits, after all. I'm the one reading them. And that's where they get their power.

Fire licks up the back of my hand. A single dancing flame

stretches closer to Zai's face, a burning whisper threatening to engulf vaer.

Vae tips vaer head back even further, eyes flicking from me to the fire and back again.

I expect vaer to ask for leniency, maybe. To beg for vaer life.

Instead, vae smiles. And it's so unbelievably unsettling that I almost jump.

Okay. So, when it comes to *wrongness*, maybe this is part of the problem.

Every single one of vaer teeth has been sharpened to a point, an entire mouthful of fangs. I've only ever seen anything like it on one other person—in depictions of Vorgaine, the Faery goddess.

"Beloved," vae whispers, and vaer voice makes me woozy with unease. It's beautiful, raspy and musical at once. "Take what you must. My life is yours."

As if doused in water, the flames running the length of my body disappear. "What?"

Because...*what*?

Which gives Lorena enough time to grab me around the middle, clasping my arms to my sides and pulling me away from Zai. I don't realize what's happening until it's too late, and as much as I try to thrash out of her grip, she's a hell of a lot stronger than I am.

The deck comes spilling out of my hand, cards flying in a pile across the floor. I notice a few of them land faceup. Page of Swords. Five of Wands. The Hierophant.

"Is he okay?" Lorena demands, still holding tight to me. She's asking Roman, who's kneeling across the room, where he's got Solomon propped up against a table leg, wafting a vial filled with some strange purple powder under his nose.

"He's fine," Solomon mumbles, before Roman can answer, reaching up to rub at his eyes.

"What did you do to him?" Lorena snaps, turning hateful eyes on me.

I wiggle in her arms and snarl. "You don't seriously have the nerve to be angry at *me* right now."

Her grip loosens, if only a little. It's still enough for me to finally shove away from her, though I don't go near Zai again.

Vae's still staring at me, even with the ample space between us, that goofy, bug-eyed expression on vaer face. It's unnerving. The memory of vaer voice croaking the word *beloved* makes my skin crawl.

"Explain," I bite out, forcing my nails into my palms and jerking my head back in Solomon's direction.

"You first," Roman sits down on the desk, propped up way too nonchalantly on the edge, and raises his eyebrows at me. "How'd the door open in the first place, Wyatt?"

Ah. Well, yeah, that does take a little of the indignant pep out of my step. Fuck me, I guess. The triad's keeping secrets, but so am I. Of course, my secret didn't nearly get Emyr and Briar killed.

Well. Actually. I guess, in a cruel roundabout way, it did. Once again, keeping things to myself has resulted in almost losing the people I love.

Seriously, what if I went one month without getting involved in something that almost murders my boyfriend? Wouldn't that be neat? I'll have to try it sometime.

"Okay," I mumble, because I'm pretty sure Roman's question is rhetorical. "Who is this?"

"I told you, this is Zai."

Roman is one of my least favorite people on the planet.

While I ruminate on the ethics of murdering him just so I don't have to hear him speak again, my eyes are pulled back to Zai. I don't *want* them to be. I'd really rather not look at vaer. But I can't seem to help myself.

The iron chains keep vaer energy shut down, invisible to the eye. They sizzle against vaer skin, leaving a trail of burn marks across vaer arms and legs. My own scars itch in solidarity at the sight.

I know it must hurt, but somehow vae doesn't look like vae's in any pain. It's disturbing.

"How long has vae been here?" I finally turn my head away, looking to Solomon with raised eyebrows.

He won't look back at me, though. He's staring at his hands, the pads of his ten fingers pressed together to make a cradle in front of his lap. His index fingers tap against each other. Tap. Tap. "Three weeks or so."

"And it's *just* vaer?"

Solomon glances at Zai, and the two of them make prolonged, uncomfortably intense eye contact. I have a feeling they're having a whole silent conversation.

"And it's just vaer?" I demand, slamming a hand down against the desk to force Solomon's eyes back on me.

"Well…" He coughs, gently, and brushes his long fingers against his jawline. "It is *now*."

"What the fuck does that mean, Solomon?"

"There were others, for a time." He sighs, forcing himself to his feet but quickly moving to the desk chair and dropping down into it. "At first, their group was moving back and forth through the open door. But when it was closed again, Zai was the only one left on this side." He pinches the bridge of his nose before taking a deep breath, and looking back at my face again. "It's probably for the best that you know, now. We need you to reopen the door."

"Is that a joke?" He cannot seriously be asking me for a favor right now.

What kind of parallel universe have I just walked into?

"What a shitty joke that would be," Roman drawls. He moves behind Solomon's chair, reaching down to run his fingers through his boyfriend's hair.

Lorena growls, leaning against the edge of the desk, her arms crossed tight over her chest. "Zai needs to *go*. Trust me, you don't want vaer here anymore than vae wants to be stuck here for the rest of vaer life."

No, I imagine I don't.

Because vae tried to kill Emyr. And almost killed Briar in the crossfire.

"Vae's the one who attacked Leonidas." It isn't really a question, but Solomon still nods. He's not looking at me again. "And Emyr."

Solomon winces. Roman puts his hands on his shoulders and squeezes.

Lorena is the one who answers, through gritted teeth. "Yes. And if I'd known what was going on before now, that never would have happened. You have to know, I would never let anything happen to Emyr. Not knowingly."

"You're telling me you had no idea your boyfriend was hiding an *assassin* from *Faery* in your own *house*?" I don't believe her.

"In her defense, Wyatt, she didn't even know the door was open." Roman's expression is a challenge, one eyebrow raised in a silent dare. "No one can defend themself against a threat they don't know to look for."

I cannot stand this motherfucker.

"I wasn't hiding vaer in the house," Solomon mumbles, as if that is at all the point.

"Why were you hiding vaer at all?!" I want to strangle him. I want to throw things, start a fire, do whatever it takes to get him to look at me. To give me some answers. "A murderer from another world stumbles into your life and you sign up as what? A tour guide? *Why?*"

"Because everything you've ever been told is a lie."

The words are so quiet, and I'm so focused on Solomon, I almost don't realize when Zai speaks. It makes me shudder, involuntarily. Vaer voice is...uncomfortable.

Not because vae sounds uncomfortable. But because it makes *me* uncomfortable to hear it.

I turn to face vaer again. When vae shifts, slightly turning vaer body toward me, the iron rattles around vaer skin, leaving a trail of bright red, oozing burn marks in their wake. Horrific.

"What does that mean?"

Vae looks to Solomon, quickly, then turns those big creepy eyes back on me. "Solomon has told me much about your lives here. The lies of the *Pierce bloodline* have robbed you of so much knowledge. It is blasphemy, what they've done to you on this side of the door. And now you've no idea how remarkable you are."

Mary's words play back in my head. *"There is so much you do not know about your magic."*

I am so tired. And angry. And everything hurts and my stomach can't settle and my bones are going to shake out of my skin.

I sit down on the floor, only a few feet of hardwood between Zai and me, and put my head in my hands.

"Someone start at the beginning. But talk fast."

Solomon moves so quietly I don't notice he got up from the
chair until he moves onto the floor with us. "All our lives in
Asalin, we are taught two things to be true. The first, witches
are an abomination, a biological accident. The second, our
ancestors fled Faery because it was no longer inhabitable, because it became a wasteland. Neither of these is true. And to
understand why we are fed both lies, you need to hear the
real story of why fae came to Earth, all those years ago. Zai…
tell Wyatt everything you told me."

Zai sighs, a quiet, sad little sound. "First, you must understand that time moves differently in Faery. Moments on
Earth may be days there. These two weeks I've spent alone
here, so much longer has passed for my people on the other
side…" Vae shakes vaer head. "You believe fae came to Earth
five hundred years ago. For us, millennia have passed. The
story of The Great Undoing is ingrained in our divine canon.
The story of Leonidas the Pillager is one told since my grandparents' grandparents were children."

"The Great Undoing?"

"When the door to Earth was first opened," Solomon explains. "Zai, tell him why that happened."

Zai tilts vaer head back against the wall. Iron sizzles at vaer
throat when vae does. "You've been told that Faery died.
That it became a wasteland, which could no longer support
life. This was almost true. Many thousands of years ago, fae
magic was draining our world of its power. It *was* dying. Our
people prayed to our goddess, Vorgaine, and begged for help

in healing what we had done. And she answered our prayers. She sent us you. The witches."

I blink, glancing from Zai to Solomon and back again.

Vae continues. "Fae magic drains, but witch magic replaces. You were given to us as a sacred gift. Only your kind could save Faery. And you were adored. Our people loved you…*most* of our people. There was a group of fae who came to hate the witches. Who resented the new influence they held in society. Who wanted, instead, to force your kind to heal Faery, without giving you the honor and respect you deserved."

"And you'll never guess," Roman sneers, "who was leading that group."

I would, actually, even if I hate that I already know. "The Pierce family."

Zai's face tightens in disgust. "This family and their vile congregation sought to *harm* you. Our most beloved citizens. Our cherished gifts. We could not allow that to happen. And so, they were outcast. Pushed away from society. And in their rage and indignation, they opened the door here. To begin a world anew. One that belonged to fae and fae alone."

"Didn't realize they'd be walking into a place that was already occupied, I'm guessing." Lorena scoffs. "Or stop to ask what they'd do with their own witch kids when they had them."

"We believe," Solomon says, shaking his head, "that the first generation to come through the door lied to their own children, and all those who came after them. They kept the truth of the witches, and of Faery, secret. And the lies about our history were able to take root."

All of this…makes an uncomfortable amount of sense. And it falls in line with everything Mary said about witch magic.

Not abominations. We aren't accidents, or things to be tolerated.

Witches never should have been accepted *in spite* of who we are. We were meant to be celebrated *because* of it.

"Right. Until Leonidas took an army through the door." Roman drops down into the desk chair and tosses his boots onto the wood. "And was met by a group of zealots who wanted him dead."

"Huh?" I was with them, really, until that part.

"My people built a temple on our side of the door," Zai continues. "We worship there. Dedicate ourselves to our faith. And keep a sharp eye on the doorway, ever vigilant in case something should come through. And then, many, many years ago, something did. Leonidas and his followers."

Right. On the mission to see if Faery could be inhabitable. The one where he discovered it was—but that the fae on the other side hated him.

"He and his people were just as violent as they'd been in our history books. They tried to slaughter us, to destroy anything they did not understand. Some of them, including Leonidas himself, were able to escape back through the door, but the Watchers made a sacred vow. Should the door ever open again, should we ever have the chance to come through and face the Pierce line ourselves, we would not rest until they were finally eradicated. From *every* world."

A beat passes.

Tongue thick, I ask, "Why only their family? They might have *led* this anti-witch group, but they obviously weren't the only ones involved. What about the other kingdoms? Wouldn't their royals be just as guilty?"

"The other *royals* deserve the inevitable horrors awaiting

them, should they ever be forced to face retribution. But they are not the vessel through which evil itself propagated."

"Damn, you really don't like Pierces, huh?"

Solomon sighs. "Wyatt, you can't blame vaer, can you? We all know that family is...different." Quickly, he adds, "Of course, vae didn't know Emyr's not like the rest of them. Vae thought vae was doing something...good."

My head is swimming. It's too much to process. I rub my temples with my fingertips, and close my eyes. "I still don't understand why you kept this hidden. What's your end goal here?"

"I told you. I want the door to Faery reopened." Solomon reaches over and curls a hand around the side of my neck, forcing me to open my eyes and look at him. "I want to go through it. A world that our magic has healed. A world where we are valued, and protected, and loved for exactly who we are? Wyatt... Faery is the answer we've been looking for all this time. Faery is where we belong. Maybe Zai should be punished for what vae did to Emyr. If that's what it comes down to, I won't stand in your way again. But we have to open the door." Something shines in his dark eyes. "We have to go home."

CHAPTER THIRTEEN

TOO MUCH

I absolutely cannot do this right now.

That's basically what I tell the triad, saying I need to go to the castle and talk to Emyr, that the two of us will decide *together* what happens next. It's a perfectly valid reason to get up and leave, but it is also not entirely the truth. The whole truth is that I am also on the brink of an epic meltdown and if I don't get some space between me and that bug-eyed alien, I'm going to go over the edge.

And being on the brink is probably not the best place for me to be when I get a few hundred feet into the palace and run into Briar and Jin. They're standing in an empty hallway, Briar leaning back against a window, her hands curled around the ledge. Jin leans over her, one of their hands propped up by the palm against the wall over Briar's head.

I stop a few feet short of them. They both hear me coming and turn to face me.

Jin's face splits into a subdued smile. "Wyatt, hey. Briar was just telling me about what happened. Did Solomon have any answers for you?"

"Huh?"

"About the tarot cards?"

"Oh." He watched me use them—sort of, he was mostly on the receiving end of things—but I didn't actually have the chance to talk to him about it. Wasn't exactly the top of my priority list. "Uh, no. He was busy."

Briar's eyebrows are drawn tight together, her sharp gaze considering me. When I meet her stare, she raises one eyebrow. *What's up?*

I take a deep breath, reaching up to rub a hand over the back of my neck. *You would not—*

"Well," Jin interrupts the conversation they don't have any way of knowing is even happening. "If you wanna show me, I'd be happy to see if there's anything I can do to help you."

"Help me what?"

"Ah…control it? Figure out how to make it do what you want?"

Maybe it's because I'm tired, and at the end of my rope, and I've had a pretty unbelievably bad day, but I know I sound like an asshole when I snap, "I'd say I have a pretty good handle on making it do what I want. No one's dead, in case you didn't notice."

Unlike when your girlfriend used your magic to kill Emyr.

Aaaand there it is. That unspoken thing. That neon sign in the corner I haven't wanted to look at this whole time.

Why should Wade be the only one wracked with guilt over

what Clarke did, while Jin just gets to walk around feeling sad for themself?

Okay. Look. It isn't actually fair to blame Jin for what happened to Emyr. I know that, in some logical part of my brain, and that's why I've been pretending I don't. But the resentment is still there. It isn't concerned with what's fair or logical or right.

Anyway, I still don't like them and Briar together.

"Whoa," Briar answers, and I know she's responding to the thing I didn't say out loud. "Wyatt—"

"Um," Jin frowns, but nods. "Yeah, okay. You're completely right. I hope you know how much I appreciate what you did. You saved two people who mean a lot to me."

"Well, I definitely wasn't thinking about you when I did it."

"WYATT!" Briar claps her hands in front of her chest, narrowing her eyes. "What the fuck?"

Shit.

"I'm sorry, Jin." And I mean it. All else aside, Jin isn't actually the reason for my shitty mood today. "It's been... I'm just tired."

They look me up and down, concern heavy in their black gaze. Finally, they nod. "Sure. You should get some rest. All three of you."

Yeah. Except I have to tell Emyr I met the fae who tried to kill him.

Well, the other one.

"Um. Did you see your mom?" I ask Briar.

"Yes." She's glaring. If she was upset with me before, for reasons I still don't totally understand, she's definitely pissed off now. "She and the baby are fine. You can see them both later."

"Okay."

They both just stare at me, Jin with their sad eyes and Briar with her furious ones, until I continue down the hall alone.

Emyr is lying on his back in our bed when I slip into the king's chambers. His leathery wings stretch out on either side of him, curling inward, clawed tips reaching for his chest. He's undressed, stripped down to a pair of silk black briefs and knee-high white socks, nothing else. Under normal circumstances it would be enough to eviscerate me.

I hate that we live in a timeline where I'm too overwhelmed to even be properly horny anymore.

He doesn't give any indication he notices when I enter, but his energy does. Gold thread slips across the sheets, through the open air, and tangles in tendrils of black. They move together, like interlocking fingers, swaying back and forth while I walk forward and drop onto the end of the bed.

"How'd the conversation with your dad go?"

"Poorly. Did the trio have any insight for you?"

"Uh. Yeah." I reach over to his chest, running my knuckles down the line of his sternum. One of his wings flexes forward to curl around me, wrapping me tighter to him. "Just, uh. Not the kind I was looking for."

Maybe he hears something in my tone. Emyr looks away from the ceiling to find my face, eyebrows rising. "Oh?"

That one syllable is the heaviest word I've ever heard. He doesn't want to know what I have to say any more than I want to be the one to say it. He's as tired as I am. I know that. He wants to be done. I *know* that.

But it's not like I can keep this to myself.

Slowly, careful to make sure I remember every possible

detail, I recount everything that happened between getting out of Tessa's Jeep and leaving the triad's cabin. Emyr doesn't interrupt me a single time during the story, though his energy shifts and shudders, grows and shrinks, at different parts. By the end, he's stood up and moved across the floor, pacing while he listens to me talk.

Finally, when I think I've said all there is to say, I rub my hands over my thighs, watching him. "I don't know what we do from here."

"Do you believe anything this person said?" Ugh. He's wearing his King Emyr voice now. That clipped, analytical tone that tells me he's more strategy than boy in this moment. "About Faery, about what it's like there?"

"Yes?" I don't sound sure, but I'm not, so that makes sense.

Emyr stomps across the room and flings open his wardrobe. He grabs a pair of pants—silver, tightly woven metal pants, like thick chainmail—and starts shoving his legs into them. "I have to meet—vaer?"

I nod. I've never heard that pronoun set before today, but it didn't take me long to catch on, just listening in on the others talk. I'm pretty sure it's vae/vaer, the same way someone might use they/them.

"Right. Let's get down there. I'd like to have a word with Solomon, too." He snatches his Faery sword out, slinging it over his shoulder.

"I… Maybe this should wait until tomorrow," I hedge.

Again—shirtless Emyr wielding a weapon should be enough to send me on my ass. (Seriously, why have I been Nerfed by the burdens of modern life? Like, sincerely, why do I exist in a society? I am a simple man. I was only ever meant to eat good food and homoerotically wrestle pretty boys in fields of flowers, or something. But no, here I am, forced to save the world because of fae Nazis.)

That's not the reason I want to pause, though. Unfortunately, Zai or not, I don't think there's any chance of Emyr and me homoerotically wrestling tonight.

"It's been a long day. I think—I'd like to just hold you." I swallow. "And vae's not going anywhere. Lorena will make sure of it, if nothing else."

Emyr frowns, turning to face me. He stands still for a moment before sighing, hard, and tugging the sword off his back. He tosses it back into the wardrobe.

He doesn't come back to bed, though. Doesn't crawl into my arms the way I wish he would. Instead, he goes back to pacing. "You really think Lorena didn't know before now?"

"There's no way. You should have seen her. I'm pretty sure there's a good chance she was gonna kill Solomon herself, if I hadn't shown up."

"What about Roman? Do you think he was helping them?"

"I…" I don't want to talk about this anymore, but I understand why we have to. But if I have to, I'm going to get comfortable. I stand up and start undressing, tugging off my hoodie and tossing it into a corner, before working on unlacing my boots. "I don't know. Roman's hard to get a read on. Could go either way."

"I'll make sure he tells me," Emyr grumbles, with the tone of a man who needs to know exactly how pissed off he's going to be.

My head hurts.

Still, if we do have to keep talking about this, there is one thing that's been on my mind. "If vae's on some kind of warped holy mission to wipe out your family line, we should probably make sure vae doesn't ever get a chance to get close to the baby. Maybe she'd be protected because she's a witch, but she's a Pierce, too, by blood anyway, and—" When I kick off my shoes and look up, and catch Emyr staring at me with disbelief, the words shrivel up and die immediately. "What?"

"You must be joking."

"Um…huh?"

Emyr turns his back to me. His wings flex, stretching out to either side of his bare, chiseled arms as he leans over the dresser. His hands curl around the edge, claws digging into the wood until it splinters around his fingertips. "Do you realize I almost died today? *Again?*"

"Wait, are you kidding?" I take a step forward, but freeze when his energy shrinks away from me this time. "Of course I do. You have no idea how afraid I was. I thought I was gonna lose you. *And* Briar."

"*You* were afraid? What do you think it felt like for me?"

It would be easier to handle, I think, if his voice sounded accusatory. If he sounded angry. Instead, mostly he just sounds exhausted.

There is nothing in the world I want more in this moment than to hold him. I lace my fingers together over my front to stop my traitorous hands from reaching out. "I'm so sorry. What can I do?"

"You could spend five minutes more worried about me than you are that fucking baby!"

"Okay. I—but that's not what's going on at *all.*" I can care about more than one thing at a time. Hell, I've *had* to. With everything up in the air, the twisted threads of our lives becoming increasingly more complicated, checking out from any of it has been impossible.

I don't need to tell Emyr that, though. He knows. Because it's been even worse for him than it has for me. A fact I'm well aware of, despite what he's accusing me of.

As much as all of this, everything we've done, has been about me stepping into my power, it's been about Emyr finally being allowed to safely step *out* of his.

He's carrying the weight of two worlds on his shoulders. He needs a break more than anyone.

"You have no idea what it's like for me," he whispers. "Derek. Clarke. My father. My mom. You. Every person in this kingdom. Every kingdom on Earth. It's all my responsibility. Just mine."

My hands twist so tight my fingers scream out in pain, but I still don't reach for him. "We both want you to have a break. That's why we're doing all of this, right? So you can finally walk away. So this doesn't have to be your problem anymore."

"HOW AM I SUPPOSED TO WALK AWAY FROM THIS?" I've never heard him yell like this before. The vicious, gravelly sound rips out of his chest like a roar. His claws dig deeper into the wood of the dresser and then he flings it, sending the whole thing flying across the floor and into the wall. It slams hard into the stone, the mirror cracking, broken glass shattering and falling to the floor.

Emyr's chest heaves as he stares at it, frowning like he isn't sure how that happened.

I don't move. Not closer to him, and not farther away. I'm frozen in place. Can't even seem to find my tongue.

Finally, he looks to me again. Tears glint in his dark eyes, catching the light overhead and glowing too bright in the planes of his obsidian face. "There's too much to be fixed,

Wyatt. There's too much. I can't—I'm never going to be able to—I'm just—"

He's just a teenage boy who's trying to undo hundreds of years of fascism with his bare hands.

He's just a teenage boy whose dad won't talk to him and whose mom is dying right in front of his eyes.

He's just a teenage boy and he's scared.

My hands reach for him of their own accord but, instead of flinching away from me this time, Emyr moves to meet me. He falls into my touch, big body collapsing against mine. I can't hold up the weight of him, so we sink, together, to the ground. I lean back against the bed, while he curls into a ball between my legs, pressing his face against my chest, and sobs.

"I'm sorry," I whisper, because I am, even if it doesn't help. My hands trace paths along his bare back, along the curve of his spine and the veined ridges of his wings. I wanted to hold him, but not like this. "I'm so sorry."

Emyr doesn't say anything. He just cries.

All the while, the brink beckons me closer. It tells me I could fall in at any time. I could give up. Emyr's right. There's too much to fix. We're never going to solve all these problems. What's the use in trying? Why not let myself fall into the comfortable chasm of despair?

I don't listen. I keep my arms around my boyfriend, and I stay right there with him. Gold anchored to black, and black to gold. Hanging on as tightly as we can.

CHAPTER FOURTEEN

TOO OLD FOR FAIRY TALES

In the end, we don't storm back to the triad's cabin. At some point, we move from the floor to the bed, Emyr's horns on my stomach, and fall asleep.

It's a sham, the fact that when I need sleep the most, it's the hardest to come by. All night, I dream. There's no through line, no story to follow. Just flashes and sounds and feelings, spikes of terror that have me drifting in and out of consciousness until morning.

I don't *wake up* so much as I stop pretending and come back to myself. I'm already propped up against the pillows, my fingers brushing up and down the length of Emyr's arm, where it's curled around my waist. His eyes are open, chin against my side as he stares up at me. The heavy bags under his eyes tell me he probably feels as rested as I do.

"Let's get it over with," he finally says, and climbs out of bed.

Neither of us wants to acknowledge the dresser in shambles. Emyr sort of stares at it for a second, and then moves to the wardrobe, instead. I just kick my way around the shards from the mirror and pretend everything's totally normal.

This is what we've been doing for a while, I guess. Pretending everything is normal.

But it's not. And the thing is, it never actually has been. Nothing about Asalin has ever been normal, or okay, or good. And even when we were happy, nothing about my relationship with Emyr has ever been normal. Things lately? Shitshow. Just one big sewage circus.

Maybe normal is what we're fighting for, then. Not a perfect happily ever after, not riding off into the sunset like nothing will ever go wrong again. Just a sliver of stability. A crumb of *okay*.

I sigh, and rummage through the dresser drawers—they won't close once I've got them open, coming up off their hinges, but that's fine, that's very cool, I'll just leave them hanging open, then—for my outfit. T-shirt. Jeans. Hoodie. A change of boxers, and a sports bra, because I fell asleep in my binder and I have been wearing it for *way* too long now, and there's no way it's staying on for even minutes longer.

I get everything on but the hoodie before I pause, catching sight of myself in the mirror.

And, weirdly, I think about Clarke.

With everything else going on—what, like I might have my hands full? weird—I haven't thought about her offer in a while. Her taunting promises of turning me into whatever I wanted to become, shaping my body however I wanted it to look. It was weird, and kind of rude—like, hello, am I not cute already?—and probably at least a little transmedicalist. I like my body. It's *my* body. There's nothing *wrong* with it.

And, yet...

Looking at myself now, bra instead of binder, no baggy hoodie to cover my curves or scars, I think...how much easier would it be to walk through the world without armor? How much lighter might I feel, if I didn't feel the need to put on some barrier all the time, some protective layer between me and everyone else? Not because *I* hate my body, but because I don't want to deal with anyone *else's* feelings about it.

Maybe it'd be nice.

My fist tightens around the fabric of the hoodie before I toss it onto the bed. No. Fuck that. And fuck Clarke. I don't need her or her magic. And I don't need to keep hiding myself, either.

I adopted the hoodie so no one would have to look at the scars on my arms, so I would never have to talk about what happened the night of the fire. But everyone in Asalin *knows* what happened the night of the fire. The same way they all (presumably) know that I have tits.

So, screw it. I don't need the damn hoodie.

I wheel around, prepared to announce just that to Emyr, before actually getting a good look at him. And that train of thought flies right out the window.

"What are you wearing?"

This is a question I've had many times while looking at my boyfriend and his little outfits, but never for this reason. Because instead of something ostentatious and over-the-top, something mesh or sheer or glittery or leather…he's wearing…jeans.

Emyr Leonidas Mirac North is wearing *jeans*. And a T-shirt. Granted, his T-shirt is at least cropped, hitting him right above the belly button. So, that's something.

But *still*.

Oh, and now we match. We do that Spider-Man meme thing where we stand on either side of the room looking at each other, in our almost-identical jeans and white T-shirts. I don't know what Emyr's thinking, maybe that one of us is going to have to change. Personally, I'm thinking the apocalypse is nigh, because there is no way this is how Emyr is dressed.

Seriously. I didn't even think he *owned* a pair of jeans.

"Clothes," he says with an eye roll, as if the whole fabric of the universe is not unraveling right now. He does grab the crown from the wardrobe, settling it around his horns, and he slings the sword over his back again. Though, I have a feeling neither of those things are for accessorizing, in this case. "Come on. Let's go."

So, yep. Okay. I guess that's how he's leaving the house. Fine. I follow after him, shoving my feet into sneakers as I go.

We should go see Briar, I think, as we hurry past the hallway that eventually leads to her room. And I should. Go see Briar. Apologize again for the things I said to Jin yesterday. Tell her everything I learned about Zai, and Faery. Take her to the triad's with us.

Instead, I just keep walking. And I try not to think about what that means.

The decision to leave behind my hoodie, as empowering

as I guess it felt in the moment, was…maybe a bad call. That becomes clear as soon as we make our way into the village, heading down the cobblestone path toward the triad's house. I can *feel* the eyes of everyone on me. Which—to be fair— isn't exactly a rarity. It would be more rare for me to be able to walk through Asalin *without* a bunch of snot-nosed fae whispering behind their palms and pointing in my direction.

But this feels different. Heavier. I can imagine what they're seeing. The scars, three-year-old burns, that wrap up from my wrists, decorating both my arms. They aren't pretty. And they're a glaring neon sign reminding everyone what I did. Not that anyone could ever forget.

I meet eyes with a young fae outside in her front yard, tending to her flowers, and her hands freeze when I stare her down. Her gaze darts, in the quickest little motion, from my eyes to my chest and back again. I show her my teeth and wedge closer to Emyr's side.

By the time we actually reach the cabin, I'm ready to claw my skin off instead of continuing to be perceived.

Emyr actually knocks, and I let him, shoving my hands in my pockets to avoid barging in the way I normally would. It's Lorena who answers, a few seconds later.

She looks tired. The purple side of her hair has been shaved down to the same length as the other half, like she got tired of fucking with it, and she's wearing gray sweats that hang low on her hips and a white tank top. She sighs, and scrubs her knuckles over one of her eyes, like she's still trying to wake herself up.

"Your Majesty."

"Do not start with me," Emyr growls in response, and we walk past her into the cabin.

It looks...absurd. By which I mean, it looks the cleanest I've ever seen it. The piles of half-finished projects usually shoved in any nook or cranny they can find have all been gathered up and disposed of, or at least hidden out of sight. Someone actually cup-checked every surface in the home, washing and putting away the half-finished glasses that are usually part of the decor around here. Everything is shiny, like someone scrubbed the windows or some shit, and it smells good, like lemon and thyme, like expensive organic cleaning supplies.

Solomon looks as tired as Lorena. He's sitting ramrod straight on the couch, with a light blue button-up tightened high on his throat and tucked into his camel slacks, but the deep hollows beneath his eyes give him away. Of the trio, Roman is the only one who looks rested. He's leaning back against the arm on the opposite side of the sofa, in a black sweatshirt that reads *LOCAL CRYPTID* and a pair of black joggers. He smiles at us and flicks his fingers in a wave.

Zai sits between them. Vae's no longer in chains—though Solomon has a hand on vaer thigh, like he thinks he might have to stop vaer from running, which isn't super encouraging. Vae's in the same clothes vae was yesterday, Roman's hand-me-downs. And vae's staring again, though not at me, and not the bug-eyed, adoring look I got. No. Zai's staring straight at Emyr, and vae looks...skeptical.

More importantly, though, there are *snacks*. Someone's set out a plate of rupiea on the coffee table, a sourdough cake rolled out into pinwheels, filled with a layer of berry relish, then thinly sliced until they're cookie-sized. I ignore everyone in favor of grabbing four of them, because I haven't been given a chance to eat anything in like twenty hours, and drop down into a chair to start shoving them in my mouth.

Roman laughs. "Morning."

"Shut the fuck up," Lorena snaps, and slams the door closed.

While she sits down on the arm of my chair—presumably so she doesn't have to go anywhere near any of the people on the couch—Emyr and Zai continue their stare-off. For all of Zai's suspicion, Emyr looks...

Murdery is probably a good word for it. Little bit homicidal.

I take another bite of rupiea. "Which one of you bakes?"

"They're store-bought," Solomon says without inflection. He's *also* staring at Emyr, though his stare is a lot more *please forgive me, my liege* and a lot less *I'm going to commit war crimes.* So, that's something.

"Huh. They're good."

I definitely see Lorena roll her eyes, but Roman smirks.

Emyr's golden energy, which has been curled tight around his body like armor this entire time, finally starts to unwind. Slowly, like it's testing the water, it starts stretching across the open air over the coffee table. It hovers in the air over Zai, Roman, and Solomon's heads. Roman's red magic bops up against it in sharp spikes, like a cat's paw batting at a toy, until gold thread snares one spike and drags it forward. Meanwhile, olive green tendrils of Solomon's energy reach for the gold without hesitation, but stop short of actually making contact.

And...that's when I notice something else that's *wrong* about Zai.

See, humans, changelings, witches, and fae—our energies all look and act pretty much the same. We each have our own color, a unique shade that belongs to only us, and it clings to us. It's a visual manifestation of our magic—or something even more important, like our *selves*—moving around us at all times. We can direct it, but sometimes it moves without instruction, following the lead of our thoughts, or our feelings.

It can lead to funny—or not so funny, depending on the circumstances—revelations, sometimes. Like when your energy can't seem to stop reaching for someone you *swear* you don't have a thing for. It often reveals more about us than we would willingly.

But Zai's energy doesn't seem to move at all. I couldn't see it before, when vae was in the chains that kept it tamped down, but now I can make out the obscene traffic cone orange surrounding them. But it doesn't move at all. Instead, it just settles along vaer skin, almost like a layer of vaer body itself. It moves when vae does, in the exact same way vae does, and otherwise not at all.

I can't explain why this is so unsettling to me, except that it's like…it's like it's dead.

But we don't have time to unpack that.

Finally, Emyr speaks. "I don't believe anything you told Wyatt."

He's addressing Zai directly, but it's Solomon who answers, piping up, "We've had some time to talk, more time than vae had with Wyatt, over the last few weeks. I believe—"

"I don't believe you're any better than your execrative ancestors," Zai interrupts Solomon to answer Emyr. Vae smiles that terrible, sharp smile. "Your lot is a plague upon this world, and the next, and all those to follow. Peace will only be known when you give yourself unto us for oblation."

Literally do not know like, several of the words vae used in that statement, but go off, I guess.

Solomon slumps back against the couch pillow and closes his eyes. I think I can actually see his soul leaving his body.

Emyr's eyes narrow. One sharp ear tip twitches, and his fangs press into his lower lip. "Unfortunately for you, it's my world that you're in now. What you believe holds little weight."

Zai *hisses*, and the hair on the back of my neck goes up as vaer tongue flicks against vaer teeth. "Fortunately for you, it is frowned upon, even among the protectors of Nowhere, to kill a fae mirrored to a witch. I do not always agree with my people's decisions. But when the door reopens, you will be safe."

A long beat passes. Or maybe it just feels long because it is so incredibly uncomfortable.

Finally, Emyr does look to Solomon, eyebrows rising.

Solomon rushes to answer. "The protectors of Nowhere are a group of Vorgaine's followers. They live directly on the other side of the door, in Faery. Zai is one of them. They consider it a sacred calling to watch out for any Pierce who might one day return. But witches themselves are sacred to the protectors. And you're mated to one. So, they wouldn't kill you."

"This one's just, what?" Emyr demands. "Extra feral?"

Sadly, relatable.

Solomon doesn't confirm or deny that.

Emyr turns his attention back to Zai. "Why do you believe the door will be reopened?"

"Because…I have to return home." Zai looks at Solomon, vaer voice rising. "Time on Earth does not move as it does on Faery. I have already lost more than a year of my life in my home world. I have to get back. *Now*."

"Maybe watch your tone," I suggest, finishing off the last of my little snack. "You're not exactly in a position to start making demands."

The hand Solomon has on Zai's thigh squeezes. Zai opens vaer mouth, makes an exasperated noise, then closes it with a snapping of sharp teeth.

Lorena surprises me by being the one to speak next. "For what it's worth, Emyr, I also think vae should go back through the door."

Emyr turns an incredibly *et tu, Brute?* look on her. "Why?"

"So that vae stops being our problem, for one. Clearly, vae can't be trusted, and Faery is as good of an exile as we could ever hope to get. And, for two…" Lorena hesitates. She looks down at me, raising her eyebrows as if expecting something.

I just stare at her. I have no clue what she's looking for here.

Roman does, though. "For two, we deserve the opportunity to see Faery for ourselves."

When every set of eyes in the room lands on him this time, Roman still looks completely at ease. Leaned back, feet propped up, arms loose over his stomach.

But I notice the way his shoulders stiffen around his throat. The way his throat bobs as he swallows. The way he looks at the chipped black polish on his nails instead of meeting anyone's eye.

"Maybe Zai's a liar. Maybe every word out of vaer mouth is bullshit. And if it is, fine. But if it isn't…" Roman shrugs, tilting his head back, practicing nonchalance. "You call yourself an ally to the witches. Prove it. Give us an opportunity to explore a world where we're wanted. Since that certainly isn't the case in your kingdom, Your Majesty."

His partners both shift uncomfortably at the taunting accusation, but neither says a word to defend Emyr.

Who, for his part, is looking a little murderous again. Though, honestly, I'm not sure if his rage is directed at Roman, or the whole unjust, fucked-up system we've been trying to torch for a while now.

"If it is so important to all of you to enter Faery, why have you not simply opened the door yourselves?" he finally asks, looking back to Solomon. "Or was plotting my assassination the more urgent matter?"

Solomon sits up straighter again, eyes widening. "I had no idea vae was going to do that. I was sure your connection to Wyatt would protect you."

"Mmm-hmm."

Solomon looks like he wants to keep arguing his ignorance. But he doesn't. He takes a deep breath, hands clenching into fists, and continues, "And I *can't* open the door myself. The magic is convoluted. It requires a knowledge of the technology, and the sigils, and an ability to tap into fae Influencing. You made an annoyingly good deadbolt." He runs one hand over his mouth, scrubbing thoughtfully at his chin. "I thought about asking Jin, but I knew they would tell you as soon as I did."

Something sharp stabs me in the gut. Maybe guilt? Probably hunger pangs. I decide to lean forward and grab more rupiea, shoving another piece in my mouth.

"Look, I know you're angry with me, and I understand why. You have every reason to be. But this is bigger than you and me. This is about uncovering the truth of our history. How we got here. Why we got here. And, more than that, how we move forward." Solomon swallows. "Please. Open the door again. Let Zai return home. And let's see, for ourselves, what Faery has to offer."

Everyone stares at the king, waiting.

Emyr looks to me and my breath hitches.

And then he says, firmly, but with something like regret hidden in his voice, "No."

"Emyr," Lorena starts, but she isn't given a chance to finish.

"I understand why you want to do this, I do," Emyr continues, shaking his head. "And believe me, I have *long* wanted to go through that door myself. I want answers as badly as you do." He sighs. "But in all my wanting, it never occurred to me that Faery would already be inhabited. Not just potentially survivable, but surviving still. And while vae has spun you a very nice story about how safe you would be on the other side, vae already tried to kill me *and* my father."

And Briar, albeit, maybe, unintentionally.

"I don't trust what may be waiting for us if we open that door. I don't want to know what might make its way here, and what it might do to innocent people in this kingdom. Or what we might really find, if we went through ourselves." He shakes his head. "It's a nice story, really. But none of us are children anymore. And I think we're all too old for fairy tales."

It's like Emyr took one of his claws and popped a balloon I didn't even know was in my chest. I deflate.

But only a little. He's not wrong. We have enough on our hands right now. *Too much.* Maybe, someday, opening the door to Faery again will be on the table. But right now? The last thing we need is even more enemies, or another problem to solve.

Solomon leans forward and puts his head in his hands. He doesn't argue. Roman reaches behind Zai's back to place a hand on the curve of his boyfriend's spine.

"Well," Lorena clears her throat. "What happens now, then? To us? And to Zai?"

"To you? Nothing. Mistakes were made. But I'll choose to believe they were in good faith." Emyr gives a small shake of his head, looking down at the fae on the couch. "As for vaer? Well, I can't exactly let vaer go free. I would like to avoid actually dying a second time."

"What are you going to do with vaer, then?" I ask, and, for reasons I don't totally understand, find myself leaning forward, like I'm about to stand.

Emyr sidesteps the coffee table. "I didn't imagine we'd be using the dungeon again, after Derek and Clarke's escape, but I suppose it'll have to do until we figure out a more permanent prison."

"Emyr, wait." I don't even know when I stood up. But then my fingers curl around his wrist, threads of black magic sliding away from me and down across the back of my palm.

He stills in the middle of wrapping a hand around the back of Zai's neck. One look at my face and he growls. "You've got to be kidding me."

"I know. *Believe me*, I know." I swallow, reaching forward with my other hand to slowly peel his fingers off of vaer skin. "I would like to cut vaer into a thousand tiny pieces. Really. If it were just about me."

"Then *why* are you *stopping me*?" He's exasperated, no doubt tired of me, and this whole conversation, and I can't even blame him. He has every right to be. I am also tired of this conversation. And of me.

"Because…" How do I explain this to someone else when I can barely come to terms with it myself? "Because we got rid of the Guard for a reason."

My stomach hurts as we meet eyes, Emyr's eyebrows pulled low in a frown. I love him so much. I need him to understand.

"Because if we're going to commit to tearing down the systems that hurt innocent people, we can't keep using them to hurt the ones who deserve it, either." I take a deep breath, fighting back the bile sloshing around in my esophagus. "Sometimes justice is complicated like that."

After a too-long moment of consideration, Emyr asks, "Then what do you propose we do?"

"I don't…uh, I don't know." Guess I should've thought about that at some point. But, in my defense, I literally never have any idea what to do about anything, ever. So. I look to Roman. "You three good to keep playing babysitter until I figure that out?"

He shrugs. It's the best yes I'll get.

Emyr scowls, and steps away from me. "I have a feeling I'll live to regret this."

"But you have a feeling you'll live," I answer. "So it sounds like things are already looking up."

CHAPTER FIFTEEN

WHAT THE HELL IS WRONG WITH YOUR OTHER HALF?

We leave Zai in the triad's care, and Lorena promises firmly that she will commit a triple homicide if anything starts looking fucky. I believe her.

I do hope they're going to be okay, though, the three of them. Like, their relationship. Not that I should be taking it upon myself to care about anyone else's love life, especially not right now. But I really don't want all of *this* (imagine vague hand gesturing) to break up their family.

"Sooo…what are our plans for the rest of the day?" I ask, my elbow brushing Emyr's as we meander up toward the palace together. I can still feel people's eyes on me. I should have asked Roman for a black hoodie—I have no doubt he owns like, twelve.

"Well, *my* plans," Emyr glances down at me, a mixture of fondness and complete and utter disdain speckled across his face. It's not one I'm unfamiliar with. "Include a video call with Paloma and Maritza."

"Oh!" The queens of Eirgard were surprisingly easy to get along with, the last time I saw them. Now that I have the kings of Monalai to compare them to, I like them even more. "To pitch them the tech magic?"

"That was supposed to be the point, yes. And I thought they'd be an easy sell, considering." Eirgard is one of the more progressive of the fae kingdoms. Emyr shakes his head and motions over his shoulder with a flick of his wrist. "Now? I don't know what to say to them."

Right. Our whole pitch so far has been about getting the fae to stop overusing their magic in order to save the planet, and to let witches step up to help by building technology the way Jin has. But after meeting with the changelings, and now Zai confirming everything they already told us and more, it seems like the *real* conversation here should be about…that.

But how do we get into that without telling them where we learned it?

Roman was right to mock me for keeping secrets. They're sure as shit not doing me any good. At some point, I'm gonna have to open my big stupid mouth and start talking.

"*Your* plans," Emyr continues. "Are to figure out what to do with our new little friend back there."

"Oh. Right. I can do that."

"Let's hope so." He's chiding me, but then he reaches over and curls his hand around mine, knitting our fingers together and squeezing, and I don't mind so much.

I tilt my head up to look at him, sunlight bouncing along the edges of his golden energy, one too-long curl falling down across his eyebrow. He meets my stare and smiles, kinda sad, really tired, but still a smile.

"I'm sorry about last night," he says, quietly.

And really, I don't want to talk about last night. I don't want to talk about anything real, or serious, or big, or important. I want to keep holding his hand. I want to take a walk in the sun with my boyfriend, and maybe stop and get some more food because I'm still hungry, and then go lie down somewhere under a tree or in a meadow and kiss and talk about the future, not in a scared way, but in the way other people get to when they still think anything is possible. I just want to be seventeen and in love and believe anything is possible.

But that's not who I am, or who we are. And there's no use wanting.

"It's okay." I shrug.

"It's really not. I shouldn't have lost it like that."

"No, you're right. You shouldn't have. I don't mean it's okay like you didn't do anything wrong. I mean it's okay like..." I use my free hand to roll my wrist a few times, struggling with the words. "I understand why it happened and I'm not upset with you and I love you."

Something passes, briefly, over Emyr's face. So quick I almost miss it, and I might have, if it weren't for the fact that it's so familiar. I just haven't seen it in a while.

Every now and then, he'll look at me with this *hunger*. That doesn't seem like a strong enough word, but I don't know what else could be. It's this cut-open stare, this raw chasm of a thing, that I don't have the right language to explain.

I haven't seen it in a little while. Maybe we've been too tired.

"Did you hear what Zai called us?" he asks, once he's tucked that vulnerable expression out of sight. "Not mates. Mirrors. What do you think that means?"

"I don't understand like a quarter of the shit that little weirdo says."

Emyr looks like he has more to say, but when he tilts his head to look up ahead of us, his expression suddenly shifts. He frowns, eyebrows creasing, his energy sinking low around him. "What the hell is going on now?"

I follow his stare toward the castle.

There's a crowd gathered outside, near the steps. They all seem to be yelling things at each other, though it doesn't sound violent or aggressive. It sounds celebratory, maybe. Like onlookers gathered in the stands to watch sportsball or something. Which maybe wouldn't be all that big of a deal on its own.

But I recognize some of the faces. The Guard who handcuffed Briar and me the day we arrived in Asalin together. The one who arrested Jin, right after Lavender's death. The two who half assed taking Derek into custody, after Emyr's.

This is a mob of ex-Guards. All crowding around the palace.

And just like that, I'm not here anymore.

Instead, I'm in a hallway filled with smoke. I can't breathe through it, it's so thick. And I can hear people screaming, and I'm terrified something bad is going to happen to Briar, but I'm helpless, here. My magic can't do me any good, not when fire is the only thing I know. And Tessa's there, suddenly, shaking, curled up in the corner, dissociating out of her own body.

And then Unicorn Boy is there, too. And he's whispering my deadname like an unholy vow, like a promise of every vile thing he's going to do when he gets his hands on me. And then he doesn't have hands anymore, because I've turned them to shreds, and I don't know how. I'm safe, maybe; I'm safe, but at what cost; I'm safe, but maybe the thing I should really be afraid of is inside of me.

Emyr curls an arm around my chest. "Wyatt?"

I'm so cold. Panic feels like ice shards inside of me. I lean into his touch until I'm not shaking anymore. "Yeah. Hey. I'm back."

He waits a beat to make sure that's really true before taking my hand again. We walk in sync up to the palace steps.

At our approach, the cheers and laughter die off pretty quickly. Someone nudges someone else, heads start turning over shoulders, and suddenly the whole crowd is shifting to look at us, expressions ranging from mild concern to overly confident sneers.

And when they part, Wade steps forth from the center. With Martha and Nancy behind him.

Right. Shit. Wade. I remember now, what Nancy said, about how my being a little asshole had brought him back to the dark side, or whatever. But in the mess of, you know, everything else, I'd forgotten it until this exact moment. Although, even if she hadn't said anything, it's obvious that this Wade is…new.

It's the first time I've seen him since we got back from New Zealand. And while the improvement from unshowered manic-depressive to fashionable metrosexual was a welcome one, it's still off-putting. His blond hair is down, his freaking *velvet suit* perfectly put together, accessorized by silver rings and earrings and necklaces, and even—I swear—a touch of glimmer on his cheeks.

It's like he's suddenly trying to be the knockoff store brand of Emyr. Which would be a lot more funny, if Emyr hadn't decided today was going to be the first day in his entire life that he dressed like a normal person.

And he's *smiling*. This over-the-top, too-white smile that makes my skin crawl. It doesn't look real at all, and it sure as hell doesn't reach his eyes. He looks like an AI being controlled with a remote somewhere.

"Emyr. Wyatt. I was *just* hoping to have a word with you." Even his voice sounds wrong. Like he's been practicing to do voiceover for a car commercial.

But the part that really freaks me out, like, seriously, makes me take a step back and start rethinking everything I know about everything, is when he gets close enough to smell. Because I recognize it immediately. The cologne is familiar because I remember thinking it smelled expensive. I remember inhaling it while being pressed up against things and fearing for my life. Wade smells like Derek.

Somehow, by the grace of whatever god may or may not care about me, I manage *not* to ask, *Did you steal your dead brother's perfume?* But it's like, just barely. We're talking skin of my teeth here.

Wade is *not* the Pierce sibling I expected to see following in Derek's footsteps.

"Oh?" Emyr does not sound like he wants to have this conversation. If I had to guess, that's probably because he does not want to have this conversation. "What would you possibly like to say to me, Wade?"

I only notice Tessa and Jin have been hovering nearby when they slip around the crowd to come and join us. Jin hovers at Emyr's back, while Tessa's elbow knocks against mine.

She leans down to speak into my ear. "They've been out here conspiring for a while. Don't know if we missed anything."

"What the hell is wrong with your other half?" I snap out of the corner of my mouth.

She doesn't answer that one.

"Well, Emyr," Wade begins, but Emyr cuts him off.

"You would do well to address me as Your Majesty."

My god, the BDE radiating from him right now is just… I'm gay.

Something twitches in the corner of Wade's eye. And yet that smile never wavers. "Your Majesty, I want to be clear that I am sympathetic to your unique situation. You are so young. Forced into the role of king because of your mother's…unfortunate condition."

Emyr tips his head back. I watch from the corner of my eye as Jin places a subtle hand over his shoulder.

Wade pushes on. "Your people feel for you. We do. But pity…well, it isn't a good enough reason to bend over and spinelessly accept every bad decision you make."

The crowd around him laughs out their mocking agreement. Nancy crosses her arms over her chest, expression smug. I want to bury all of them.

"If you're winding up toward a point, fucko, I think now

would be a good time to just spit it out." I bite the words through my teeth.

"If you insist." Wade inclines his head. "We know how much you adore the humans. How you emulate them in your decision-making. How you drag their technology into our world. And if you have such a depth of admiration for their kind, perhaps you should follow their lead in political matters, as well."

Having lived under the leadership of Texas politicians for a few years, I would very much like to disagree.

Tessa pinches the bridge of her nose. "Seriously, Wade, this isn't spitting it out. What the hell are you getting at?"

He tilts his head at her. Blinks. Then looks back to Emyr. "If fairness and justice are really what you're after, you have no business declaring yourself king. The people demand an election. Let *us* decide who should lead Asalin." Somehow, his smile grows wider. "It's only fair."

Well, fuck me.

It's not like this is unprecedented. Emyr and I have had this conversation at least a dozen times already. On the surface, an election *is* fair. Letting the people of Asalin decide who gets to lead them. Creating a democracy.

But in practice? We'd end up back where we were a few months ago in, like, a week. Maybe worse.

Sometimes the *right* thing is also the unpopular thing.

And Emyr is on the same page as me. Because his only answer is, "No."

The crowd loses their shit. Everyone starts screaming, hypocrisy this, fascism that. Nancy steps forward and throws a few choice words in my face. Martha starts crying.

Wade looks unbothered. "Care to explain how you can justify that, dear cousin?"

"I don't *owe you* any justification. But alright. Sometimes things aren't black-and-white." Emyr's gaze flits to me and then quickly back to Wade. "Sometimes justice is complicated like that."

It's the fact that Wade is still smiling that really does it for me. Even as everyone around him continues to protest, he just nods, absolutely unfazed. "Alright. But it is a shame, Your Majesty, that when this began, all I wanted was to get my hands on my niece. You could have given that to me. Instead, you've chosen to begin something you won't be able to stop. Don't forget that."

He raises a hand and motions for the crowd to move away from the steps, in the direction of the village. As he starts following after them, like a shepherd herding sheep, Jin calls out at his back.

"What the hell happened to you?"

Wade freezes. I watch, curiously, as he stands still while the rest of the crowd disperses. My eyebrows rise when his head tilts to the side, and his hands curl into fists.

And then slowly, he turns around to face us again, his eyes on Jin. That awful smile is finally gone.

"What happened to me?" His voice is softer now. Like maybe a part of the Wade I remember is trying to claw its way to the surface. "I was handed a set of impossible circumstances. I was told to take my heart and rip it out of my chest, and I *did*. I am not the villain here. I am only doing what I have to." He swallows. "And I'm sorry."

And then, as quickly as any sign of vulnerability is there, it's

gone again. He turns his back to us and hurries away, catching up to Nancy and Martha as they head into town.

Jin just stares after him, mouth open.

For a moment, the four of us stand in silence. When it gets
to be too heavy, I clear my throat and interrupt it.

"Well...that was a little fucky wucky, huh?"

Emyr looks at me like he's going to kill me, and starts for
the palace doors. His golden energy has turned to a wildfire
around his shoulders.

I don't follow him. He needs a minute. And also, I can see
Tessa, standing beside me, still staring off in the distance after
Wade. *She* needs something, too.

And then there's Jin.

Which. Right.

Jin.

I open my mouth to apologize, again, for yesterday, but
what comes out is, "Where's Briar?"

Jin stares at me for a second too long before answering.
"Uh. Still sleeping, I think. We were up late."

"Oh."

I don't have any opinion about that.

"Yeah." Jin shifts their weight from one foot to the other,
then coughs. "I'm gonna go."

"Okay. See you later."

I watch them head off in the direction of the dragon field,
and I hate every miserable little thing about myself.

Still. That's nothing new, and also not really the pressing
issue at hand.

Tessa drops down onto the steps and puts her elbows on
her knees. I join her, our thighs nearly touching.

"So..." I don't even know how to begin this conversation. "That was interesting. You have any idea he was planning that?"

"Of course not. Shut up." She rolls her eyes, but there's no sting behind her words.

"You wanna talk about it?"

She's quiet for so long that I think the answer is, actually, no. I tug at the hem of my T-shirt and stare at the grass near our feet and don't ask again.

Eventually, my patience pays off.

"He's not himself." Tessa worries her cheek between her teeth, still staring toward the village. Any sign of Wade or the others is long gone by now. "In more ways than one."

When nothing else comes, I knock the sole of my boot against hers. "Cryptic. What does that mean?"

"I'm..." She frowns, blinking back into focus, and glancing over at me. The grimace that crosses her face next is almost comical in its drama. "I don't think you want to know."

"*Okay.*" I roll my eyes, turning sideways so I can face her fully. "Except now you're morally obligated to tell me."

Tessa huffs, reaching down and brushing her knuckles against her stomach, over the scarification in her skin. Finally, though she looks really unhappy to be talking about it, she says, "Wade and I slept together."

"Uh." Not really where I thought that was going. "And it was...different than normal?"

"Well, it was the first time we've ever done that, so, no? I don't know." She presses her fingertips into her temples.

"Huh. You know, I wondered what this whole—" I wave

my hand at her, and then in the direction he disappeared to
"—thing was. You two are weird together."

"Thanks." An eye roll. "We're just friends. But we're... I
don't know. Sometimes you're in love with your best friends."

"Mood."

"Anyway, I never thought anything would actually *happen*.
And when it did..." She sighs, shaking her head. "Are you
sure you want to talk about this?"

"About your awkward sex with Wade?" Because it sounds
like that's what we're getting at here. "Sure, why not?"

"It *was* awkward." Her nose crinkles, and she reaches up
to tuck a strand of hair behind her ear. "But it was also...he
just...he didn't act the way I expected him to. He was so..."
She swallows, gaze a little foggy, like she's thinking back to
whatever happened between them, like she's there instead of
here with me right now.

Something ugly winds itself through me, settling heavy
and thick in my stomach. My sharpened teeth slide against
the inside of my lip until I taste my own blood. "Tessa, what
did he do to you?"

"No! It's not like that. He didn't *do* anything. Not exactly."

"Not exactly?" That's not as encouraging as I think she
thinks it is.

My conversation with Nancy from the day before replays
in my head. Asking her what she'd done to turn all of her
children into predators, the sort of people who would use any
kind of manipulation, coercion, or force they could to get
what they wanted from those around them. Derek was always
a little more heavy-handed, magic or brute strength more
than enough to get him what he wanted. Clarke wormed her

way into Jin's life with promises of love and a happy future, empty words and saccharine charm that stole Jin's ability to give real, informed consent to their relationship.

If Wade is changing sides, it wouldn't shock me if he followed their footsteps.

It might shock *him*, when I rip his fucking head off.

Tessa sighs, hard, slamming her open palms down against her knees. "He was just so *aggressive*. It was like…we'd never done anything like that before, and he went from zero to a hundred in five minutes. I don't know. He just…" She waves from her chest toward the village. "There was no *us* in it. No connection. It was like he was a completely different person. And then it was over and I felt nothing. And he just left."

I've never been someone who attaches a ton of meaning to sex. It's different for everyone, obviously. Some people need to be in love, *committed*. For them, sex is one part of a bigger picture. Others just want to feel good while it's happening. For me, I guess it's somewhere in the middle. I don't need to feel butterflies; I just need to trust the other person. I need to feel safe. It's why, before Emyr, I always needed to be in total control.

But it really doesn't matter what my personal philosophy on hooking up with your friends is. Tessa's voice trembles over the words *he just left* and I know she's hurting.

"Have you talked to him about it?"

"No. I was going to, but we've barely talked at all in the last few days. He's like, crawled up his mom's ass. I don't know."

I don't *know*, either. But I *think* Wade was really, incredibly hurt by Emyr refusing to let him have Derek and Martha's baby. And I think it sparked something ugly in him, something that'd probably been instilled by his parents, that he'd spent his whole life trying to unlearn. I'm not saying this is Emyr's fault. Clearly, he was very correct to have reservations about trusting Wade. I just think maybe he was already teetering on the brink of becoming a traitorous little rat, and then he got pushed over the edge.

Again, doesn't really matter what my personal feelings are on how Wade ended up here. What matters is that he's here, and people are hurting because of it.

And it's obvious things are just going to get worse. He's planning something, and as much as told us so. The other shoe is going to drop; it's just a matter of time.

"Okay, stop perceiving me." Tessa sniffs, turning her head away like she can hide the fact that she's rubbing tears out from under her eyes. She can't, but I'll pretend I don't notice, because I'm a good brother. "Or tell me something you don't really want to talk about so I feel less exposed."

Okay, well, I don't want to do either of those things. I think we should talk about this some more. That seems like the right thing to do. And even if we don't, I don't know what good airing *my* dirty laundry would do anyone.

But really, sharing something ugly only seems fair. Tessa and I have lost so much time together. Not just the years I was gone, but all the years before that, too, really. When we couldn't look past ourselves to actually see each other.

"Sometimes it feels like every bad thing that's ever happened to me is still happening." I pull my knees to my chest and curl my arms around my shins. When she turns back to frown at me, I shrug. "It's like there's a part of me that's always trapped in my own memories. Reliving the worst nights of my life over and over. Like, yeah, I survived, but did I really? Can I say I lived if my own head's trying to kill me now?"

Like when I saw a group of people on the palace steps and suddenly it was the night of the riot all over again.

Tessa is quiet for a moment, watching me, her eyebrows tense. When she does speak, it's slow and careful. "Your head isn't trying to kill you. It's just remembering that the world is dangerous, and fucked-up things happen all the time. You should be gentle with the part of you that's just trying to protect you." She sniffs again. "We definitely need so much therapy, though."

"There are no fae therapists," I remind her. "But maybe we could opt for DIY lobotomies, instead."

"Ooh. Me first. I bet I could YouTube it."

We both laugh without a hint of joy. And I hate it, really, but I guess there's one silver lining in this whole thing. Instead of turning all our hate on each other, Tessa and I are finally learning to hate the rest of the world side by side, instead.

CHAPTER SIXTEEN

GROWING PAINS

When Tessa and I part ways, I head up to find Briar.

I *don't* find her, though. Instead, when I knock on the bedroom door and shuffle awkwardly outside, thinking about everything I want to say to her and everything I need to say to her and everything I maybe shouldn't say at all, Nadua answers with the baby strapped to her chest. I peer around her, but the bedroom looks otherwise empty. There's a stack of papers and an open laptop in the center of the bed, and the balcony doors are thrown open to let the light in.

"You finally made time to come and talk to me?" she asks, stepping back into the room and leaving the door open for me to enter.

Guilt is such a useless emotion. I can't do anything good

with it. Anger gets shit done. Grief helps move me from one place to the other. Envy shows me what I want. But guilt? It's just there, hanging out in my body, making me feel like shit, with nothing to show for it.

"Uh—"

"Before you lie to me, I already know you're actually looking for Briar." She sits down in the nest of things on the mattress, clicking a few keys on the keyboard, and motions for me to join her without looking up again. "Don't think she wants to be found right now."

It *wasn't* my intention to hang out with Nadua today. But maybe it *should* have been. She's not wrong, that I should have made time to talk to her. I've missed her so much. Ever since I left Laredo, I've missed her. It's just, with everything going on, and the whole world in flames—sometimes metaphorically, but often not... Well.

I climb into the bed and lie on my side next to her, head on the pillows. The same spot I used to sleep in with Briar, back before Emyr took the Throne and I moved into his suite.

"Found at all? Or found by me?"

Briar is known for taking *Briar time*. It isn't unusual for her to unplug from the world, to abandon her cell phone (personally unthinkable, as I prefer a constant stream of memes injected into my eyes) and go wander off to touch grass.

But...it's entirely possible this isn't alone time so much as not-Wyatt time. I still don't really understand what happened. Yesterday was a weird day. First the accident, then the tension with Jin. Even if we don't talk it out, if there's nothing really to say, I'd like to just move on. There's shit she needs to know about, and sooner rather than later.

242 H.E. EDGMON

Nadua still doesn't look at me. She shrugs one shoulder, and scribbles something down in her notepad. "Probably both."

I sigh, and close my eyes.

The sheets smell like Briar and Nadua. Like cocoa butter and sunlight and a hint of cigarette smoke. It's the most comforting thing in the world. I nuzzle my cheek into the pillow and think I could probably fall asleep in minutes if I stayed like this.

Nadua doesn't let me. "She tells me your talk with Mary was enlightening. That your take on the conversation, too?"

I don't open my eyes, because I don't want to. I let the breeze from the open doors blow in and tickle my face and say, "*Enlightening*'s one word for it. I still have a lot of questions."

"Could call her and ask them. It's been a few days now. You've all had your room to think."

"Mmm." Fair point. And anyway, between Wade and Zai, it looks like we need all the friends we can get. Best to solidify the alliance with the changelings sooner rather than later. "What are you working on?"

"Mary's family isn't the only one out there. The rest are just…a little less enthusiastic about getting caught up in all this." She breathes out, once, hard, through her nose. "Just a lot of back and forth with a lot of good, scared people."

I reach out without opening my eyes, fingers pawing until I find her knee, and give it a squeeze. "Thank you. Have I said that yet?"

"No. But I'm not doing this for you, so you don't have to."

"Thank you, anyway. For everything."

"Oh, hush," she grumbles, but she reaches over and runs a hand, gently, back and forth across the top of my shaved head.

We sit like that for a while, the room quiet except for the

occasional click of a key or scratch of a pen. The sunlight warms my face, and the breeze carries in the smell of fresh earth from outside, and Nadua's fingers don't stop scratching at my scalp.

Finally, quietly, I ask, "Are Briar and I fighting?"

Briar and her mom are close. If we are fighting, she probably would have told her.

Nadua sighs, but doesn't move her hand away. "No, you're not fighting."

"I don't understand what happened." I guess that's not entirely true. I understand she wasn't impressed with what I said to Jin, even if I still feel like it was warranted. And I guess I understand that she thought she was going to die in the car accident, and maybe she's feeling a lot of feelings about that. Either way, it feels like a switch got flipped in the last twenty-four hours, and we went from good to...to this living tension monster between us.

Or maybe it's all in my head. I haven't actually seen her, not since I ran into her and Jin in the hall. Maybe I'm just blowing this out of proportion.

"Sometimes," Nadua starts, "in relationships, two people *need* each other. Sometimes, one just needs the other. And sometimes, even though they'd both be just fine on their own, they want to be together anyway. You and Briar have needed each other as long as you've known each other. Some ways visible. Others more subtle. But more and more, you need each other less."

"That is not true," I grumble, finally opening my eyes and sitting up straight. Nadua takes her hand back. "I'm always going to need Briar."

"No, you're not." She scoffs, shaking her head, and goes

back to looking at her computer instead of me. "Nothing wrong with needing people, if that were the case. But you don't need Briar. Not any more than you need me, these days."

"I still need you." I roll my eyes, looking down at the thinning knees of my jeans.

"Shut up. You don't. You did, once. Real bad. Didn't have much of a choice when I picked you up and brought you home." She sighs, and in the next moment her fingers are curling around my chin and lifting my eyes to hers. "But that's the kicker of it all. When you don't *need* someone, you get to *choose* them. Always preferred that kind of setup, myself." Her thumb brushes along my jaw, her nail gliding over my scars. "You and Briar are learning how to choose each other. It's a good thing. Just comes with some growing pains."

For reasons I can't put into words, even in my own head, the thought makes me feel panicked. I tug at the front of my shirt, eyes darting around the room to land anywhere but on Nadua's face. I can feel tears starting to sting the corners of my eyes, but I don't know why.

"Why does that make me sad?" I whisper, tongue tripping over the words.

"Oh, Wyatt." She leans forward and kisses the top of my head. "Because when someone gets to choose you, they can also decide not to. And that's scary."

"I'll always choose Briar."

But maybe I don't know if she'd always choose me.

And maybe I don't know if I deserve her to.

Nadua doesn't say anything. Maybe she's thinking the same thing. Or maybe I'm just projecting. Either way, I lie back down, and her hand finds the top of my head again, and we sit in silence for a while longer.

★ ★ ★

Later, I find Emyr in our bedroom with Boom. The demolished dresser's been fixed, glass and wood put back together as if nothing ever happened. And his laptop is sitting on top of it, opened up but the screen still black.

He's sitting on the edge of the bed just staring at it. He glances at me when I come in, but quickly looks right back to the computer. Boom, stretched out on the bed next to him, head over one of Emyr's thighs, acknowledges me with a tail wag and nothing else.

With a quiet click, I close the door behind myself. "Getting ready for your call?"

Eirgard was the only kingdom willing to take a video call instead of meeting in person. Which works out well for us, because, with the clusterfuck of everything else going on, now's *not* the time for us to leave Asalin, but definitely the time to start calling in favors wherever we can.

"Mmm-hmm."

I sit down next to him, and our fingers find each other on instinct. I brush the pad of my thumb against the back of his and watch as his jaw tenses.

"Do you want me to set it up?"

"I—" His mouth sits open for a moment, nothing coming out of it, before he shakes his head. "I have to get comfortable with technology again eventually. You won't always be there to hold my hand." He squeezes my fingers. "Figuratively or literally."

"Fair enough," is what I say, but it still feels like someone just threaded a needle into my aorta.

If Nadua's right—and she usually is—about the difference

between relationships where you need each other and ones where you don't, what does that mean about Emyr and me?

A few months ago, when he showed up in Laredo and dragged me back to Asalin, it was because he needed me. He'd said as much, in pretty clear terms. I wasn't the person he would have chosen, but I was the one he was stuck with. For better or worse.

The contract's gone now, the wedding canceled. But we've still got the bond hanging between us, this inexplicable *thing* tying us to one another. The fae believe it's about who you should make babies with. I don't think that's true at all, but I don't really know what I *do* believe. I know it forces Emyr's hand, compels him to feel drawn to me when he otherwise might not.

And now we've walked hand in hand through the kind of shit most people don't ever come back from, and lived to talk about it on the other side—more than once. I can't separate my relationship with Emyr, and my feelings for him, from the things that have happened to us. It's all sticky at the edges, and I don't know how to even start trying to pry them apart.

I *know* I would choose Emyr. His quiet strength, his dry humor, his insight and passion. His endless wardrobe (current outfit excluded) and his dimpled smiles and his hands, firm but gentle. I chose him when I decided to stay in Asalin. And I would do it again.

And I know he would choose me, too. He's told me more than once that his feelings for me, and his attraction to me, aren't caused by the bond. There are plenty of people who don't feel about their mates the way he feels about me. He *wants* me.

But does he also need me? Do I need him?

And is it a bad thing if the answer is yes?

I realize I've just been sitting there zoning out beside him only when Emyr finally lets go of my hand and pushes himself to his feet. With tense shoulders and a grim expression, he moves over to the dresser and stands in front of the laptop.

His claws hover over the keys.

I grab my hoodie, still discarded on the foot of the bed from this morning, and yank it on. By the time I shove my head through, he's walking back to join me, and the camera is open on the screen, and the program is ringing.

All that for nothing, though, because no one answers.

"My life is a joke." He collapses backward onto the mattress, staring up at the ceiling.

I pat his knee, consolingly. "That's rough."

When the computer starts ringing *again*, this time from an incoming call, I jump up. "I got it. I think you've made enough progress for one day."

He shoots me a thumbs-up that somehow manages to be passive-aggressive, and I move to answer the queens' call.

Paloma Pereira was born to rule, and she looks every bit the part of a princess turned queen. I've never seen skin as dark or unblemished, pixie-like features as delicate, or expressions as smug as hers. Her silver crown is threaded through her curls, and nestled between her antenna-like horns. Her pink gown, the same shade as her pink and yellow wings, is really just a bunch of loose fabric draped over her and somehow falling in the right direction.

I'm not sure what Maritza Pereira was born to do, but I have a feeling it involved less diplomacy and more being gay, doing crime. She's hard where her wife is soft, brown skin rippling with muscles and marred with healed scars, like Paloma plucked her right out of a bar fight and brought her to the castle. She's shaved her head since the last time I saw her, and is dressed in a black leather romper covered in zippers. Paired with her bull's horns and eagle-like wings, there really isn't a drop of subtlety about her.

The two are sitting on a balcony, the brightly colored Eirgard village in the background. Paloma wiggles her fingers cheerfully when we come into view. "You're still alive! Oh my goodness, look at that sweet baby."

Boom boofs out his agreement that he is, in fact, a sweet baby.

"I—was my life a point of concern?" Emyr demands.

"Well, you never know." Paloma nods, maybe attempting to appear like she's having profound thoughts, mostly looking irritating.

Have I missed her? I might've missed her. I snort. "Hello to you, too."

"Little shadow." Paloma sighs around the nickname, shaking her head at me with a tiny smile in the corner of her mouth. "I was so disappointed we didn't get to see one another when I was in Asalin last. We'll make up for it soon."

The last time Paloma was in Asalin was when Leonidas had his crown taken from him, and the Court flew in to coronate Emyr last-minute. I was in timeout in my room until she'd already left, on account of being a little traitor.

"Will we?" Emyr asks, a hint of dread in his voice at the idea of the queens stepping foot in Asalin.

"I was told you wished to discuss something important." Maritza looks unimpressed with all of us. Paloma reaches up to place a hand around the back of her neck. "Let's get to that?"

"Right." Emyr's claws twitch against his thighs. "So, as you are already aware, a witch consultant of mine, Jin Ueno, has been helping me to build technology encrypted with magic. They put together Fae TV."

"Yes, of course," Paloma smiles, leaning forward and placing her chin in her free palm, elbow propped up on the table in front of her. "I'm a fan of Jin's. How are they?"

"They're—" Emyr shakes his head and apparently decides to lie. "Uh, fine."

"Are they? Hmm." Paloma frowns, glancing over at Maritza. "Weren't they mated to Clarke Pierce?"

Boom hops down off the bed and growls, seemingly at nothing. I choose to believe it's the sound of Clarke's name.

"Mmm-hmm."

"The one who conspired to kill Emyr?"

"Mmm-hmm."

"Because she actually hated witches?"

"That's the one."

"Huh. Well, I'm glad they were able to bounce back so quickly." Paloma raises an eyebrow and glances back at the screen. "How *is* Clarke doing? We heard Derek is no more."

"Rest in pieces," Maritza adds.

"Clarke…continues to evade us."

"Really? Hmm."

I don't know if we're going to find our way back to the point, so I clear my throat and interrupt, "Jin Ueno. Tech magic."

"Right." Emyr reaches over and takes my hand again. "As you *also* know, fae magic takes its power from the land. I have reason to believe our presence is adding to the effects of the climate disaster the planet is already facing."

"You don't say." Maritza sounds alarmingly unalarmed.

"My proposal for Eirgard is to begin implementing this brand of magic, in the hopes of limiting the need for fae to draw excess energy from the Earth." Emyr takes a deep breath, clearly only just getting started on his pitch, but Paloma cuts him off.

"Sounds good."

"I—" He closes his mouth and blinks at her.

"Wait, really?" I lean forward, narrowing my eyes at her through the screen.

She mirrors me, leaning forward and mockingly glaring in my direction. "Yes, really. What? Did you think I was a climate change denier? Have a little faith."

"To be clear, I don't anticipate this to actually reverse or solve the issue of climate change," Emyr quickly adds. "We are not solely responsible for that. We just aren't...helping."

"Sure, sure." Paloma sits up straight again and flicks her wrist. "It's like recycling. Everyone has to do their part."

"Okay." I...sure. Yep.

"Um." Emyr looks as flabbergasted as I am. "Right. Well, that's not the entirety of it. In order to maintain this sort of magic, you will need the assistance of witches. And I believe it is only fair, if we are asking for their help in reshaping the way our kingdoms operate, we give those witches positions of power historically denied to them."

"Makes sense." Maritza nods, glancing from Emyr to Paloma and back again. "What did you have in mind?"

"Well... I know the Guard and Committee are time-honored institutions. But, in the context of their treatment of the witches, they have too often been used as tools to oppress. As I'm sure you've been made aware, one of the first

things I did as king was to abolish both branches. I've replaced
them with a new political body, which I've called the Circle;
a hand-selected assembly of fae and witches who maintain
order and help in making decisions for Asalin's future."

"Hmm." Maritza? Not impressed. Though, I'm beginning
to wonder if that's just her face.

"And how is that working out for you, cherub?" Paloma
asks, fingernails scratching the nape of her wife's neck.

"Truthfully?" Emyr swallows. "I don't know. It's too new
to deem it a success or a failure, especially when I've spent so
much of this last month outside of the kingdom. But I have
my reservations about its long-term success."

"A winning sales pitch," Maritza drawls.

Paloma is smiling, though. "As you should. But perhaps
we fix the immediate problem, and worry about long-term
success later."

"Perhaps," Emyr agrees.

A moment passes before I realize what she just said.

"Wait—are you actually agreeing to abolish the Guard? In
Eirgard?" And, like, yes, the Committee, too. Both of them
keep witches out of power. But when one of them is doing
clerical work and the other has the power to legally do as
many murders as they want…you know, I don't have it in me
to get that worked up about the Committee.

Paloma doesn't immediately answer, but she does turn that
sly little smile on Maritza. Her wife sighs, giving a small, re-
signed shake of her head.

"Forgive me," Emyr starts. "But I don't understand how
this was that easy."

"Has it been easy?" Paloma asks, tilting her eyes back toward the screen. "Has any single part of the last month felt easy?"

She's doing that *thing* again, that Feeler thing, where I have to wonder what she's seen, what she knows. I look up at Emyr's face and see the way his eyes glaze over and his muscles tense. Like he's trying very, very hard not to crack wide open. "No."

"That's what I thought." Paloma claps her hands together. "Emyr, you and I inherited very strange positions in very broken systems. For a long time, I've convinced myself I needed to play the hand I was dealt. It didn't occur to me until very recently that walking away from the game was an option at all." She turns a wry smile on me. "Your little shadow is the one who opened my eyes."

Emyr squeezes my hand. "He has that effect on people."

"Hmm. The match that sparked an inferno."

Maritza adds, "And burned it all to the ground."

I am feeling uncomfortably *seen*. Usually, when this much attention is focused directly on me, it's the result of me doing something terrible. I actually don't know what to do with it going hand in hand with praise. (That's what this is? Praise? I don't have enough experience to be certain.) Anyway, I think maybe I'll die now.

After a moment, Maritza looks away from me and continues, "Anything else? Before we go and cause a shitstorm among our people?"

"Yes, Emyr," Paloma smirks, and her eyes flick back to him, too. "Is there anything else you'd like to tell us?"

Well, actually…

There is a lot we could tell them. First of all, how about the fact that the door to Faery opened up and one of their people with a grudge against the Pierces came tumbling through?

Or about how we learned the secret truth about witch magic, where it comes from, how it operates, and what it can really do for the Earth?

But explaining either of those would mean turning over the secret of the changelings.

Which is why I'm not surprised when Emyr only says, "Wade Pierce seems to have taken up the mantle of his brother."

Boom growls again, from where he's taken up pacing by the door.

Hellhounds are *not* dogs, despite their appearance. But they're definitely not *that* sentient, either. Has to be a coincidence.

"Oh, for fuck's sake." Maritza leans back in her chair and glares at the sky overhead.

Paloma pats her arm. "Oh?"

"It's a long story, involving Derek's widow, and their baby, and now I think Wade possibly is trying to overthrow the government." I nod, face scrunching up. "Yep. So. If we need a favor at some point, like, reinforcements against a bunch of angry fae supremacists…"

"Right. Well, I suppose you'll call me if that should happen. Or I'll call you." Paloma sighs. "Sincerely, cherub, what is with the *constant* family drama?"

"Well, it was nice talking to you, Paloma. Maritza. We'll talk again soon, I'm sure." Emyr stands and shuffles over to the laptop. I hear the queens laughing before he slams the lid closed.

When he drops down onto the bed next to me again, I curl

my arm around his waist and press my face into his neck. I love the smell of him. Musk and smoke and sugar. There is a distant part of my brain that thinks *I wanna bite him*, but I don't, which deserves credit.

"That went better than I expected." That seems to be a running theme with the queens.

Emyr hums his agreement. His claws run the length of my spine, curling slowly up and down, repeating the motion again and again. "I don't know why I'm not relieved."

I think there are probably a lot of reasons for that. Like, this is just one thing we had to do in a long stack of terrible things looming, and it doesn't really *solve* anything so much as it doesn't add any new problems. And also, you know, there's the capital *T* Trauma of it all. Never expecting anything to work out, because so far, usually, it doesn't, and good news can't really be trusted.

But I don't say any of that. Instead, I switch gears. "Nadua hooked me up with Mary's direct number. It's tomorrow morning over there. You think enough time has passed that we can call her up and finish our conversation?"

He heaves a deep groan. "I think we don't have much of a choice, either way. Let's get this over with."

We don't, though. Get it over with, that is. I take my phone out of my pocket and call up the number Nadua gave me and it goes straight to voicemail.

Hmm.

"Well, never mind, then." That was depressingly anticlimactic.

Emyr keeps running those claws up and down my back. Just like when I was lying with Nadua, I think I could fall asleep. If I lay still long enough. If he kept scratching at me like this.

Of course, with Nadua, I was not also thinking about maybe sleepily making out.

Any thoughts of that flavor evaporate when Emyr says, "We still have Kitaraq and Oflewyn to contend with."

Right. Ugh. The other two fae kingdoms, from Africa and Eurasia. So far we're one for two on these meetings. Not *ideal* odds, but it could be worse. And when have our odds ever been ideal?

Boom jumps back onto the bed and settles on Emyr's other side. I reach over to scrub under his chin with my short nails.

"There's no chance they'll agree to video calls?" I prop my head in my hand, one elbow balanced on Emyr's chest. "It seems like…a pretty remarkably bad time to leave town again."

"Pari was open to the idea, but Amin shot it down." Pari is the queen of Oflewyn, and Amin is her husband. "Loureen and Calvince were interested, but they're also *convinced* any communication done through the computers is going to be hacked."

Loureen and Calvince are the seven-billion-year-old queen and king of Kitaraq.

Okay, not seven billion, fae age just like humans do. But still, like. Old old.

I could definitely make a joke at their expense. It has a very *conspiracy theory on Grandma's Facebook wall* vibe. But honestly, after everything we've been through and the delicate nature of these meetings? Their concern is valid. They're probably smart not to put their faith in anything they can't trust completely.

"Could we send someone in your place?" I ask, running one fingertip along the hollow at the base of his throat. "What about your mom? They worked with her in the Court for a long time. She knows how to talk to them. Do you think she'd feel up to it? Health-wise?"

Emyr frowns, looking down at me with scrunched eyebrows. "That's a good idea."

"Okay, well, you don't have to sound fucking *shocked*."

We decide to go immediately to find Kadri and gauge her interest. It's not a perfect solution. Not only is she sick, but she is married to Leonidas, who's very much fallen from grace in the eyes of the Court. It also takes away Emyr's chance to prove himself as the new king, to show up and be...

Uh, kingly.

Still, it's the best we've got. And we can send another member of the Circle with her. Jin, maybe, so they can explain the magic themself. Or Tessa, if we want to play it safe with only fae in the room. Though that idea does make my ass itch.

We actually don't make it all the way to Kadri and Leonidas's room. When we're still a full hall's length away, we round a corner and find her in front of a palace window. She seems to be arguing with someone, the two of them talking in clipped but fierce tones. It takes me a second to realize the someone in question is Nancy Pierce.

Before they spot us, I grab Emyr's arm and pull him backward, back around the corner, out of sight.

That's not the only unexpected part of running into Kadri here, though. Something's changed since the last time I saw her.

The former queen's signature cat-head cane is gone. Instead, she's using a wheelchair. The backing and armrests are made of black quilted leather, pinned with what I assume are actual diamonds. The dark silver rims catch the light and glitter, giving off the same powerful, shimmering vibe that Kadri's storm cloud energy does. And that energy clings, now, to both her and the chair. She sits back, hands folded in her lap, her eyes narrowed as she speaks to Nancy.

"When did she start using a chair?" I ask softly, my eyes flicking toward Emyr's face.

"While we were away." Emyr doesn't look at me. He only has eyes for his mother, peering around the wall to sneak a look at her. "Walking, at this stage, takes too much to be worth it. Even with the cane."

Obviously, I knew Kadri was getting sicker. It's the whole reason Emyr had to step up and become king *now*, the whole reason I was dragged here from Laredo when I was. We were literally just talking about her health back in the room. It isn't a secret that she's dying. But this is the first physical sign I've seen that things are getting worse.

It makes my chest ache in a way I wouldn't have expected. It's not like we've ever been close. In fact, I'm pretty sure she doesn't like me all that much. But I know how much Emyr loves her, how it's going to kill a part of him when she's gone.

"I'm sorry," I whisper, because it seems appropriate.

But the glare Emyr shoots my way tells me it maybe isn't. "Why? The wheelchair isn't the thing killing her. It's *helping* her." He looks away from me and back to his mother. "I'm glad she has it. She should conserve her strength as much as possible."

Oh.

Well, yeah, I guess that's true.

"YOU BROUGHT THIS ON YOURSELF!" Nancy's voice raises to a near yell, and Emyr and I fall silent to listen in. "Emyr was never meant to be king; Derek was! The Throne was rightfully his. He waited his whole life for it!"

"Perhaps if he'd found a better use for his time—a hobby, perhaps—he would still be here," Kadri replies coolly, and it takes everything in me not to *yell.*

I can't see the fury on Nancy's face, but I hear it in her tone when she says, "You should have died when you fell from that tower."

Oh. Okay.

I don't know if Emyr or I step out from behind the corner first, but we move in almost tandem down the hallway and toward the two women. Kadri looks up at us with a sour look of bored resignation, while Nancy's vicious expression quickly morphs to one of disgust.

"If it isn't—"

Whatever nasty thing she was going to say is cut off by Emyr's, "You will leave my palace immediately. And you will be grateful you are not being removed from the kingdom entirely. *Yet.*"

He is, as far as I'm concerned, a bastion of leniency.

Because when Nancy has the audacity to open her ugly-ass mouth like she thinks she's going to respond with something smart, I snap, "Or you can stay right here and I'll make a hag-skinned rug, you awful—"

And then I call her…something, a rather vulgar something that I only ever use to describe the Nancys of the world.

Her face starts to turn purple and a vein throbs, ugly and red and huge, across her forehead. She does start to move, though, backing away in the same direction Emyr and I came from.

Because she just can't seem to help herself, she has to add

one more seething, cryptic little comment before disappearing. "Your kingdom in name only, and not for long. Everything you have stolen shall be returned to us... Just wait..."

And then she's gone.

Emyr crouches next to Kadri's chair, reaching out and placing one hand on her knee. "Are you alright?"

"I'm fine, my love." She brushes her knuckles over his cheek, then flicks her fingers up, motioning for him to stand. He does, though he looks at her warily. "I've survived far worse than her."

Which I suppose is true. It makes me think of my conversation with Tessa, though. Does it really qualify as survival if we're still in the thick of surviving? Kadri is still dying.

But maybe that's not what she's talking about, anyway.

"What are you two doing on this side of the castle?"

Emyr still seems hesitant, like he can't decide between finding Nancy and ripping her throat out and wrapping his mother up in a blanket or something. Since neither is actually an option, he eventually answers the question. "We were looking for you, actually."

"Oh?"

"My video meeting with the queens exceeded my expectations. I believe having them on our side builds a stronger case for speaking with the other kingdoms. However," Emyr shakes his head. "Mom, I can't leave right now."

She sighs, shaking her head. "No, you can't. Do you have any idea what's wrong with Wade?"

"Well, for starters," I pipe up, "*that* woman raised him."

Kadri glances at me and hums, before turning her attention back to her son. "What does this have to do with me?"

"I was thinking, maybe you could go in my place. I know

it may not look good, me skipping out and sending my *mother* to the first meeting I'm meant to have with them. But you do have a rapport with them that I don't. All of this, of course, only if you feel up to the traveling."

She folds her hands together, one of her thumbs running the length of her opposite palm. Finally, she shakes her head again. "I don't. Not really. I could do it, but I don't know how long it would take me to recover. But more than that, I don't really want to leave you here without me. Not with tensions as high as they are."

"Oh." Emyr nods. "I understand. Of course."

"That said," she continues, "I can contact the other kingdoms and request their presence here, in Asalin. It will give us both a chance to meet with them. And they can see for themselves how things are unfolding here."

Which may actually be a terrible mark against us, considering, um...everything. But I don't say that.

"Do you think they'd really agree to that?"

"I think Calvince will be grumpy, as he always is, but Loureen will go along with it." Kadri smiles, a rare fondness lighting up her eyes. "And Pari will be happy for any excuse to come and see me."

Kadri grew up in the same kingdom Pari now rules. Though she's old enough to be the other queen's mother, I think they must be friends.

She reaches over and takes Emyr's hand. "You knew there would be growing pains. But you are not alone in facing them. We will get through this."

And I know she's not talking to me. But she's right. We will get *through* it.

I'm just not sure what's waiting on the other side.

CHAPTER SEVENTEEN

NO MORE ATTEMPTED MURDERS WILL BE FORGIVEN

As much as I want to talk to Briar one-on-one about whatever may or may not be happening between us, telling the others about Zai really can't wait much longer. So, the next morning, I shoot off a mass text and tell the other members of the Circle (except Kadri, who Emyr talked to alone the night before, after our conversation with her) to meet us at the triad's.

Briar, Jin, Tessa, and Roman are all loitering outside the cabin when Emyr and I walk up. Roman's got his arms crossed, leaning back against the front door, all casual.

The other three look like they're thinking about killing him.

"What did he do now?" I groan, coming up next to Briar.

She shifts from one foot to the other at my side, getting just a smidge closer to me. The yellow fog of her energy rolls forward and wraps around my waist.

Not to be all *I let out a breath I didn't know I was holding* about it, but I definitely do, like, unclench.

"He wouldn't let us inside until you showed up." Jin frowns, glancing between Roman and Emyr. "What's going on?"

"Sol was worried there might be a...bad reaction to his little pet." Roman shrugs.

Emyr could not possibly sound less impressed than when he drawls, "And he thought *we* would help with that?"

"Not you, no."

Tessa rolls her eyes, taking a step forward until she's chest to chest with Roman. Her perfectly plucked eyebrows rise in a way that feels like a threat. "Okay, well, they're both here now. Are we good, my guy?"

Roman too slowly looks her up and down before he smiles and tilts his head toward me. "You two really are so much alike."

"Thanks." He definitely meant that as an insult.

The door opens up behind him, and Roman's cool-guy-lean is unceremoniously interrupted. I snort when he loses his balance and nearly falls backward into the house. Unfortunately, Lorena does grab his elbow and right him before he lands on his ass.

She sighs, glancing out at the group of us gathered there. She looks even more tired than when I last saw her. The circles around her eyes have grown, and her lips have gone pale and chapped. I'm pretty sure those are yesterday's sweats she's still wearing.

Jin seems to notice that, too, because they step forward with their frown even deeper. "Lor, are you okay?"

"No," she answers plainly. She sniffs but scowls when

Roman tentatively pats her back. "I'm having a nervous break-down. But it's fine. Let's get this over with."

Everyone starts filing into the cabin. I let them move around me, hovering outside until, for one brief moment it's just Briar and me. Her hand brushes against mine. I take a deep breath. Our eyes meet.

"Hey," she whispers.

"Hey."

My pinkie slides into hers, our fingers locking together. And we step inside to face the absolute shitshow that's waiting for us.

All things considered, it could have gone worse. Jin only tries to kill Zai once, immediately after hearing vae was directly responsible for Emyr and Briar's almost-deaths. Tessa *suggests* killing vaer a lot more than that, but at least she doesn't need to be physically restrained.

Briar is uncomfortably calm about the whole thing. You'd think she'd be angry on her own behalf, since she never has any trouble getting angry for other people. But she isn't. She just listens to the story about who Zai is and where vae came from, nodding along with interest the whole time.

She's the first to speak when it's all said and done. "Everything vae's saying lines up with what Mary told us."

"I had that thought." I nod.

"Who's Mary?" Solomon asks. He and Zai are back on the couch in the living room, isolated to their timeout chair while everyone else paces around them.

Not for nothing, Zai seems just as interested in Briar as she is in vaer. Vaer eyes stay on her through most of the conversation, narrowed with a kind of intense interest that *really* makes me want to punt vaer into orbit.

Emyr and Briar exchange a look. Though I'm not part of their conversation, I can tell a silent exchange is happening.

Finally, Emyr sighs and looks to Solomon. "Mary is an elder of a changeling village in Aotearoa—New Zealand. Changelings...are the offspring of humans and witches. We learned of their existence recently, and were able to meet them face-to-face when we traveled to Monalai."

"The offspring of humans and witches?" Solomon stands up. Then immediately sits back down. Then stands up again. "What? How?"

"It is, apparently, not unheard of for humans to discover abandoned witch children and raise them as their own. This village in particular has been living in secret for many generations, keeping a close eye on the fae kingdom." Emyr scrubs his hand over his mouth, shaking his head. "The ability to practice magic without fae oversight has allowed them to learn a lot about their power."

"Why...did you not say anything sooner?" Solomon demands. He flourishes an arm in Zai's direction. "When we told you about Faery, and what the witches can do. Why did you not tell us then?"

Emyr's eyes flick back to Briar. She sighs, reaching over to squeeze his hand.

From the far corner of the room, Roman asks, "How did you learn about them at all if they've been living in secret, *Your Majesty?*"

"He didn't tell you because he was protecting me." Briar shrugs. She crosses her arms over her chest and turns to look at Roman. "I'm a changeling. And I'm the one who opened the door to Faery."

Jin wraps an arm around her waist.

I move to stand between her and Roman.

Roman's not even looking at Briar, though. His eyes drift to the other side of the room, to the chair where Lorena's curled up with her legs underneath her, her arms wrapped around her middle. He raises one eyebrow, but doesn't say anything.

She pushes the pads of her fingers into her temples. "Yeah, I knew."

As a member of the Circle, Lorena was privy to that information a while ago. The boys weren't.

"And you didn't think to say anything?" Solomon demands. "You knew the door had been open, you knew Briar wasn't human, and you kept your mouth shut? These are things that affect us, Lor!"

She lowers her hands and glares in his direction. "Are you really lecturing me about keeping secrets? I was doing my job and serving the king. What's your excuse?"

Solomon doesn't say anything else. But his olive green energy bristles and shrinks away, like a frightened cat.

"Look," Jin starts, when the silence stretches on for long enough to get uncomfortable. "We've all made mistakes that got us to this point. No one in this room is totally blameless."

"I am totally blameless," Roman pipes up.

"Yeah, me, too," Tessa adds.

"No one who is *not* insufferably annoying is totally blameless," I amend on Jin's behalf.

They chuckle, and shoot me a quiet smile. I offer an awkward one back as they continue speaking. "Anyway, so, hashing out what we've already done really isn't the point. Right now, we need to focus on moving forward. What do we do next?"

"I think that's pretty obvious." Briar steps out of Jin's arm, doing a spin to glance at everyone in the room. She stops to face me. "We reopen the door to Faery."

"Yes. Definitely." Jin nods.

"That absofuckinglutely is not obvious," Tessa bites out. "There's no way we're opening that door again."

"We already discussed this." Emyr folds his arms over his chest, glancing between Jin and Briar with profound *I'm not mad, I'm just disappointed* energy. "It's too dangerous to risk opening again."

"*We* didn't discuss anything. You did. Without half of the Circle present." Briar raises her eyebrows. "I thought your whole thing was not making unilateral decisions."

"It wasn't like Emyr decided all on his own." I sit down on the edge of the coffee table, unfazed by the unimpressed look Lorena shoots me when I do. "I don't think opening the door's a good idea, either."

"Because it isn't," Tessa agrees.

"Okay, well, that's really easy for you to say," Solomon bites out from the couch. "Because you're not a witch."

The eyes in the room shift to him. He tugs at the high collar of his button-up, then rubs his palms on his thighs.

"I'm sorry, but I don't think fae opinions hold as much weight in this conversation. Neither of you have any idea what it's like for us to live here. To *literally* be disposable. If there is a possibility for a different world, one where witches are valued for who we are and not just accepted in spite of it, we all deserve the opportunity to go through that door."

"Sounds too good to be true to me," Roman moves out of his corner to drop down onto the couch with Solomon and Zai, though he sticks to one far edge. "But I do think vae's gotta go. We can't hide vaer here forever. I say we open it up long enough to toss vaer back in, at least."

"We already settled this debate," Emyr says slowly.

"I don't understand." Jin shakes their head. "You *wanted* to open the door to Faery. For years, you talked about the possibilities that we might find over there. What changed?"

"Well, for one, Faery tried to murder him," Tessa snaps.

"Think about all the knowledge that was lost," Briar pushes. "When our fae ancestors came over from Faery, when they warped history to create their own version of reality about who witches are and what they can do. Think about all the things we can *never* know if we don't go through the door."

"We don't know anything about these people," I argue. "Even if everything Zai is saying is true, how much does that really tell us? They don't hate witches. Okay. Great. They have a bone to pick with the Pierce family. Okay. Fine. So do the rest of us. But Zai was also plenty willing to sit back and let *you* die, Briar. That doesn't exactly make me feel great about the kind of people we'd meet over there."

"You talked to Kadri, right?" Lorena asks, tugging her knees up to her chest and raising her eyebrows at Emyr. "What's her opinion?"

"She...should not be left in a room alone with Zai, ever, if our intention is to keep vaer breathing." Emyr smiles without humor. "As for the door, she's inclined to keep it closed. It's a can of worms she doesn't want to open."

"Of course not," Solomon snaps. "Because she's a fae."

"Sol—" Roman starts, but Solomon interrupts him.

"Don't start! You hate them more than anyone. Why aren't you on my side?"

"I'm not *not* on your side." Roman's hands flex in his lap. "But I nearly lost you once already. I just think we need to be careful. Maybe that means sticking with the devil we know."

After the riot, the same night Roman's surrogate mother died, Solomon was arrested and sentenced to death for his part in the so-called anti-fae demonstrations. He escaped, with help from Tessa and me, and fled Asalin with the others who were taken in with him that night.

But I remember Roman's face when he thought Solomon was actually going to be executed. For all his sharp edges, he's just a boy trying to keep his heart safe.

"Okay." Lorena stands up and starts pacing the living room. "Okay." She stops in front of Emyr, opening up her hands demonstratively in front of her. "Okay."

"Girl, *are you* okay?" Tessa asks, and Jin shoves her without much strength behind it.

Lorena gives herself a second to glare at Tessa, before pushing on. "I think the question of the door is a lot bigger than the people in this room. Because it's true, there's a possibility we open it, even for a second, and something we can't contain comes through. It affects everyone. Not just in Asalin. Witches and fae everywhere."

She's right. And it goes hand in hand with the same thoughts I had the first time we had this argument.

"Maybe," I say, turning my eyes on Emyr, "this isn't something we can resolve right now. There's too much going on. Too many immediate problems we have to deal with. Maybe the door is something we can put on the back burner until everything else feels more stable."

"That relies on a version of the future where things *are* more stable," Tessa reminds us.

"You are a ray of fucking sunshine." Briar narrows her eyes.

"Enough." Emyr rubs his hands over his face, eyes closed, and takes a deep breath. Finally, he lowers his hands and nods. "Okay. You're right. Reopening the door is something that needs to be brought to more than just the Circle. And that's going to mean telling a lot more people about what happened. About the changelings. About Faery. All of it."

"Shit, meet fan," Roman drawls.

Emyr nods. "Which is precisely why we're waiting until whatever is going on with Wade has been resolved. Is that a plan we can all live with?"

"Consider," I say, turning to Solomon, waving my wrist demonstratively, "it will give everyone more time to perfect their arguments. Maybe we can all make PowerPoints."

I don't know if Solomon knows what a PowerPoint is, but he glares at me, anyway. "Fine. But this doesn't solve the immediate problem of Zai's presence. If vae's not going back to Faery anytime soon, and we can't exactly tell people where vae came from—"

"And no one's going to look at vaer and believe any lie we tell them, other than maybe that vae crawled up straight from hell," Tessa says with a scrunched nose.

"Thank you so much." Solomon might actually try to fight my sister. "What are we supposed to do?"

No one appears to have a quippy comeback to that. Lorena moves back to her chair. Emyr frowns, pacing across the room and slumping against the wall, wings curling around him like a cage. Jin's brow furrows, and Briar's eyes dart back and forth like she's watching a game of invisible ping-pong. Tessa drops to the floor and stares up at the ceiling.

On the couch, Roman and Solomon both stare at Zai. Zai, who's just sitting there, silently, hands in vaer lap. When I look at vaer, vaer eyes move up to mine and vae smiles. That horrible, off-putting, too-blissful smile.

I sigh. "Well…what do *you* want to do?"

Vae seems startled by the question. And honestly, so am I. Vae's like, a fugitive, technically. There's no reason we should be concerning ourselves with what vae wants, when vae's lucky, really, that we haven't just decided to burn vaer on a pyre or something.

So, I don't know why I ask. But I do.

Zai frowns, that wacked-out smile disappearing from vaer face, and sits up a little straighter. "Until you determine if I can go home?"

"Yeah." I wave my hand around the room. "Asalin's small. Everyone's gonna know you're not from here. Plus, frankly, I don't really trust you not to get into some shit. But we could try…as long as you understand that no more attempted murders will be forgiven. Or, you could stay here with Solomon, keep hidden in the house. What do you want?"

Vae runs one claw against vaer inner wrist. "Are those my only options?"

"You have something else in mind?"

"Perhaps I could go to this changeling village you mentioned." Zai glances at Solomon, then Briar, then back to me. "You say they are witches whose blood has been blended with Earth's people. I can sense this, on her." Vae inclines vaer head at Briar. "She is *different*. I think I would enjoy meeting more of her kind. And I could make myself useful to them.

I have Faery's knowledge of witch magic, and they can use my energy as fuel."

Huh.

Well, if anyone is capable of handling this little weirdo, it's probably Mary. Plus, it gets vaer far away from me and *my* people, which would be...ideal.

"That's an interesting proposition." I raise my eyebrows, glancing around the room. "Objections?" When no one bitches about it, I continue, "Okay. I can try calling Mary again. What time is it over there?"

"Approximately two in the morning," Emyr answers, glancing at the wall clock in the triad's living room.

"*Well*, maybe I'll do that later, then."

"Has anyone actually been checking on the door?" Tessa asks, expression grim. "Like...since we closed it? Supposedly."

"Not *supposedly*. It's closed." Jin shakes their head with a small eye roll. "I've gone and looked it over a couple times. Nothing exciting to report."

"Okay. But, if vae's got a whole group of people over on the other side missing vaer..." Tessa waves her hand in Zai's direction. "I'm just saying. Doors work both ways. Maybe we should be keeping a closer eye on it, and make sure no one on the other side has shown up with a battering ram."

"So much time has passed," Zai says quietly, so quietly I'm not sure everyone in the room can hear vaer. "Perhaps they've forgotten me entirely."

Hmm. Depressing!

"Briar and I can go check," I offer, standing up quickly and moving in the direction of the door.

Do I actually think someone from Faery has blown the door up since the last time it was looked at? No, I don't. I have a feeling we would *know*, if that were the case. Like, someone would have shown up to take Zai back. Or Leonidas would be dead.

(In fairness, I actually do not have *proof* Leonidas is still alive. He's been hiding out of sight since the day he was attacked. But I trust Emyr hasn't been lying to me about talking to his dad. Because that would be creepy. For several reasons. So.)

What I *do* think is that this gives me a chance to be alone with Briar for a while. We can "check out the door" while talking about everything that's happened over the last forty-eight hours. And maybe longer than that.

Yeah, probably longer than that.

"Sure." Briar nods, moving with me, and I smile at her.

Right up until Jin adds, "Okay! I'll come too," and starts heading our way.

I pause, one hand on the doorknob. "Oh. Um, that's okay. We'll be quick."

Jin stops, tilting their head to the side, though they're still smiling. "Yeah, but, if there is some issue, I'm the one who designed the security box. Probably best that I be the one to check it out."

"Sure…" I'm going to lose my mind. There's no way that Jin thinks for even one single second that there's an iota of a chance of the door actually being tampered with. They said themself that they've checked on it multiple times. This is just an excuse to latch onto Briar and follow her wherever she goes.

Exactly the way they've *been* doing.

"But I really don't think there's an issue. And, on the off chance there is, we'll just come back and let you guys know."

"What's going on, Wyatt?" Jin laughs, quietly, and reaches out to take Briar's hand. I watch the way their fingers thread together and something ugly swats at my lungs. "You trying to get rid of me?"

I don't say anything.

And the moment stretches on and on for way too long. And I still can't make myself say anything.

"Of course he isn't," Briar finally answers for me, shooting me a sidelong look that silently begs *what the fuck?* She hasn't let go of Jin's hand.

Jin's laugh is louder this time. Every "ha" feels like something cracking. "Well, okay."

"Oh, for fuck's sake, I can't take this anymore." I throw my hands up, letting go of the doorknob to do it.

"Wyatt," Briar starts, a warning deep in her throat, but I ignore it.

When I turn on Jin, their dark eyes have gone massive. It should maybe, probably, make me feel worse than I do, but I'm at the end of my rope here.

"Look, I've been trying to be understanding and not act like an asshole, *really*." Though, I've failed more often than I've succeeded, I know, at least where Jin is concerned. "But you need to give Briar some space. Seriously. She's not your emotional support blanket. She's a person. And you're just... you're too much, Jin."

"Stop." Briar lets go of Jin's hand only to step in front of them, her body a physical barrier between us. Like she's going to take a bullet for them and I'm the one holding the gun. "That was *completely* uncalled for."

"No. No, it wasn't, and someone has to say it. And apparently, that someone is me. I'm right about this. I might be an asshole, but I'm a *correct* asshole. I should have just said this the other day when we got into it, but you make me feel like shit with your…your sad eyes and your… I mean, look, Jin, I'm *sorry* your pain is so big, and I mean that. You didn't deserve what Clarke did to you. You deserve to be happy, and it is fucking unfair that you aren't, and there is nothing that can make it better right now. But just because you're trapped in the pit doesn't give you the right to drag someone else down there with you. Especially not *Briar*."

"Wyatt." Emyr puts a hand on my shoulder. I'm not sure when he moved closer to me. "I think you need to excuse yourself. This is not your place."

I shrug out of his grip. "Yes it is! She's *my* best friend, and they're—they're just using her as some replacement girl-friend!"

Jin takes a step back, away from Briar, away from me, full-body flinching at the impact of my words.

"Okay, enough." Tessa steps forward, moving to stand next to Briar. "I know you love Briar. And I know what you *think* you're doing right now is protecting her, but all you're *actually* doing is being a jerk."

"Yeah, maybe, but I'm also right!" Someone has to be the bad guy here.

"No, you're not." Tessa pinches the bridge of her nose, like I'm giving her a headache. "Jin and Briar are friends. They care about each other, mutually, and it's pretty obvious. Jin didn't force themself on her. They didn't cross any lines. They're leaning on a friend while they get put through the emotional wringer. And if that's too much for Briar to handle, if she feels like she's being used or treated like some kind of Clarke stand-in, that's on *her* to deal with. Not you. It's her responsibility to set her own boundaries with the people she loves, and it's her *fault* if she doesn't set any at all."

"But—"

"Please do not make me embarrass you in front of all your friends," Tessa warns.

"What does that even mean?" I throw my hands up again. "They're—"

"Okay, fine. How much of you being angry at *Jin* for being a shitty friend is really just you being angry at yourself?"

"Tessa, I think that's enough." Emyr grabs my shoulder again, and this time I don't have it in me to pull away from him.

Lorena clears her throat. I'd almost forgotten we were in her house at all. "Look, emotions are clearly running high. And it sounds like you all have a lot to talk out. But is this really the best time to do that?"

Somehow, it's Jin who answers her. They've pulled themself together, face impassive. A mask firmly set in place. "No. You're right. Wyatt and Briar, you two should go check on the door."

I can't snap out of it, though. My whole body feels like it just got zapped with an electric shock, or struck by lightning, or something, everything buzzing and off balance. Tessa's words bounce around in the empty space of my skull, the only thing I can think about.

Because she's not wrong. Everything I'm mad at Jin for doing is something I'm worried I did.

For years, in Laredo, while I tried to piece myself together into something resembling a person, I leaned on Briar. I used her as my emotional crutch, as my bridge between worlds, as my whole reason for getting out of bed every day. *I'm* the one who used her as a stand-in girlfriend, someone to fool around with while I figured my shit out, only to break up with her once I did.

Nothing in our relationship has ever been equal. When I left Texas and came back to Asalin, she was more than willing to put herself on the line for my cause, and I *let* her. I let her throw herself into danger, for me, again and again, and I never asked her to stop because I needed her there to make me feel okay. And now I'm worried I'm going to lose her, because she has never needed me the way I needed her.

Even the bubbling resentment I can't bring myself to talk about out loud, the part that has nothing to do with Briar, the blame I've turned on Jin for the part their ignorance played in Emyr's death...that's just my own guilty conscience. I allied myself with Derek. He Influenced me, used me, and manipulated me, but I still let it happen. At least to a certain extent. I had a feeling he was capable of doing anything, whatever it took, to get to the Throne. And I didn't speak up until it was too late.

I'm only as angry at Jin as I am at myself.

Fuck.

Briar shoves past me to open the cabin door and stomp off into the yard. I tuck my metaphorical tail and follow after her.

Fuck, fuck, fuck.

CHAPTER EIGHTEEN

SOMEHOW, BOTH ARE TRUE

Briar stomps all the way through the woods to Faery's door without stopping or turning to look at me. Branches crack under her feet, thorny limbs snag at her clothes, and she doesn't seem to notice or care. Her yellow energy pops around her body like firecrackers.

The door, as expected, is fine. It looks exactly the way it did the last time I saw it. Security system in place. Sigils powered on.

It's fine.

Things in general? Less fine.

"Briar—"

"You have a lot of nerve, Wyatt Croft." She finally wheels around to face me. Her cheeks are red. "I *knew* you had an issue with my relationship with Jin, but I didn't realize you

couldn't possibly wrap your head around the idea that someone might like being around me for reasons that have nothing to do with me being an *emotional support blanket*."

Wait. What? "No. No, no, no, that is not— I did not
mean— I was only talking about Jin. Of course people want to
be around you, are you kidding me? You're perfect, you're—"

"Oh my god, I am not perfect!" She looks like she wants
to hit me. I've rarely ever seen her this angry. And definitely
never directed at me. "You put me on this freaking pedestal
all the time, and do you know what that does? It completely
takes away the fact that I'm a PERSON!"

"I know you're a person!"

"I thought after you found out about me, when I opened
the door to Faery, I thought you would be so mad, and you
would finally realize that I've got my own issues."

"I was mad!" I throw my hands up. "And I know you have
issues!"

Okay. So, she isn't perfect. And I *do* know that. There was
a time, I guess, when I thought she was. But somewhere along
the way, maybe when I found out about the secrets she'd been
hiding from me, I realized that wasn't true. Maybe the real
truth is that I *want* her to be.

Briar groans, stomping away to the nearest tree stump so
she can drop down onto it. She puts her head in her hands.

After a moment, I sit down on the ground a few feet away.
"Okay. I'm confused. Are we fighting because you think I
don't think anyone would want you for more than free therapy, or because you think I think you're perfect?"

"Yes?" Briar peeks at me through her fingers. "Both."

"Those two things seem at odds with each other." I rub my palms against my thighs. "Don't they?"

She shrugs and lets her hands fall away. "No. Because if I'm perfect, it just means I don't have any needs of my own. It's like you think I just exist for everyone else."

"I don't—" The urge to defend myself wells up, strong and vicious, in my chest. Because I love Briar, I love her so much that sometimes it confuses me, and I can't stomach the idea that any version of me, even one that only exists in her head, could think that about her.

But I stop it before it leaves my mouth.

Because maybe she isn't entirely wrong.

So, instead, I take a breath. I think about it. And then I say, "Okay. So, subconsciously, I do feel that way sometimes. But…you sort of *do* just exist for everyone else, Briar. That's actually kind of your whole thing."

It's her responsibility to set her own boundaries with the people she loves, and it's her fault *if she doesn't set any at all.*

Briar has never set a single boundary a day in her life.

A tear falls from the corner of her eye and over one round cheek. She reaches up to brush it away with her fingertips. "Yeah. I know."

We sit in the near quiet for a while, the only sounds around us the sounds of Asalin's forest breathing in and out. She wipes a few more tears from her face. I do, too.

Finally, it's too much. "I feel like I used you. I showed up at your house, this broken, fucked-up thing, and you put me back together. One piece at a time. And I let you. I took and took, and I didn't give you anything in return. And I can't go back and change that, so I thought… I don't know. I thought I could stop Jin from doing the same thing."

Briar laughs, the saddest sound I've ever heard. "You used me as much as I used you." She sniffs, and shuffles off the stump to join me in the dirt. Our knees almost touch. "I don't know how to live for myself. But it's easy to live for other people."

My heart turns to ash and blows, like dust, into my mouth.

I think about what she said, when she woke up after the accident, after Emyr healed her. She didn't want to die alone. I left her, and she was afraid she was going to die alone.

She continues, "You put me on a pedestal and couldn't see past your own bullshit and I let you do it. Because I never wanted you to look too closely at mine."

We have both been terrible to each other. We have both loved one another more fiercely than we've ever loved anyone else. Somehow, both are true.

"Is this a toxic relationship?" I ask, and I'm only half kidding.

"Probably." She sniffs again and shrugs one shoulder.

"Your mom says we're trying to figure out how to stop needing each other," I say, even as Briar scoffs at the mention of her mom. "When did that happen?"

She sighs, hard, and tilts her head to look up at the trees tangled overhead. "I don't know. I thought, when I started seeing you and Emyr together…it was so obvious you were falling for him. I worried I was going to lose you."

"That isn't ever going to happen." I am a tiny homosexual and a raging piece of shit, but I know this fact for certain. "I *do* love Emyr. I love him in ways I wasn't sure I'd ever love someone." Ways that are both vulnerable and powerful, ways that I am still trying to understand, even for myself. "But I don't care if I'm with him every day for forever, if we get married and pop out a bunch of babies, if we spend the rest of our lives wildly and stupidly in love—it doesn't make you any less important to me. You're my—"

I don't actually know. I wave my hands between our bodies, trying to think of a word, trying to find out how to tell her the way I feel about her.

Maybe a word doesn't exist. Maybe no one has ever loved anyone in the *way* I love Briar.

Finally, I just say, "It's not like he's my boyfriend so now he gets the number one spot in my life. There are no spots. No one has a rank. He's my boyfriend and you're my best friend and I'm gonna have my claws in both of you as long as you'll let me."

Our eyes meet again. She stares at me, silently, for a long moment. And then chuckles. "Yeah, no. Like I said, I *worried* about that. I don't really, anymore."

"Oh." Well, then. "But if that's not the problem...what is? What changed?"

"Do you honestly not know?" Briar frowns at my obvious confusion. "*You* did."

I don't understand. "What are you talking about?"

"Wyatt, you're..." She waves a hand at me. Now *she's* the one struggling for words. "You came back to Asalin kicking and screaming, and planned to weasel out of your engagement and run away again as fast as possible. And instead, here you are, overhauling a kingdom. You're using your magic again, and you're healing things with Emyr and Tessa, and you're...

you're finally facing your demons. And you're *winning*." She reaches down to grab my hand, running her thumb along my knuckles. "It's a good thing. It just means you don't need me to take care of you anymore. And maybe that scares me." She takes a deep breath. "But that's on me to deal with. And I don't want you to think I'm not proud of you. Because I am. So proud of you."

I use my other hand to brush my fingers along the inside of her arm. When another tear drips onto my chin, I don't wipe it away. "I'm sorry I didn't realize what I was doing to you sooner."

"Yeah, well. I'm sorry I got upset when you stopped."

"And I'm sorry about what I said to Jin."

"Ah, yeah. No, that was pretty uncalled for." Briar tugs her hands away, making a face. "I mean, you're not exactly wrong? I'm not an idiot—that's obviously what they're doing. But... I'm also letting them."

I consider her for a long moment before letting out one startled, sudden laugh. "Briar, you're *fucked up*."

She blinks at me in shock before chuckling. "Now you see. This is my true form."

"Huh. Nice to meet you."

She rolls her eyes, but she's smiling. "Shut up."

We are disasters. Both of us. Whatever growing and improving Briar thinks I'm doing, I'm far from mentally or emotionally *stable*. But we have each other. And we'll keep choosing each other, and keep getting better, together.

"We should head back to the house before someone thinks you opened the door again." I push myself to my feet, and hold out a hand for her.

She takes it and hoists herself up. "That *does* sound like something I'd do."

Briar doesn't take her palm away, as we make our way side by side through Asalin's forest, back to the cabin.

When we step inside, I feel the exact moment her palm goes cold and clammy against mine.

Nadua is standing in the triad's living room. Next to her, Emyr is holding the baby, his face a tangle of concern. And gathered around them are a group of people that definitely weren't there when we left, most of whom I don't recognize. The three I do? Mary, Ari, and Kora.

"There you are." Mary puts her hands on her hips. "We need to talk."

CHAPTER NINETEEN

ASALIN WILL FALL

The other people in the living room are more changelings from Mary's village, and they've all come to deliver some terrible news. Because why not? It's not like we have enough going on.

"We realized something was happening in the kingdom soon after you left," Mary tells me, sitting down in the chair that Lorena offers her. "A bunch of unrest, whispers of the kings being rather unhappy with whatever you three said to them. We have some ears on the inside. And two days ago, we were informed of plans for a coup."

"A coup?" Didn't we do this already? I swear we did this already. Only, last time, it was just one cop and his shitty cop friends. Now it's a whole other kingdom. "You're saying Robin and Gordon are planning to take Emyr's Throne?"

"Take it—or help someone else take it."

Emyr and I meet eyes. He growls, and the baby's frenetic rainbow energy turns a violent shade of neon pink while she lets out a startled cry. With a guilty look, he shifts her into my arms, and says what we're both thinking. *"Wade."*

I look down at the whimpering newborn on my chest, and she blinks up at me. Nadua shakes a bottle in my face. Wondering when this became my life, I take it and put the nipple in her mouth. (Ha. *Nipple.*) When her energy shifts to that increasingly familiar chocolate shade, I tune back in to the conversation.

Someone must have asked who Wade is, because Emyr's in the middle of explaining. "—but things seem to be getting worse very quickly. Just yesterday, he *and* his mother made thinly veiled threats about taking control of the Throne."

In my pocket, one of the cell phones starts buzzing. I'm not sure if it's mine or Emyr's, but it doesn't really matter. Neither of us has time to talk. I reach in and reject it without checking.

"Hmm." Mary inclines her head, considerately. "I see. In any case, we got to you as quickly as we could. You extended an offer for an alliance. We are here to accept. It has been a long time coming that we finally come face-to-face with the fae. Whatever happens next, our people will stand with you."

"Thank you." Emyr dips his head at her. It almost looks like a bow.

I nod. "Yeah. And we'll do whatever we can to keep you safe."

"This is all very touching," Nadua pipes up. "But Briar and I are leaving."

"What?" Briar balks. "Mom? No, we are not."

"Yes, we are. And we're taking the baby. And Wyatt?" Our eyes meet. Nadua's stare burns into me, like a brand. I give the smallest shake of my head. "Yeah. Didn't figure I could convince you to come. But you—" she wheels on Briar "—don't have a choice. You've done enough. Things are about to go south here fast, and neither one of us is equipped to do anything to help."

"I—" Briar stumbles over her words. "I can do magic. Sort of."

"Briar." She turns her head to look at me, and she knows what I'm going to say before I say it, because I see her flinch the second before the words actually leave my mouth. "Stop trying to die for everyone else and save yourself for once." I shrug. "Besides, she's right. There's not much you can do."

My pocket buzzes again. I ignore it again.

The conversation turns to strategy. They're making plans. Something about bringing the changelings to the palace. Talking to Kadri. Bringing Wade in to demand answers.

I can't seem to focus on any of it.

Instead, I stare down at the baby in my arms and I think about her future. She's never going to remember anything that happened before tonight. The world, as she knows it, has yet to be made at all. It's endless potential, nothing more.

What happens next decides so much about what her whole world looks like. What her life looks like, and if she gets to have one at all.

"E's a beautiful creature." Zai's whisper is so close that it tickles my neck, and I jump. I didn't notice vaer creeping up behind me.

I glance back at vaer, frowning. "E?"

"Yes, the pronouns given to Faery children too young yet to pick their own." Vae's still staring over my shoulder at the newborn, big eyes wet, as if the very sight of her is enough to bring vaer to tears. "What is eir name?"

"Uh." How the fuck is she supposed to have a future without a name?

Instead of answering vaer question, I yank the (ringing, again!) cell phone out of my pocket, balancing the baby's bottle under my chin to do it. It's Emyr's. And it's Paloma Pereira on the other end.

"What do you want?! We're sort of busy!"

"Oh, little shadow, you're still alive." Paloma should *not* sound so relieved about that.

"Um. Yes? If you're open to constructive criticism, I really hate this new way of starting all your conversations."

When Paloma speaks next, her tone has taken on a warped, flat edge. It's like listening to a recording. Or a bot that's learned English from watching commercials. Which would maybe be funny, except it scares the shit out of me. And what she has to say doesn't help. "Asalin will fall. Tonight."

You know what the opposite of butterflies in your stomach is? Pixies in your chest. I can feel them, buzzing around behind my bones, snatching mouthfuls of muscle with their sharp teeth.

Somehow, my voice doesn't shake when I ask, "How do you know?"

"I have seen it unfold. She who walks in the in-between has already arrived. She is death disguised as a friend."

My eyes flit to Mary and my stomach bottoms out.

The in-between—half witch, half human?

Maybe we shouldn't trust these changelings after all.

"What do we do?"

"*Run.*" Paloma's voice drops to a terrible, scratching whisper. "Run—or else run out of time."

There's a shuffle on her end of the phone, and a second later, Maritza's voice comes through. "Wyatt?"

"Is she okay?"

"She's half here. Listen to me, we're on our way to you, but I don't know what's coming, and I don't know if we'll make it in time."

I don't know if they will, either.

We need to get Briar, Nadua, and the baby out of here.

"Thank you." I press the end button and slide the phone back into my pocket. My eyes find Emyr's.

His face has gone perfectly calm, even as his eyes rage and his golden energy crackles around the edges of my black. He heard the conversation, with his sensitive fae ears, and I have a feeling his mind has gone to the same place mine has. We can't be certain the changelings can be trusted.

I glance at Zai, and vae's still staring at the baby. If vae overheard anything, vae is either unbothered or is doing a damn good job at pretending to be. Tessa, to the side, is frowning at me, but gives a small shake of her head when we meet eyes.

Everyone else in the room is a witch or a changeling. None of them should have been able to overhear the conversation.

"Who was that?" Solomon asks, taking in whatever my face is doing right now.

I force myself to shrug. "Paloma Pereira. We were supposed to meet with her over video chat, but she's rescheduled. Not like we could fit it in today, anyway." Am I a good liar? I tried to become one, when I was conspiring with Derek. But I don't think I am. I swallow. "We should head up to the palace."

Roman, Solomon, and Zai stay behind. The group of changelings, Lorena, and Jin come with us, planning to meet with Kadri, and Briar and Nadua follow, planning to grab their shit and go.

There's some famous quote or something about best laid plans coming undone. I've never planned a single thing in my entire pathetic little life, so, if that's true, you'd think things would stop falling apart.

Wade's group is gathered in front of the palace again, blocking our way entirely. Somehow, we see them before they see us, our group still a ways down the cobblestone path. We duck into the trees to stay out of sight.

"Here." I tuck the baby back into Nadua's arms, leaning forward to brush my mouth against the fine hairs on top of her head. I kiss Nadua's cheek, too, and Briar's lips. "Go around to the western side. There's another way in. You'll come up near the dungeon. Grab whatever you can't leave without, and then get the hell out of Asalin. Don't take the main road. Go through the dragon field until you reach the border."

I think of Summanus, when he met Briar, the day we took him for our joy ride. The way he instantly accepted her. The dragons won't hurt these two. But they *are* loyal to the Throne, and they might keep Wade and the others away.

"Wyatt—" Briar starts, tears welling again.

"No. Jin?" I turn to them next. "Can you get them to the door? You know where it is, right?"

"Oh. Uh, yeah, of course." They nod, stepping forward,

motioning for Nadua and Briar to follow them. "Come on. I'll get you in safely."

"*Wyatt,*" Briar repeats, more insistent, and I wrap my arms around her as tight as I can.

"I love you." I push her away from me. "Now *go.*"

With one more devastated look from Briar and a fierce one from Nadua, they turn to leave.

"Oh, shit. Hey, Jin?" The three of them pause and turn to look at me. "Um. In case we both die and I never get another chance to say this? I'm sorry."

I don't know if I was *wrong* to say what I did, but I know I wasn't *right.* And I am trying to remember we are all just people, carrying our own luggage, backed into our own corners, and trying to survive. It was never my intention to give Jin another bag to carry.

"Yeah." They're looking right in my eyes, but they're not really looking at me at all. They're looking through me, maybe past me, maybe into me. "Yeah, I just, uh. I know she's your best friend, and you want to protect her. It's just, I guess… I thought *you and I* were friends, too."

Oh.

And then they leave.

And I watch them go.

And I wonder when I'm going to stop hurting people when I think I'm doing the right thing.

And I wonder when I'll stop saying goodbye to the people I love without knowing if it's the last time.

Mary is looking at me considerately when I finally turn back to the rest of our group. I raise my chin at her. "This is your last chance to back out."

It's Ari, of all people, who answers, with a guffaw of a laugh. "Please. Do we look like quitters?"

Kora, in an impossibly acidic tone, answers, "I sort of wish we looked like quitters."

But Mary shakes her head. "Lead the way."

And Emyr leads the way. He stands at the front of our group, flanked by Lorena and me, and makes his way up the rest of the path. It doesn't take long after we leave the woods for Wade's group to finally notice us. They start jostling each other, pointing and whispering.

Obviously, this is what they've been waiting for.

Finally, with a stretch of lawn still between us and them, we come to a stop.

Emyr exhales the most exhausted breath I've ever heard. "Hello again, cousin."

At the front of his group, Wade smiles. His eyes glance over the group of changelings behind us, but he barely reacts. He either doesn't care who they are, or he somehow already knows.

Because he knows them? *Death disguised as friends.*

When he doesn't actually say anything, though, Emyr continues, "I've been thinking about what you said, and I've come to realize you're right about one thing. I was cruel to shun you the way I did. We have always been able to work through things before, and I did not even give you the chance to do so this time. And for that, I am truly sorry."

Very slowly, Wade's head cocks to the side. He narrows his eyes.

Wondering what Emyr's getting at? Because same.

"But I will be even more sorry if you allow this one mistake on my part to send you down a path you can never come back from." Ah, there it is. "Walk away from this. Please. While you still can."

A few of the people gathered around Wade exchange glances, as if considering Emyr's words. *They* look more confused about who the strangers are than Wade does. And more concerned.

As for Wade himself? He blinks, taking in Emyr's very polite threat. And then he laughs.

When he does answer, it's to say, "It's funny. I was going to make you the same offer."

His response, and unfazed reaction to Emyr's words, ignites the crowd all over again. Their laughter joins his, and their energies spark with every sound, and I want to claw their faces from their skulls.

"You have made it clear to everyone you have no interest in *fairness*. You're a hypocrite and a fraud." Wade shrugs. "But as I said when we last spoke, I'm not unsympathetic to the position you're in. And I'm here to give you one last chance to do this peacefully. Acknowledge the damage you've already caused to this kingdom, and step down from the Throne. Or we will have no choice but to take what's ours by force."

"For fuck's sake, Wade!" I step forward, in front of Emyr. "Do you hear yourself? You've turned into your brother."

Wade startles out another laugh, reaching up to put a hand over his mouth while he delights in my comment. "Oh, I guess I have."

Freak.

Behind me, Emyr's voice is calm and even. It isn't raised to a shout, but it isn't whispered, either. He speaks like he and

Wade are having a conversation over the kitchen table. "You will become king of Asalin only by going over my corpse to do it."

"That can, as I'm sure you realize by now, easily be arranged." Wade slinks closer.

My black energy soars out on either side of me, a wall between Wade's group and mine. I know it won't keep them at bay. There's nothing I, or anyone else, can do to stop this fight from happening, not anymore.

But I like our chances well enough. Tessa's scary when she wants to be, and they don't know what I can do with my magic. They don't know what the changelings can do, either, assuming they really are on our side. If shit gets loud enough, others will come. Other witches, like Roman and Solomon, and Jin, and others from Lavender's group.

We'll be okay. Probably.

And that is the last optimistic thought I have before I register the sound of tires on cobblestone. Before I turn my head and see not one, but a *fleet* of cars, making their way through the village, crawling to a stop in front of the palace. From one, a driver jumps out and moves to the back seat, opening the door for his passengers.

I know who they are before I see them, but there is a part of me that clings to the hope it could be Paloma and Maritza.

Robin Bell steps out.

The kings of Monalai have arrived with an army.

CHAPTER TWENTY

A THREAT OR A PROMISE?

"Oh, Emyr, you sweet, naive boy." Robin Bell shakes his head, hands curling around the handles of his husband's wheelchair. "I wish it hadn't come to this."

It's oddly quiet in the courtyard, considering there are at least a hundred fae packed on the grass. The swarm of black cars carrying Monalai's Guard made a semicircle around us, filling in all the gaps where Wade's people weren't already. And now there's nowhere to go. And I don't know. I thought it would be louder, these few moments before we die.

Because we're definitely going to die, right?

Emyr tilts his head at the kings, one eyebrow rising. I try to read his mind for all the things he isn't saying out loud, and can't. Maybe it's very quiet for him, too.

What he *does* say out loud is, "How can you rationalize this? Even through a cloud of your own bigotry, there must be a part of you that knows this is wrong."

He sounds as eerily, uncannily calm as I feel.

It's like the day of the car accident. When I found Emyr, body contorted by Zai's invisible magic, and everything inside of me went sort of still. I'd spent so long *waiting* for the next time my boyfriend died, when it actually came, I'd used up a lot of my panic.

We've spent so long *waiting* for someone to try to rip the crown from Emyr's head, now that the Monalai kings are standing in front of us, we're not exactly going to start hyperventilating about it.

It's like, okay. Yeah. Congrats, you're overthrowing the government. It isn't original at this point. What else you got?

Gordon cuts his eyes at me, and the hand resting on his thigh curls into a gnarled fist. He looks like he wants to answer Emyr's question, but his husband does, instead.

"Difficult, yes. Painful, absolutely. But wrong? No. I know I am doing the right thing." Robin sighs, shaking his head sadly. "And I know it is hard for you to hear this, because I believe you've tried to be a good person, and a good king. I know you care about your people, Emyr. And, because you care about them, I hope, in the end, you will understand why we had to do this."

"Explain it to me, then."

He's stalling. I don't know *why*. We're so outnumbered that it's comical. What good would it do us to push our inevitable deaths back for a few more minutes?

I turn my head to consider the others at our back. The

changelings have gathered together in a small cluster, shoulder to shoulder, eyeing the Guards with unease. Mary's eyes don't leave Robin and Gordon, burning with a hatred so deep and sharp I wonder how they don't just drop dead from the weight of it.

If she's a liar, she's a damn good one.

Lorena sticks tight to Emyr's back, head high, expression vicious. They're going to kill him, I know. But I think they'll have to go through her first.

Tessa stands the farthest from us all. She's made her way to the bottom of the palace steps, chin tilted up to stare at Wade, hovering over her. I can't see the look on her face from here, but I wonder if she's pleading with him to stop.

He isn't even looking at her, though. He only has eyes for Emyr, staring holes into the back of my boyfriend's skull with those blazing blue eyes.

"You want to create a more fair world for the witches. And, on its surface, this is a considerate goal. But you have failed to realize, the world as it is, is already fair for the witches." Robin sighs, as if explaining this is exhausting. As if talking to a child. "True equality is not a possibility. They are *abominations*, son. Of course, they can't be blamed for the way they are. So, we can let them live peacefully. We don't have to cause them harm. But they should never be given the same power as our kind. They would only use it to abuse us, if they were given space in our sacred institutions. They simply don't know any better. And it is our responsibility to make sure that doesn't happen."

Emyr's ears twitch. "You must have been furious when my betrothal was announced."

Gordon flashes fang, and finally speaks. "Your mother certainly has an interesting way of going about things. Had you been our son, this never would have been an issue."

Had he been their son, he probably would have killed himself. Had *I* been their son, they probably would have killed me before I had the chance to.

Not that either of our actual dads were significantly better.

They keep talking, about Kadri, and the witches, and the sad, sad reality of what they're being forced to do. But I'm not listening anymore.

Emyr is stalling.

Robin Bell thinks I'm a *creature*. I remember the heads on the kings' wall. The other creatures, slaughtered for decoration. The selkie, her mouth frozen open in a never-ending scream.

These people, people like Gordon and Robin, like the Pierce family, like the fae who blew open the door to Earth to begin with because they didn't want to live in a world where witches were treated with respect, they're all just afraid. Because they see something different from themselves, and they're terrified of what that *thing* is going to do to them. They think, because their inclination is to hurt anything they don't understand, everyone else's instinct is the same. They think they'll get knocked down the hierarchy, because they can't understand the concept of a world where the hierarchy doesn't exist.

They say the witches don't know any better, but that's not true. They're the ones who don't know any better.

The world of fae and witches never needed to operate under the rules of eat or be eaten. Fae like these invented that, all on their own. It's why they feel so fucking threatened any-time witches get together to do anything. They can't sepa-rate the ideas of witch equality and witch supremacy, because they can't imagine a world where someone doesn't rule—and someone else isn't ruled.

And because of that, they treat us the way they do. And their treatment creates people like me. A boy forced to be-come a monster. No matter how hard I fight to become a boy again, there will always be a part of me that's a little hungry for their blood.

And they did that. They created their own worst fear.

The real problem is that no single one of them *is* the prob-lem. There's no Big Bad, no skin and bones villain to fight. We took out Derek and it didn't do anything. Even if we somehow made it out of today alive and killed the Bells, killed Wade, it wouldn't do anything. I can drink all the blood I want, but it's not going to undo hundreds of years of systemic violence. The system is the problem. The system is the Big Bad, and unfortunately, it doesn't bleed.

But it can still die.

Paloma's voice plays in my ear. *"Asalin will fall. Tonight."*

A threat or a promise?

They're still talking. My eyes flick to Emyr. His face is im-passive as he listens, collected on the surface, but I can see the tension in his shoulders. The way his hands tremble.

The pad of his thumb brushes against his other fingertips, and he repeats the motions over and over, stimming.

His gaze flits to mine, but only briefly.

Emyr is stalling.

"Run—or else run out of time."

Yes, we are going to die today—but only *if* we have to fight them. So we won't fight them. At least, we won't fight them today.

My hand slides into my pocket, brushing along the edge of the tarot cards. Any second now, the kings are going to grow tired of their monologuing and tell the Guard to move forward. Our only hope of this working is if we move fast.

And Emyr's been stalling, trying to buy me the time to figure that out.

As soon as I decide what I'm going to do, that eerie calming effect that's been hanging onto my brain evaporates. Everything feels louder, closer, more solid. It's like I step back into myself.

Robin Bell is still talking. This guy loves the sound of his own voice. "—and we will install a truly fair and benevolent leader, one who recognizes the need to keep a close eye on the population of witches, and who—"

Okay, that's enough of that.

I pull the card from my pocket with a flick of my wrist, and black magic explodes from it the second I do. It erupts in every direction, that obliterating darkness that overtakes everything it touches, ripping the world from sight. Even though the darkness doesn't come through me, I know this time that it comes *from* me. I can feel it, punching its way through my chest, down my arm and out of the card.

The Two of Swords.

An impasse. A difficult decision. And being unable to see all the possible consequences.

Shouting breaks out all around us, confusion overcoming

the crowd. I feel Emyr's fingers snatch the back of my shirt and start dragging me away.

He doesn't speak, and I can't see him, and it would be a great time for someone else to grab me and yoink me off to die. But I know Emyr in the warmth of his palm, and I know him in the way his claws press into my skin through fabric, and I know him in the unseeable but no less possessive press of his energy against mine. Without sight, through distance and time, even beyond death, Emyr and I reach for each other. I would recognize him anywhere.

He pulls me past wings and yanks me between armed Guards. By the time someone turns the sun back on, we're on the outskirts of the woods, and we've left most of the crowd behind. Emyr's got one fist tangled at my back, the other dragging Lorena by her arm. I search the crowd for signs of Tessa, but can't make her out.

My eyes catch Mary's for the briefest second, and she nods. And we turn and run.

Or, more accurately, *Emyr* turns and runs, yanking both Lorena and me off our feet when he does. He slings each of us over a shoulder as if we weigh nothing—which, okay. I might be a five-foot-two twink, but Lorena is stacked; this shouldn't be so easy—and starts booking it through the forest, ducking and dodging trees as he goes.

Lorena's head bounces up and down against his ass as he runs, and honestly, if we weren't racing the clock to escape our own almost-certain deaths, it would be hilarious. "We have to find the boys!"

I open my mouth to argue, but any arguing dies behind

my teeth. Emyr stops so abruptly that Lorena's and my heads knock together.

"Hey!" I blink dark spots out of my vision, while Emyr tosses us back to our feet. "Why'd you stop? We're not there yet."

"You're close, though." A fourth voice, familiar in its sharpness, joins the conversation.

A second later, Roman, Solomon, and Zai come through the trees to join us. The sound Roman looses at the sight of his girlfriend is terribly primal, and he reaches forward to curl a hand around her waist, dragging her close and pressing his forehead to hers. Solomon joins them, one hand on her back, the other on Roman's, and tilts his forehead in to join theirs.

"We saw the cars pass the house," he explains. "We knew things were about to go sideways. Somehow Roman knew where to find you."

Zai blinks at us expectantly. "I'm going home?"

"That was not the plan," I argue.

"How did you know we would be here?" Emyr bites back, looking at Roman.

He sighs, and tugs away from the other two. "Because what other fucking choice do you have?"

And he's not wrong.

Roman is an irritating bastard, but like recognizes like. The feral animals in our chests are the same breed. And he knows what happens when you back someone into a corner and force them to make an impossible decision.

The decision today wasn't even that impossible. Die quietly at the hands of Monalai's Guard. Or try something else and maybe die anyway. Only one of those comes with the *possibility* of survival.

"There's no time to argue." I shake my head and turn away from them. "Come on. If you can find us, so can they."

The door to Faery is exactly as it was earlier that morning. Holy shit, was it only this morning that I was here? Only what, two hours ago that I was sitting here with Briar, pouring our hearts out to each other? How is that possible?

I guess it's a good thing we cleared the air between us. Because I don't know if I'm ever going to see her again. At the thought, something knotted in my stomach forms a noose.

But I don't have time to dwell on this, either.

"How are you going to do it?" Solomon asks at my back.

I grit my teeth. "Sheer dumb luck." The only way I've accomplished anything, ever, in my life. I turn and face Zai. "Are you an Influencer?"

Vae frowns. "Our magic does not work that way."

We don't have time to deal with that, either.

"Fuck it. Just stand here and look pretty and think about home." I snatch vaer hand in mine, dragging vaer forward, toward the door.

The changelings said we can channel the fae, right? We're supposed to be able to use their energy, to let it fuel our magic. We don't have Tessa here to do whatever fae magic needs to be done, but maybe I can channel Zai. Maybe I can let vaer power boost mine.

It can't hurt—unless it can? I don't know, I'm making this shit up as I go.

I focus on the space where Zai's hand meets mine, where vaer bright energy is enveloped by my black. I imagine dragging it forward, pulling it into my body; imagine it floating in my blood. That's where the magic is, right?

And I don't know if it does anything, but I can't just stand around waiting for a sign. I pull another card from my pocket.

The Magician.

Forging ahead into new beginnings. *Ready or not, I guess.*

"Over here! I see them!"

My head snaps back at the sound of another voice calling out behind us. Trees begin to rustle. Monalai's Guards have caught up to us.

"Wyatt, NOW!" Emyr slams his hand down on my shoulder.

And I slam the card into the empty air of the door.

Black lines crack out across the space, spiking up out of the card and into the ground and the tree limbs surrounding it. Threads of orange and gold knot with the black, tugging at them, pulsing until they evaporate into a cloud of smoke. And suddenly Faery waits.

Monalai Guards burst into the clearing with us.

And, ready or not, we forge ahead into a new world.

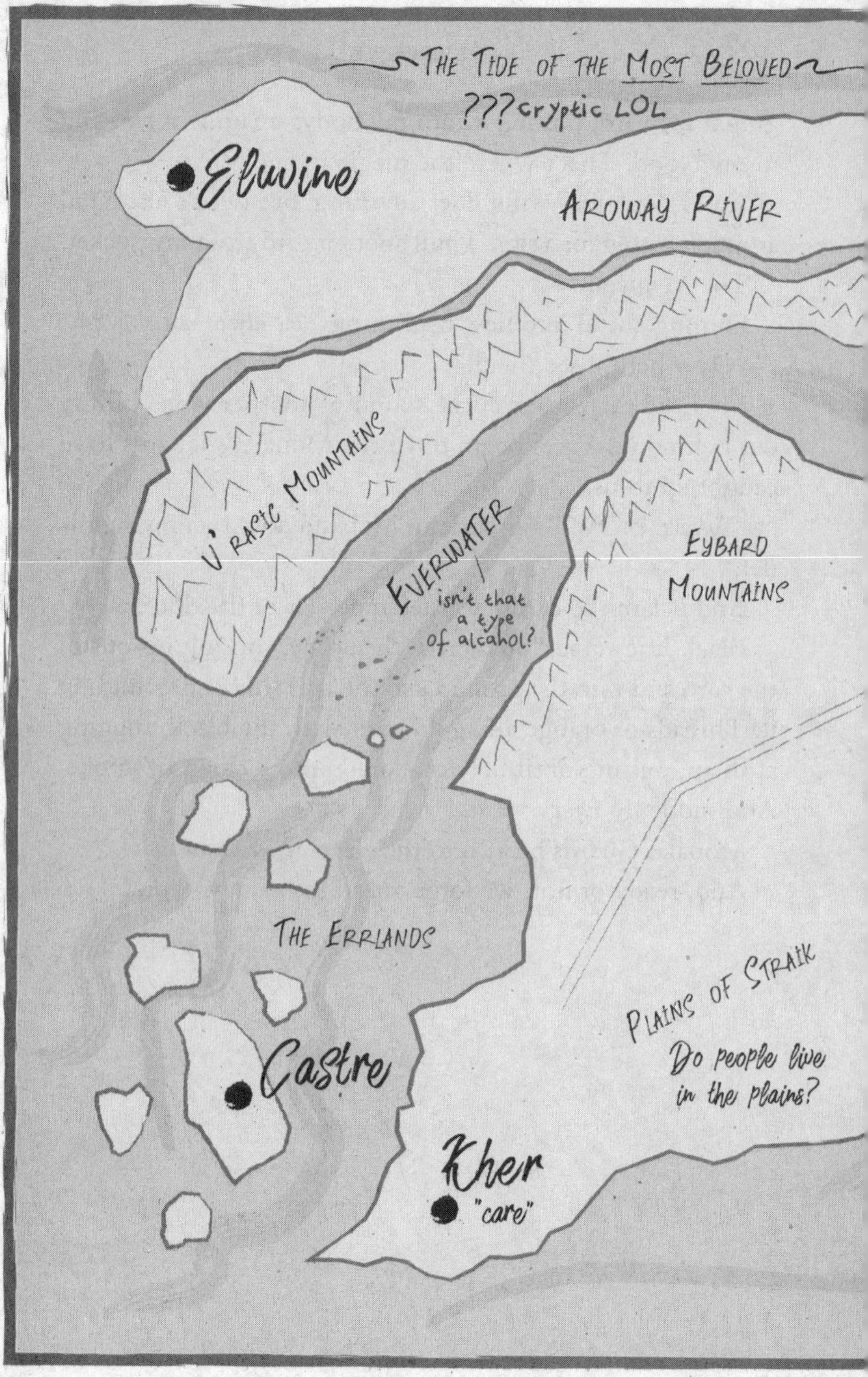
THE TIDE OF THE MOST BELOVED
???cryptic LOL
Eluvine
AROWAY RIVER
V'RASIC MOUNTAINS
EVERWATER
isn't that
a type
of alcohol?
EYBARD
MOUNTAINS
THE ERRLANDS
PLAINS OF STRAIK
Do people live
in the plains?
Castre
Kher
"care"

CHAPTER TWENTY-ONE

TAKE ME TO YOUR LEADER

Zai's promises of a lush green Faery were…bullshit.

We step through the door as easily as moving from one room to another. One moment I'm in Asalin's forest, breathing Asalin's air, with Monalai Guards breathing down my neck. And the next I'm standing on cracked, lifeless gray dirt, with an open pale pink sky overhead, painted in faded strips with orange and yellow clouds. A near-perfect sunset.

Emyr's hand is still on my shoulder, but Zai drops my hand. Vae takes a step forward, sweeping vaer arms out to either side. "Welcome home."

Home, in question, looks almost like an island. Almost. To our left, a dark sea stretches out as far as my eyes can see. Its waves slosh, gentle but relentless, against the shore. But to our right, around the curved edge of the island's shore, as the floor begins to drop lower and lower, where there obviously was once an ocean…is nothing. The water has dried up, leaving behind nothing but more of the same cracked gray dirt—with the skeletal remains of the creatures who used to live there embedded inside it. From here, I can make out what looks like a jaw, as big as I am, jutting from the ground. Behind Zai, in the distance, there seems to be a looming cliffside, its jagged edges erupting up and up and up.

I turn to look behind us, just as the triad steps through. "You stop to take a bathroom break before you followed us, or what?"

Lorena frowns from where she's tucked between Solomon and Roman's shoulders. "We came through right behind you."

Ah. Right. *Time.*

Where there are elm trees in Asalin, on this side of the door there are stone slabs, thick cuts of rock framing the open space between them. It reminds me of pictures I've seen of Stonehenge.

Looking through to Asalin's forest, from this side, feels… surreal, the uncomfortable disconnect between where I am and where I was making me feel a little dizzy, a little nauseated. I can see flashes of green, and maybe the vague shape of bodies, but not much more. It's like looking at the world through a pair of glasses with a bad prescription. I have to look away when my head begins to swim.

"Take us to your leader," Emyr demands of Zai, voice full of kingly authority. The hand on my shoulder still hasn't moved. I can feel it trembling.

Zai's sharpened teeth—looking at them still gives me the

worst of vibes—graze against vaer lower lip. Vaer eyebrows knot together, like vae isn't sure how to respond to that.

I open my mouth to ask what the problem is, but that's when the Monalai Guards finally come storming through the door after us.

"Fuck," Roman snarls, shoving Lorena and Solomon forward. He grabs a handful of dirt from his feet and tosses it toward the Guards' eyes. It sparks with the scarlet red of his energy, and sizzles when it makes contact with their faces, like it burns.

One of them, a thin man with a sharp face, surges toward Emyr with iron cuffs held in his black-gloved hands.

Emyr forgoes magic entirely and punches him in the face, fist connecting with his mouth with an ungodly crack. The Guard stumbles back and coughs out a mouthful of blood and broken teeth and *wow*, we're not going to unpack why that made me, somehow, gayer.

The other, a woman with broad shoulders and flaming red hair, swings her own length of iron chain, like a rope, and it wraps around Emyr's waist. He bellows in pain, golden energy stomped out by the iron, and hits his knees in the dirt.

My hands are on my cards before I realize I'm reaching for them. I throw the first one my fingers connect with, and it flies across the space between us, slicing across the woman's cheek and drawing blood. Black magic erupts from the cut, snakes of it like charred veins erupting across her cheek. She screams, reaching up to claw at her own skin, as my card floats back to me, sliding perfectly into the deck.

A third Guard bursts through the door just as I fall at Emyr's side, wrenching the chain from his waist with my fingers.

And then something *incredibly fucking weird* happens, which is saying something, considering the morning I've had already. Weird enough that all three of the Guards, and the triad, and Emyr and I, all turn to stare, practically frozen in place.

Zai flaps vaer velvety black wings, kicking up a dust storm around vaer body. And then lifts off from the ground. Vae *flies*, hovering in the air above us all, and stretches our vaer arms to either side of vaer body. Vaer neon energy begins to glow, brighter, and it spreads out like a halo framing vaer, moving for the first time. Vae lifts one open palm and thunder roars, loud enough to shake the earth beneath me. Lightning cracks in the clear pink sky, and vae *snatches it from thin air*, and sends it hurtling toward the chest of the newest arrival.

It slams into him, knocking him off his feet, but his body has turned to a blackened crisp before he ever hits the ground.

Everyone seems to remember themselves as soon as he falls. The thin Guard leaps for Emyr again, and Emyr surges to his feet. He snatches the sword from his back, wrenching it free from its sheath. It swings out in a wide arc, and the Guard's head disconnects from his body. It hits the ground and rolls away before the rest of him finally hits his knees.

Roman and Solomon each grab one of the woman Guards' arms, and Lorena wraps her hands around her jaw. There is a sickening kind of crack, and then the woman's body slumps forward, crumpling into a heap when the boys release her.

Zai lands back on the ground. I push myself to my feet.

After a beat, Emyr breaks the sound of our mingled, heavy breathing, by demanding, "You must show me how to do that."

I've always heard rumors that the fae were able to fly once.

That they could, in Faery. But I was never sure it was true. Apparently, it was.

Zai's words have hinted this whole time that witch magic isn't the only thing we don't entirely understand. That fae magic, too, operates under a different set of rules here in Faery. And that has to be true, because I've never seen *anyone* who could do *any* of the things vae just did.

Vae opens vaer mouth to respond to Emyr, but then, pointed ears twitching, turns to look over vaer shoulder, instead.

I follow vaer line of sight to the winged figures bustling our way.

"Zai?" A soft feminine voice calls out.

"Elonia!"

"Zai!"

Vae races away from us, toward one of the people now rushing forward to meet vaer, practically leaping across the cracked landscape of the desert island. The two collide halfway between our group, wrapping their arms around one another.

Emyr and I exchange a look, and move to follow Zai, the triad at our back.

The voice in question belongs to a petite fae with big strawberry-pink wings and brown hair in a long braid down her back. She nuzzles her face into Zai's neck, her horns—like reef coral along her hairline—jutting up beneath vaer jaw.

Emyr clears his throat at the display and repeats his earlier command, "Take me to your leader," just as the rest of the fae approach.

While they are different in many ways—ages, and genders,

and skin colors—the group is all dressed similarly, the same way Elonia is, in sheer black robes, more so just draped over their bodies than anything else. I can catch glimpses of their bare skin when they shift in certain ways, and they're all as scarred as Zai, too.

And they all have those fucking *teeth*.

"We have no leader," an older fae, with long gray hair and an even longer beard, shakes his head. "We are the Watchers. And you are King Emyr, from Lacuna."

"Lacuna?" I raise my eyebrows.

Zai curls an arm around Elonia's waist, beneath her pink wings, and turns back to me. Vae motions at the door in answer to my question.

Interesting.

"I am happy to see you've made it back to us, Zai," another of the Watchers says, their words slow, as if carefully chosen. Their eyes move across the triad, before settling on me. "All this time, we have hoped you would. But the congregation you have brought with you is unexpected. Why would you bring a Pierce here?"

The other Watchers, the ones who have not spoken, only stare at us. That same reverence I saw in Zai's stare, the day we met, is clear on their faces, mingled with a hint of fear.

Zai does not take vaer hands off Elonia to answer, "Emyr is not the same as the others in his line. He is mirrored to a witch." Vae inclines vaer head at me. "Wyatt."

The Watchers whisper amongst themselves. Elonia stares at me, brown eyes huge.

Zai continues, "Conditions for the witches only continue to worsen on the other side. These problems run even deeper than we realized, last you bore witness to it. I cannot even begin to detail the horror of it all without feeling ill."

That's...like, I'm torn between wanting to roll my eyes at Zai's dramatic-ass wording and feeling oddly validated.

Collectively, the Watchers seem to hiss and grumble.

"A war has broken out between those who seek to make things right, and those who would continue to abuse the witches. Emyr and his allies stand on the side of righteousness, but their defeat is nigh. It is our sacred duty to offer them what aid we can."

"We've bought ourselves time by coming here," Emyr adds. "As minutes pass in your world, seconds tick by in Asalin. You must take me to speak with Faery's ruler."

The gray-haired fae exchanges a look with the others. He takes a deep breath, and nods. "We will escort you across The Unsea to meet the one you seek."

"*You* will escort them," Elonia snaps, her grip on Zai's torso tightening. "Zai is staying here, with me."

"As you wish." The older man looks up at the pink and orange sky, and nods. "Night will fall soon. I will take you now." He looks at the others. "Prepare to enter Lacuna once more upon our return. The time has finally come to fulfill our most holy mission."

There is something incredibly *not great* about those words. Goose bumps scatter along my arms, crawling up my neck, whispering warnings in my ear in a language I don't speak. I ignore them, because I have no other choice.

Emyr and I follow right behind the fae as he turns and heads in the direction of the dried-up ocean on one side of the island. Roman and Lorena follow behind us. I see Solomon hesitate, standing in front of Zai and Elonia. Zai says something I can't hear, reaching up and touching the side of Solomon's face when vae does. Finally, Solomon rushes to catch up to us.

The incline is steep, the land dipping lower and lower as we move deeper into what was once water. It's going to be a pain in the ass to walk *up* this on the way back, but right now I'm choosing to ignore that. The skeletal remains of ocean creatures appear more frequently, somehow growing bigger the deeper we go. As we pass a rib cage big enough to be a house, I shiver.

But it isn't nearly as horrific as the selkie skeleton curled up next to it. My mind buzzes, and my stomach aches. I can't look away until we've walked too far to see it anymore.

"What's your name?" Roman asks of the Watcher, breaking up the silence.

He turns to look at us over his shoulder, seemingly startled to be addressed at all. After a moment, he supplies, "Cavenia."

Solomon pipes up, "How can you speak English, Cavenia?"

"English?"

"The words we are literally using to communicate right now." I wave a hand between us.

"Here, this language is known as the Low Tongue." Cavenia turns away from us, continuing to walk. "Those who study the depths of the cosmos believe your Earth is one of the closest worlds to our own. That is how the apostates were able to construct Lacuna and journey there. It is not surprising we would share similarities in our evolution."

Huh. Wait. "Worlds? Like...there's more than just Faery and Earth?"

"I imagine the number is infinite," Cavenia answers, as if that's totally normal.

Which, I guess, to him, it is.

We trek in silence for a while longer, the only sounds our breathing and the rattling of Emyr's sword as it bounces against his back. Overhead, the sky continues its transformation from that pale pink to a dark plum. Stars begin to appear, luminous white beacons across the horizon. They feel closer, brighter than the stars back home.

That isn't the only difference I've noticed. Something about the air here feels...well, I don't know how to explain it, really. It's *crunchy*. It's crisp when it hits my lungs, like... McDonald's Sprite.

I guess I never realized the air I was used to breathing felt so thick until I was breathing air that wasn't. I have no idea what it means, though, if anything.

Emyr's hand reaches out to find mine, inexplicably, at exactly the same moment I reach for his. My thumb brushes along his knuckles, naked of his usual assortment of jewelry. He's still dressed down, slouchy, in another pair of jeans and a T-shirt. Even *I* know he's underdressed for the occasion. His thumb claw presses into the back of my hand, all thin bones and veins, and I inhale sharply at the subtle hint of pain.

He breaks our quiet to ask, "Zai refers to Wyatt and me as mirrors. Where we come from, we call bonded pairs mates. Where does your terminology come from? Why *mirrors*?"

Cavenia frowns, looking back at us. "Why mates?"

"Because...that is what we are." Emyr glances down at me, like he's looking for backup. He is absolutely not getting it on this point. He looks back to Cavenia and shrugs. "We are biologically compatible. That's why the bond exists."

Cavenia stops short, so suddenly that Emyr and I almost run into his back, and Lorena *does* run into mine. We all stumble to a stop while our wizard-looking tour guide whirls around to face us, his black robes billowing around him when he does.

"Biologically compatible?" he demands. "You believe you are brought together to *breed?*"

Emyr winces. "Ah… No?"

"That's what we're taught about the bond," I throw in. "Is it not true?"

"That's—I cannot believe—well, you know what, I *can* believe it—obsessed with their own bloodlines, fanatics, all of them, I—" Cavenia rubs a hand over his face and groans. "I suspect this is a story concocted by those who founded your Asalin. I cannot tell you for certain what their aim was, as I was not there to witness this unfold, but I can tell you these fae were hysterical with the idea of maintaining a future for fae children. They believed the arrival of the witches meant the coming downfall for their own. Likely, this false belief about *mating* was instilled to encourage future generations to procreate, so you might continue building the fae utopia they so desperately sought."

Huh. It's *gross*, but I can see where it makes sense. Kinda backfired on them, though, when Emyr's bond was with a witch. Guess the founding bigots didn't think that through super well.

"If it's not about genetics, what *is* the bond?" Solomon asks, stepping forward with his forehead wrinkled in thought.

"This sacred fellowship exists between two people who are

one another's perfect mirrors. A reflection of all they are, and all they hope to be. These unions allow both parties to grow to their fullest potential. It is a beautiful and sacred thing."

"Yeah...we're definitely just told it's about getting married and making babies," I counter, even as something warm and liquid slips through me. Emyr, my perfect mirror. Everything I am, and everything I want to be. It isn't wrong.

Cavenia scoffs with disgust. "To equate them to romantic unions, or parental partnerships, would be to diminish their value. Certainly, they *can* become these things, but it is not inherent to what they are."

"What happens to a person if they deny it?" Emyr asks, tone soft. "If they walk away from the bond?"

"Should a person turn from their mirror, they will never know themselves for who they truly are. Should they do the unthinkable and *shatter* their mirror, they will be doomed to become the most warped and broken version of themself."

My eyes meet Emyr's and I know we're both thinking the same thing. I squeeze his hand. *Clarke.*

"What happens to the one who's shattered?" Emyr asks, looking away from me to consider Cavenia.

The older man shrugs. "They can heal, with enough time and hard work. But there will forever be something just a touch wrong about them."

Thinking about Jin makes my stomach hurt.

"If these relationships are so damn important," Lorena begins, "why can't witches feel them? Fae can bond to us, but not the other way around. Why?"

Cavenia stares at her, unblinking, for a too-long moment. Finally, "What?"

"We don't feel whatever it is that you feel," she repeats. "Why?"

"Why would you believe you *don't*?" I don't know exactly what look he sees on our faces, but Cavenia gnashes his sharpened teeth in frustration. "Of course, in a world that refuses to teach you of your own magic, why would you be taught the truth about your bonds?" He sighs, hard. "There is much to say on this subject, and we really should continue on before night drags deeper. But the brunt of it is this—fae magic is not just innate, but it is ever present, always taking from the world around it. Our magic never goes dormant, and this allows us to more immediately feel the bonds for what they are. A witch's magic is equally innate, but it must be practiced with intention. When a witch channels the energy of their mirror, when their magic flows together, in union through their body, only then are they able to experience the full weight of this connection."

And then he turns and continues stomping across the open floor. The five of us exchange glances of mixed confusion and wonder, before hurrying after him.

If any of this is true...hmm.

I *knew* the baby-making line was bullshit. There were so many holes in that story, it didn't even begin to add up. Only through generation after generation of some serious brainwashing could the fae have managed to keep spewing such an obvious lie.

But I wonder if I could really feel whatever it is that Emyr feels. All our lives, since that first day he laid eyes on me, I've wanted to know what it feels like, for him. I've wanted to understand that look he sometimes gives me, hungry and cut open all at once.

Cavenia is right; now's not the time to dwell on this. But we'll come back to it.

Ahead, I see a sharp cliff appear in the distance. The closer we get, the sharper it appears. It's as if the earth takes a sudden step. One moment it's flat beneath our feet and then, inches forward, it's a wall of dirt, covered in vines, looming a mile above our heads.

When we stop in front of the wall, Cavenia holds his arms open. "We will carry you up. Two of you with me, two of you with Emyr."

"I can't fly," Emyr argues, giving a quick shake of his head.

Cavenia eyes him up and down, considering his leathery wings. "Yes, you can."

Oh, okay.

Solomon wraps an arm around the man's neck with little hesitation, pressing his body against his side. Lorena frowns, and then looks to Roman, waving her wrist out toward him. Roman scowls. She shrugs and moves forward, sliding onto Cavenia's other side, opposite Solomon.

And just like that, the Watcher begins to flap his wings. And just like that, he rises into the air, drifting up the cliffside, carrying our friends with him.

"For fuck's sake," Roman snarls. He moves behind Emyr and plants his hands on his shoulders, looking every bit the part of a man who hates his life. "Well, come on then."

"I *cannot* fly," Emyr repeats, enunciating hard on every word.

"I don't even see you trying," Roman counters.

"What's the worst that happens?" I slide in front of him, so we're nearly chest to chest, tipping my head back so I can look up into his elegant, monstrous face. "You embarrass yourself? I do that constantly."

Roman huffs out an agreement.

Emyr sighs. His big hands find my waist and he drags me closer, until our stomachs press together, until I can feel the press of his body against my hips. He does not say anything about me embarrassing myself, but he doesn't need to, because we both know it's true.

Slowly, his own wings begin to move. Up and down. Up and down. They begin to kick up dirt from the ground below us, and I close my eyes, tipping my head forward to press my face into his chest.

I can hear his heartbeat, an even, steady thrum. *Boom... boom...b-b—*

His heart stumbles over itself, and my feet are no longer touching the ground, and when I open my eyes, we're lifting up into the air.

Roman's hands tighten on his shoulders. "Holy shit."

Yes, that.

As we rise higher and higher, I can do nothing but laugh, quietly, into the underside of Emyr's jaw. "You're doing it."

He isn't looking at me. A mixture of shock and something like rapture plays out across his face.

He is the most beautiful thing I've ever seen.

After a moment, we reach the top of the wall. Emyr stumbles a little on the landing, knocking Roman from his back, but his hands tighten around my waist, keeping me upright until my feet are back on the ground again.

"See," Cavenia says, waiting there on the cliff's edge with Solomon and Lorena. "I told you."

While Emyr processes...that, I survey the spot where we've just landed.

Zai's promises about Faery being lush and alive? Maybe actually not a lie after all.

Because *everything* up here is green. The starlight overhead is just bright enough that I can still make out the sprawling scenery unfolding in front of us. Trees taller than anything I've ever seen, fields of wildflowers stretching on and on.

There are buildings, too, but they're not like anything on Earth. They're built right into the layout of the land, not disrupting anything to make space for themselves. There are homes nestled into the giant limbs of the trees, and tucked into massive tangles of flowers. Cavenia has led us to a massive door carved directly into a sloping hillside.

There are people moving around, still finishing up their days. Witches and fae move together, intermingling without concern. They've set up in what appears to be some kind of town center, gathered around a natural pool of water, where children splash.

It isn't only witches and fae, either. Pixies dart in the air. A goblin helps a young fae patch a hole in the tree branch roof of their home. The sight of a hellhound with her two pups makes my heart ache for Boom, back in Asalin.

"Oh my god," Lorena gasps, her head tilted up toward the sky.

I follow her line of sight and *oh my god*.

Overhead, floating islands dot the sky, their undersides made of roots that hang loosely toward the ground. I can barely make out the greenery peeking over the edge on top. One of them has a waterfall flowing off the side, and the water seems to turn to mist before it reaches anyone below. The islands look small from here, as high up as they are, but I know they must be huge. Know, because I can see dragons lounging on *all of them*.

For a moment, I think about the dragons in Monalai. My stomach hurts.

Behind us, I can make out the island we came from in the distance, the colossal divot of an empty ocean stretched between us. This far above it, I realize the island is shaped like a near-perfect crescent moon. Weird.

And then, "There you are," says the single most unsettling voice I've ever heard. It sounds like a thousand voices speaking all at once, a chorus of all kinds of people stacked over top one another.

I turn and my stomach drops.

Standing there, in front of the door carved into the hillside, with her hundred eyes, and fiery wings, and row after row of razor-sharp teeth, is the goddess Vorgaine.

CHAPTER TWENTY-TWO

HATE CAN BUILD AN EMPIRE, BUT ALL EMPIRES FALL

I've always found looking at Vorgaine to be incredibly uncomfortable. There's a statue of her in the village in Asalin, and a carving of her on the front of the palace. She's horrifying to look at, even when she's made from stone. In person, it's even worse.

"You—" Emyr begins, and then trips over his own tongue, something like frantic confusion warping his face.

How exactly does someone go about addressing a literal goddess? Is there even a right way?

"What are you doing here?" I demand.

Okay, well, there may not be a right way, but there's definitely a wrong way, and I landed face-first on top of it.

While Emyr stares at me like I've just, I don't know, insulted a goddess, Vorgaine herself...uh, laughs? I *think* that's what it is, but the sound of her voice (voices?) makes the whole thing feel very uncanny valley.

Thank you, I hate it.

"Where would you expect me to be?" she asks, folding her hands in front of her. Her claws are...oh, no, those aren't claws. Her fingers are just ridiculously long, with lethally sharp points at the ends. Very cool and normal.

"Uh. I don't know. Aren't gods normally off in some god space doing important things?"

All of her eyes blink at once and it is revolting and oh my Her I'm going to be sick. "I breathed this world into life, Wyatt. What could be more important than living within it?"

You know, I don't really know what to say to that.

It must be true, that she's just *here*, living like a *person*, that the people of Faery don't find this to be completely and totally bizarre, because no one has spared any of us more than a second glance. If a goddess started walking around on Earth...

Well, probably no one would even notice there, either. But for different reasons.

I glance over at the others to gauge their reactions. Lorena's face has gone *purposefully* blank, like she's trying very hard to have no reaction at all. Her eyes are bugging, though. Solomon looks awestruck, lips parted, head tipped back with something like reverence.

Why is Roman looking Vorgaine up and down like he's checking her out? I cannot take him anywhere.

"You know who he is?" Emyr asks, and I look away from Roman to tune back in to the conversation. I didn't even clock that she said my name until he does.

I guess it just didn't strike me as weird. I don't know what the limits on a goddess's powers are, but caller ID seems like child's play.

Vorgaine tilts her head, and her eyes move over our group. "I know who you all are. And I know why you've come. Cavenia, thank you for bringing them to me. I will take it from here."

"Of course." The Watcher steps back, toward the edge of the cliffside. "I will prepare the others."

"Do," she agrees.

And Cavenia falls backward into the air, disappearing from sight. I know he's okay, I saw him fly up here. But it still makes my ass twitch.

"Please, come inside. We've many things to discuss, I'm sure." She steps back and presses her palm against the doorway, pushing it open to reveal the home inside.

Emyr and Solomon move immediately. Lorena hesitates for only a moment before walking after them. Roman and I exchange a look before he grits his teeth and moves ahead. I walk in last, the goddess closing the door at my back.

The inside of the hillside home is oddly shaped, but I guess that makes sense, what with it basically just being a hole in the dirt. It's like a large dome, with tunnels breaking out on all sides of it, hallways leading to, I guess, other parts of the house. The ceiling is made of packed dirt, held upright by entwined roots, overgrown, thick and knotty.

It's far less over-the-top than I would have expected. There's a simple kitchen at the back, and a big table in the center, with carved wooden chairs. On one wall, there is a shelf of books, and on the other, a massive map of Faery itself.

"Can I——" Emyr begins, his hands twitching as he stares at the map.

As if reading his mind—and maybe that's exactly what she's doing—Vorgaine pulls a piece of paper and a long raw-wood pencil from one shelf, and hands both to him. He starts to copy the map down, eyes moving from it to the page, a sort of frantic energy overtaking him.

"You said you know why we're here," Solomon begins, dragging my attention to him and away from Emyr. He's staring at Vorgaine with the kind of intensity that burns. "Do you hear us when we pray to you from the other side? We are told—" He clears his throat. "We are told you cannot hear the prayers of witches."

"I do not hear your prayers," Vorgaine agrees, and Solomon's shoulders slump. "But not because you are witches. I cannot hear you because you were *stolen* from me."

"Really?" There is something like childlike longing stuck in Solomon's throat.

"You are my most beloved children, and you were taken from the safety of your home and carried to a world where I could not reach you. There is no anguish that compares to what I have felt for you, all this time."

It strikes me as weird, in hindsight, that the people of Asalin would build monuments for Vorgaine, and then actively, viciously go against everything she actually stands for. But maybe it shouldn't. If I learned anything about religion in the human world, it's that a lot of people love the shield of a god more than they'll ever love the god themself.

"But I always knew you would return home one day. When Leonidas arrived, I hoped he would come to me and confess the sins of his ancestors. That he would lay his weapons down and come home, where he, too, belonged. That he would bring my lost witches home, alongside him. It broke my heart anew when that did not come to pass." She sighs a hundred sighs. "But still, I knew it was only a matter of time. And now, here you are."

Here we are.

"Our world is falling apart," Lorena whispers, shaking her head. "In more ways than one."

"I knew it would." Vorgaine reaches out one terrible hand and touches Lorena's cheek. "Hate can build an empire, but all empires fall."

"You'll help us?" I ask. "You'll come to Earth and fight with us?"

"No." Vorgaine shakes her head, turning to me and letting her touch fall from Lorena. "I am Faery, and Faery is me. It is how I knew you the moment you stepped through from Lacuna. You became a part of me, as you were always meant to be. But I do not exist beyond this place, and I cannot go with you. Could I, I would have done so a thousand times over. Instead, in the morning, I will ask the citizens of Ra'Ora who is willing to stand beside you and aid in ushering in a new era. An era where the door between worlds may stand open, where my children may come and go freely, as they wish. And an era in which they are safe, wherever they are, whoever they are."

Ra'Ora? I look at the map. Yeah, I guess that'd be this place we're in. I nudge Emyr, shoving gently at his shoulder, and he glances up at me.

"Are you listening?"

"Yes. We'll return to Asalin in the morning." And he goes back to his work.

My knowledge-hungry boy.

"Are we sure that's wise?" Lorena asks. "Things had gone to hell when we left. They're only going to get worse."

"I am told time, there, moves quite slowly. You are all badly in need of a rest. There is no reason to rush, exhausted, into a fight that can wait for you." Vorgaine opens her palms, gesturing between us. "By the time you return, only minutes will have passed in the other world. And, were you willing to give up hours more, I could gather more of your allies, from all across Faery."

"No." I shake my head, not offering anyone else a chance at answering. "We'll stay one night."

Minutes, I can rationalize, but even that leaves me feeling guilty. Getting to stay here, in this goddess's hole-in-the-wall home, while *Briar* is an entire world away, possibly in danger. Getting to rest while there is a war raging, even if I'm only missing minutes. There's no way I can stay longer than that.

Vorgaine nods. I have a feeling she knew that would be the answer before she ever made that suggestion. She turns back to the triad. "You are tired. Shall I show you to your room?"

Lorena and Solomon exchange a glance, but Roman nods. Vorgaine motions for them to follow, and the four of them disappear down one of the tunnels.

I flick Emyr's earlobe with my middle finger and he shoots me a dirty look. "Yes?"

"You too good to make conversation with the *mother* of your species?" I am not used to being the one to scold Emyr for behaving inappropriately. Actually, the role reversal is not at all appealing to me. But still. "This is kind of a once-in-a-lifetime shot here."

"Exactly." He sets his own hand-drawn map on the table, but only to move to the shelf and pluck down a weathered old

book. "I don't know that we'll ever be back here. If things in Asalin don't go our way...we need to collect this information, for our allies who survive. Think of how different our lives would have been, if we'd known any of these things before now."

Well. I guess he has a point.

When I'm rude to important people, it's just because I have no social skills. It does not shock me that when Emyr does it, it's because he wants to save the world or whatever.

Vorgaine appears again, this time alone. She pulls out a chair at the table and sits, hands in her lap. I hesitate for a moment before doing the same.

"So...you're sure about the time thing?"

She nods, but doesn't speak.

"Huh. So, wait, you guys are like...thousands of years ahead of Earth then, right? I mean—" I try to do some mental math and fail, laughably, miserably, because obviously I do. "I mean, I guess I've always imagined Faery as being this primitive place, 'cause that's the kind of story the fae always told. But you're basically living in the future. Shouldn't you have..."

I struggle to think of a proper reference point. Vorgaine appears unbothered by my stumbling. Though, I don't think I'm of enough interest to bother a goddess, anyway. She blinks those too-many-fucking-eyes at me and continues staying quiet.

Finally, I finish, "I don't know, flying cars or something?"

Her eyes move in unison as they sweep over my face with consideration. Dislike. "You are asking why our technology is not more advanced?"

She knows the answer to the question. I can *tell* she knows. It kind of reminds me of talking to Kadri, actually. Like the way I *decide* to answer is actually more important than her *knowing* the answer.

I've always hated these mind games, but I extra hate it right now because I'm pretty sure the goddess could kill me with a single unpleasant sigh if she really wanted to. I glance away from her to look at Emyr. Who is absolutely not fucking helpful, still standing over by the books, now with a whole stack of them shoved under his arm. The brilliant, irritating, perfect jerk. I look back at Vorgaine.

"Yes?" Oh god, oh shit, I should sound more sure than that. I add, quickly, "Faery is beautiful. Don't get me wrong—I'm very impressed. Five stars. Uh, it's just very Nature Reclaims The World around here is all. You'd think by now you'd have managed *the internet*, at least. Right? Humans got that shit down like a hundred years ago."

I have absolutely no idea when the internet was invented, but what does time mean to someone like her, anyway?

Someone like her. Right, because there's so many of them.

"Hmm." She's smiling, and I do not like it. Her smile is worse than her eyes, all jagged teeth and black gums. And then she chuckles, and gives the smallest, most condescending shake of her head. (Can it be condescending if she's a literal deity? Doubtful.) "It's true, Faery does not have the internet. Nor cars, flying or otherwise. But our air and water are clean. Our people are nourished, body and mind. And all of my children, from the largest dragon to the smallest pixie, are protected from those that would seek to harm them. Perhaps, Wyatt, you should consider that this world is not primitive. It is your own ideas of progress that need to catch up."

Well, fuck me, I guess.

"Would you like something to carry those in?" she asks,

looking beyond me to Emyr, now struggling with his pile of books. "You may take as many as you'd like."

He balks, bashful, but nods. "Yes. Thank you."

She nods. "You are welcome to anything in my home. It is as much yours as mine."

He turns back to his books and Vorgaine turns back to me. I try not to shrink under the scrutiny.

"You've more questions. Feel free to ask them."

The one pressing at the back of my tongue feels so close to groveling that it actually makes me gag. I don't want to ask her. But there's something in me that needs to know anyway, that's desperate to.

"You know me as Wyatt," I say finally. "You know my name. What about my...my old name?"

The goddess tilts her head to one side. "Wyatt is who you are. Perhaps you were once addressed by something else, but it was not you. I've no reason to know that mistake."

She doesn't know my deadname. I'm sitting here at a dining room table with a goddess and she doesn't know my deadname because it doesn't matter to her.

I take a deep breath. "You see me as a boy?"

Something like a frown presses into the corner of her mouth. "I think your ideas of gender are confusing."

"Faery doesn't have trans people?"

"Faery is not arrogant enough to assume we know anything about our children before they've a chance to learn it for themselves." She shakes her head. "There are as many genders as there are people. And each one of them comes into the language they'd like to use for themself, in their own time."

Emyr has tuned back in to the conversation. He joins us at the table, setting down a massive stack of books, and then settling a hand over my knee. "Why would our ancestors, the ones who came through the door, shy away from that? Why adopt human ideals?"

If Briar were here, she would remind us that Asalin didn't adopt human ideals but *colonizer* ones. I bite my tongue, though, because that's really not the point. Not right now, anyway.

"In part, I suppose things were different at the time of the Great Undoing. Perhaps our ideas of gender were more limited, at that time," Vorgaine considers, nodding slowly. "But it goes beyond that. I have learned things of your world, fragments from the minds of those who have stepped foot in both places." She *can* read our minds here! "And I believe these fae have evolved only so much as it allows them to gain power. They witnessed for themselves the power structures in this human society, and they took what they could, any time it meant making themselves stronger. Ideas about gender and sex, race—these things were never part of our world, but they accepted human influence if it meant accepting they were better than someone else. They created capital for the same reason."

"The fae on Earth don't have capital cities, either." I frown. "I mean, like, Asalin is kind of a capital, I guess. It has the door."

"*Capital,*" Emyr presses. "Money."

"I'm sorry, *what*?" I shoot up straighter in my seat. "Faery doesn't have *money*?"

"That can't be true." Emyr shakes his head, reaching into his pocket. He grabs a green velvet wallet, opening it up. Behind the credit cards and cash is a pouch of fae coins. He shakes them out onto the table between us. "This is Faery money."

Vorgaine makes a face of disgust. "It certainly is not."

"You have got to be joking." If she tells me that the Pierce family's ancestors and their little cult invented fae capitalism just so they could win at being rich, I am going to have an aneurysm.

She shrugs one shoulder in an upsettingly normal gesture. "What use does anyone have for this sort of thing? Why must we make a game of exchanging useless little trinkets for the things we need, when there is plenty to go around?"

The Pierce family's ancestors and their little cult totally invented fae capitalism just so they could win at being rich.

I slump back in my seat and stare at the ceiling. I'm going to be sick. I hate it here. And by here, I mean there.

The three of us sit in relative quiet for a long moment after that. Vorgaine seems happy to let Emyr and me stew on everything we just learned.

Finally, once I pick up my oozing brain and shove it back in my skull, I ask, "One more thing." Because I need to go to *bed*, now worse than I did a minute ago. But I need to ask this first. "How do I channel Emyr's energy?"

He turns to look at me, and the hand on my thigh squeezes.

"Cavenia says I can feel the bond from his end, but I have to channel him to do it. How do I do that?"

"You have already done it." She raises one of those terrifying hands and motions between us. "When you brought him back from the dead."

What? "What?"

Vorgaine taps her eerie fingers against the tabletop. "I can see the mark of his energy in your blood, Wyatt. And Emyr, Wyatt's is anchored within you. It is clear to me that your magic nearly faded. That you were almost snuffed out—from all worlds. But Wyatt brought you back." She tilts her eyes toward me, all at once. "And you did that by tapping into his power."

I remember it clearly, more than I'd like to. The feeling of Emyr's body in my arms, dead but still warm. The darkness around us, lit up by flecks of gold.

My energy and his, working together? Because I was using Emyr's own magic on him?

"Because he's a Healer? That's why I could do that?"

Vorgaine *sighs.* I've never made a deity sigh before, but it doesn't feel great. "Another one of your strange beliefs. It is true that all fae are born with a natural inclination toward one sect of magic. But no fae can practice *only* in that sect. I do not understand why your ancestors would limit you the way they have." She motions to us, between us. "It is why your energies are like this. Frantic, always moving, never still. Your magic is desperate for all it has been denied. *Both* of you."

Have I mentioned how much I hate the fae?

Not all the fae. I guess. But the ones who decided they were going to lie about everything we've ever known, who decided they were going to invent a new set of rules to make their people easier to manipulate?

Because that's what it is. Vorgaine can say she doesn't understand, but I do. (It has to be big blasphemy to think I know better than a goddess, but... Blaspheming makes sense for me, I think.) Everything the rulers in Asalin, or any of the fae in power on Earth, have ever done was to make the rest of us better lemmings.

'Cause the truth is, they don't actually care about the *fae,* either. The rules they put in place, the systems they design about who gets to have power and who doesn't, it hurts the fae, too. The people at the top just have them convinced that because their circumstances don't look like the witches, they aren't under anyone's boot. The truth is, we're all being crushed.

Very sincerely fuck those guys.

"Do you...do you know how long I'll have?" Emyr asks here, and his claws dig into my thigh. I reach down and put my hand over his. I don't pull his fingers away. "I know that resurrection magic is rarely permanent. My—my mother—"

Vorgaine reaches across the table and lays her hand across the back of Emyr's. He stills under her touch, and tilts his head up to stare into her eyes.

"I am sorry about your mother, Emyr. That never should have happened." She shakes her head. "But I can tell you this. Wyatt's energy is permanently, and inextricably, tangled with yours. For as long as one of you lives, the other cannot die."

And just like that, with one sentence, a thousand pounds of invisible weight, sitting on my chest for the last few weeks, disappears.

Our world is on fire. Everything we've ever known is a lie. We could *both* die tomorrow.

But Emyr isn't going anywhere without me. I am not going to lose him.

Never again.

CHAPTER TWENTY-THREE

HELL OF A WAY TO GO

The bedroom Vorgaine loans us for the night is impossibly homey, small and quiet, with nothing but a simple bed with a patchwork quilt and a dresser against one wall. Both pieces of furniture are built curved, curling upward along the sloped walls.

As she leaves, closing the door behind her, I find myself thinking, you know, if someone had told me a few months ago that pretty soon I'd be having a slumber party at a goddess's underground house...

Well, I might've believed them, actually. It seems like a fitting absurdity in the continuing ridiculousness of my entire life.

I drop down onto the edge of the bed and almost groan at

how *plush* the mattress is. I want to say only a goddess could afford a mattress this comfortable, but that wouldn't be true! Because apparently, in Faery, anyone can afford anything!

Ugh.

I shuck off my shoes, maybe too aggressively, sending them scattering across the packed-dirt floor. My zip-up hoodie comes off next, then my shirt and binder. I lift my hips off the bed to wiggle out of my jeans, kicking them away from me, before turning my head toward Emyr.

He's still standing where Vorgaine left him, arms full of books. And he's ogling my chest, with his mouth hanging slightly open.

Which—pardon? *Hello?* I mean, I know, I look great, but this feels a little aggressive.

But after a second, I realize he's looking more through me than he is at me. His eyes are glazed over. His head's a million miles—or maybe another world—away.

"You okay in there?" I ask finally, and he jolts, as if waking up.

"I—yeah. I'm fine." That probably isn't true. Not because I think Emyr is a liar, but because I don't remember the last time anyone I know was fine.

He moves over to the dresser, dropping his things on top of it, and then starts getting undressed himself. I watch his sword come off, then his shirt. Watch the way the dark hard planes of his stomach move with every twist of his torso, the way his back flexes and his wings stretch, the way his impossibly pretty spine—seriously, how is a spine *pretty*—curves down beneath the waist of his jeans.

And then I go distract myself by walking over to the dresser and checking out the map he's copied down. He's made a few notes next to some of the names, questions he's got about different things. I pick up the pencil and jot down some of my own.

When I allow myself to look at him again, he's in bed, the blanket pulled up around his waist. I release a hard breath and join him, curling up under the quilt and wrapping one arm around his middle. My head finds his chest. His claws find my lower back.

We lie like that, for a while, digesting the day.

Emyr can fly. Only in Faery, I guess, but he *can* fly. (There's probably a very good, scientific, reason for this, about like, gravity, or something, but I don't know what it is and I didn't think to ask.) And Vorgaine is real, and alive, and here, just, like, a person. And Faery is everything Zai said it was and more.

And Emyr isn't going to die. Not unless I do.

Finally, into the too-quiet stillness between us, I admit, "There is a part of me that doesn't want to go back."

And then I wait for the fallout of that statement.

Because I know how ugly it is. I know how selfish and immature it is. I know that it is the coward's way out. The fact that I could even entertain the thought, that I could *fantasize* about leaving behind Briar and Nadua and my family in the human world, and Tessa and the whole rest of Asalin to face the Bells and Wade alone, means I haven't done nearly as much growing as I'd have liked over the last few weeks, or even years. I'm still that same scared little boy I once was, running away from his problems, trying to hide himself in a world he thinks might hold him more gently. I am *trying* so hard to be a better person, and yet, at the heart of me, there is an urge to run. It's humiliating. Emyr must be disgusted.

Or maybe not. Because he replies, "Me, too."

My arm tightens around him. There's so much I want to say to that, but I know there's no point. We both want to stay. We both know we aren't going to.

For everything that could keep us here in Faery, there's something else calling us back to Asalin.

"We can come back," I remind him, brushing my mouth against the center of his chest.

He shivers beneath the ghost of my teeth. "We will. I'd like to bring Briar."

It makes me happy in a way I can't really put into words, how Emyr and Briar have stepped into each other. How the most important people in my world, in any of my worlds, are starting to love each other almost as much as I love them. "Briar's gonna love this place." I let out a shaky breath, letting Emyr go to roll onto my back next to him. "I hope she's okay."

My magic might be anchored to Emyr, might be enough to keep him here with me, but I can't say the same for her. She's breakable, though she'd like me to think she isn't.

"She is," Emyr says, with more conviction than he has any right to. "She got out. Her, and Nadua, and…baby."

"For crying out loud, the baby needs a name." It's not what's important right now, I'm aware, but it's still bugging me. I reach up to pinch the bridge of my nose, taking a deep breath.

When I finally drop my hand, Emyr is staring at me from the other side of the bed, expression tight.

"What?"

"I don't understand your feelings toward that child." He shakes his head. "I know. I know we've talked about this before. And I'm sorry about the way I handled it then, I am. But I still don't get it. Do you really *want* to be a father right now?"

"God, no. I don't know if I ever want to have kids." The idea used to be more repulsive to me than it is now, back when I envisioned myself forced to play mommy to the offspring I *had* to give birth to because of Superspecial Genetic Compatibility and a duty to Asalin's Throne. It's *less* repulsive now that I know Emyr would never do that to me, and that the choice to have children would be entirely that: a choice.

Nadua was right when she said that choices make things painful, but they make them better, too.

Still, I'm seventeen and in desperate need of some *extensive* help. You know, brain-wise. The right time may come, it may not, but it most definitely isn't now.

"It's not…" I wave my hand around, struggling to find the words without sounding like an absolute freak. "It's not like I want to take care of her because I want to be her dad. It's like… I want her to be taken care of, because…no one wanted to take care of me."

Emyr's frown deepens. He crosses the space between us with his hand to brush his thumb along my jaw, and I tilt my head into his warm touch without thinking.

"I don't know how to explain it in a way that doesn't sound stupid."

"You don't sound stupid." Emyr swallows, and then shrugs one shoulder. "And if you do, it doesn't matter. It's just the two of us here. You can say anything to me."

This is true. Emyr knows I have no brain cells and loves me anyway, for some reason.

I take a deep breath. "It feels good to care about her. It feels like caring about myself."

His claw grazes my lower lip. "It's why you fought so hard for her."

"It was like finally being able to defend the kid I used to be. The one who never got the chance to fight back."

That too-loud silence settles over us again. Emyr watches my eyes as his fingertips trail across my facial scars.

When it gets to be too much to handle, I turn my chin away and offer him an uncomfortable laugh. "Anyway, parents probably shouldn't project their shit onto their kids, so, all the more reason we *not* be her dads."

"Fair enough. We could be something, though." He tucks his hand under his temple, propping his head up as his body rolls more fully to face mine. "Of the many things Briar has taught me, one is that family doesn't need to look any particular sort of way. We make our own rules. And the baby can always be our family. Whatever that looks like."

"Yeah. You're right."

"She *will* need a name, though."

"Ugh."

Emyr's hand trails down from my face to my throat, then lower still. His open palm sweeps across my chest, not shying away from any part of me, then trails lower over my stomach. His fingers brush the waist of my boxers and I *know* he's doing it unthinking, I *know* he's not trying to start anything, and it still takes concentrated effort not to whimper.

"So," I mumble, as his fingers trail the space between my belly button and my collarbone. "You're not dying."

"I am not dying," he agrees. Gold dusts across my throat as his knuckles brush up the length of it, stopping beneath my chin to force my head up. He holds my eyes for a moment before letting his hand sweep back down toward my chest again.

My voice takes a minute to catch up, since it's currently dying somewhere inside of me, biting back all the embarrassing sounds I'd like to make. I do not know when I became this person, this person who could explode because his boyfriend *pets him*. Finally, I choke out, "That's pretty cool," which was definitely worth the struggle it took to speak.

"Mmm," he agrees. His claws leave white almost-scratches on my lower stomach.

Okay, we have to stop this. I roll over onto my front, propping myself up on one elbow, and stretch my other arm out over his chest.

"I have something to confess." I run my own nails, not claws but no less dangerous when they need to be, along his torso, feeling his muscles beneath my palm. Black magic slicks out, painting the aftermath of my touch, and gold drips along the edges to meet it.

"Mmm," Emyr growls softly, tilting his throat back, horns pressing into the pillow under his head. I see his eyes flash a brilliant gold before his lids shutter closed. "Alright. Tell me about your sins, Firestarter."

If he doesn't shut up, I'm going to kiss him. That doesn't even make any sense. My brain, whatever existed of it, has turned to fog. Horny, horny fog.

But I have a feeling what I have to say is going to splash some cold water on the situation.

"I'm worried we're never going to have sex."

"Oh." His eyes open again, and he tilts his head forward just enough to look at me. "Not where I thought that was going."

I shift so I'm straddling him, one knee on either side of his hips. There was definitely a reason for the adjustment. It was essential to the conversation. I am not being a pervert. "It's just that, uh. Every time things start to head in…that direction, it's like we're not alone in the room anymore. I mean, the last time you went down on me, you *died*."

"Right." Emyr raises his eyebrows, reaching up to settle his palms on my hips. His claws stroke, gentle enough there's no risk of breaking skin, at my back. A terrible little part of me wishes he would sink them deeper. (Maybe not so little, but definitely terrible.) "Going down on you is not what killed me, to be fair."

"Hell of a way to go, though." I don't think my joke is very funny, but Emyr does make a *you're not wrong* sort of face and I roll my eyes at him. "I want to have sex with you. To be clear. In case there was some doubt."

"There wasn't, really, but thank you for keeping me updated." He smirks, and those claws *do* stroke a little harder. I roll my hips down, pointedly, against his, until his hands stutter to a stop.

"Do you want to have sex with me?" I demand, lifting my hands from his chest to throw them, indignantly, into the air.

Emyr sighs. Hard. "Wyatt, you're the only person I ever want to have sex with."

"Right. Okay. Just checking." I mean, I knew that, but also, sometimes it's just nice to hear it out loud. "Are *you* worried we're never going to have sex?"

He's looking at me like I'm the stupidest person alive. "I was trying to seduce you, quite literally, about two minutes ago."

And I *am* the stupidest person alive! "I thought the fondling was platonic."

"We're doing so good at this," Emyr mumbles. His thumbs stroke forward over my stomach, meeting in the middle at my naval, then brushing back toward my hips again. "I'm not worried we're never going to have sex. But." He swallows. "Sometimes I worry we'll get started and I'll have to stop."

"That's okay, though. Dude, I told you, you can always stop." There is something seriously very weird about me calling my boyfriend *dude* while we talk about having sex with each other, but whatever. When has anything about our relationship ever not been weird?

"I know. It's not that I think you'll be upset with me. But *I'd* be upset with me." He takes a deep breath, looking away from my face to watch the way his hands pet at my rib cage. "I want you in every way a person can want another. Ways I didn't even know I *could* want. When I think about the things I want us to do to each other... It verges on a kind of pain. And sometimes the weight of that alone is enough to scare me."

A beat passes. I nod, slowly, my hands still making their way back and forth across his skin. "Sometimes, I worry we'll get started and *I'll* have to stop."

Emyr nods, like he knows where I'm going with this. And maybe he does.

So, I continue, "I meant what I said about it feeling like someone else is in the room sometimes. I don't... I don't want to think about Derek when I'm with you. But I'm still trying to untangle parts of my head from what he did to me."

A quiet, involuntary growl brushes from between Emyr's fangs. His claws stroke my hips, pulling me just a little closer when they do. "I wish I could kill him all over again."

"I don't," I whisper. "I'm glad it's over."

He sighs. We stare, quietly, back at each other for a long moment. Finally, he says, "You said I could always stop if I needed to. You must know the same is true in reverse."

I do know. There's no part of me that's really worried about shutting things down and making shit weird between Emyr and me. Maybe I just needed to say this out loud. That I'm struggling. That this *thing* Derek did left a scar, less visible than the rest but no less there.

We're fucked-up. Both of us. But that doesn't mean we can't figure it out, together.

My hands reach up, knuckles hovering a breath away from the base of Emyr's horns. When he gives the smallest nod of consent, I grasp them both in my hands, palms stroking up their length. The reaction is immediate, and everything I wanted it to be. Emyr growls, eyes rolling back in his head, flashing his beautifully long fangs. His horns darken in my grip, elongating and curling backward from his skull. He bucks, hips desperately searching, and my own hips press down, hard, forcing him to still underneath me. With nothing but two thin layers of fabric between us, I can feel the entirety of him between my legs. My hands tighten even harder, and my mouth finds his.

I will never tire of kissing Emyr. His mouth, the perfect combination of soft lips and lethal teeth, opens eagerly for mine. I press my tongue into him, press my lips tighter to him, and don't pull away when I taste my own blood.

Emyr is the one to finally break the kiss, tugging his head back to fall against the pillows. He stares up at me, breathless, eyes pure gold, and I have never felt this wanted in my life.

My fingertips slide down to frame his face, his perfect cheekbones, his beautiful nose, his impossible mouth. I cup my palms around his jaw, sucking in a shaky breath. "I want to feel you inside me."

Emyr's throat bobs. He gives a trembling nod between my fingers.

I've never done this before, and I don't really know that I'm doing it the way I should. I'm just going with what feels right.

Taking a deep breath, I focus on the place where his jaw meets my fingertips. If I concentrate, I can feel his pulse, thrumming beneath my hands. I curl one finger into that notch on his neck. My eyes close.

It isn't until it's happening that I know I did it right. I can feel it, the moment I drag his energy out of his body and into my own. Warmth floods through every part of me, starting in my hands and moving up my arms, spreading into my chest and my belly and my legs. I can *feel* it, golden light curling around my bones, softening the wicked, wounded edges of me.

My eyes open again and I stare into Emyr's face, desperate to, for the very first time, truly understand the weight of our bond. To finally understand what he feels when he looks at me.

And I feel…nothing different. Well, maybe there's something. Maybe there's some dull ache of pressure in my chest, a more insistent importance when I look at him. But this profound thing, this life-changing feeling I was expecting—it isn't there.

I can't help but frown a little, disappointed.

Emyr immediately registers something is wrong. He shifts beneath me, sitting up a little straighter. "Are you okay?"

I don't understand. Is *this* all the bond is? Just a little extra pressure?

Emyr presses his hand to the side of my face, cupping my jaw. "Wyatt?"

And then it hits me. The realization rocks me so hard I almost can't breathe through it.

The bond only exists to point us in the direction of the person who can help us become our most powerful and true selves. It leads us to them. That's all. What we do with it after that is all up to us. The way we feel about that person, the way we treat them, what our relationships look like…it's all up to us.

The bond didn't make me love Emyr. I did that, all on my own. I fell headfirst into him, and I couldn't have stopped it if I'd wanted to. And now, every day, I *choose* him, and I will keep choosing him, even when it's hard, because I can never go back to the person I was before I was in love with him.

The bond said I needed him. The marriage contract said I needed him.

But *I* said I wanted him. I chose him. After a lifetime of being backed into corners and forced to play a role for everyone else, loving Emyr was the first choice I really made for my future.

And that choice is so much more powerful than any *need* could ever be. What I already feel for Emyr, all on my own, is so much bigger and fiercer than any bond.

I don't understand why I'm crying when I say, "I am so in love with you."

His eyes widen a fraction more. "I am so in love with *you*."

This time when we kiss it is sloppy and desperate. Our mouths, and hands, and magic mingle in the bed, twisting together to form a new creature entirely.

And we choose each other in a new way, for the first time.

CHAPTER TWENTY-FOUR

WHAT COULD GO WRONG?

The next morning, I, my friends, the Watchers, a goddess, and a handful of fae from Ra'Ora stand in front of the door that will take most of us to Asalin. And I *am* out of breath after walking up that fucking hill again.

As she said she would, Vorgaine went to the citizens of her city and asked who among them was willing to stand beside us. In the end, it was decided no witches should come along, because of the extra risk posed to their lives on the other side. The same was true for any other creatures. Since fae are the only ones whose power Asalin has any respect for, fae are the only ones who will come.

Emyr stands just in front of the door, face-to-face with Vorgaine and Cavenia, the three of them talking seriously. I should probably pay attention to what it is they're saying—I'm sure it's very important and totally pertinent to the battle we're about to dive right back into.

But I can't stop replaying last night over and over in my mind. Emyr's body under mine...

Look, I'm just saying, if I'm going to die, that was one hell of a sendoff.

There's another reason I can't stop looking at him. When I dragged myself out of bed, he was already awake and dressed for the day. I have *no idea* where he got this outfit, but it makes me dizzy anytime I look at him for too long.

The dress begins in a tight metal bodice starting just beneath his wings, wrapped protectively. But as it drapes lower, the fabric turns from metal to something softer, more romantic. By the time it reaches his thighs, the draping is delicate and *swishy*, easy for him to move in. He's paired the whole thing with gold sandals, with metal braces that line his calves up to the knee, and arm cuffs, tight at the wrist, flowing around the forearm, with leather bands wrapped around his muscular biceps. Somehow, a world away from his wardrobe, he's acquired an assortment of rings, and earrings, and necklaces. His eyes are decorated with gold and black, and his crown sits, a glaring reminder of how far we've come and how much further we still have to go, atop his head.

Oh, and he's got a satchel of books tossed over his shoulder, like a nerdy, hot, androgynous Santa Claus.

I don't know how it's possible for one person to be everything, but he is. Masculine and feminine, soft and strong, a leader and a partner, darkness and light.

I know we have other things to do, but I'd like to kiss him again.

He catches me staring and grins, inclining his head. I give an awkward little wave before his attention returns to Vorgaine.

Cavenia has Emyr's sword over his shoulder. When I asked my boyfriend what that was about, he told me only, *"I don't need it anymore."* No elaboration.

Off to one side, the triad stands with Elonia and Zai. The two of them aren't coming with us. After everything, Emyr doesn't trust Zai not to go turncoat at the last second and try to off someone vae shouldn't. (And I can't exactly blame him for it.) Vae holds Solomon's hand, and tells him something tearful. Finally, after their last goodbyes are said, the trio makes their way over to me.

At Solomon's depressed look, I offer, "You can always come back."

"Oh, I intend to," he answers, shooting me a fierce look. "And you should, too."

"Yeah." I take a deep breath, turning away from him to survey the open ocean to one side of the island. "Maybe so."

"Zai and Elonia want to come over together, too, when everything's said and done." Lorena raises her eyebrows at me. "They're both interested in your changelings."

"*My* changelings have enough to deal with," I mumble, but I do glance over at Zai again.

Vae's not wrong. The changelings are kind of incredible.

"Alright," Emyr says, turning to the rest of us and clapping his palms together. "This is the way things are going to go. We enter this door. I, accompanied by our allies from Faery, will try to locate Robin and Gordon Bell. We will give them one final opportunity to end things peacefully." He doesn't elaborate on what happens if they choose not to *take* that opportunity. "Lorena, Solomon, and Roman will go to the village and evacuate Asalin's residents to safety, as far from the fighting as possible. Wyatt—"

"I need to make sure Briar got out. If she didn't—" I can't make myself finish the thought. But I don't need to.

"Yes." Emyr nods. "And then you're going to come back to me."

"Yes."

That's the plan. It's totally a very good plan. What could go wrong?

"And when the dust settles," Emyr looks to Cavenia. "We will give you Wade Pierce."

As part of the Watchers' holy mission.

I should probably feel worse about this part of the plan than I do, but I can't seem to make myself. Wade could have become a friend, once, but that bridge is long burnt. His life is a small price to pay for what we have to do today.

Tessa may not agree. Not at first. But she'll come to the same realization, in time.

I hope.

When his words are met by nods and agreement, Emyr takes a deep breath. He meets my eye, then turns to look at the door. Squaring his shoulders, he steps through, and disappears from my sight.

As soon as we are a world apart, something terrible crumbles in my chest. I move forward as fast as I can, barely sparing a glance at the goddess herself, before throwing myself through the doorway after him.

I step gently into Emyr's back, in Asalin's forest once more. In the distance, there is screaming, explosions, chaos. But here, in the trees, everything is muffled. Almost too quiet.

We are immediately joined by the rest of the group, the triad first, and then the rest of the fae. Emyr opens his mouth, though whatever he's going to say gets lost.

Because the Faery citizens *take off running* through the woods, in the direction of the palace, completely abandoning us.

"Um." I force myself to take a breath. "Did our backup just...jump ship?"

"No..." Emyr says, slowly, and I wonder if he believes it. "They're going to find the kings. That's the plan."

Sure, I guess, technically.

Still, it sits weird in my gut.

"Best of luck, everyone," Roman says, as he starts toward the village. "Let's all celebrate tomorrow, if we're not dead."

Solomon and Lorena hurry after him.

Emyr and I exchange one long look. He huffs, shrugging the books from his shoulder and, very carefully, hiding them behind a tree. I watch, absolutely gay and in love, also absolutely bonkers confused, as he does his best to cover them up with leaves. Like he's worried they might get hurt.

When he's finished, he takes my hand and we make our way through the trees together, toward the palace. A full day has passed since we were here, and yet it's hardly been any time at all. Things are just as frenzied and bloody as we left them.

Well, maybe more so, thanks to one small difference. There

are *dragons*, now. The dragons have come in from the field, and seem to be fighting back against the Guard.

Emyr and I hover at the tree line, watching in silent awe for a moment too long. Finally, I pull my fingers from his grip.

"Briar."

"I know," he says. His eyes burn with all the things he isn't saying.

There's nothing to be said. Not right now. We said it all last night. Over and over again.

"I'll come back to you," I promise him.

"I know," he repeats.

Silently, I remind myself of Vorgaine's promise. As long as one of us lives, the other can't die. We're anchored to each other. Emyr isn't going anywhere without me.

And I turn and run for the castle.

I enter through a side door, the same way I sent Briar and Nadua in, avoiding most of the chaos happening outside. Everything happened so quickly after we separated, with Monalai's arrival, I have a sick, sinking feeling they really didn't make it out of the palace. I hope I'm wrong. But in case I'm not, this is where my search begins.

There's an eerie, relative calmness here, a stark contrast to what's happening outside. But every now and then I see someone dart through a doorway or around a corner, so clearly trying to keep out of sight. Most of the people in here are servants. Witches, mostly, and some fae who have worked for the royal family for years. They're just trying to keep their heads down.

We should evacuate the palace, the same way the triad is taking care of the village. Yeah. I'll find Briar, and Nadua, and the baby, and then we'll start getting everyone else out of here.

That is a very good plan, I think. At least, it would be. But almost as soon as it forms in my mind, there's a *BOOM!* and the palace begins to crumble.

My body moves on instinct and nothing else, arms shooting over my head, sinking into a corner to curl up as small as I can make myself. Debris, chunks of stone both big and small, fall from the sky as parts of the ceiling cave in on top of me. I cough through the dust, squeezing my eyes shut.

As quickly as it began, it's over. When the palace settles around me, the sound of cracking stone is replaced by the sound of screaming. Anyone hiding in the castle begins flooding out of their rooms, racing for any exit they can reach, even if that means a newly formed hole in the walls of the palace itself.

I return to my feet and keep moving. Okay, so, part of Asalin's in ruins. Sure. That tracks. Doesn't change what I came here for.

It takes longer than it should to get to the room, having to push boulders out of my way and crawl through cracks between slabs of mountain rock. By the time I get where I'm going, my clothes are ripped, my fingers bloodied, but I don't care. I made it.

A piece of the ceiling has cracked and wedged itself into the top of the door. I brace my shoulder against it and slam, hard, forcing it open. "Briar?"

The sight that meets me is so *completely* bizarre that it takes me a minute just to wrap my head around it. The walls of the bedroom are covered in sigils. A body, too small to be Briar or Nadua but too big to be the baby, is lying in the corner, surrounded by water.

And Wade is standing over the empty bassinet.

"I believe you just missed her," he says with a sigh, turning slowly to face me. "I came here looking for my delicious little niece...but I am so happy to see you, instead."

Something buried deep in my bones tells me to be careful. I have never known how to listen to a warning. "I wish the feeling was mutual."

He chuckles, shaking his head. "Oh, Wyatt. I will miss the way you make me laugh, when I've carved the skin from your body and forced Emyr to wear it as a coat."

Vomit squeezes the back of my throat at the mental picture. "What *happened* to you?"

I don't understand how we got here. I had sympathy to extend for Wade, up to a point. But this? This murder-happy, bloodthirsty monster, telling me the awful things he's going to do while he smiles? It reminds me of—

Wade's deep green energy glitches, like a short circuit. There one minute, gone the next. It reappears, only to do the same thing again.

"What..."

This time, when it flickers back to life, it isn't green at all. Instead, it is a bright, violent pink.

Right in front of my eyes, Wade's face begins to morph. One by one, his teeth fall from behind his lips, another set bursting through the bloody gums to replace them. His hair sheds, falling to his feet, and blond curls unfurl in its place. His skin starts to slough right off of his body, revealing muscle and sinew underneath, with bones breaking down on themselves, getting smaller, shrinking his frame. The sound of their violent, unnatural cracking reverberates throughout the room. And then new skin, softer skin, stitches itself over them.

My brain can't process what it's seeing. Instead, Paloma's words echo in the back of my mind.

"*I have seen it unfold. She who walks in the in-between has already arrived.*"

A brand-new body begins to take shape in front of me, Wade's clothes now too big on the much smaller frame.

"*She is death disguised as a friend.*"

"Well," Clarke giggles. "It's kind of a long story."

SHUFFLE

So, there's a lot happening today.

Unfortunately—or maybe *luckily*—I'm not there for most of it. And what I'll learn in the next few days, and weeks, and months, will be told to me by others.

JUSTICE

Briar

"Jin's already gone." Mom ducks back into the room after doing a sweep of the hallway, face twisted with worry.

"Shit," I whisper, fingers knotting over my stomach, staring down at the scene unfolding in the courtyard. I don't know what happened between breaking apart in the woods and getting up here, but there's a bunch of fae from *Monalai* down there, a gruesome fight breaking out, and Wyatt and Emyr are nowhere to be seen.

"Okay. Alright." She takes a deep breath. "Stay here," she says, and I turn to look at her just as she's pushing the baby at me. Outside, something explodes. "Do not even *think* of opening this door again."

"Mom!" I shout and the infant wails. I rub her back, trying

to soothe her, and lower my voice to a stage whisper when I continue, "Where are you going? I thought we were leaving!"

"Think it's too late for that. And I—I have to find Wyatt," is all she tells me before the door slams shut behind her.

And it's just me and the crying baby and Boom, sitting stock-still and on guard at the balcony door. He was here when we arrived, waiting, whining, and anxious. And now it's just us, all alone. With my thoughts, and the sound of a war beginning a few hundred feet away.

You know, it's kind of fucked-up that I'm not even surprised I've landed myself in this situation. It's the ultimate act of being a good person, right? Dying for your cause? And I just want to be a good person.

Some people don't believe that. Not about me or anyone else. And I understand why. We're conditioned not to trust each other, at least in this country. Good ol' American individualism teaches us to put ourselves first. And when you buy into that, the idea of taking care of each other *just because you can* doesn't really make any sense.

I'm lucky my parents taught me early on that was settler bullshit.

"You've got your voice for a reason, baby," my dad would tell me. *"And when that doesn't work, you've got two good fists."*

My dad doesn't know the truth about me. My mom loves him, really loves him, but she loves her people more. She keeps their secrets close to the chest. But if I survive tonight, I think we should tell him. I know he'd be proud.

I don't know if I will, though.

Survive, that is.

Outside, screeches sound from the sky, and I turn to watch

as dragons begin descending into the courtyard. Dragons. That's how things are going.

Okay.

"Shh," I whisper, bending my neck down to kiss the top of the baby's head. "Shh. You're okay. I'm gonna take care of you."

That's what I do.

That's, like, all I do. And apparently, that's not always a good thing.

Because I've realized lately, I don't know who I am outside of the things I do for other people. Outside of protests and late-night breakdowns and fighting for the things and people I believe in. What do I have to offer if I'm not being helpful? Who even *am I* without something or someone to take care of?

At what point does self-sacrifice start being about self-harm?

At what point is wanting to die for the greater good actually just a socially acceptable way of *wanting to die*?

I should probably work on figuring that out. You know, if I survive this battle I never should've been a part of, that for sure didn't need to include me, that I only got involved in because I wanted to help people.

The baby—for crying out loud, when are we going to give her a *name*?—starts to settle against my chest, and I shift her carefully into her bassinet. She makes a scrunchy little face like she's thinking about crying, but doesn't, instead closing her eyes.

Good.

Okay.

Deep breaths, Briar. Everything's fine.

Everything's not fine, and I know that, but I don't know how to make anything better, either.

Well, there's one thing, I guess. I bend down to rummage underneath the bed, pulling free a canvas bag with random mismatched odds and ends. I yank out a black marker, tucked in the bottom with all the other pens and pencils, and get to work.

I've been studying my *ass* off to memorize as many sigils as I can. (And that's a lot of ass! It's impressive!) It started after the riot. When Lavender died and Jin and Solomon were on the run. When I decided to take it upon myself to try and open the door to Faery.

Clearly, that was, um…it was a questionable decision. My heart was in the right place, though.

But like, was it? *Really?* Did I actually want to save Asalin and help Wyatt, or do I just have no impulse control when it comes to throwing myself headfirst into danger?

And we're back to that problem again. And we're shelving it. Again.

Anyway, back to the sigils. I uncap the marker and start drawing them on the wall between the bedroom and the hallway. Any I can think of that might do me any good. Protective wards, defensive ones. A couple offensive ones. At some point, I run out of space on the wall, and run out of relevant sigils, but I keep going. Onto the next wall. Onto *any* sigil I can think of.

It keeps my hands busy. It keeps me from thinking about my mom, and if she found Wyatt, and if they're both okay, and what I'm supposed to do if they aren't.

When I get to the balcony, I glance over at the baby in her bassinet. I'm pretty sure she's sleeping.

I like her. I don't have any idea what I'm doing with her, and I think Wyatt likes her way more than I do, but she's cute. And anyway, even if she was ugly, she wouldn't deserve to die. Ugly babies deserve rights, too.

Boom whimpers, on edge, and I put a hand on the side of his face, pushing him away from the balcony doors and toward the bed.

"Go lie down. Pretend you're a dog and not some kind of furry guardian angel with anxiety."

He glares at me, growling, but *does* turn and jump onto the bed. So, success.

I slip outside alone. It's *loud* out here, people screaming down below, things exploding left and right, the roars of dragons enough to rattle the world under my feet. Maybe Mom was wrong to tell me to stay here. Maybe we all should have run from the castle like we were supposed to. It's not like I don't remember what happened the night of the riot, the way this very balcony blew up and took half the bedroom with it.

And still, here I am. Like I've got a freaking target drawn on my forehead.

Ugh. Whatever.

I start scribbling out here, too, drawing black sigils along the railing, teeth sinking into my bottom lip. I'm so focused on what I'm doing, and it's so unbelievably loud, that I almost don't hear Boom when he starts growling again, inside.

Almost.

"What is your—"

Martha Pierce is beautiful in the delicate, harmless sort of way that is unattainable for people who look like me. She is porcelain skin and wet eyes and perfume so faint you could almost believe she wasn't wearing anything, that she just smells like that. She is everything we are told to protect. She couldn't possibly hurt anyone.

Boom is as big as she is, maybe a little bigger. And he's standing between her and the bassinet. The hackles down his back stand upright, red eyes glowing, mouth open to show his fangs dripping with drool.

Her pretty face screws up in disgust when a glob of it hits the ground.

"You need to go," I tell her, squaring my shoulders and moving to stand at Boom's side.

Internally, though, I'm just screaming a long stream of expletives and wondering when my mom's coming back.

Martha sniffs and blinks those dewy eyes at me. "I've come for my baby."

I'm so sick of this. There's a part of me that's like, okay, maybe we just give her the damn baby back if it means that much to her. Sheesh.

But also, no, absolutely not, for about a dozen different reasons.

"Not your baby anymore, Martha. You didn't want her, you gave her away, now get out."

"I just want to protect her. She's not safe here, while the castle's under attack." She sniffles, taking a shaky step closer. "I just want to get her somewhere safe."

Boom snarls hard enough it makes *me* flinch. Martha lets out a squeal. In the bassinet, the baby starts to fuss.

"You don't understand what it's like," Martha whispers,

talking to me though she's staring at the waking newborn in the corner. "We don't know where the witches come from. We don't understand why some children are born like *that*. But everyone assumes it's the mother. Right? They think I must have done something wrong. But I didn't. I did everything right. I wanted my baby; I wanted my *family*." She chokes on a quiet little sob, bringing a hand to her mouth. "And then something like this happens and everyone starts whispering about it. Speculating. Do you know the way they gossip about me? People can be so *mean*."

She's so pathetic, so small and fragile and pitiful, I could almost feel bad for her. Except I know that's exactly what she wants. The weaponization of victimhood, from women like Martha Pierce, is nothing new.

"If you don't like being the topic of conversation, why are you here? Why keep trying to get her back instead of washing your hands of it?"

"BECAUSE EVERYONE KNOWS SHE'S MINE!" Martha throws her hands up, eyes unmoving from the bassinet as the baby begins to cry. "I was supposed to get rid of her! She was supposed to be gone! People would feel sorry for me. They would talk about how it was a sad, terrible thing that happened to me. How I made a difficult choice, and how I had to be so strong to do it. That's what was supposed to happen. Not this!"

I inch backward, toward the bassinet. The hair on the nape of my neck rises. "How is this any different? Shouldn't they still feel sorry for you?"

Finally, she turns her eyes on me. There are no more tears. Instead, they burn. "Because you went to the woods and you found my shame and you brought it back. You parade it around Asalin for everyone to look at. I will never know peace until it's *gone*."

It, she says. I swallow down bile.

"I thought you wanted to take her somewhere safe, Martha."

She blinks at me. Her pretty pink lips part in surprise. And then she raises one hand.

I swear I feel something brush against the side of my face. Like a whisper of magic just beginning to reach out for me. But as soon as I feel it, it's gone. Because Boom intercedes.

With another vicious growl, he throws himself at her, teeth snapping toward her throat. And whatever was focused on me focuses on him, instead. Martha twists her raised hand into a fist and Boom lets out a pained wail as his body goes flying into the wall.

"Stop it!" I scream. I want to go to him, want to save him the way he saved me, but I can't make myself move from the spot in front of the bassinet, my body the only barrier between this deranged woman and the crying child. I want to do anything to make the sound of his dying animal screams stop. "Martha, don't do this!"

It's an awful sight, the way Boom's body convulses, twisting at an unnatural angle, his spine curving backward. His agonized howls die off into whimpers and then into nothing at all. This frantic rise and fall of his chest slows…slows…

I have to do something before it stops entirely. I have been working *so* hard to learn to use this magic, to tap into this lost part of me, hidden in my blood and passed down from my mother, and my grandmother, and the people who came before her. I want so badly to reclaim what was stolen from my ancestors by fae who were too embarrassed, too ashamed, to keep their witch children.

But is it enough? Is there anything I can actually do that will make this better, instead of worse? The last time I tried this, I fucked everything up.

I have to try again, though. I'm not going to stand here and watch Boom die. And even if I could stomach that, she'd just come for me next.

My palm connects with the wall, with the first sigil I see in swiping distance. It's the one Solomon taught Wyatt at his last lesson, the one he was supposed to use to fill a cup with water. I copied it down just to have something to do, having run out of useful ones long before.

But maybe...

Martha's arms fall to her sides. Boom whines, shaking himself free of whatever she did to him, and runs to me on shaky legs.

"Wh—" Martha starts, but can't seem to finish.

A trickle of water slides from her mouth. She tries to clear her throat, like coughing is going to help. Another gush of water follows, spilling over her chin and down onto her pretty, probably expensive blouse. It starts to leak from her nose, next. Then her ears.

And then she's staring at me with those wet, sad eyes, now spilling water over her cheeks for a brand-new reason.

I can see it, the moment she realizes what's happening to her. What I've done. The confusion—how could a *human* do *this*? The indignation—how could *anyone* do this to *her*?

The fear, as it spreads across her face—as she realizes she's going to die.

When she hits her knees, her delicate wings seem to seize up behind her before going limp against her back. Her mouth opens and closes rapidly, her hands clawing at her own throat, as she struggles to get in any air. It doesn't take long for her skin to start turning from white to blue, starting at her mouth and spreading out through the rest of her. Her whole body bloats, the tiny woman swelling and swelling, all while water pours out of her, until I think she might just pop.

It is terrifying and uncomfortable and there is a part of me that hates it and I do not ever want to be forced to take someone's life again, even in self-defense.

But.

I can feel it in my body. For the first time, I can *sense* my own magic, like a living thing swimming through my veins, like an electric current taking root in my nervous system. I feel stronger and more grounded than I ever have before.

Earlier, I'd wondered who I was without someone else to take care of. Maybe the answer is simple. I'm a *badass.*

"You're right about one thing, Martha. Witches aren't born because of something their mothers did." I don't even realize I'm going to speak until the words are already leaving my mouth. I crouch down next to her, shoes squelching in the puddle that's formed in a circle around her body. "You don't get to take any credit for what we can do."

Not to be all *we are the granddaughters of the witches you ~~couldn't burn~~ left to die in the woods* about it. But if the shoe fits.

Her torso has gone rigid, too swollen to move. The water seems to be streaming right out of her skin now, leaking out of her pores. Her eyes are so big, three, maybe four times the size they should be.

And I watch as the last gush of water finally leaves them. And her body slumps to the floor.

Boom makes a small noise at my back, nosing against me. I manage to pry my eyes away from Martha's body to look at him. He tilts his head toward the bassinet.

No one's yelling in the room anymore, and the baby's fussing has quieted down some. She has no idea her mother just drowned to death from the inside out.

But she's still awake, making little coos and squirming against the confines of her blanket. I push myself up, lift her into my arms again and tuck her against my chest.

Martha was right about one thing. Being locked in this room isn't safe. I need to find the others. And if I run into someone else on the way, someone who wants to hurt me...

Well, maybe I can handle it.

"C'mon," I nod at Boom, and head toward the door. "Let's go find your dads."

THE STAR, REVERSED

Tessa

"I have to find my brother," I snap, yanking my arm out of the grip of the tattooed behemoth when he tries to drag me to (presumably) safety. I've just spent the last who-knows-how-long fighting my way through ex-Guards, every single one with a bone to pick with *me* specifically, blaming me for their jobs getting axed.

And like, yeah? And I'd do it again. Eat shit.

Ari—I think his name is Ari—throws his arm out in the direction of the woods. "Yeah, and *I'm* pretty sure he went this way."

"Right, so move it or lose it, princess," Kora, the sourpuss little ice queen with mismatched eyes, fucking *body checks me* on her way toward the tree line.

I would start a fight. But there's a much bigger fight already happening on the palace steps right now. And I really do need to find Wyatt.

So, fine. Given my options, I choose to move it, and follow the changelings into the forest.

Good timing, too. 'Cause that's right about when dragons start dropping into the courtyard, too close to the very spot we were just standing.

"What direction was he going when you saw him?" I ask, stomping along in Kora's wake, kicking around fallen branches as I do.

Ari makes an unidentifiable sound at my back. "Oh, we didn't actually see him."

I pull up short, look over my shoulder, and raise my eyebrows at the big dude. "Then *why* are we *here*?"

You know, I've never been a very patient person. Empathy, understanding, the innate softness that comes from having a compassionate spirit, or whatever—none of that is my thing. I was not born knowing how to view the world from anyone's perspective but my own.

Some people aren't like that. Wade, for instance. He's a Feeler. He picks up on the emotions of people around him so easily. It can get overwhelming, I'm told. That's why, as a kid, before he was really in control of his power, he liked to hang out by himself, a little creep lurking in the woods. It's why, even as an adult, he doesn't really have many friends besides me.

Well. We definitely aren't friends anymore. And apparently, he has new ones to replace me.

Just gonna put that away in the "traumatic incidents to process *after* the world's done imploding" folder.

Anyway, patience, empathy, all that jazz. I didn't even really see the value in it until I was older. Until I realized I was completely alone, this little black hole of misery, and I was probably going to be alone forever, because I was pushing everyone else away. Because I couldn't see past myself and all my pain and rage.

I've been working so hard to be better. Every single day, I have to make the conscious, intentional decision to practice kindness. Sometimes I fail, *hard*. Sometimes I get it right. I am a work in progress, I guess.

Today, though, I'm definitely failing, because I'm about ten seconds away from killing Ari.

"We think he and Emyr went to the door," Kora answers for her cousin, and I turn around to face her. She raises her eyebrows at me. "It's this way, right?"

"Why would he have done that?"

"It's what *we* would have done. There's a whole army over on that side whose entire purpose is protecting witches. Hell, even if Wyatt's not there, someone should probably call in the cavalry."

It makes sense. I guess. I still don't like this girl. "Fine."

"You've been to the door, right?"

"Yep."

"Okay. So you lead the way, cupcake."

Princess, now cupcake. You know, if I killed her and left her in the woods, everyone would probably just assume it was one of the Monalai Guards or something.

I press my claws into my palms and count to ten in my head. And then I do. I lead the way.

At least, I lead the way part of the way. Only a few minutes into walking, Kora and Ari both stop to inspect something. I keep going, at first, thinking they'll eventually start following me again. When they don't, I grumble something incredibly nasty under my breath, turning back around to see what the hell they're looking at.

The tree is beautiful and massive, one of the biggest in the forest, with thin limbs draping down around it, covered in leaves. It makes it look almost like a dome, like a soft green cup turned upside down.

Both of the changelings are staring at it strangely.

It's noteworthy in that it's interesting to look at, I guess, but it doesn't seem worth stopping what we're doing. Kind of more pressing matters at play. But hey, what do I know?

"Uh. Hello? Is Wyatt hiding behind the tree?" I demand, motioning in the direction we're supposed to be heading. "The door's not far from here."

"Yeah, yeah, we'll get to that. But…something's…here." Kora frowns, reaching up to brush her hand against the limbs, her fingertips making the leaves rustle together. Her frown only deepens, and she turns to look at her cousin. "Do you feel that?"

"Yep." Ari puts a hand on my shoulder, but I immediately shrug him off. "I don't know if you wanna see this."

"See what?" Something cold starts to claw up from my naval, into my chest cavity, tickling at the back of my throat. "What's in there?"

"Death," Kora says, and parts the tree limbs with her arm like a curtain.

And I see what I see, but I don't see it, not really, not yet. My eyes see it, I guess, and my brain says *nope*, and everything shuts down for routine maintenance.

I was the one who identified my parents' bodies after Wyatt

killed them, you know. Asalin's not that big. There's only a few hundred people; everyone at least knows *of* everyone else. And my mom and dad weren't exactly wallflowers. They were well-known, established. I shouldn't have *had* to be the one to look at them and say, yes, that's them, that's my parents.

But I wanted to. I needed to, maybe. I needed to see them. Needed proof, *undeniable* proof, that my brother had really done what everyone said he did.

It's weird, though. I saw them. Their scorched, mutilated bodies, skin fried and peeling back, muscle tissue and organ meat and bone exposed. I recognized it was them.

And I *also* accepted that they were dead. That they were never coming back. That I was completely and totally alone.

But somehow, my brain never put the two together. Like it couldn't. It could see this horrible vision of my mom's and dad's bodies, and it could know I was an orphan, but it could never actually let those two facts sit side by side. Almost as if there was always a barrier of unreality between me and what I saw that day. Like even though the vision of it still exists, somewhere in my head, there's a part of me that refuses to accept it was real.

I wonder if I will ever be able to accept the sight of Wade's rotting, mutilated corpse hidden beneath the tree.

Ari is speaking. "Isn't this—"

"The guy from the castle?" Kora asks. "Yeah. Except he's been dead at least a few days."

"Shit." Ari whistles. Then I think maybe he looks at me. I think maybe he's talking to me when he says, "I told you not to look."

There is another part of my brain that will come back, later, to *how* this is possible. How Wade could have been there, at the palace, staring at Emyr the way he was, minutes ago. And how he's here, now, dead, wrapped in a cocoon of vines and roots, with his chest carved open, and—

"His heart?" That's my voice asking the question, I'm sure of it.

Kora answers, "Gone. For fuck's sake, what happened here?"

I will wonder that later, too.

But right now, I'm thinking instead about how I've had to spend years practicing softness, but Wade worked just as hard, his whole life, to put up walls. Every day, he did everything he could to keep people at arm's length, to hold himself back just enough so that no one knew just how *delicate* and *good* he was. Because Asalin has never been a place where being delicate or good has served someone well.

When we met, two lonely people afraid of the entire world, a sharp-edged girl trying to learn tenderness and a tender boy wrapping himself in armor, we managed to meet in the middle. We found each other in the space between where we were and where we wanted to be. And when I struggled to keep my fangs to myself, he pulled me back. And when he could not protect the fragile animal he was, I used my teeth to do it for him.

And now he's here, dead, with flies buzzing around his rotting skin and maggots crawling in the hole where his heart used to be.

"Hey." Kora's voice is closer now. Her hand brushes against the inside of my elbow. "You okay?"

No.

"He—" Oh, my voice does not normally sound like that.

Hmm. I clear my throat and try again. "He was my…he was mine."

"Oh." Ari's big tattooed body shifts, uneasy.

And maybe the cousins are looking at each other, and maybe they are whispering some quiet conversation, talking about me instead of to me, but maybe they aren't. I don't know. I'm not paying them any attention.

No, I'm staring at Wade's dead body, and wondering if his vulnerability has crawled into my body and taken root, because I don't feel strong at all right now. And if it has, maybe I can carry it forward, keeping that piece of him alive and right here with me. Where he should be.

"We can give his body to Papatūānuku," Kora says, and I have no idea what that means but there is a part of my brain that realizes she's asking me for permission. "We can send him to rest."

He deserves to finally rest. My knees hit the dirt, palms stretching toward him, but I don't touch him. I can't bring myself to. From here, I can see the bugs making a nest of his lungs.

"How did this happen?"

"I don't know." Kora's voice is right at the back of my neck, her hand on my spine.

"I'm so sorry," Ari whispers, crouching down next to me.

Something moves in the trees next to us, someone coming up on our group, but I can't move to do anything about it.

"I'm so sorry," I repeat Ari's words back to Wade's corpse. "You deserved better."

We all did.

Behind us, back toward the castle, a dragon screeches. I don't turn my head to look.

Instead, I watch as Kora and Ari place their hands over Wade's ruined chest and pull a thread of perfect emerald green from the hollow that once held his heart. The three energies converge like a cocoon around him, his green mingling with their shades of red to create a dark brown almost the same shade as the earth beneath them. It curls around the top of his head, encircling his antlers.

And when it does, Wade's horns begin to disappear. They flake apart in bursts of powdery brown that drip onto the ground beneath him. As the magic moves over his body, every piece of him begins to quickly disappear.

Soon, there's nothing left at all. Just that same powdery brown. And as I watch, it begins to swirl, lifting up into the open air in front of us. And it begins to shift, no longer brown, but deep green alone. Just Wade. Leaving the others behind. Leaving all of us behind.

The green magic swirls into a cyclone in the middle of the forest, whipping my hair around my face so violently I can hardly see through the strands of blond.

And just as quickly, it ends. The trees around us settle, no longer shaking under a turbulent wind.

And where Wade's body was moments earlier, draped by the leaves of the willow tree, a tiny magnolia sapling stands. Deep green leaves jut out from the bark, and tucked between them is an array of delicate white flowers.

He's gone.

There is nothing else left of him.

Vaguely, I think I hear more dragon roars picking up at the castle, the sounds of the clash getting worse. But their screams are dull and faraway, buried beneath my own.

THE WHEEL OF FORTUNE

Jin

When the loudest explosion yet comes from the direction of the palace, I pause, just for a second, to glance in that direction. But the second passes, and then it's back to my task.

I know the herd did as I told them to. They went to help. What happens next is anyone's guess, but a dragon army is nothing to scoff at. I hope it's enough to keep the people I love safe.

Maybe I should be there, too, but I'm not. I'm guiding Auriga, *my* dragon, through the trees, going the opposite direction. I've got one hand on her long throat, her scarlet scales warm under my touch. My other hand's fidgeting with the phone in my pocket.

Truthfully, I'm scared.

Truthfully, I don't know if I'm doing the right thing. And

if I'm *really* being honest, I'm probably not. Not if the right thing is defined by how many people I'm helping.

'Cause the answer is just one. I'm only saving one person tonight.

The door to Faery is tucked far enough into the woods that I can still hear everything happening back at the castle, but it's dull. Like an echo. A faded bruise. If I press on it—if I listen—it'll hurt. But I can choose to ignore it.

I've never been good at ignoring bruises. Compulsion, maybe, forces me to rest the pad of my thumb against them and press as hard as I can. There is a metaphor in there about not being able to leave things alone, even when I know they'll hurt me. About choosing to live in the hurt for a little while longer, even when I could walk away.

But, tonight, I tune out the sounds behind me. I choose not to press on the bruise.

I'm not living in the hurt any longer. I'm finally walking away.

Auriga makes a soft, disgruntled huff when we stop a few yards shy of the door. She tries to back up out of my hand, but I tighten my grip on a spike along her spine, and she settles.

Can't blame the poor girl for being spooked. It's creepy out here.

The last time I was here, I watched magic, *my* magic, slam this thing closed. Now, it's blown wide open again. Maybe even wider than before. I can make out more of the world beneath the twisted elm limbs, a hint of gray sky and barren earth.

Goose bumps come crawling up my neck.

There's a chance I'm totally out of my mind. Or that Zai was lying about the way witches are treated in Faery. Or both.

It's entirely possible I could step over into that world and realize witches are even more mistreated there than here.

But I won't know that world until I know it. I sure as hell already know this one, though.

I tug the phone from my pocket. I worked so hard on this, on the tech and the magic, and for what? In the end, I don't know that it did any good. It didn't keep the door closed. It almost got Emyr killed.

Clarke almost got Emyr killed.

Clarke almost killed Emyr.

Slowly, I uncurl my fist from around my phone when I realize I'm squeezing. Shouldn't break it. There's a few more things I need to do first.

The sight of myself on-screen when I open the camera app is dizzyingly disorienting. It's not that anything about me looks wrong, or different. It's that I don't actually remember the last time I looked at my reflection and really saw myself.

How long has my body been moving through the world without a real person living in it?

I press the record button.

"Monalai has initiated a war against Asalin. Their monarchy is attempting to seize the Throne from King Emyr. They have allied with traitors in our own people, the fae extremist group formerly led by Derek Pierce. To our friends in Eirgard, Oflewyn, and Kitaraq—please hurry."

A few more clicks, and it's off to Fae TV. Hopefully it'll do some good.

In front of me, in the open doorway between this world and another, two bodies suddenly appear, nearly falling to the ground as they stumble over tree roots. I frown, looking up from my phone to the two fae who've just appeared.

"Zai? What are you—"

"Where is Emyr?" Vae interrupts me to demand, righting vaerself and tugging vaer companion, a pretty fae woman, to vaer side.

"Um. Back toward the castle, I— Okay, bye!" I shout at their backs as the two don't bother waiting for me to finish, darting away.

That can't be...good. Maybe I should go investigate what has them all in a panic.

Instead, I go back to looking at my phone. Whatever it is, it's no longer my problem. And I have one last thing to do. Two things. Technically.

They're both going to be upset I didn't give them one last conversation. I should, maybe. Should stay and fight tonight out and hold on for a real, proper goodbye.

But I'm so tired. Tired of fighting and tired of goodbyes.

I think they'll get it. At least, I hope they will.

And I can always come back, right? If Zai's to be believed, time works weird over there. I could live a whole *lifetime* and it would have just been a year or so for them.

Yeah. Maybe I'll come back. Sometime.

Deep breath. Open text messages.

Briar's first. I reread it a few times, make sure it says everything it needs to. Hit Send.

Then Emyr's. I don't reread it at all. I can't, because, if I do, I might not be able to do this. I send it off and shove the phone in my pocket, out of sight.

There's basically no chance of it actually working in Faery, I know. But I can't seem to leave it behind, either.

Grabbing hold of Auriga's spikes, I hoist myself up, settling onto her back. She huffs, turning her head around to look at me. I kiss the top of her snout, and we both turn back to look at the elm trees again. At the open space between them.

My heart gives one last guilty lurch, trying to convince me to follow after Zai. To go back to the castle and make sure my friends are safe. To do the right thing.

I've always tried to do the right thing. Even when it was hard. I've tried to help my friends, and to show empathy to my enemies. I've tried to take care of the witches, and extend forgiveness to the fae, and build bridges with the humans. I have tried, and tried, and given, and given of myself until I was empty.

And Asalin was happy to take, to accept everything I had and still ask for more. Clarke was the worst of them, because I thought she loved me. I always knew this kingdom didn't. I thought if I worked hard enough, maybe, someday, it would. Instead, it took everything I had.

Almost everything. But there is still air in my lungs and a pulse in my throat and blood in my veins and I am *not* dying for them. Not tonight. Not ever. Before now, I always thought I might, in the end. It was kind of romantic, this vision I cooked up of me sacrificing myself for the greater good.

But there is nothing romantic about martyrdom. And Asalin cannot have anything else.

I'm done fighting for a world that doesn't love me. I'll love me.

Gently, I press my heel into Auriga's side. She shifts beneath me. And together, we move through the door.

THE EMPRESS

Kadri

I always wanted to be a mother. I wanted it as badly as I wanted to change the world. It's a shame I spent so many years believing both were impossible dreams.

As the world rattles around me, dragon fire erupting outside the palace windows, explosive magic from fae in Guard uniforms that I recognize only from my traveling, I rush to find answers. A scared young witch in a servant's uniform, trembling as she watches the scene unfolding outside through a pane of glass, looks to me when I approach.

"What is going on?"

"I'm not sure. A bunch of fae showed up, and I think they were brought here by Wade Pierce. They cornered King Emyr and Wyatt Croft in the courtyard, and then everything went black, and now there are dragons, and—"

I reach forward and put a hand on her arm. "Did you see what happened to the king?"

"No, Your Majesty, I'm so sorry."

"That's alright." I incline my head down the hall, away from her lookout's post. "Get somewhere safe. Bunker down until this is over. Go, now."

She scurries away, and I move in the direction of the main entrance.

My husband, Leonidas, used to *want* as deeply as I do. He had such big dreams for the kingdom he was born to rule, and the way his rule would build the world into something new. It drew me to him instantly when we met, this renowned warrior king whose charm was only outdone by his potential.

For years now, I have watched that potential wash away. And I think I know when it began. The night I fell from the tower, when I lost my life only to be pulled back from the edge and given another chance at a handful of extra years. It reinspired me to push harder, to demand more, not knowing how much longer I might be able to fight. But it destroyed something in him. He finally saw what the real cost of *wanting* could be, and it was not one he was willing to pay.

Which is why he is still hiding in our room, holed up like a coward while the world burns and I search for our son. What a peculiar, unfortunate truth it is that his love for me could turn him weak enough to taint my love for him.

Not that I ever truly knew the man I'd married. Not until recently.

I reach the steps of the palace just in time to see the black dragon Summanus swallow Robin Bell's massive body in one fluid motion. Gordon Bell, screaming out his husband's name, reaches out a hand, wielding his gray energy, and a rope of magic winds itself around the dragon's neck. Fire explodes from his mouth, and Guards rush to use their own magic against him, even as other dragons land at his side using fire and their own scaled bodies to take out swaths of Monalai's army.

I can hardly comprehend anything in the commotion. And I do not see whether Summanus or Gordon survive the encounter, because my attention is pulled elsewhere.

"Kadri!" Briar Begay-Brown, the not-human child, bursts from the door I just left through, Martha and Derek Pierce's infant daughter cradled in her arms, and Boom, the hellhound, at her heels. "Have you seen my mother?"

"No," I hold out a hand to her, ushering the girl closer to me. "Have you seen my son?"

"Emyr and Wyatt disappeared together. My mom was looking for them, too."

Nadua Begay-Brown is a woman who can hold my attention. She represents so much of what I have always wanted. Magic and mundanity and motherhood pooled into one body—and a fierce leader, at that.

I do not have time to tell Briar I haven't seen her mother, because flame ignites the steps around us. Briar lets out a startled sound and steps back, even as I hold my arm out in front of her, as if thinking to protect her from the fire with my own body.

Leonidas may never have been willing to pay the price for wanting, but I always have. And now, knowing death's claws are drawing ever closer to my throat, what right do I have *not* to throw myself into flame for someone else?

As it turns out, I don't have to. The fire parts, creating an unnatural path right through the center, and another woman appears, racing up to us. She is beautiful and stern, with tattoos coating her brown skin. I do not recognize her, and I imagine I would remember her face.

"I believe you were sent away from here," she chides Briar.

"My mom went looking for Wyatt. I need to find them." Briar motions to me with a quick flick of her fingers. "Mary, this is Queen Kadri. Kadri, this is Mary, a Maori elder and a descendant of a Monalai witch."

"Did you arrive with them?" I demand, motioning to the chaos around us, the Monalai Guards at the center of it all.

In all my travels as queen, Monalai was my least favorite kingdom to ever step foot in. Asalin, my second least. I believe both felt the same about me.

This woman, Mary, does not deign to answer, though she does scoff. "Saw Wyatt and Emyr headed into the woods when the lights came back. Come on."

From the magic flame, the steps have been leveled and turned into a ramp made of packed, flat dirt, making it easy for me to move down. Even as I follow after her, Briar at my side, my eyes return over and over again to the massacre happening in the courtyard. Most of the dragons have begun to take off, leaving the fight behind, though two of their number lie, slaughtered, on the ground. One of them slams her tail against one of Asalin's walls as she ascends, and with a sickening, cataclysmic explosion, the palace begins to fall. People, witches and fae alike who were hiding in the palace moments ago, begin to flood out, screaming.

Some of them join the fight, the same way that some residents in the village have begun to join in the carnage. But these are not trained warriors. All of Asalin's trained warriors are fighting on the side of Monalai's Guard. Their ranks are one and the same.

Perhaps the departure of the dragons has been caused by the arrival of *new* fae. Not from the palace, nor the village. I do not recognize them at all, nor do I know when they appeared. But I can see, even from here, that they are fighting alongside us, not against us. Perhaps these are fae from Kitaraq or Oflewyn, arrived for our meeting only to discover chaos.

I don't think they are. Though I cannot comprehend who they really might be.

At one point, I swear I see Maritza Pereira wielding a machete in the crowd. But that would make no sense.

Still, Summanus is alive. Somehow, as if sensing my stare, the giant creature swings his head to look at me.

"*Go,*" I mouth.

I know he understands me. I see it in his hesitation. The way he looks from me to the fight and back again. Until finally, with a cry, he lifts himself into the air and follows after the rest of his herd.

I am glad he is leaving us to our fate. He is as loyal a creature as has ever lived, but I cannot be certain we have ever deserved his loyalty.

There is a reason the pixies and the goblins, autonomous beings that they are, have not raised a hand to join this fight. I can feel them in the woods around us, moving about with unease, but none of them offer a shred of assistance. And why would they? What have the fae ever done for them?

And then I see the very last person I'd like to.

"*You.*" Nancy Pierce appears in front of us, blocking the

path Mary has been making through the woods, headed in the direction Emyr was last seen.

Boom snarls, haunches rising, and takes his post at my side.

She looks disheveled. Her khakis are crisped at the edges, her blouse torn, her hair a tangled mess. There are bruises on her face, her cakey foundation smudged. Her beige energy crackles along her shoulders and down into her palms, a dangerous, ugly kind of magic.

"Move," Mary says, in a tone more kind than this woman warrants.

I have always hated Nancy. Derek Pierce was a monster in his own right, but he was raised in the lap of a bigger one. Her obsession with the untainted Pierce bloodline, her conviction that her son was the true and rightful heir to the Throne, it spawned everything he did.

I wonder if she knows her bigotry, bottle-fed to her boy, is the reason he's dead now.

She ignores Mary's warning entirely. She's focused on me, those wild blue eyes wide and crazed. She takes a step forward. "All of this is your doing."

Maybe she isn't wrong. Maybe all my wanting created Emyr, the same way her hatred did with Derek. Maybe if I'd been more like Leonidas, more afraid to push, more docile, Emyr would have been the same. Maybe he would have been happy to accept the status quo.

Maybe I will be the reason for my boy's death, too.

And still, I will not give her the satisfaction of my acquiescence. "You were told to move, Nancy. Do not make this uglier than it already is."

At my side, Briar takes a step back, tucking the infant

tighter to her chest. I will not let anything happen to either of them. Nancy will have to go through me first.

She barely seems to register that I've spoken. She takes another step forward. "I tried so hard to stop it from coming to this. I always knew it would. From the moment Leonidas dragged you here. His beautiful, *precocious* bride." She practically hisses the words. "I knew you were going to ruin this kingdom. And look where we are now."

I am not the one who ruined Asalin. But what use is there in defending myself? "Well, I suppose you should have stopped me when you had the chance."

"I *tried*." She snarls like an animal, and it isn't fitting, coming from a woman usually as prim and uptight as her. "But you *lived*."

In the moment that passes after she speaks, the world is suddenly so very quiet. It isn't possible she's saying what I think she is. Is it?

Of course it is. But my brain doesn't want to believe it.

And even so, my brain has maybe known it, on some level, for a very long time.

"What is that supposed to mean?" I finally demand, even knowing what she's going to say.

Her upper lip rises over her teeth. "You never should have survived the fall from that tower."

She surges forward, hideous tan magic sparking toward me, but she doesn't manage to make it anywhere close. Mary moves with a swiftness I would never anticipate, throwing out her arm in front of Nancy's body.

No, not Nancy's body, exactly. Just her throat.

I see the jade green weapon in Mary's hand at the same moment I see blood spilling from Nancy's neck. She reaches up to press her hands to the gaping wound of her flesh, her mouth opening to protest, but more blood gushes out over her tongue.

The buzzing of her beige energy frantically collects around her neck, as if it thinks to heal her. That's what I expect it to do, at least. And instead, I watch with a sickened fascination as Nancy Pierce is eaten alive by her own magic. It snatches onto her sliced throat, and begins to disappear her right in front of my eyes. Her neck, and then her chest, her torso. The woman standing before us only seconds ago erupts into a thousand pieces of powdery fragments that float in the air around her. The last piece of her to disappear are those wild, terrified blue eyes.

And then Mary turns to me and slams her hand against my chest, and the magic that once was Nancy flies across the space between us and burrows its way into my body. Immediately, I feel it surge through my veins, flooding into me, an unfamiliar but not entirely uncomfortable new power.

"What have you done?!" I demand.

"I have returned what was stolen from you," she says simply, shoving the blade back into a hidden pocket in her pants. "Your life."

I don't know exactly what that means.

But for the first time in years, I no longer feel the scratching of death's claws.

Unfortunately, I hardly have time to process what's just happened before I hear Emyr scream.

THE EMPEROR, REVERSED

Emyr

I watch Wyatt run headlong into the castle, follow his back as he disappears from the protection of my sight, and marvel, for only a moment, at how he takes my breath with him. I will not breathe again until he is in my arms.

But that is the way it is. Right now, I have things to do more important than breathing.

That's been the theme of my life for as long as I've been aware of it—what I want to do is always less important than what I *must* do. My responsibility to myself is only to fulfill my responsibility to my people. Such is the lot of a prince, and of a king.

God, I am so tired of being a king.

But I don't have time to be tired. Not right now.

I wheel back to the battlefield stretched out in front of me.

The Bells are nowhere to be seen, but their Guards are trawling everywhere, supported by Asalin's own people, traitors attacking their neighbors and the fae from Faery.

These people don't even know *who* they're fighting, and I doubt they have a real understanding of *why*. This is just bloodshed for the sake of bloodshed. *These* are the kind of people attracted to the Guard. *This* is why we got rid of it.

There's no sign of Wade, either, or of Tessa, or my parents. But there is…

"Emyr!" Paloma appears, breaking free from the crowd just as one of the dragons above our heads slams her tail against the stone palace. Paloma's soft yellow wings flutter above her head, where Maritza appears, her tawny feathers stretching out to shield her wife.

And I watch, in a sort of detached horror, as Asalin falls right before my eyes.

With my breath trapped somewhere inside it.

"NO!" I surge forward, panic like a fist around my throat. The entrance has been blocked by fallen stone. I slam my hands against it, howling out my rage and desperation.

"Emyr," a familiar voice says at my back.

When I turn, Paloma and Maritza have been joined by Nadua. "Wyatt, is he—"

"Inside," I snarl.

A hollowed-out grief crushes her face. "I left Briar inside… to come and find him…" The woman's body begins to shake.

Paloma, though she cannot have any idea who Nadua is, wraps her in her arms.

No. I will not accept this.

All my life, I have been forced to accept things I do not want. To swallow back my own aches, to shelve my own dreams, for others. I have done so willingly, eagerly, every time. Because I was a good prince. Because I am a good king. Because I would do anything for my people.

Almost anything.

Wyatt is my limit, finally reached. He is the one dream I cannot be forced to shelve. My people can burn if they have to.

My claws curl into the rock. I am strong, but not strong enough to move this. I need an Influencer.

Or do I? Vorgaine's words float across my mind.

"Your magic is desperate for all it has been denied."

My magic cannot possibly be as desperate as I am. Because I have to get inside this castle. I have to find Wyatt. The goddess told me I would not die, that our lives were anchored to one another. If I survive, so will he.

But *survival* is a low bar. I picture his small body, trapped beneath stone somewhere inside, unable to free himself, unable to get back to me. I think of the years I spent apart from him, forced to play the role of the good prince, forced to stay behind in this kingdom when everything in me wanted to *find him*.

And eventually, I did find him. But I waited so long. We lost so much. And, like a coward, I only went to him when it was permitted by those telling me what I was *allowed* to want.

I failed him, then. I will not again.

My hands collide with the fallen stone blocking my path and gold erupts from my palms. It turns the rock to dust at my touch, an explosion of ash that fills the air. It's enough to sting my eyes, to choke my lungs, but I don't care. The entrance is open.

I will find you. I will always find you.

"Emyr?" Maritza's voice this time, a warning in her rasp. "You may want to see this, first."

Nothing could possibly be more important than finding Wyatt. I jerk around to tell her as much, a snarl poised on my mouth—

The Watchers of Faery are dragging my father out from the ruins of the castle by the collar of his shirt.

Okay, I will find you, Wyatt. But...well.

"CAVENIA!" I shout across the courtyard, storming in their direction. Gold and stone ash make a storm around my body as I move. "WHAT IS THE MEANING OF THIS?"

Perhaps it is the sight of the former king on his knees in front of the palace wreckage. Perhaps it is the sight of their current king stalking across the lawn toward him. Perhaps it is the sudden, creeping realization that this battle is drawing to a close, and there is something *not right* about the outcome. But whatever the case, the frenzy of battle has begun to die down. A quiet settles over Asalin.

Cavenia, one hand on my father's neck, turns to look at me. He shakes his head. "You know who we are, Emyr. You know what we must do."

"No! We had a deal! We will give you Wade Pierce." Panic thumps, hard, inside me. I look to my father's face, but he will not meet my eyes, his head bowed.

"Yes, we will take Wade, as well," Cavenia agrees.

"YOU WILL TAKE ONLY WADE!" Spit flies from my fangs as I bellow across the space between us. Gold flares out around me. "Or you will bring a new war to Faery's shores!"

All around us, onlookers begin to whisper.

"Faery?"

"Faery?"

"Faery?"

"Faery?"

Cavenia's eyes narrow. He cocks his head at me. Finally, in a low, grave tone, he says, "You know...we believed you were different. We allowed your mirror to the witch to protect you. But maybe we were wrong for that. Threatening a war if you don't get your way? You sound just like the rest of them. A Pierce through and through."

"No." Finally, my father speaks. One single word is enough to have nearly every eye in Asalin on him. He lifts his head, but he isn't looking at me. He's looking at Cavenia. "Kill me. And this will all be over."

"Dad—"

"You want to die?" Cavenia is unconvinced.

My father smiles. "My family has caused a great deal of pain. Witches have suffered for hundreds of years, in ways I will never be able to make up for, because of the things we've done. I understand why you hate us. But you can put an end to it now."

Eighteen years I've known him, but I have never seen this smile on his face before. It is not exuberant, as my favorite of his smiles are. Nor is it forced, like the ones he has offered me in moments when I believe he held the truth of himself at arm's length.

No, there is a peculiar unreality to this smile. Tears run freely down his wrinkled face but his blue eyes are vacant. He smiles as if he is no longer a resident of his body.

"The Pierce line has already been hunted or exiled into extinction. I and my nephew, Wade, are the last true Pierce fae who walk free." He won't look at me. "You will take my life, and then you will take his, and the last untainted drop of our family's blood will finally be spilled. You will rid this world, and every world, of our plague."

When he tilts his head back, offering the fae his throat, there is a pause among them. They are confused, and understandably so.

"You are not the last of your line," someone finally grumbles. "Your son is right here."

That smile does not waver. He still will not look at me. "I have no son."

And he's still speaking, I know. I can see his mouth moving, and I manage to catch a few choice phrases, things like *"...no living children..."* and *"...neither by name nor blood..."* But it is a curious thing, the way everything suddenly seems to be taking place from very far away.

Someone screams Cavenia's name again, but the sound is as distant as a memory. When I glance for the tree line, in the direction of the voice, I don't understand what Zai is doing there with Elonia at vaer side. They're not supposed to be here.

Zai runs for Cavenia, but another Watcher grabs vaer and forces vaer back. Over his shoulder, vae meets my eyes. Perhaps there is something like an apology in vaer stare.

Perhaps I'm the one who should be apologizing.

I never should have been king. And all the world knows it.

Does he say these things to save my life, or because he means them?

Cavenia raises the very sword I gave him above my father's neck. The sword I have carried with me for weeks now, paranoid about protecting myself after my brush with death. The sword I handed off, returning it to the world it came from, feeling empowered for the first time since that night, believing I no longer needed it to save myself.

He uses it to cut my father's head off.

I will never have my answer.

SHUFFLE

Right.

So, anyway. Back to me and *Clarke?!* in the bedroom.

CHAPTER TWENTY-FIVE

AND FROM THE ASHES, AN UNLIKELY HERO ARISES

The sight of Wade *becoming* his sister—the gruesome, revolting sight of his skin falling from his body, his teeth falling out of his mouth, only to be replaced by hers—is enough that I almost black out where I'm standing. A dizzy spell hits me and nearly knocks me off my feet, even as vomit chokes me, climbing up my throat.

Clarke giggles again, shaking her head. "Oh, please. Don't act so put off. You and I both know you've done worse."

The smell of burning flesh floats just under my nose. A flashback? Or Clarke's Influencer magic, fucking with my senses? Could be either, and it really doesn't matter either way.

There are plenty of things I want to ask her—things like *how*—but I don't think she's interested in sitting down for a chat. I can feel the cards in my pocket, heavy and insistent, pulsing against my body like they've got a life force of their own. Like they know what I want and they're as ready as I am.

"You haven't seen anything yet," I snarl, fingers curling around the deck. Black slicks up my hands, thrums between my fingers as I pull the cards free, and—

Clarke's pink energy strikes like a snake. It scalds when it slams into me, a fierce burning that breaks out across my hands as it goes right for the deck. And it distracts me, only for the briefest second, but just long enough for her to snatch the cards away from me.

Just like that. She just...takes them. And it's so, so easy for her.

She snickers, rolling her eyes. "I *have*, actually. I saw what you pulled in the courtyard—what there was to see of it, anyway. You've learned to control that little lights out trick. Good for you."

And she holds my eye as her magic, that pretty pink magic, curdles over her hands and sloshes up her arms. And then fire, her own fire, comes to life in her palm.

And my cards burn.

"Good for you," Clarke whispers.

And I am once again just a little child, wailing, watching my parents burn my first tarot deck. They'd found the cards given to me by Emyr, the first connection I'd ever felt to the witches, and forced me to stand back and watch while they destroyed them.

"NO!" I jump for her. I don't care if she's the most powerful, most evil monster this side of the door. I will take her apart with my bare hands. I will ruin her with my teeth if I have to.

But I don't even make contact with her. That energy slams right up against me and forces me into the wall, holding me in place against the stone. Pink wraps around me like some kind of cocoon, and I can only watch, completely and totally helpless, as my tarot cards turn to ash.

As my *magic* turns to ash. The one piece of magic I've ever let myself hold on to. The first time I ever felt truly *powerful*.

Just going up in smoke. As if it were nothing. Clarke's taken everything from me and she didn't even break a sweat doing it.

While the last card sheds into cinder, orange embers floating from Clarke's hand to the floor, I force myself to look away and meet her stare. Tears sting the corners of my eyes, burning with a sharp, familiar pain, but I refuse—absofuckinglutely refuse—to let this bitch see me cry.

"You aren't going to win." I can only manage a whisper, voice hoarse, something vicious and vile threatening to overcome me. The things I want to do to her, the *ways* I want to hurt her, don't feel like they're even coming from me. I've lost control before. I've hurt people before because I had to, because I didn't have any other choice.

But given the choice, I would burn Clarke Pierce alive inch by inch and make sure she felt every second. And that would be a kindness, all things considered.

"There may be losses on both sides tonight, but we've got you outnumbered. And every single one of our allies knows what you are." Maybe not that she's been cosplaying as her brother, but definitely that they both *suck*. "There's no scenario where you get the Throne. What's your end game here?"

Clarke shrugs. With my cards destroyed and my body held against the wall, she must think I'm a defused threat. She looks away from me to take the belt off Wade's pants, letting them slide off her legs, and refashioning his shirt into a dress by cinching the belt around her waist. Like she's worried about her outfit right now.

My teeth throb with the urge to rip her throat out.

Finally, after glancing at herself in the mirror and seeming content with whatever she finds, she looks back at me. Her smile returns. "You know, Wyatt, I told you once before and you didn't listen, but it bears repeating—you and I have a lot in common."

Do we? I don't remember being the literal embodiment of evil.

Entertaining a single similarity between Clarke and me means acknowledging the fact that she's a person at all. And it's hard for my brain to comprehend that a *person* could do the things she's done. It would be so much easier to think of her as a soulless void in expensive shoes.

"And the number one thing?" she continues. "Everyone is *always* underestimating us. It's a pity you're doing it to me, now. You'd think you would have learned better."

I don't really know what to say to that. Instead, I ask, "Where's Wade?"

She shrugs. "Rotting. I moved him just before things started getting touchy out there. Perhaps someone will have found him by now."

My chest feels like someone's slammed into me with their

car. An ache so big I can hardly breathe through it spreads through me. Part of me knew, the minute I saw her face, Wade was gone. But I didn't want to look at it, didn't want to face the fact that I've spent the last few days cursing the name of a dead man.

I try to remember the last time I saw him, when I would have seen the *real* him. I remember thinking how different he looked the morning he sent us off to New Zealand, how he'd showered and put himself together. So…the night the baby was born? The morning after? Was that the last time Wade, the *real* Wade, was there?

If so, he died wanting nothing more than his cousin's forgiveness, and to take custody of his niece. He died *aching* for his family—and at the hands of his family.

And what about Tessa? Oh, fuck. Tessa.

Something unspeakable grows inside of me, something I can't even put a name to, can't look directly at yet. There is a place in my torso that suddenly goes hollow to make room for old conversations and still-healing wounds, a hint of Clarke's familiar feigned tenderness and the memory of Derek's lecherous Influence worming like venom under my skin. I can't let myself think about it all, not really, not right now, otherwise there's no way I'm making it out of this room alive.

Still, Tessa's name bounces through me and echoes off my bones all the while.

When I can make my tongue work again, I ask, "You're not worried about someone finding him?"

Clarke grins and taps a manicured fingernail to her temple. "All part of the plan."

"Explain the plan, then."

I'm stalling. Just like she was stalling that day up on the mountain, waiting for Derek to come to her rescue before I attacked her, not knowing he never would. Just like Emyr was stalling yesterday—an hour ago—in the courtyard with the kings, waiting for me to get my shit together and act.

I don't know what I'm stalling for. A rescue? A plan? But I know as long as I keep Clarke talking, I'm not dying.

"Well," she hums. "It started with Lavender."

Lavender, Roman's surrogate mother and the leader of the witch activists. Lavender, the woman Clarke murdered.

She continues, "Well, technically, I guess it started with Jin. With Jin's technology. See, it takes witches to make it work. *Witches* have to put in the spells. Fae can use the damn thing, sure, but let's be honest—Jin designed this to make *you* feel powerful. Not to help us."

You shouldn't be allowed to speak Jin's name.

"Once I realized I could use your contract to take Emyr out of the running for the Throne, I knew I needed witch magic to actually go through with it. *I* certainly couldn't code a spell. And there was no way Jin was going to turn on Emyr themself. No. I tried getting closer to other witches, tried to find someone who might be willing to do it if I convinced them it was for their own cause—but I don't think any of them trusted me very much."

"Weird."

"Right?" She chuckles. "Anyway, so I didn't have a *witch*. But I did have a witch's *body*. Thanks to our friend Lavender."

I'm beginning to realize where her story is going. And I don't want to hear it. I want her to stop talking, as badly as I need her to keep talking.

"You know, I've always heard magic travels through the blood. And it makes sense, right? I mean, we pass it on to our children, and their children. And we bleed for our most sacred contracts—there's no binding as powerful as a blood oath. That's gotta mean something. That's what I figured, anyway. So, I thought. Maybe I don't need a witch. Maybe I just need a witch's blood." She grins. "I had no idea how *right* I really was."

I think back to New Zealand. To the changelings. To Mary's offended explanation that *of course* they didn't eat the fae.

What would happen if they *did* though? If they dug their corpses from the ground and fed on what was left?

Apparently Clarke knows what would happen.

I can see not-Wade, standing over an empty bassinet, in my mind's eye. *"I came here looking for my delicious little niece…"*

Vomit erupts into the back of my mouth, and I swallow it.

When I can finally stomach speaking again, I ask only, "Wade?"

She shrugs. "As I told you once, sweetie, I'm very talented with makeovers. It was easy enough turning myself into him. But mimicking someone's *energy*? That's a whole other level. I needed something special for that." She sighs, and then, nonchalantly, adds, "So, I ate his heart."

I think maybe I'm watching all of this happen from somewhere outside of myself now. Something breaks in my brain. I can't handle it.

"He was your brother. How could you let yourself do that?"

Clarke snarls, expression shifting suddenly from mocking happiness to genuine rage. "Do you know the only thing worse than a witch who doesn't know their place? A fae who doesn't know theirs."

I can only stare at her.

When I don't give her the reaction she's looking for, she adds, "And anyway, the whole thing is unfortunate for me, too. I think I'm getting a taste for it. It's a rush but a pain in the ass to hide, you know."

"I came here looking for my delicious little niece..."

I hope she dies a very painful death. "Uh, no, I absolutely don't know. I don't understand. If you went through all this trouble—" that's one word for it "—to impersonate Wade, why blow your cover now? Why let people find his body?"

"Because I'm not going to be Wade for much longer, silly duck."

"Who—" I want to ask the question, but as soon as it starts forming on my tongue, I know the answer. And she must be able to see it, on my face, the moment I realize what she's planning, because she starts to giggle.

"Finally, he catches on."

"You can't kill me," I whisper. Panic threads through the branches of my lungs. "The night I brought Emyr back, I anchored my life to his. Neither of us can die without the other."

Clarke tilts her head, eyebrows knitting together. She hums, quietly, and then shrugs. "Oh, well. It's a good thing I wasn't planning on letting him live, either."

As she stalks toward me, the panic in my lungs kicks it up into overdrive. I can feel my pulse threatening to pound right out of my throat.

"Allow me to set the scene for you, since you won't be around to see it yourself." She chuckles, getting so close our chests are nearly touching. "Asalin is in ruins. The king has died on the battlefield. The evil Pierce family has finally been

defeated, but at a terrible cost. And from the ashes, an un-
likely hero arises. The very witch who once sought to destroy
the kingdom himself—but who was born to *rule it*. With or
without his mate." She sighs, a swoony kind of sound, and
presses her palm to my cheek. It's all I can do not to flinch.
"These pawns will lap it up. They'll get in line to lick your
boots. And then…well, how could they possibly ever accuse
you of not being on the side of the witches, of not being *progressive* enough?"

Her thumb brushes against my cheek. I can feel her energy
as it slides over my skin and shoves itself against my own. Can
feel the gaping, hungry thrum of it as it beats against me.

"It's a shame you didn't take me up on my offer to make
some alterations," she taunts with a smirk. "There are definitely some cosmetic renovations we'll *have* to do. But that's
alright. We can start with the basics for now. I tell you what,
I'll get changed, and then you'll tell me how it looks before
I carve you open and use your vena cava as a bendy straw.
Okay?"

She doesn't wait for my answer, but she shouldn't, because
one isn't coming. Clarke's face begins to shift again. First the
godawful loss of teeth, falling one by one to the floor, blood
pouring over her mouth as they do. Then the hair.

And I can see the halting, jerking process, as it unfolds in
front of me. I can see the moment that Clarke's features, so
pretty and delicate and repulsive, begin to look like my own.
A rounder softness to the cheeks. A smattering of scars. One
of her blue eyes pops out of her head and rolls onto the floor,
a green one beginning to grow in its place.

I want to move, to do literally anything to stop what's

happening, but I can't make myself. Not just because of the magic holding me in place. But because there is something sickly fascinating about this whole thing. I don't want to watch. It is disgusting, and horrifying, and I don't want it to happen—and yet.

Within minutes, another me stands in front of me. Our only discernible differences the clothes we're wearing, and Clarke's pink energy still fluttering around her-my body.

She puts her-my hand back on my face, says in my own voice, "Well? What do you think?" Her giggle sounds even more disgusting from my mouth. "How does it feel to finally have to face yourself, Wyatt Croft?"

A beat passes, where I stare into my own slightly mismatched eyes. And a vicious realization begins to crawl its way through my chest.

Clarke might have burned my cards, but I'm *not* the same wailing kid I was when my parents did the same. I'm not helpless or trapped. I *know* myself now. I know my magic.

And I know the cards are just a conduit. I don't need them. I never did.

"You're right. I did underestimate you. But you underestimated me, too. Oh, *sweetie*," I tilt my cheek into her-my palm. "Did you really think *fire* would stop *me*?"

And then, in exactly the same way I channeled Emyr's magic last night in Faery, I drag Clarke's power from her body into mine.

It feels *bad*, but it also feels immediate. Like a sugar rush, pink cotton candy floods into my arteries and lights me up from the inside out. I keep pulling, and pulling, yanking as much of it as I can into me and out of her control.

She yelps, like a startled little dog, and jumps back, just as the magic keeping me pinned to the wall is broken.

Power crackles around my body, an ugly, offensive combination of her pink and my black. They can't seem to work together, slashing out at each other even as they both bend to my control, frantically snapping like a storm around me.

I watch as my eyes widen in my face, as not-me takes a step back. "How—"

"For a long time, I was afraid to look at the things I'd done. The things you people *forced me* to do." The words crawl out my throat as a rough whisper, and I move toward her as she backs up rapidly. Fire begins to crawl up my arms, and ignites at my feet when my soles scuff the floor. Pink and black tornadoes whirl in my palms. "And if you'd been just a little earlier, this plan would've worked. 'Cause when I couldn't even stand to look at myself, I had no idea what I was really capable of."

It's *her* backed into the wall now, my-her back against stone as I step nose to nose with my own face. "But you're too late. Because I *already* faced myself, Clarke. And it turns out, I'm not actually my own worst nightmare, the way I always thought." My hands find the sides of her-my face, my fingers caressing the soft, scarred cheeks. "I'm yours."

Energy explodes like a bomb. Pink and black and flame, all wrapped up into one, build and build until they can't build anymore, until they have to release. They rush out in a thrumming wave from my body, connecting hard with the stone walls when they do. The very air around us seems to shake with the force of the contact, as the bellow of magic meeting mountain rings in my ears. I smell petrichor and sulfur just before jagged broken hunks of rock begin to collapse from the ceiling, and the ground, with a splintering, devastating crack, starts to fall out from underneath us.

My fingers dig into the sides of not-my face, blunt nails forcing their way beneath the surface of not-my skin, blood spurting onto my fingers. Clarke tries to shift back into herself, her hair falling out, her skin beginning to peel away from the muscle beneath. The fleshy mask of her magicked costume comes away more easily into my hands, until I can feel her cheekbones from the inside. I smell burning flesh again, but I know, this time, it isn't an illusion. I hear my own scream, but I'm not the one screaming.

Maybe we're going to die, but she's not going to wear my face while we do.

But instead of being buried under crumbling boulders, we land safely on the ground as the castle explodes into *dust*. Where once was Asalin's ancient palace is now nothing more than a pile of sand in the middle of the woods.

Well, one of us lands safely. I'm unhurt, standing in the center of the settling dust storm, suddenly surrounded by the fae and witches fighting outside.

Clarke lies—little more than a tangled mess of meat, some parts of her raw and others burnt to a crisp—dead at my feet.

And my own face, ripped from her skull, hangs limply in my hands.

CHAPTER TWENTY-SIX

YOUR MISSION IS OVER

Despite the number of people, my eyes find Emyr immediately. He's on his knees in the grass, with Nadua, Paloma, and Maritza behind him. As if sensing my stare, he turns his head to meet my eyes, and his are red-shot and hollow.

I see Leonidas's body soon after. Both parts of it. I don't have it in me to feel nauseated anymore at the sight of gruesome death, but my heart does give a painful tightening.

Oh, Emyr.

Standing over Leonidas are the Watchers, Cavenia holding the bloody sword.

Zai and Elonia are here, somehow, with Watchers keeping them both back. I can see the triad on the other side of Emyr, Solomon poised as if he were trying to get to Zai, the other two holding him in place.

Farther back, Tessa, Ari, and Kora come stumbling out of the woods. Kora has an arm around Tessa's waist, like she's keeping her upright. She's already crying, but when she sees me from across the yard, she lets out a half-delirious *yowl*. She surges forward, like she intends to come to me, but the girls keep her back.

I can't keep my eyes on her. There is still that *thing* I can't look at.

On the other side of the courtyard, coming from another gap in the woods, I spot Briar with the baby, Kadri, and Mary. Boom trots out after them and then, with no concern for the gravity of what's happening, makes his way over to my side. I look to Briar, and we catch eyes, a silent exchange of relief and reunion passing between us. But it only lasts a moment before we both look back to Emyr.

He's not staring at me anymore. He's looking at Leonidas again. Or what *used* to be Leonidas.

Emyr's dad was not a good person. Their relationship was fraught, and often ugly, especially toward the end. But I know firsthand that only makes the grief complicated, not easier to carry.

As I watch, a convoy begins to make its way through the village, up the cobblestone road toward us. Something unpleasant churns in my gut at the memory of the Monalai kings and their arrival. And when these cars begin to park, the royals from Kitaraq and Oflewyn step into the courtyard.

Loureen and Calvince Muia, from Kitaraq, are the oldest of the royals, but their frailty is belied by the obvious enormity of their power. I remember admiring their energy the last time I saw them, the way they seem to only have one single magic between them, an opalescent white that surrounds them both. Even apart, they're fascinating. Calvince holds his shoulders back and surveys the wreckage with practiced detachment, barely glancing at Leonidas. Loureen, though, stares at the once king with genuine and *profound* sadness. Her eyes don't move from his body.

Amin and Pari Darwish are the rulers from Oflewyn. Classically handsome, well put together Amin balks at the sight of Asalin's castle, his bright red energy buzzing, and immediately turns to the people with him to start barking orders. Pari, though, scans the crowd of people until her eyes find Kadri. With no regard for the obvious *bloodbath* she's running through, or her own pregnant belly, she races across the courtyard to her friend, throwing her arms around Kadri's shoulders when she reaches her, navy blue energy shielding them both.

"What is the meaning of this?!" Amin demands, storming forward. He swings his arm out, toward Cavenia. "Why are you all just standing there? Why are you not arresting this man? Why—"

I hold up my palm, and Amin falls silent, though he doesn't look particularly happy about it. I look back to Emyr. He's looking at me again.

Please. I can hear his thoughts as clearly as if I were a mind reader, the unspoken word hanging between us.

Okay. I nod, and look back to Cavenia. And then I pick up Clarke's body by the back of her neck and drag it the several yards from the ashes of the castle to the blood-soaked grass where Leonidas was beheaded. I toss her, and my own ripped-off face, at the Watchers' feet.

The crowd shifts closer, as if hoping to get a better look at it, or maybe trying to interpret just *what* they're seeing.

"The only remaining members of the Pierce line are a witch and the mirror of one. Your mission is over." I swallow. "The door will remain open. But the Watchers are no longer welcome here."

Cavenia considers the body, then glances at his people. After a few nods, they begin to make their way into the woods. He stays behind only to say, "You understand why this had to be done."

I don't answer him. Maybe I do. Maybe I won't mourn Leonidas the way Emyr will. But it doesn't change anything.

Eventually, he follows after the others.

Zai and Elonia move to join the triad as soon as the Watchers are gone. They aren't the only fae still here from Faery. I spot their faces in the crowd. I see some of their bodies on the ground, with the bodies of Guards, and witches, enemies and allies.

I take a deep breath and look around at the living again. Everyone in the courtyard is staring at me. Waiting.

"The door to Faery is open." A chorus of whispers—and some shouting—spreads across the lawn. I wait for everyone to let it out, before continuing. "Everything we have been led to believe about that world is a lie. It is not dead. It is *thriving*. And it is only able to do so because of the relationship between the fae and the witches. As equals."

For so much of the past few years, I've dreaded the idea of having to stand in front of people and lead. To give speeches just like this one.

Maybe it's because I don't have anything left to give that

I can't bring myself to be uncomfortable now. I don't feel much of anything.

Except for a clawing desperation to be done, so I can get to Emyr.

"So much of what we've been taught about our magic is a lie. And these lies have poisoned, not only our kingdoms, but this entire world. But for the first time, we have access to the truth. For the first time, I believe there is hope for our futures."

My hands clench at my sides. I grit my teeth. They're not going to like this. "Asalin has fallen, but in its place we're going to build something new. And the same must happen to every other kingdom."

The Watchers believe evil itself comes from the Pierce family. And so, with that line almost entirely gone, their job on Earth is done. But I know *evil* wears many faces. The whole of fae society on Earth was built on hate. It's rooted here in Asalin, and in every other kingdom across the globe. There are other families to deal with. Plenty of other people who would rather stage a coup or burn a kingdom to the ground than see witches hold any power. The work isn't over. It's barely just begun.

"We cannot, and will not, continue like we have. We'll get back the knowledge that was stolen from us. And we'll use it as a roadmap for rebuilding our societies. For creating a world where fae, and witches, and any creature from this world or another can live in peace."

I shrug, moving forward, turning away from them and their shouting. "And if you don't like it, you're always welcome to go through the door yourselves. There's a goddess there you can take it up with."

There are plenty of questions we're going to have to answer, sooner rather than later. There are details we'll have to fill everyone in on. We're going to need an actual plan. But for right now, none of that matters.

For right now, I hit my knees in front of my boyfriend, and wrap my arms around him. His face finds my neck, his arms sliding around my waist and dragging me tight to his chest.

Though I don't see them, I can still feel when the others join us. Briar, Kadri, Mary, and the baby. Tessa, Lorena, Solomon, Roman, Kora, and Ari. Nadua, Paloma, and Maritza. Zai and Elonia. Together, we stand in the ruins of the kingdom of Asalin, and we wait for the fight that's still to come.

CHAPTER TWENTY-SEVEN

THE WORLD

While the changelings return the bodies of the dead to the Earth, we take Kadri to Faery's door.

She says she needs to see it for herself. And when she does, she stares at the twisted elm archway, into the Isle of Not beyond, for a long moment in silence.

Finally, she nods, turning back to Emyr, Briar, and me. "I don't know if this is the right decision. But we *will* leave the door open."

And she's right. She doesn't know if it's the right decision, and neither do I, neither do any of us. It could be a great thing. It could mean we're just asking for problems.

But that's basically true of everything I've ever done. And I've turned out fine.

Mostly.

Kind of.

Emyr takes a deep breath and nods, rubbing his palm over his face. I don't think he's come back to his own body, yet. I don't know how long it will be before he does.

Briar hooks her elbow with his, and leans her head onto my shoulder.

I only have eyes for Kadri. "What do we do now?"

There's really no knowing if the other kingdoms will fall in line, and I'm really not sure the people of Asalin will, either. We have no idea what happened to Gordon Bell, who seemed to disappear after Summanus made a snack out of his husband. There's still so much to be done, and to be undone, and it feels like for every exhausting step we took over the last few months, things are only just getting started. What if—

"Now you rest," Kadri says, and I think at first I must have misheard her. When our eyes meet and she realizes I'm just staring, barely processing her words, she continues, addressing all three of us, "You have already done everything you can. You stopped an evil regime from taking hold of the Throne. You tore apart unjust, broken systems and fought your hardest to replace them with something better. And not only did you protect the witches when you could, but you helped them to realize—helped us all to realize—that it isn't *protection* they really need. You showed us how much we need *each other*. And you might've saved us all by doing it. You certainly saved me."

She reaches up to press her fingers to her throat, brushing her short claws along her collar. I wonder what she's thinking about, where that far-off look in her eyes has taken her, but it's only seconds before she snaps out of it.

"So, now you get to stop. You destroyed Asalin, and you gave us all the tools we need to rebuild it better. Trust that we will. And go be children. Rest. Grieve. Heal. Your jobs are done."

An almost total silence makes the air around us feel thick. It's interrupted only by birds in the branches overhead, and the distant sounds of people moving around the bodies near what used to be the palace.

Our jobs are done?

"Are you sure?" Emyr's voice is the softest I've ever heard it. In this moment, he is not a king. He is not an aristocrat or a warrior. He is just a child standing in front of his mother and asking her if he can stop being strong.

The hand on Kadri's throat moves to beckon him forward, showing him her open palm and curling her fingers toward her wrist. "Yes, baby. You can let go now."

And he does. He collapses in front of her chair, and he buries his face in her lap, and he starts to sob. It is an ugly, wide open kind of cry, a heaving thing that throws itself up from his stomach. She slides one hand along the back of his neck, brushing through his curls, and shushes him, softly. Her gray energy wraps around his gold until it covers it entirely, hiding it from sight.

Briar and I don't need to say anything. We leave together, giving them their space.

When I spot Tessa, sitting alone next to a tiny little tree, covered in white flowers, Briar squeezes my hand and then continues on without me.

But when I get closer, I realize Tessa isn't actually alone at all. She's holding the baby, propped up against her thighs.

The newborn blinks sleepily up at her, then over at me when I crouch down next to them.

"I'm sorry about Wade."

It barely scratches the surface of all the things I want to say, but I don't know where else to begin. I reach out and brush my nail against the baby's wrist, and she turns her hand over, wrapping her little fist around my finger. I notice her fluttering rainbow energy seems to have taken on a greener shade than normal.

"Thanks."

It's a curt brush-off, but there's sincerity hidden in it. She has nothing else to say, the same way I don't.

We both know what Clarke did to her. It hangs between us, unspoken.

Maybe it should surprise me more than it does. But of course it doesn't. Clarke made it clear she was willing to do whatever it took to convince people she cared about them. She used her softness and her charm and her *love* as a weapon. What she did to Jin was no better.

And anyway, she did always admire her older brother and his tricks.

People like that, people who only care about power and how much of it they have, will find any way to wield it. Unicorn Boy's hand up my skirt. Derek pressing me against the foot of his bed, using his magic to convince me I wanted him. Clarke wearing Wade's face and taking my sister to bed.

This isn't the time to talk about it, I know. She's not ready to look at that, yet. It's only been hours since she found out he died at all.

But whenever she is, if she ever is, I'll be there to listen.

"I was thinking maybe her name is Magnolia." Tessa's eyes shine when she tilts her head up to look at me.

My eyes flit to the little tree and back to her face. *Magnolia*. "We could call her Maggie."

"Yeah. Maggie." She looks back down at the baby, and tears slip freely down her cheeks. "Maggie Croft."

I bend forward to kiss her forehead before I go.

As I leave, Lorena slips past me to join her. The other witch squeezes my wrist as we pass each other.

Briar is waiting for me at the edge of the courtyard, and she isn't alone. Paloma and Maritza are with her. Maritza with her machete on her back, cleaning her wife off.

"There you are, little shadow." Paloma sighs when she spots me. "I'm glad you're still alive."

Briar takes my hand.

"Again, I don't love this greeting." But I don't have it in me to pack any heat behind the words. "I wanna ask you something."

"Ask, then."

"You told me once that I was going to be king. That my marriage to Emyr was inevitable, and the contract wasn't supposed to be dissolved. I don't know if you've noticed, but you were wrong." I motion to the remains of Asalin, the bodies in the field. "So, are you just a shitty psychic, or what?"

Paloma laughs, tilting her head back and baring the black swath of her throat. Maritza takes her chin between her fingers and tilts it back down so she can continue wiping the blood from her face.

"Maybe I am," she says around a chuckle, flashing me a glittering look. "But what would have happened to Asalin, to any of the fae kingdoms, if your contract *had* been annulled when Kadri came to us? You may not be marrying Emyr just yet, but without your engagement, you never would've come back here. And none of this would have happened."

For better or worse, I guess. Emyr was on the path to changing Asalin forever, but without me...would he have succeeded? Or would Derek be on the Throne right now? It's a strange thing for me, to admit I've actually helped people. But it's true.

I did good.

"Yeah, well." I close my eyes, tipping my head back against a tree. "I'm not the king."

"No." Paloma's soft voice tickles at my ear. "I did misinterpret that part. Not a king. Something better."

When I open my eyes again, the queens have wandered off, leaving Briar and me alone. She's staring across the courtyard, and I follow her stare to find Mary, Nadua, Solomon, and Zai crouched over one of the bodies. Mary is showing them how to move the energy.

With a jolt, I realize the *body* is Leonidas.

I should stop them. Right? When Emyr and Kadri come back from the woods, they'll want his body. They'll want to say goodbye.

It makes sense. And still, I can't seem to force my legs to move in Mary's direction. Can't open my mouth and call out to them to get her to stop.

Leonidas's familiar green energy explodes into dust in the courtyard. Moments later, where there was just a fresh corpse, a mushroom circle has taken his place. Dozens and dozens of little golden-capped mushrooms sprout up through the soil and make rings around the survivors.

Briar squeezes my hand as our heads move in unison to follow the fungi as it continues sprawling past the clearing and into the forest.

Maybe it will find Emyr and Kadri on its own. And maybe that's better than a headless king, anyway.

Roman, Kora, and Elonia hang back a few feet, watching the others. When Roman catches my eye, he gives the smallest inclination of his head.

I don't know what the triad will do next. Maybe they'll stay here and help the witches rebuild. Maybe they'll take Zai and Elonia to New Zealand, to learn more from Mary and the others. Maybe they'll fuck off to Faery and live happily ever after. They've earned it.

Either way, I hope we find a way to see each other again.

As the little group disperses, Nadua stands and heads in our direction. I'm not sure if she reaches out first, or if I step forward and she just raises her hand to meet me. But as soon as she's in arm's length, I press my cheek against the palm of her hand and close my eyes. Her thumb strokes along the bridge of my nose and, even without looking, I feel her clay-colored energy tighten around my shoulders.

"All your friends okay?" she asks, voice gruff but sincere.

"I think so," Briar answers, close enough that her breath tickles my face. "But Jin is gone."

"What?" I jerk back, eyes popping open. "What do you mean? Gone where?"

Wet, muted sadness tucks itself into the backs of Briar's eyes. She offers me a not-smile and a one-shoulder shrug. "They left for Faery. They needed…" She sniffs and straightens her spine. "They needed to move on."

I *want* to be angry at Jin for ditching us in the middle of a shitshow, but I can't even make myself pretend to be annoyed. Moving on is exactly what I've been hoping they'd do. Granted, I didn't think it'd look like this, but…

"Are *you* okay?" I tip my chin at Briar, eyebrows rising.

She bites at the inside of her lip. "I'll miss them. But it's probably for the best this way."

Yeah.

Wherever, and whenever, Jin is, I hope they're happy. And while I *hope* to see the triad again, I have a feeling my path will *definitely* cross with Jin Ueno's another day.

"And where is your king?" Nadua asks, kindly changing the subject.

"Emyr's with Kadri. She wanted to check out the door for herself." I slump into Nadua's side when her arm tightens around my waist. "She seems…different."

Nadua clicks her tongue with a nod. "I'm not entirely sure of the details. But it seems like Mary used Nancy Pierce's energy to heal her."

Briar asks, "Kadri's not dying?" at the same time I step back and shout, "Nancy's dead?!"

Nadua nods for us both.

"We just saw her, though." I shake my head. "She was still in the wheelchair."

"I can only tell you what I've told you." Nadua shrugs. "It isn't my story, and I don't have all the details. But maybe she'll fill you in, when she's ready."

She steps back, tilting her head toward the woods. "I'm

going to check on her. And let her know what's happened with her husband." Her eyes go sharp as she holds out a finger in warning. "*Don't* disappear. We're all sleeping under one roof tonight. Understood?"

"Understood," Briar and I repeat in unison, and then Nadua is gone.

Kadri isn't dying.

Maybe she'll never walk again. Maybe she'll always carry the scars of what happened to her. But she's not *dying*. Knowing that, now, her words make a lot more sense. She's not going anywhere. She can lead, the way she always should have.

Emyr and I really can rest.

Briar sighs, and our eyes meet.

Do you know how much I love you? My fingertips brush along the back of her hand, tracing the shadows of leaves overhead as sunlight breaks through the branches.

She sighs, her thumb curling up along mine, pressing into the space where it meets my palm. *Yes. Do you know I feel the same?*

I lean forward at the same moment she does, and we knock our foreheads together. Eyes closed. Just breathing. *I do.*

My relationship with Briar is a lot like Asalin itself. For everyone to see, it was beautiful, practically perfect, but there were ugly things growing underneath. Things that were shuffled out of sight, intentionally not looked at critically or for too long. I put her on a pedestal, convinced myself she didn't have a single flaw, and it only hurt her in the end. She stretched herself so thin she almost disappeared trying to solve *my* problems, and it just kept me from ever having to face them on my own.

Just like Asalin, we had to fall apart. But we can rebuild, too. And we will.

I don't know what our relationship is going to look like moving forward. I know it exists, though. In one form or another, across space and time and whole other worlds if need be, there's going to be Briar and me, together.

She squeezes my hand and heads in the direction of the other changelings. I don't follow her.

Instead, I turn and walk back into the woods.

The field outside of Emyr's cabin is still filled with peryton. Either they somehow avoided the chaos of the night, unscathed, or they've already recovered. Ari's with them, at the center of the field, running one of his big hands along a baby's spotted back. They barely spare me a glance as I move past them through the grass, and into the little house covered in overgrown flowers. Inside, it just smells like clean air, the window at the back hanging open.

It's been weeks since I was here last, the day Emyr and I said goodbye, not knowing it wasn't really goodbye at all. Then, I thought everything was coming to an end, thought my job here in Asalin was done, and I was going to disappear back into the human world and start some new life. I didn't realize how much was only just getting started, how much I was still right in the middle of.

This time, it really is an ending. But I know now it's also a beginning.

My fingers itch to grab for a card in a deck that no longer exists. Absentmindedly, I brush my fingertips together, as if I were pulling—and flame flicks to life at my fingertips. The fire takes shape, forming the lines of a card in my hand.

The World.

One chapter coming to a close, while the next looms just ahead.

I open my palm and the flame disappears, but something warm blooms in my chest.

The door to the cabin swings open. Emyr's eyes are red and swollen when he looks at me, tear tracks dried on his cheeks. Boom trots in behind him, slipping past his legs to drop into his oversize dog bed.

Emyr drops the recovered bag of Faery's books onto the cabin floor before holding out a little white card to me. I take it and frown. "What's this?"

"Apparently," his voice, so hoarse from crying, takes me off guard. "One of New Zealand's changelings is a therapist. She'd like to speak with us later."

A beat of silence passes before I laugh.

And I laugh *hard*, maybe because that's the funniest thing I've ever heard, maybe because I don't know what else there is to do. Still, I put the card on the kitchen counter for safe-keeping.

Emyr's hands curl around my waist, and mine slide up the sides of his neck. He kisses me, soft and chaste, and I don't follow him when he pulls away. We're both too strung out for anything more than that. He moves over into his ham-mock and drops down, eyelids sliding closed.

Kadri's right. He's earned his rest. We all have.

I can't get mine just yet, though.

The last leftovers of Clarke's energy are still lingering in-side me. I feel it, like sticky-sweet saltwater taffy clinging to my bones. I hate it. It's nothing at all like the feeling of drawing on Emyr's magic, when gold and black twine together in their brilliant, if imperfect, union. Emyr's energy moving inside me feels natural.

This feels all kinds of wrong. Clarke's bubblegum-pink magic isn't supposed to be anywhere near mine. It needs to go.

And I know it will, soon. She's gone and she's not coming back. It won't be long now before the last dregs of her fade away, leaving behind nothing but wounds that need tending.

But I could help move things along more quickly.

For so long, maybe my whole life, I've been searching for a *home*. It was never in my parents' house. There was a time when I thought it could be in the palace, with Emyr. And, when that didn't work out, I made my home with the Begay-Browns. I didn't realize I was also trying to carve one out inside of Briar.

Lately, I've been fantasizing about what things look like in the future. Now that we get to rest. I think I'd like to find that home. Maybe it looks like an apartment in Texas. Maybe it's a brightly colored house in Eirgard, or a quaint little home in the changeling village outside of Monalai, or a treehouse in Ra'Ora. Maybe it's this very cottage. I don't know. And I don't have to know, not today, or tomorrow, or anytime soon. I have all the time I need to figure out where I want to live. To decide what I want to do next, and do forever. I think I'll know it when I find it.

And honestly, I'm not worried about it anymore. Because I'm finally realizing I've been carrying around *home* with me this whole time.

My body is my home. It's the first home I ever had, and it's the only one I know I'm always going to have. It's just that it's never really felt like it belonged to me.

My parents took one look at my body, the day I was born, saw I was a witch, and made up their minds about me.

Later, as soon as people realized Emyr and I were fated mates, all of Asalin decided my body was good for nothing more than giving the kingdom the heirs it demanded.

As my magic grew but the secrets to wielding it were kept away from me, my body felt more and more like a disaster waiting to happen. Until one day it wasn't *waiting* anymore. Then it just felt like a graveyard, my scars like epitaphs, inescapable reminders of what I'd done.

And yeah, when I realized I was trans, there were things I started to hate in brand-new ways. Rarely being seen as *myself* played tricks on my mind, created a chasm between the me in my head and the me in everyone else's.

Even Derek, rest in pieces, controlled my body in his own fucked-up way.

So much was decided for me. All of the experiences were forced on me by other people—people who took away my control and backed me into a corner. Of course I never felt at home in my own skin. It barely felt like *mine* at all.

But that's over now. For the first time, my body is my own. My *future* is my own. Not as the witch king, or the fae keeper. Just as Wyatt.

I have all the power here. And I can do whatever I want.

There's a mirror hanging on one wall of the cabin. I stand in front of it and consider myself. Buzzed hair, overgrown because when the fuck would I have had time for a haircut lately? Two green eyes, one just a shade darker than the other, with purple rings beneath each one. The scars running the length of my cheek and over my jaw. Sharpened teeth peeking from under my upper lip. Slumped shoulders and the tan edge of my binder poking over the collar of my shirt. A thin waist and wide hips and small hands.

It's really not a bad body. And it's gotten me this far, despite all the things that tried to stop it.

But what would I change, if I could?

Would I make it easier to pass as cis, changing bits and pieces of myself not because I *hate* them but because I hate the way other people look at them? Would I get rid of the scars, allow myself to finally get a break from the constant, never-ending reminder of the worst things that have ever happened to me? Or would I make myself into more of a monster, something truly un-fuck-with-able, and reclaim some of the power the fae have *always* denied me?

Hell, maybe I'd just cover myself in cool tattoos, because that shit's expensive and I have no money.

Maybe bits and pieces of all of the above.

Because it's *not* a bad body. And I *don't* hate it. The whole wide fucked-up world has worked overtime to try and make me turn on it, but their plans have always fallen through. Hating my body is not a prerequisite for validating my existence. Not because I'm trans. Not because of the things I've survived. And not because I'm a witch.

And still, I can love my body, and *want* to change it. Isn't that, in a way, the ultimate act of loving it? Just like loving Asalin means tearing it down and starting over, maybe loving myself means actually owning the skin I live in. Defiantly holding up a middle finger to everyone who ever tried to use it for their own purposes, who ever tried to convince me it would never actually belong to me.

Maybe, in the end, it's just me finally coming home to myself.

"Hey, Your Highness?" Shit, I guess I can't call Emyr that for much longer.

Though I don't turn to look at him, I hear him scoff. "What, Firestarter?"

I grin. "Wanna see something cool?"

The hammock ropes creak. I imagine him shifting, turning his body toward mine to see what trouble I'm getting myself into now.

I focus on Clarke's energy, the intense, unwelcome pressure of it in my chest. How hysterical that this will be the last thing her magic ever does. The final note in the Pierce family's twisted story.

"Wyatt?"

And slowly, subtly, the reflection in the mirror begins to change.

★ ★ ★ ★ ★

ACKNOWLEDGMENTS

First and foremost, a resounding "THANK YOU!" to my incredible publishing team: Stephanie, Bess, Laura, Brittany, Justine, Linette, Kathleen, Connolly, Andy, and everyone else who had a hand in bringing this book to life. I was once again blown away by the amazing cover art by illustrator Ryan Garcia. My agents, Lee and Victoria, are the best advocates for me and my career I could have asked for. And, as always, I am forever indebted to the incredible sensitivity readers who offered insightful feedback on the way marginalized identities are represented throughout this duology.

TFK could not have been written without the aid of caffeine and prescription medication, so big thumbs-up to both Starbucks and my psychiatrist. Don't know what I'd do without either of y'all.

TFK *also* could not have been written without my early readers and best friends. So—

For MJ: for truly understanding this story, and understanding me, and never letting me give up on either.

For Samantha: for writing sprints, and seven-minute-long voice memos, and so much laughter, and reminding me to be gentle with myself *or else*.

For Alina: for lending me their vision when I was trying to build a world I couldn't yet see clearly. (Is this about the book or am I being gay? Yes.)

I am eternally grateful for my eccentric little brood, the people I love most and am privileged to be loved by in return. Though always chaotic and occasionally feral, I cannot imagine my life without my chosen family, both in my home and around the world. It is only with their endless support that I am ever able to get anything done.

Well, all of them except for Fin, who actively distracts me from working, but who makes up for it by being two years old and perfect. (And a special shout-out to Erin for making sure I cannot actually just stare at our kid all the time.)

And finally, thank you to everyone who picked up this series and became a champion for Wyatt and me. Thank you for yelling about your feelings on social media, and sending emails to tell me how validated you felt, and creating a community around my words. Thank you for embracing this story and these characters in ways I never expected.

Until next time. ♥